OLD-FASHIONED HUNTSMAN

High Table Hijinks Book Two

CHRISTOPHER JOHNS

MOUNTAINDALE
PRESS

This story is dedicated to those who are still fighting the good fight. Those of you who have come to stand before your own monsters and are still here. Because I've been there too. I've stared my demons in the face before, and having been blessed enough to have friends there to back the shit I talk with me, I know how it feels. You're a badass. And don't you ever go a single second without recognizing that, or think that someone important to you doesn't care. Because even though I may not know you personally yet—I'm here. I'll listen. And I for damn sure care.

Thank you for being who you are, and for letting me be who I am with you through these words.

Let's go have a story, yeah?

ACKNOWLEDGMENTS

First I would like to acknowledge my team, those of you who have stood with me in the trenches of my own mind and fought these stories with me even when I screamed and shouted that I wanted to stop, or that it was enough. You pushed me into better grounds and through the fight. Thank you. To my readers, I hope that you see these words, hear these voices, and know that every single word—each syllable—was crafted with you at heart by all of us. Without you, our jobs would be boring. Thank you.

CATCHING BACK UP

Things for Marcus Bola—Marine-turned-bartender—at a nice Columbus bar called the High Table, near the Campus area, had been... interesting before.

The majority of his platoon had died during an escort mission to a newly discovered temple gone horribly wrong. Then he was basically told that he couldn't trust the Marine Corps to keep him safe, because those brothers and sisters who survived had been sent up shit's creek to the wizard and... disappeared.

Having to lay low somewhere they couldn't find him very easily, with people who wouldn't be taken as hostages to get him to comply with anything weird, his only option was to come live with his uncle and get a normal job.

Far be it from him to stick to the plan, as the High Table was the furthest thing from a normal bar you could likely find. It catered to supernatural and preternatural creatures, had staff that consisted of Oni, lycanthropes, a jinn with a knack for sarcasm, a chocolate-loving brownie housekeeper, and a several-armed cook. Yeah, your average, everyday bar.

But the real kicker was the mysterious necklace that he

found during that hellish mission overseas that cost so many lives. Contained within that item was a magical creature that awoke within his consciousness, Galaxy. Marcus' mysterious new patron knew nothing of herself other than that he and she could protect each other, and that she could grow and, with her, so could he.

While the bar was a neutral ground meant for the patrons to come and blow off steam, while keeping humanity and themselves safe, that didn't mean that it was without problems.

Marcus and his friends, Cassia, Arden, and Merlin—a Warden trainee who had belonged to a now-dead nephilim—discovered a plot to take Columbus, then Ohio, over with a new magically made drug called "Divinity." Manufactured by the mafia-like son of a Seelie noble, Marcus and his friends fought back to the point where their enemy resorted to finding Connell, his estranged son and the heir to the Unseelie Winter Court, to take as a hostage.

After a successful but bloody battle to reclaim what was lost, Marcus was offered the opportunity to become something even stronger by the High Table Council.

The Huntsman.

CHAPTER ONE

Sunlight streamed into the room as not-so-subtle snoring rang out and almost echoed off the walls from the bed. Cassia, in her Oni form, took up the majority of my bed where she slumbered.

I smiled at her, red skin smooth in most places, but scarred in others. Her purple lips hung open as she took a deep, snarling breath in and let it loose in a huff that blew some of her jet-black hair up and away from her face. The blanket covered her loosely, doing little to hide her massive assets and curves. Cuddled closely to her on the inside of her right arm lay Galaxy in her night-colored, star-covered elven form. She slept easily with a look of contentment on her face that made me wonder if she enjoyed sleeping next to Cass more than she liked sleeping with me. Granted, she really didn't need to sleep at all.

She grumbled something unintelligible and cuddled closer to the larger woman before one of her eyes opened. *I know all of what happened already. She's been asleep the entire time, but will wake soon. How do you feel on the matter?*

I frowned, sitting on the corner of the large desk I had in my room before I closed my eyes. *They made it sound like this was a venture that had happened before, but that hadn't been successfully managed. It sounds like it could be highly dangerous according to Uncle Yen, and I know that you're eager to go.*

My eagerness is a product of my need to grow and get stronger. I opened my eyes and she looked over at me, her eyes trained on my face now. *I will not force you to go immediately, and from the sound of things, Merlin may yet need us here for a day or so still.*

Out loud, I asked, "What's wrong with Merlin?"

She stilled and glanced back at Cassia who had woken up and frowned before saying, "He told me that the Wardens have called him for a full report, but that he needs to come alone or with proof of Varlin's demise."

"Alone *or* with proof?" I grimaced, that made no sense. "So then he needs us to come with him?"

"They will likely try to kill us for killing one of theirs." Cassia grunted and sat up, smacking her lips tiredly. "I'd be surprised if they didn't have him killed for failing to avenge his trainer."

My lips turned down in a scowl. This was a little bit of a predicament, and it put Merlin in harm's way.

"We can save him, if we teach him how to fight." Galaxy stood up and snapped her fingers, clothes appearing on her body. "Are the two of you going to go to the gym this morning?"

Cassia stood up and let the blanket fall from her as she smiled. "Yup." She tilted her head at me. "Why are you dressed like that?"

I filled her in on what happened and the slight drowsiness that had been present in her features melted away. She shifted into her human form, and began to pace. She was really just a smaller version of herself in human form, sans horn and her hair a chestnut color this time, which was cut shaggy. She bent over and pulled a pair of shorts on and then a tank top before turning around to face me. "That's a lot."

"What do you know of the Wild Hunt?" Galaxy asked and sat on the bed, watching the other woman carefully.

"They're a story told to all the bad little monster children in this world and Grestal to scare them into being 'good.'" She shook her head and sat down. "They're the stuff of nightmares and, honestly, they are an entity that is to be feared."

"But do you know anything specific?" She shook her head and I glanced at Galaxy. "Research to do, can you get on that?"

"Of course." She smiled and went to my books, then pointed to my desk. "Your funds from last night are there."

"What do you mean?" I turned and found my tip jar and also a large bag on the table. "What's with the bag?"

"Spoils of war." Galaxy grinned at me before I unzipped it. Inside were coins, bags, and wads of cash. "Those all came off the bodies of the fallen that you all had a hand in killing last night."

"Well, this will definitely pay for the gun range." I smiled and patted it. "See if Uncle Yen can put it all in human currency?"

She nodded once and motioned that we should be off as she cracked a physical book open and began to sift through pages.

Cassia stepped aside while I changed into shorts and a t-shirt to go workout with her. As we walked down the stairs she said, "Guns won't work in Grestal at all." She turned to me and added. "All technology, really."

"What?" I stared at her as if she were crazed. She nodded and I just sputtered, "B—but how am I supposed to fight?"

"Magic and blades?" She chuckled, then frowned at me. "What?"

I groaned and she snorted when I said, "That means I'll need to train more with Kenshi."

She laughed all the way out the door, the bright sunlit day greeting us warmly as our feet hit the sidewalk. We walked down the road about fifty feet and into the direct side of a building, brick wall and all. Though that was just a glamour used to hide the entrance to the security team's gym and training facility. It was fully decked out with all the equipment they would ever need to stay ready to defend the High Table, including a chow hall and barracks.

She had me training with Kenshi again, alone for this first bit before Merlin was supposed to arrive for his lesson.

Kenshi, the demon of an Oni that he was, brutalized me once more while training. Cutting me and stabbing me when I couldn't adequately defend myself or react in time. He let on that he wasn't disappointed, but he could tell from when I started cursing at him a bit more vehemently that he was getting to me.

"Fine, bubba Marcus." Kenshi growled and stepped toward me, my right arm raising to stab at him. He laughed and swatted my hand aside. "No. Watch. Follow. Learn."

He took me through motions and movements that made little sense to me until he put them all together and attacked me slowly. A downward strike to push the attacker's blade away, a step toward them and a slash with the blade held facing away from the body followed by a stab low when they were exposed.

"Good." He resumed his thrashing until he was satisfied that I was thoroughly bested, at least that was what it felt like, then released me to the tender mercies of his sister Cassia.

Who was almost as fervent as her brother that someone's all be put into training.

"Push, Marcus." Cassia growled at me. "Push!"

My chest burned like crazy as she encouraged me to bench more. I was just this side of 1,200 pounds and this was the ninth repetition and floundering on the tenth.

"Dig deep!" A bass voice bellowed from across the room. "Push yourself!"

I snarled and grunted before releasing a pent-up yell of rage as I put the tenth rep up and Cassia brought it back to the rack. My muscles spasmed a bit, but otherwise I felt great.

"Great work!" Cassia touched my chest appreciatively, a little breathier than she had been. "So strong."

Indeed. Galaxy purred as a notification popped into my field of vision.

+1 Brawn.

"Oh shit!" I grinned and she frowned at me. "I bumped up my Brawn by a point for that!"

Her eyebrows shot up and she grinned. "More. Lift more!"

I groaned and she forced me to push myself further until I failed a rep for squats and could lift no more. Panting, I looked up at her. "No more."

She sulked a little. "Fine." Her eyes lit up as she leaned closer so that she could look me in the eyes. "Do you want to fight?"

"Good God, do you ever rest, woman?" Another woman's voice made Cassia jump and look back to see Arden standing there with a slightly bruised Merlin. "He's covered in sweat and filth."

"That's not what I was asking him to do, we use the term scrap for that." She glanced at me, "Not that I would mind that either."

I blushed and stood up, my muscles protesting loudly. "Hey guys."

Arden, whose fiery red hair gave away a little about her heritage as a flame jinn, smiled at me. She wore a pair of short shorts and a tank top like Cassia, her willowy figure filling her clothes out a little less, but she wasn't bad looking in the slightest. "Hey. Merlin just finished his lesson with Kenshi, the brute. Want to go somewhere and chat?"

"Food?" Merlin asked hopefully. His boyish delight at the prospect of food made me snort and clap him on the shoulder. He was still wearing Arden's hand-me-downs, including the beaten and worn shoes.

"Yeah, buddy." I pulled him toward the stairs for food. We could all do for some food, after all. Especially me, having healed the injuries I'd gotten from Kenshi and then the wear on my muscles had eaten into my reserves too.

We stood in line to get our food, piling plates onto trays with eggs, bacon, sausage links, and biscuits with a little gravy on them. I had to laugh when Merlin went back up to the line and got another plate for a large cinnamon roll, bringing it back with a grin.

"Such a kid." I grinned at him.

He stuck his tongue out at me and I rolled my eyes.

Hard to believe that Galaxy had rebuilt his body after he took a magical death blow that I managed to dodge. He had brown hair and equally brown eyes that glimmered with mirth. I hated to admit it, but I'd never really cared what he looked like before, but now?

Now it was like I was looking at my little brother and I could memorize everything about him.

You only feel this way because you feel responsible for his death, Marcus, Galaxy whispered through my mind. *Remember, he's better off now. He has his full, untainted memories of his life before and knows that the Wardens are responsible for his being an orphan. He doesn't blame you.*

Is that because he was remade by you, or because he doesn't know that he took that blow in my stead? She fell silent and I knew instantly it was because she knew I wouldn't trust what she said on it. I was too volatile when it came to the boy right now due to my emotions. She thought I would come around—that I'd see reason.

Instead, I saw a kid who I felt responsible for.

"You're going to need some better civvies if you expect to go to the range with us, Merlin." I took a bite of my food and he almost choked on his.

He looked down and forced himself to swallow his food. "When are we going?"

"That's part of what we need to chat about." Arden put a guiding hand on his shoulder to calm him. "First, we need to know when you talk to the Wardens?"

"I'm supposed to go and find the nearest one as soon as I possibly can." He shrugged, then added, "It's a pretty bureaucratic system though, so likely all the Wardens around here have no clue yet. So I can wait until tomorrow."

"Okay, so how do we help you make it so that they don't kill you and all of us?" Cassia asked before shoving some food into her gullet. She swallowed quickly and grinned before saying, "Not that I'm worried about you or anything. Benched a hundred pounds today. How's that for a bookworm?"

"Cass, you're supposed to be building his confidence—not making him sound like an immortal." Arden chastised her friend with a severe frown.

"I am not!" She pointed at Merlin. "He's not spent one damn point that he has on anything! That's just his own raw ability."

I frowned, joined swiftly by Arden who looked at him in shock and asked, "Is that true?"

Merlin nodded and I grinned ear to ear. "Awesome!"

"Not bad for only seventeen." He grinned and puffed up his chest, that was until I spat out my coffee and both Cass and Arden started to choke on their food. "What's wrong?"

"You're *how old*?" Cassia cried and stared at him. "But… but you looked older."

"That's a spell all Order of the Staff mages learn to be able to operate on their own." He shrugged. "You seriously never realized I was younger?"

"I think it may have been that we never had the opportunity to really dwell on it until now," I whispered and blinked. "Well, you can't legally have a gun now, but that's neither here nor there."

He sulked a bit, so I offered, "I'll still teach you how to shoot, Merlin, you just can't *own* a gun until you're older." He seemed a bit more at ease with that and I had to ask, "What do the other Orders do?"

"Sword doesn't allow their Wardens to go out until they're twenty-one and the Heart doesn't need to go out until they see fit." He shrugged and ate a little more while he thought about it. "I don't think the majority of their trainees see the light of day until they're ready to run a locale? Though I'm not too sure."

That was… good to know? Though, knowing what they did

to Merlin—all those kids were probably orphaned or taken from their families for nothing more than the Orders' personal gains.

"I can't see anyone having given you an I.D. card either." I rolled my eyes and he flipped his hand over, producing one. "Jesus, kid, what else are you hiding?"

"A lot?" He whipped his other hand out and his staff appeared. "I'll need a sword if I'm to try out for the other Order and be safe."

"Knowing what you do, why don't you quit the Orders and work for us?" Cassia's question was quiet, almost sullen, as she picked at the food left on her plate.

"Because if I do, that will make me a target. I need to serve at least a few years to take any suspicion off me if I do decide to leave." Merlin leaned his staff against the table, then scratched his chin. "I could also be useful in gathering intel for you guys, as well as researching Galaxy."

"Which we appreciate," I said with a smile. "Thank you. We'll work out how to get you taken care of. In the meantime, today, we can go and get you a sword and do some shooting lessons."

"You missed an entire chunk of that conversation." Arden rolled her eyes and when I glared at her to go on, she did just that. "He still has all his starting points, Marcus. Though five were taken for other things, according to Galaxy, as it was necessary to get his memories back to their original state—he still has fifteen points to use and more for the experience that he got for all the killing at the compound."

"Oh, shit." I blinked at him and watched as he opened his Status screen to show it to us.

Merlin

Galaxy spawned

Galaxy spawned? I blinked at that and figured it must have been given to him as a means of saying that he was blessed by Galaxy. Or reborn because of her. Going back into his stats, I whistled.

Level 3
Stats
Brawn: 0
Dexterity: 2
Physique: 1
Mana: 23
Charisma: 2
Points to spend: 25
Spells Known
N.A.

"Sucks that I can't see your spell list." Merlin smiled at my sulking and I just shook my head. "Shit, Merlin, you could completely rebuild yourself. You could be almost as strong as me. Stronger even."

"You see his Mana?" Cassia whispered emphatically. "Look at the little glass cannon!"

I chuckled and he blushed a bit. "So, what build did you want to go for?"

"Charisma is a dump stat, unless you want to be a little more likable, or to be able to lie better—you can't lie for shit." Arden crossed her arms and stared down at him, then scoffed and rolled her eyes as he leered back smugly. "It was a spell, and you have high magical affiliations—no more."

"Suuuure." He laughed and just shook his head. "I really don't know. I could imagine that the average Sword Warden has high Brawn, Physique, and Dexterity, with middling Mana just because they use some magic to augment their abilities."

"Well, you definitely want to up your endurance and physical abilities." Cassia rubbed her chin thoughtfully. "I don't know the difference between the Wardens, but getting killed by that weak-ass magic attack was hardly good, was it?"

I turned to her so fast my neck cracked and adjusted, her face mirroring my displeasure. "Dude, what the hell—why would you say that to him?"

"Too soon?" She looked a little embarrassed as I nodded emphatically and Arden just shook her head. "Sorry, Merlin."

"Oni care about battle prowess." The boy shrugged. "Bubba Kenshi took the time to teach me a little about your culture during my lesson. He says that you only push me so hard because you like me."

I laughed, then scowled. "How come he teaches you about culture and beats the dog piss out of me?"

"He likes you more?" Merlin offered with a half-hearted shrug and a laugh.

"Well shit, that changes everything." I grinned, resolving to show Kenshi *just how much* I liked him, the next time we had a lesson. "I'd pump some points into your Physique, at least five to be safe. The other twenty points can easily be split between your other stats. Just know that anything over, like, a three or four is superhuman."

He nodded and fiddled with his points before he seemed satisfied. "Ten Brawn and Dexterity, six Physique, twenty-five Mana, and left Charisma alone for now."

"Congratulations on points spent." I smiled at him, Galaxy watching us both reminding me. "And don't forget, spending your spell points on a spell can net you bigger returns if you fill it completely."

"I had wondered what some of the stars next to a majority of my spells meant." He grinned.

"You have spells already maxed out?" He went to answer. "Stop! I don't want to know. Just… Let's just go get some money and go shopping for you, though you can't wear those clothes even if they are comfortable."

Arden held up a hand bashfully, and we glanced her way as she poked her two index fingers together. "I may or may not have already gone shopping for him this morning while you all were working out…"

"Arden!" Cassia snarled and stood up from the table. "You know I want you to work out more!"

"I know, but he needed this!" She looked like she was about to swing at Cassia when someone cleared their throat. I didn't even need to look to know that it was Gunny, and he was not going to have another brawl in his chow hall.

They both sat back down and spoke more quietly. "I know he does, but you need to take protecting yourself seriously!"

"I'm a Jinn, Cass. We fight with magic and speed!" Arden's hissed reply was just as vehement as Cassia's had been and both continued to glare at each other.

I leaned forward and muttered, "It doesn't matter right now, we're all going to be training here soon with our trip to Grestal coming up."

Arden blinked and Merlin stopped snickering to stare at me as Arden asked, "Come again?"

I leaned back to look around for listeners before motioning that we leave. Arden took Merlin to shower while Cassia and I did the same up in my room.

"She's not going to want to come," Cassia said after she finished washing her hair.

"Arden?" She nodded. "Why?"

"She hates Grestal; it's where her family was bottled and sold."

What the hell is she saying? "You make it sound like they were a soft drink."

"It's what jinn call being forced into a lamp, Marcus." She sighed and turned me to wash my back for me. "They killed her brother, then bound her sister, mother, and father to lamps to sell. Somehow, Arden wound up in Egypt and the Middle East, where she was able to bargain for her freedom with some trickery. Still, she's never been back to Grestal and refuses to go."

"What if we looked for her family along with the mantle?" I wondered.

Cassia stopped moving and lifted my chin to make me look back at her. "Are you serious?"

"Why not?" I shrugged, uncertain why she was being so weird. "She's our friend. She's helped save my bacon a few times already; it's not like I don't want to repay her kindness."

She turned me fully and kissed me on the mouth so hard

that I started to grow woozy from the hot water and lack of air. "Woah."

"I am really starting to wonder where you've been all my life, Marcus Bola." Her breathless whisper made me smile and though my hands started to move to her, a loud knock on my door made me stop and sigh. "What wonderful timing."

I heard the sarcasm in her tone and just laughed as I shut the water off. We toweled ourselves dry and dressed quick. She wore a pair of jeans that could have been painted on and a cut-off anime shirt that bared her strong midriff.

I wore a pair of comfortable jeans the same color as hers, surprisingly, and a gray tee. I also wore my inner-pants holster for my Fae Frame. I still had some high iron content rounds left for it, so I loaded those before stepping into my room where Arden and Merlin sat with Galaxy.

Arden wore a cute black skirt with a yellow tank top, Merlin wore a nice pair of shorts and a black security shirt that looked good on his frame. Since we had seen him, he had put on a little mass too thanks to the points spent; his lean body was now much more athletic-looking and muscular. Like he'd been lifting heavy for a while.

Galaxy read what she had in her hands while Arden and Merlin stared at us.

"I've been offered the position of Huntsman."

"What?" Arden howled, her eyes wide. "A human? *Huntsman?*"

"What's that?" Merlin seemed confused, but it was Galaxy who answered.

"From what I've been able to gather from various texts and tomes that I've... acquired recently, the Huntsman is the leader of the Wild Hunt." She frowned and shook her head. "No, Merlin, not like that Witcher game. This is an entity that had been beholden to the High Table for some time, though what exactly did it do?" She shrugged. "It varied from tale to tale."

"I don't know much other than what Cassia likely does." Arden crossed her arms and stared at me. "The Hunt is the boogeyman of the supernatural world. They were last rumored to have stopped the Cull."

"The war between the supernatural creatures, humans, and dragons?" Merlin's eyes flew open wide. "It's one of the largest sections of our history curriculum!"

"What?" They taught that in school?

"The Orders all stood with the supernatural creatures, myths, monsters, and even some of the lesser gods to fight off the hordes of the dragon queen." He smiled and clapped his hands, spreading them and a large book appeared between his outstretched palms. He snatched it out of the air and tossed it to Galaxy. "This should help you get some more insight. There's a little missing from what I can remember, but the missing bit is really where there was a falling out between the monsters and humans. The Wardens having been born and forged of the fire of the conflict to watch over the innocents of the world and protect humanity and other monsters from another Cull."

"That falling out must have been monumental." I grumbled, shaking my head and scratching my ear. "Listen, I don't know what it all entails, but I think something else is afoot somewhere. Councilmember Serpath told me that once I had the item to take control of the Wild Hunt, I'd go to work immediately."

"Serpath?" Arden frowned and I nodded. "What was the councilmember of High Table Middle East so afraid of that she had to ask you for help?"

"I don't know, but some of the council didn't like me telling them to get off their asses and get to know their patrons and protect them, so there's a little opposition." I smiled as they rolled their eyes. "It's me, guys. Come on."

"And the last known location of the relic that the last Huntsman had to signify his reign was lost in Grestal," Galaxy said, then held up a couple envelopes. One, she tossed straight at me. "This first one is the funds from your tips and the spoils of last night. This one is for Merlin from Councilmember

Amelia, and this one is for all of us who wish to seek out the relic."

"I'm not going to Grestal." Arden lifted her head.

"Marcus said that he would help you find your family," Cassia blurted, my eyes widening at her as she lifted her hand to her mouth. "Sorry, did you want to tell her?"

"He what?" Her eyes blazed as she stared at Cass, likely knowing that she would have been the one to blabber to me about her life. "I don't know what she let slip, but my family is the least of my worries going back to that hellish place."

"Arden, I need you for this." I motioned to Cassia. "I know that I couldn't keep her away if I wanted to, and I know that no matter what I do, Merlin will sneak along with us. We need you." She seemed like she was ready to bolt, but I added. "You're our party member, Arden. You have power you didn't before and you can be so much more than you were before, when they did that to you."

I scratched my head and went for it. "We don't even need to go for the relic first. We can find the monsters that bound you to that lamp and get your revenge. We can keep it from happening to anyone ever again at their hands."

"You mean that?" she breathed and I nodded, motioning to Galaxy. "Does he?"

"He thinks that killing them will help you get over your fear, yes." Galaxy turned the page of the book in her lap, then looked up at Arden. "He also believes that the extra experience it could net you will help you prepare for the journey to gather more power. You win, he wins—you all win. Now let me read and research in peace."

I rolled my eyes at her and she ignored me. Arden stared at me. Hard. Finally she walked to the door and muttered, "I'll think about it."

Cassia went to follow her, but I held a hand up. "She's hurting right now, Marcus. She needs to fight."

"She needs to think," I corrected her. "You want to fight because she's hurting and it's where you do your best thinking."

She grimaced at me and crossed her arms. "Smartass."

I smiled at her and patted her shoulder. "Let's go get some stuff to kill things with then, how's that?"

"Better." She smiled and grabbed my hand. She turned to Merlin and nodded approvingly. "I didn't get the chance to tell you, but I like that shirt on you."

He grinned and we were on our way out the door and off to collect some things to kill with.

CHAPTER TWO

We pulled into the lot at the Forge, smiling when I got out because I remembered to not bring anything that they didn't make, so they couldn't tease me for it and tear it apart. The building was as unassuming as last time, and Merlin almost grimaced when I told him what to expect, as if he couldn't believe that this place was really what I said.

We walked in, Merlin trailing behind, and once again we were greeted by the sound of hammers banging on metal and metal machining and shearing. It was a little louder today, it seemed, than last time.

I glanced back and saw that his eyes were wide and his mouth hung open at the sight of all the dwarves working deftly.

Cassia took us to the elevator, much like she had last time, and pressed the button to get to the sales floor. The door closed and opened almost instantly and Merlin hissed, "Teleportation?"

Jayvali, caring for a sword at the nearest desk snorted. "Nah, just damned-fine craftsmanship!" The dwarven man looked up at us and smiled. "Cass and Marcus, how was the hunt this past morning?"

"They all died and here we are." Cassia grinned back at the man and he just snorted again. "You expect anything less?"

"Nah, never have, Cassia—never would." He looked directly at me and grinned. "Carrying a dirty weapon in my shop now, Marcus?"

"Only because I plan to use it to teach Merlin here how to care for his weapons once he learns how to shoot." I grinned at him and he looked behind me, his smile faded. "What's wrong?"

"The Wardens stay clear of our shops, as they like to do their own work and we like it that way too." His voice had dropped an octave, becoming more growl than speech as he regarded the boy. "I s'pose you'll be reporting our shop to your Order?"

Merlin did his best to smile and said, "If I wanted to report you, I wouldn't be with my friends here." He pointed to the sword that Jay was cleaning. "Besides, I need a sword fit to fight with."

"I don't sell to Wardens." Jay scowled and turned to look at me. "Marcus, lad, I like you. Cass done right with you, I swears it. But this one? Shite."

"He's just a kid, Jayvali," I murmured and leaned closer. "One who died when I should have. He's like a little brother to me now, and I mean to see him equipped with the best goods that I know—and that's your stuff."

"Nope." He leaned back and crossed his arms. "Can't do it."

"What if we were to let you know that the Wild Hunt means to make a return, and that if you look the other way for Merlin and him *only*, we could convince the Huntsman to come here for his weapons?" Cassia raised an eyebrow at the dwarf, who looked gobsmacked.

He grabbed his beard and pulled it, his jaw drifting down with it a little. "You mean that? The Hunt be nigh on returning?"

Cassia nodded, not saying any more.

"I'll need it in writing." He blinked and tripped over his feet as he went to the back portion of the room where they kept a large set of filing cabinets. He flipped through a few folders and pulled one out. He returned with a single sheet of paper and started to look for something to write with. "Where's that blasted quill!"

"Quill?" I snorted, and pulled a pen out of my pocket. "It's the twenty-first century—here's a pen."

"Quills use the signer's blood to seal a contract," Merlin explained and produced one such quill. "Here, Jayvali, use mine."

Jay turned and glowered at the young man and took it. He jabbed his left thumb with it and stared at Merlin. "How many statements have you forced my kind to write with this quill? How many lives has it confirmed and consigned?"

"None, I'm only a trainee," Merlin answered bashfully, embarrassed.

"Was that necessary, Jay?" I growled at him.

He blanched a little, his scowl turning to a look of slight discomfort. "No. I didn't know."

Merlin shrugged. "You never asked."

"Maybe lead with that before a dwarf runs his mouth, hey?" Merlin smiled and motioned to the blank sheet of paper as the dwarf spoke. "I know."

Jay turned his gaze to the sky and spoke slowly, "I, Jayvali of the Forge in Columbus, Ohio, have been given word of an event to take place, and upon said event being completed, demand compensation for work and service given beforehand to a third party I would not normally work with. I sign in my blood, witnessed by two I'd call friends and another sworn to uphold his kind's laws, in good faith of compensation being appropriate to my service and my show of honor."

As he spoke, the words filtered onto the sheet of paper in front of him that mirrored his sentiment. As he finished, a single line and an X appeared beneath it where he made his mark. He presented the quill to Cassia who took it, pricked her finger, and lifted her head as Jay had done.

"I, Cassia, head of security for the High Table Columbus Branch, have given word of an event to take place to the best of my knowledge, and as such have promised to compensate the above for his service and work when it comes to fruition. I sign my blood, witnessed by two who I call friend and one with whom I share my bed, in the hopes that I will be able to uphold my end of the bargain, my death being all to stop me from completing it—should my honor be so besmirched."

She reached down and signed beneath the last line before two more lines appeared in a section that said *witnesses.*

Merlin lifted the quill that Cassia had carefully set onto the counter. "I, Merlin of the Order of the Staff, trainee Warden and protector of the innocent, do hereby witness this contract and declare both parties of willing consent and able mind to enter it. May all benefit from this."

He nicked his finger and signed his name in a spidery, flowing script before he turned and offered the quill to me. "Just say something to that effect, your heart should guide you."

Nodding my head, I lifted the quill that felt surprisingly heavy in my hand and spoke from the heart. "I, Marcus Bola, sergeant of the Marines and blessed of Galaxy, protector of the High Table and its patrons, do hereby swear and affirm as witness that this document was signed and sworn to before me. With my signature, I hope that all parties involved live long and prosper."

Cassia snorted and Jay just facepalmed as I nicked my index finger and signed—poorly. He lifted the document and sighed. "That'll do it."

He lifted the contract and slammed it against the wall where it stuck before turning around. "Well then, boy." Jay eyed Merlin and spoke to him with the same professional courtesy a tradesman spoke to a difficult customer might. "What kind of sword were you lookin' for?"

"I honestly have no idea, but I will defer to the expert's judgement on what he thinks is best." Merlin looked hopefully at the dwarf who cocked an eyebrow and looked at both of us before taking him over to the rack for swords.

"Does it have to be a sword?" Jay asked politely enough as he pulled a few items from the rack to set on the nearest counter. "I'll admit I don't know much of the Orders' specifi-cations."

"It doesn't have to *only* be a sword," Merlin admitted uncer-tainly, looking at all of the options he had. "But I do know that I need to have a sword as a symbol of my station as a Warden of the Order and that whatever I get needs to be able to harm supernatural creatures. Like an Oni weapon."

"Not looking for anything fancy?" Jay raised his eyebrow, piling several weapons that he had taken from the rack back on. Merlin simply shook his head and Jay whistled low. "Good. Got just the things for you."

He went to the far end of the rack and pulled a simple-looking short sword from behind a couple larger swords and set it on the counter before going to the rack for less... sword-like weapons. He pulled a simple axe out and held it up, the light blue metal of the head catching the light and shimmering, reflected it around the room. He nodded to himself and pulled it behind the counter.

"These are the best two options I can present you. If you want something fancier, I can get it out for you." Jay stared at Merlin hard as his selections were pored over.

"These are perfect!" Merlin touched the sword and smiled. "I don't need pretty; I need it to function."

A small smile moved Jay's beard, his tongue likely loosened by Merlin's honesty and pure nature. "I chose the axe because it's a good weapon. Simple to use and if someone sees you lugging that thing around, they'll know you mean to kill them."

"That's great." Merlin lifted both of them and Jay's eyes bulged as he seemed to have no issues with the axe, which was almost as large as Merlin was. "I wonder if Kenshi can teach me how to use one of these too?"

Jay looked like he'd had a stroke, grabbing his beard and gnashing his teeth as Merlin retreated with his weapons. Finally, the dwarf wheezed, "He knows Kenshi?"

Cass nodded and smiled. "Bubba Kenshi has devoted himself to teaching Merlin the Way of the Blade. Marcus too."

I crossed my arms and scowled. "All that asshole does is beat me, cut me, and yell at me." I smiled at the end to let her know I was teasing. "He's a pretty ruthless instructor, that's for sure."

For a second, I thought Jay was going to keel over, but he managed to compose himself, smoothing his hand over his clothes and beard. "And how are *your* weapons doing, Marcus?"

"Funny you should ask me that." I pulled the severely bent rifle that was Thumper out of my inventory and placed it on the counter. "I got into a bit of a scuffle during our outing and I need Thumper fixed. Can you do that for me?"

"What in the *bloody dragon fuck happened to my baby?*" Jay cried, his hands flying to his head in distress before he launched himself over the counter at me. "You *bastard!*"

I fended him off as best I could while trying desperately not to hurt him, calling out, "One of those junky elves hit her instead of me, it was a noble sacrifice!"

He roared, "I'll sacrifice you!" He reached for an axe on a nearby wall, snarling at me. "Hold still so I can end your suffering!"

"That'll be all, Jayvali," a lighthearted voice called out over the thudding in my heart. I turned to see a vibrantly dressed dwarven woman staring at us in front of the elevator. "Take her to the smiths and see if they can work on her."

"Bu—Mistress, he harmed our work!" He pointed at me and seethed, tears in his eyes. "Downright negligent!"

"You heard him as well as I that he was attacked by an inhumanly strong creature who hit his weapon instead of him," she reasoned calmly. "I will mind the sale for now. Go."

Jayvali hung his head, not even noticing that he had dropped the axe in his grasp onto the floor so that he could go and collect my former rifle as if it were the most precious thing he'd ever held and trudged out of the room.

"Forgive him, he's very protective of his work, and Thumper was so close to being a master-crafted weapon." The woman picked up the axe and put it back onto the rack that it belonged in. "Dropped a weapon like that too? Must have truly been upset. Nearly lost his mind over it." Her gaze slid over us all before she explained, "I felt the contract being imposed on the Forge and thought I would come to investigate."

She stared openly at us, her lavender eyes unnerving as she scrutinized us. "Imagine my surprise when I find a trusted ally of the Forge, an unknown benefactor, and a would-be Warden." She raised a hand and stopped us from saying anything. "As I'm sure you can guess, I run this establishment. I hold no particular ill will toward the Wardens, nor do I intend to harm any of you for supposed carelessness with our work—all it does is add money to our coffers."

Ah, a shrewd business woman. Though how did she know so much about us? "Your eyes are beautiful," I said lamely, hoping the compliment would allow me some insight.

"They are, and they see through much." She smiled at me and it felt as if she was looking through me. "Is there anything else I can help you all with today?"

"I was wondering if I might be able to pick up a gun for the boy, something simple, likely similar to a Beretta. Or even another Fae Frame like the one I carry."

She moved around the counters like she knew the place better than even Jay did, but since she owned the place, she likely did. She pulled out a Fae Frame, another Silvaero like my other pistol and then a third pistol that looked exactly like a Beretta 92X full size. It was beautiful.

"This is an RH Steltz Magnifico." She cleared the weapon and locked the slide to the rear. "Standard combat sights with the white dots for easy sight attainment with a red dot on the front sight. Comes with a rail that most accessories such as flashlights and laser sights will attach to, as well as an exaggerated bevel for the magazine, allowing swifter magazine changes."

I whistled low and motioned to the weapon, showing Merlin how to ensure that the weapon was unloaded and on safe. He caught on quickly, manipulating it and checking everything.

"First time handling a firearm?" the woman asked and Merlin nodded. "We have an indoor range that we allow our customers to test fire guns before purchasing. Helps us maintain our armory and ensures our potential patrons get the best bang for their buck."

Cassia snorted and started to laugh, making the dwarven woman smile. "I wondered if anyone would enjoy that as much as I did."

I laughed too, and looked at her. "I'm Marcus. These are Cassia and Merlin."

She held her hand out and I shook it. "My name is Magdalena."

"Pleasure to meet you." She smiled at me and gathered the three pistols and motioned that we follow her. We stood in the elevator as she pressed six, the door closed and opened immediately to a long indoor range that was empty except for an attendant who looked to be Merlin's age.

"Torre, these are my guests." Magdalena smiled nicely and motioned to her haul. He nodded and went to a large set of containers where he pulled out several magazines and boxes of ammunition before bringing them over to the lane we would be using before fading back into the background. "Take your time. I'm certain that someone as knowledgeable as you knows how to train someone who is completely new?"

I nodded and she backed up. "Take your time."

"Thank you." I lifted the Magnifico and showed it to Merlin. "We'll start with this one."

He watched as I loaded the magazines for it after finding

the right kind, then had him load another three. He wasn't used to it, but adapted quickly and had it done quickly.

"You right- or left-handed?" He raised his left hand and I smiled. "Southpaw? Nice."

I laughed and handed him the gun, but someone tapped on my shoulder. It was the attendant, Torre. "S'cuse me, sir. I got a lefty Magnifico here if he wants to try it?"

"Is there a difference?" Merlin asked politely and the dwarf nodded. "What's that?"

"The magazine release is on the right side of the grip so you can manipulate it with your left hand like the right-handed folks do." He pointed to the button and smiled. "Makes it a little easier to work it out. Slide lock is still on the left side, but it's a little easier for us."

"Thanks, Torre, I appreciate the help." Merlin took the Magnifico from him and I relinquished the other we had been given.

"Now, first thing you do when someone hands you a weapon?" I asked him and he paused as I watched him expectantly.

"Check it and clear it?"

I nodded and he pulled the slide back, struggling for a second to lock it to the rear until I tapped the slide lock and had him press it up. Once it was back and checked, I had him set it on the table.

"I'm going to teach you a little ditty." He frowned at me and I held up my index finger to count. "Treat. Never. Keep. Keep."

Cassia asked, "What's that mean?"

"Glad you asked." I smiled and turned to Merlin. "Treat every weapon as if it were loaded. Never point your weapon at anything you do not intend to shoot. Keep your finger straight and off the trigger until you're ready to fire. Keep your weapon on safe until you intend to fire. The last rule is more one of foresight and use in crowded areas—know your target and what lies beyond."

Merlin looked to be committing these to memory and I waited until his eyes had refocused on me.

Down range there was already a man-shaped silhouette target attached to a pin, so I pointed at that. "What we will work on right now is getting that good sight alignment."

I smiled at the chance to relive my days at the range. "Shooter! When I say 'target,' you will pick up that unloaded pistol and sight in on your target. The key to good sight alignment is this—build your castle!"

He looked at me, clearly confused, so I lifted the gun and showed him the rear sights and the front sight. "Align these like you would build a castle wall. Equal points of light on either side, and perfectly flush along the top."

"What about the target?" Merlin asked and I shook my head.

"Doesn't matter right now." I placed the gun on the table and pointed to Cassia as I cleared the Silvaero for her. "You can do this too."

She scowled, but shrugged and placed the weapon in easy reach for herself.

I stepped back and bellowed, "Taaaaaargets!"

Merlin panicked at my raised voice and fumbled the weapon a little bit, but finally managed to get it up and pointed down range. A soft chuckle escaped me and I smiled. *Was this how I was the first time I handled a pistol?*

Likely, Galaxy chided me and I smiled again. *Teach them well.*

I stepped over to Merlin and corrected his stance, isoceles was what I used for shooting with a pistol and it was a solid base in my opinion. From there, I corrected his grip and the positioning of his arms. I flicked his finger roughly. "Get that finger off the fucking trigger, son."

"Sorry, sir." His instant response made me want to gag. He realized my displeasure and said, "Sorry, old habits."

I smirked. "Same. I forget that you fight different monsters and it confuses me sometimes. The Marine Corps was a simpler time." I poked his index finger. "Straight and off the trigger, okay?"

He nodded and I had him set the weapon down and lift it a few more times to get used to how his hands were supposed to be positioned on the grip. "Firm, don't grip too tight, but don't limp wrist it either, okay? You'll see what I mean here soon."

I checked Cassia's form and found that she was just as proficient with a pistol as she was a massive club.

She winked at me and said, "Warriors know."

I grinned and shook my head, running them through the drill three more times quickly for them to get a feel for it.

After that, I had Merlin practice loading and unloading the pistol with a magazine, charging the empty weapon as if it were firing. He was shaken, but as we moved from motion and movement to the next, he grew steadier and looked to be enjoying himself.

Finally I felt it was time. "Shooters!" I bellowed louder to be heard over the ear protection that Torre had given us excitedly. "Loading a magazine of ten rounds, load! Maaaaaake ready."

Merlin and Cass slammed their magazines home into the well and slapped the slides of their respective pistols back. Merlin slapping his chest on the follow through like I'd shown him.

"Shooters, firing one round—*one round only*—on my command into the target before you." I waited for what likely felt like forever to them before I hollered. "Stand *by*!"

Merlin flinched and I grinned as I waited for him to return to his ready position before roaring, "Taaaaargets!"

Both of them raised their pistols, safety clicked off when they made ready, and fired a single round into the target. Both went to put their pistols down and I snarled, "Keep them up! Keep them up and at the ready!"

They flinched and I surged forward, pointing at the horizon line. "You never know when or if there will be another target, so you keep that weapon up and at the ready until you check to see that the coast is clear."

They both nodded and I backed up, Torre already having brought the targets forward. Cassia's round was in the white to the right of the silhouette and Merlin's was in the black, but low and to the right.

I had them clear their weapons and turn to look at me. "When you're lining up your sights, are you relaxing or are you anticipating the shot and recoil?"

"What's the difference?" Cassia asked and I pointed to her target. "You're squeezing your trigger way too hard; that's the only reason you could be shooting that far right if you're aiming center mass."

She lifted her pistol up and aimed it down range. "This is how I do it." She had me watch and I noticed that the second pad of her finger was on the trigger.

"Pull your finger out until you have that little nub right here —" I touched the small bump on the center of her finger opposite where the white of her nail cuticle was. "—on the trigger, then it's a slow, steady squeeze. Let the shot surprise you."

I looked over at Merlin and said simply, "You're anticipating the shot and leaning into the gun when you squeeze the trigger. That target is blurred and the sights are crystal clear, okay? Let's do it again!"

I had them fire single shots again and there was improvement on Cassia's end, but Merlin anticipated his shot again. So I had him hold the weapon up and I stood next to him, staring at his arms and hands while I told him to fire. He had a full magazine and I told him to fire randomly. The kid was perfect.

The only issue he had was with anticipating the recoil and trying to control it.

So, I stuck my finger on his and made him watch the target. Any time I pressed on his finger and he flinched, Cassia smacked him over the head. It was simple, childish, and likely incredibly dangerous to do to someone with a loaded gun. But after the third smack, he tried to relax more.

His last shot was perfect. "Fuckin'-A!" I grinned at him as

he rubbed his head sullenly. "I do believe we got through that thick skull."

"I don't understand what the issue is if I hit the black and it's a little low." He frowned at me, his eyes worried as I hit him with a consternated look.

"Think of the round like a specific kind of spell." I pointed down range and he frowned. I cast Bolt and missed the target by a foot. "If you miss a vital spot, sure it hurts like hell, but it won't stop anyone unless they're human. And even then, a shot to an unnecessary fatty bit like a love handle or muffin top is hardly going to stop someone trying to kill you. That, and you'd be wasting a shot."

He seemed to get it, but I rammed it home. "Wasted rounds are like wasted spells—they can get you killed."

He nodded like that made perfect sense. "Perfect practice makes perfect."

I grinned at him as he said that. "That's right." I patted his shoulder and he looked at the gun. "I know it's different, and not necessarily what you signed up for, but I want you to carry it with you. If for nothing more than my peace of mind."

"And mine," Cassia added smiling. "I don't care for guns, as there's no hand given sentiment behind them, but you would do well with them." She frowned. "Though in Grestal, it won't help at all since it won't work."

"Okay," Merlin agreed. "I'll take this one then."

"Excellent choice, Merlin." Magdalena's voice came to us from behind Cassia. We turned to find the dwarven woman watching us. "You said that you were planning a trip into Grestal?"

I nodded and she smiled. "While our more modern weaponry is not feasible in that magic-rich environment, I would suggest a weapon for everyone. Jayvali told me that you have an Oni-blooded blade, but only in the form of a knife, is this accurate?"

"Yes, it is." She nodded and I added, "I'm Touched as well, if that matters."

"Just as well, we have a new type of sword that we would like to try out, and since you've given us insight before, we would be eager to have you test it out." She motioned that we follow her once more and toward the elevator we went. She paused and looked back at Torre. "Torre, if you would please clean the weapons used, and package them for sale for me?"

"I'll get right on it, mistress, have 'em ready for you at the counter before you get back." He smiled and waved us away before he turned to his work and chuckled to himself before bellowing, "Taaaaargets! Haha, what a riot."

I laughed and shook my head. Our ways were strange, but I missed them. Magdalena joined us and pressed a button for a floor I couldn't make out and before the door opened once more, she issued a statement. "Mistress Magdalena and three guests, all of whom are contracted to the Forge to a degree."

While it wasn't a lie, it made me a little concerned. "Something going on?"

"We take security of this section of our Forge very seriously, as some of our more... *aggressive* creations are made and housed here." She smiled at me sweetly, lavender eyes sparkling. "I trust it would suffice to say that if word got out about anything you see today, I would personally kill all of you?"

"It's about what is expected for me these days," I retorted and she giggled. "Show us the goods, I'm curious now."

She ducked her head and the elevator doors opened onto a massive area that had traditional-looking forges with green and blue flames that looked to be alive. There were tables and machines in there too, with what looked like alchemist supplies and chemistry sets. I had to admit I was a little worried now, as every eye in the room was on us.

Looking around, I saw that there were more people than just dwarves here. Other, smaller, figures worked at some of the stations with delicate-looking tools.

I recognized one's style of ears, but as I tried to get a closer look, Magdalena said, "Please, don't stare at our goblin masters.

They can be quite temperamental and their work is highly volatile at times."

"Goblins?" Merlin whispered with wonder in his voice that made me pause. "What are they working on?"

"That I cannot tell you." Magdalena smiled and ushered us off to the far back corner and pushed us into a ring of tables. "Please, wait here while I have the items in question brought to you."

She left us, and as soon as she was out of earshot I turned to Merlin and Cassia. "I thought goblins were the evil sort?"

"They can be if denied materials to pursue their various crafts." Merlin shrugged and nodded to one that looked to have rounded on a coworker who came too close to his work. "Goblins are some of the most driven, devious creators in this world or Grestal. Their work is highly sought after and can be amazing, rivaling dwarves. I wouldn't be surprised if it was a goblin god of sorts who made the relic that bestows the mantle of the Huntsman."

"Oh, that's so cool." I frowned and scratched my chin, about to ask more questions, but our host rejoined us with two of the goblin crafters in tow.

Their bent and small figures lugged a middling-sized object covered by a thick cloth. Looking closer, their green skin was sallow and sickly looking, warts and growths on their noses and ears making me flinch as I looked at them.

Merlin bowed to them as they hefted their haul onto the table, his voice calm and clear, "Thank you, gentlemen—you're very handsome."

I blinked at him and noticed that the goblins smacked each other and looked back at the boy bashfully, making motions for him to stop like they were embarrassed or something.

Magdalena raised an appreciating brow at Merlin while her workers stepped back. "I see you know something of goblin culture."

"I was more adept at learning of other cultures than some of my peers, but looking back at it now, I think I know why."

She looked like she was waiting for him to reveal more, but he didn't.

She lifted the heavy cloth off the object and revealed a sword, the blade blackened and open in the center from the hilt to about an inch and a half from the pointed tip. Symbols and shapes decorated the blade just on the inside of the finely honed edge.

"This is a new style of weapon that we have worked to create with our goblin tinkerers." She motioned to the goblins who produced a vial of something that glowed amber within and screwed it into a small hole at the hilt of the sword.

Once it was secured, Magdalena lifted it up and braced her feet in what looked to be a practiced stance. "With these vials, we can imbue the blades with magical properties."

"And you want us to test it?" I asked skeptically.

"We want you to test it, and the vials that we will provide you." She stabbed the sword straight and the blade tip glowed with amber energy as the center of it glowed the same way. "The vials we give you will need to be filled with as many types of energy as can be managed, and then used to see how the sword holds up to the stresses of combat and magic."

"Is it going to shatter on one of us?" I raised an eyebrow at her and the goblins shared a look that definitely made it seem like they hadn't a clue. "Is there a benefit to this?"

"You get to try out a new weapon that will be highly versatile if it pays off, and we will give you a discount on any purchase you make today," Magdalena offered readily enough, offering the weapon to me.

I had to admit, I was a little upset that I was just now finding out about this and had thought about upgrading my Blade spell all the way. Would it matter, or was it just a wasted spell purchase?

I took the sword and moved with it the way that Kenshi had shown me. It was a little off balance. I attributed that to the design having a gap in the metal of the blade, or it could have been the simple fact that it was a heavier weapon than the blade I was used to.

I held it up in front of my face and tapped the vial, noting no cracks or imperfections. It was a little wider and longer than my index finger and now only had about half as much amber energy inside it.

"These don't last very long," I pointed out and the goblins nodded, speaking in their own tongue.

"He says that they were meant to be turned off and on in combat." Magdalena reached out and touched the sword, closing her eyes and the energy filtered away. "The energy looked to escape a bit, but if you can find a more manageable way to work with it, we will reward you handsomely."

"What is it about guns that makes them unable to be used in Grestal?" I asked suddenly.

Merlin lifted a hand, stating as if recalling a textbook answer, "Human-made weapons such as pistols and rifles requiring the use of black powder will not fire well in the magic-laden realm, because black powder is a material having been formed in Grestal and takes on a different property when exposed to the atmosphere of Earth."

He looked at me and said, "Basically speaking, the gun would blow up in your hand because black powder is so much more volatile in Grestal."

"Even with us taking down the amount of gunpowder used to make a single round, the explosion would be enough to destroy the inner workings of most guns, or won't be enough to propel the round to a target further than a foot away," Magdalena explained as if expecting some pushback. "We've tried."

"What about using a small spell, or enchantment to propel it?" I blinked at them and they frowned. "I don't know too much about the process of it, magically speaking, and I'm sure it sounds stupid, but can't you go through and enchant things like that?"

I touched the sword and tilted my chin up at Magdalena.

"You turned the magic on and off with a thought, that had to be a specific sort of spell coding, right?" I pulled out my Fae Frame and cleared it. "What if there was spell work you could do to make the right kind of conditions shoot a projectile forward?"

Magdalena froze as the goblins muttered to each other, then said something to her. "Even if we took the time to come up with a way of doing something that time consuming and difficult, the ammunition wouldn't be of any use to or against magical creatures."

I shrugged and pointed to the vial in the center of the experimental sword. "Why not make smaller versions of this that can hold magic and be used like a spell? Fire damage, ice—what have you."

The goblins screeched and spoke frantically to each other, one of them stomping closer to me and pointing accusingly, Magdalena translating, "He wants to know how you came up with that idea. And if you have any idea how costly it would be to manufacture."

"It seemed logical given how things work. All you did was show me something that led me to wanting to have my guns on me." I offered the sword back to them and shook my head. "As far as the logistics are concerned? You could all have a new glass-making machine built and put together to mass produce the smaller vials in little to no time, I have that kind of faith in you. You could make it inexpensive given enough time."

They eyed me suspiciously and I sighed. "Look, I know you're secretive about this stuff, and I know I'm not an expert, it just seemed like a logical progression to me. I'm not looking for anything and I don't care if you do start working on prototypes for it. It was just a thought."

They all looked to ease back down, some of the other goblins and dwarves having drifted closer at the excitement and noise.

"And what of our offer to take the sword as an experiment?" Magdalena asked after a brief silence.

"We can try to do the thing with the sword, but I'll admit that I have a spell that is a sword and it's a lot easier to use." I opened my hands and held my palms out as I explained. "I'm not much of a swordsman either, so I don't know what good I could do with it."

"Then what of young Merlin?" Magdalena offered with a hopeful glance at the Warden in training.

"I'm not much of a swordsman either, but if I can try it out, I don't mind." Merlin held his hand out and took the sword from the dwarf. He stepped away from us and moved the sword from hand to hand, falling into the stance that Kenshi had shown him. He moved awkwardly at first, but began to improve slowly. "Yeah, I'll take it and experiment with it."

"Excellent, thank you so much." Magdalena looked relieved and nodded to the goblins who sprinted away to collect something from a table and brought it back. It was a bag that they held out for Merlin to take.

"This bag contains fifty vials like that one." Magdalena pointed to the one in the sword. "They will draw ambient mana into themselves slowly if exposed to any, like in the various areas of Grestal. If you insert an empty one into the sword, *theoretically* it should draw and store the mana of the victim. Though how efficiently, we aren't sure."

"Can I get a contract specifying what you want done and freeing me of liability should anything happen to the prototype in my care?" He smiled at her and she scowled, but agreed.

She did the same thing with Merlin as had been done already by Jay. Apparently, they wanted at least twenty-five different kinds of uses if possible, and for him to try to drain something's mana at least twice. If he agreed to take part in the experiment, they said they would give us a discount and that they wouldn't hold him responsible for losing it or any damage to the sword or the vials.

We went back to the shop area and I looked at all the swords, failing to find one that I wanted. Cassia whispered,

"Kenshi will sell you one of his if you want. He makes many kinds that he doesn't sell to these guys."

I grinned at her and winked as I paid for Merlin's sword, axe, gun, magazines, and several boxes of ammunition. All in all, it cost around twelve thousand dollars after the discount, the sword and the axe being the most expensive pieces, but it was alright, since with my tips and the money we had made from the elves, I had around twenty-five thousand to begin with.

After we had everything, Merlin made it all vanish, and we were on our way back to the High Table.

CHAPTER THREE

In the car, I took out that envelope and opened it to see what I could find out about where we were headed.

The letter was written in a scrawling and somehow still-neat script that was a little irritating to read, but it had to have been important.

Marcus and those brave enough to follow,

Or, rather, those foolish enough to follow. Forgive me, but this is not the time to beat around the bush, as they say in the human world.

My support does come with a cost, as I am certain that you are aware. There are forces at work against both the High Table and we Grestallans, as well as against the whole of the world and—while it is a stretch—the Wild Hunt can help keep those forces at bay for a time.

There are those on the council who would use you as pawns in their games, and to gain much personally. If your fervor to protect and serve is such that you continue to work as you have and displayed in that meeting, I dare say that their machinations will hold little sway over you.

The item you seek has not been seen for thousands of years, but I am confident I may have found a lead for you in the elemental plains, northwest of Virani in a set of ruins. Forgive me, I could not find more information without drawing attention to myself or you.

Hopefully,
Anon.

"Well, shit," I sighed and handed the letter back to Merlin for him to read.

Cassia pulled into the parking lot and told him to read it out loud, so he did. Her face screwed up, her mouth thin and her eyes narrowed. "It has to be someone we know, right?"

"I don't know. Do you recognize the handwriting?" She shook her head and I frowned, leaning back. "Then we have nothin' more to go on than that."

"Could be a trap." Merlin huffed and scanned the page again. "No magical signature of any sort and no scent. Whoever gave this to us was careful."

"Which is suspicious, but some intel is better than no intel." Thinking back to the temple slaughter, I shivered and got out of the car. "Let's go see Galaxy, then I can prepare for my shift tonight."

They got out of the car and joined me in walking to the front of the bar.

Keith the werewolf security guard smiled at me. "What's up, Massacre?"

I snorted and rolled my eyes. "Got back from gearing up a little. What're you up to?"

"Oh, you know." He looked around at the empty sidewalk, then pointedly at the door before smirking at me. "Security stuff. Skatin'."

"I'm right here," Cassia growled at him and he just waved her off.

"You know that first shift is skatesville." He laughed as she growled again, then hit me with a serious look. "Yen told me to have you come see him when I saw you. Should be in his office."

The door opened, Uncle Yen glaring out at me, making Keith shrug. "Or I'm a liar and there he is."

"Shut up, puppy," Uncle Yen snarled angrily and Keith closed his mouth with an audible click. "Marcus, get in here."

My stomach dropped and I thought I'd majorly fucked something up as I trudged into the open bar. A torrential wave of sound buffeted me as several people yelled, "Surprise!"

"What the fuck!" I roared back, noticing that it was the majority of the staff, security, and several customers that I liked. Out of the corner of my eye I caught a glimpse of Galaxy smirking next to the karaoke set up. "The hell is all this?"

Uncle Yen had tears in his eyes as he muttered, "A going away party, kid." He sniffed and rubbed his eyes. "I'll miss you."

"I'm not going to go to Grestal and die, Uncle Yen." He just shook his head and waved me off. "I have to work tonight."

"Nope!" Keith chipperly called through the door. "Place is closed with an exclusive list for tonight, you'll be drinking and reminiscing with your pals and new family."

"Uncle Yen, come on, this is ridiculous," I pleaded and he just pulled me into a hug. "I'm just going to look for this thing. I'm going to be alright!"

"No one has come back in thousands of years, Marcus!" he roared, tears falling down his face. "I won't try to stop you from going, but God damnit, I will send you off with care!"

"I'm going with him, Yenasi," Cassia said as she grabbed my hand. "I swear I'll do my best to keep him safe."

He stared at her for a moment, then nodded. "Appoint your replacement, fill them in on the role they will be taking."

"My beta is already aware of what's going on." Cassia raised her chin and I mouthed *beta?* "Hiro will be on duty tonight so I can be here, and everything I do, he does just as well. Except for fight. No one can beat me in a fight."

"You sure about that, girl?" Jolly rasped at her with a lopsided grin on his face. "Only got one arm, and I bet I could take you."

The former alpha and security head had cleaned himself up a lot. His cheeks and chin cleared of beard and stubble with a neat goatee left behind. His locs had been cared for and tied back, the sides of his head shaved smooth. He grinned and looked younger than he did when we first met.

"Looking good, Jolly." I smiled at him and pulled him into a hug. "I appreciate you fighting with us to help save Connell."

"Any time, Marcus." He rested his hand on my shoulder and winked at me. "You be careful in Grestal. Everything has its place, but there are places that will try to have you, so keep your shit together. Got me?"

I nodded and whispered, "Keep an eye on my uncle 'til I get back?"

"Always." He smirked and grabbed my tearful uncle by the shoulder. "Let's go and get you some tissues and a beer, eh?"

He was off with nary another word that I could hear and I just shook my head before making my way toward Galaxy. She met us with a smile, then informed us, "Arden won't be on shift tonight either, or here. She has sequestered herself in her home so that she can dwell on her decision some more. She tells me nothing else."

"Thank you." I sighed and asked, "Anymore luck on more information about the Wild Hunt?"

"Just what I can find in a lot of media, video games, and fictional books." She shrugged, "The man that you met with the Fae as a guard is an author, it seems. He wrote a book that had mentioned the Wild Hunt in it, though from what I could gather it was a thread that was barely unraveled. Perhaps he, or his Fae companion, could be of use in this matter?"

"Maybe?" I blinked at her. "I'm not sure how to get a hold of him though."

"No need to worry, I found him on the book of many faces." She tapped what looked to be a brand-new phone a few times with her thumbs and smiled. Then she frowned. "It seems he's under the impression that if he goes to a bar with a woman of any sort, his fiancée will murder him. Though he appreciates the invitation."

I laughed. "Sounds about right. If you were able to find him, I'll be able to."

Pulling out my phone, I opened the app that I used probably the least since I got back from the hospital and started looking for the guy with help from Galaxy.

Within minutes, I had a message from him asking me for the address and that he'd meet us if he could.

I walked over to Keith and told him that I was expecting a human acquaintance to come here and to let him in.

He stared at me skeptically, but I just shrugged and told him he was okay so far as I knew of.

Lucifer came over to me, concern on his slightly gaunt, angular face. "They say that you mean to journey into Grestal?" He leaned against the bar next to me, his long dark hair swaying as he moved. "You still owe me songs, my friend."

I nodded to the karaoke equipment having been set up already. "I think they mean for that to be paid tonight." He smiled and so did I. Despite the fact that this guy was literally Satan, he was alright. Definitely someone that I'd call a fast friend. "You picked what songs I'll be singing for you?"

I held up three fingers and his smile widened to a boyish grin, making me groan. "Are they really that heinous?"

"No?" He raised an eyebrow, then chuckled. "They're songs that I like, but many people may not know. The first one is *Lover I don't have to love*, originally performed by Bright Eyes, but I first heard it as a cover by a band called TFDI."

"I think I've heard that one!" I smiled; he did have great taste. "Real sultry tones, a breathier singer?"

"That's the one!" He clapped in delight. "I think you'll do it well."

"You have two more, any ideas?" I pressed him but he simply smiled and raised his hand for the bartender, Xerxes, to come and take an order.

"Hey Luci, Marcus!" he greeted us happily. "What'll you have?" He stopped Luci. "Please tell me you want something other than a Bloody Mary again?"

I laughed and Luci looked wounded. "I like them! How about a Manhattan for me and an... Old Fashioned for Marcus?"

"Coming right up, boys!" Xerxes started mixing the drinks as we turned back to each other.

"Thanks for that." I smiled and watched as the werewolf made our drinks to perfection. He was good at his craft. "And thanks again for helping us get Connell back how you could."

He waved it away. "I was offered a deal too good to pass on, no more." He put a hand on my forearm and muttered, "You used my assistance to dance around my question. Why do you go to Grestal?"

"We're going to be looking for the Huntsman's mantle," I answered honestly. "The council seems to think I would make a good candidate to become the leader of the Wild Hunt, and I think I could do some real good with it."

"There hasn't been a Huntsman who lasted any longer than a few years that didn't go almost completely insane, Marcus," Lucifer whispered back. Xerxes gave us our drinks and Lucifer nodded to him politely. "The last one killed and ate an entire dragon before he was... put down."

"Do you know why?" He shook his head and I took a sip of my drink. The Old Fashioned was a damn fine drink still. "I have to risk it. Even if I don't find it, they'll kick me out of the High Table if I fail to become the Huntsman."

"Would that be so bad?" Lucifer wondered aloud, staring at me as he took a drink, then another and finished his. "Damn, that's good. Would it be so bad to not be here as an employee?"

"I'd lose the protection of the Table, and it would mean that the Seelie and their whole Summer Court could come after me with nothing in their way." I took a larger drink of mine. "Either way, I'm a dead man, so I may as well commit."

"I'd protect you," he said without a second thought. "You could come and be my personal bartender. I'd shower you in all the alcohol you've never dreamed of and so much more."

I laughed and pulled him into a hug, clapping him on the back. "You know what? If I can't find the mantle, I'll take it." I paused after I pulled back. "You do know that would mean having to let Cass and Arden come to spend time with us, right?"

He smirked. "I knew they'd weasel their way into my home eventually. Quite the small price to pay for a personal bartender and a safe friend, don't you think?" He clapped and grinned at me. "Would that make you my Maze?"

I snorted, almost spilling my drink. "I think it would."

He sighed and closed his eyes. "Father, I adore that show."

I shook my head and clapped his shoulder. "Think of those other two songs for me, eh?"

He nodded and raised his hand for Xerxes to bring another round before he waved to me while I walked away.

I stopped near Galaxy. "You okay?"

"I find this all to be much more than should be happening, but now that I have you physically here, we must speak." She pulled me to the corner of the room, my drink in hand, and sat us at a table.

"Is this about what Servant said to you?"

She nodded and switched to speaking in my mind. *He told me that I looked to be closely related to his queen. So much so that I could be her twin.*

I blinked and frowned. *How is that possible?*

I do not know, but he holds hope that I could eventually get his master and his queen reunited on a planet I've never heard of. She took a drink of my Old Fashioned and smiled. "This is good."

"I thought so too." I smiled in return and mentally asked, *Is that something that you could do?*

If I were to become powerful enough, yes. Though he mentioned there being interference of some sort from the gods here. She sighed and stared at the door. *I know that Grestal is a real place even more densely packed with mana than this world is. Depending on our time there, I could gain much—we could gain much. Not to mention this mantle of the Huntsman.*

It will be interesting, that's for sure. I took a drink of my alcohol and grimaced at the bitterness of it being diluted by the ice. The bane of a good drink, ice. *Is that all he said to you?*

No. He said that should I find out more about myself, he would be interested to know more. He even offered to teach us magic for a price.

What price is that? I was eager to learn a little more about the creature, considering it was Fae and not of this world to begin with.

Helping to protect his master—King Zeke. Should there be a reason to call for aid. She stilled and closed her eyes. "They're here."

I blinked and looked up from her to see Keith letting the man in, his head freshly shaved and his eyes searching through the crowd. "Hey!" I called over the din and he turned my way. He wore a pair of gray shorts, a black t-shirt, and a pair of white Converse.

Servant is contained in his shadow, Galaxy warned me and I nodded.

"Hey, Marcus, right?" He reached out and grasped my hand firmly, but not the kind of grip that would be a challenge to a lot of Marines like us. "How're you doin', brother?"

"Good!" I grinned at him. "Got a little trip out of town planned in a few days, so the staff are throwing me a going away. Can I get you anything to drink?"

"Sure! I drove here, so I can't have too much." He smiled and turned to Galaxy bashfully. "Sorry about that, but getting asked to the bar to talk about my books with anyone would be weird to my fiancée—take into consideration that you're a beautiful lady and I'm pretty sure I'd be burying myself."

She laughed as I walked away from the table. "That's quite alright. Wouldn't want to hurt your queen."

He laughed too and I went to get him a drink. I tried beer first, something flavorful, and then another Old Fashioned for me, then decided to get one for the table. Who can resist?

I returned with the tray of drinks where our guest was speaking excitedly about something. "Sorry about the wait. Here's a cold one for you, one of our fruitier beers and an Old Fashioned for all of us."

"Thanks!" He lifted his beer and made a toast. "To new friends and strange worlds."

I couldn't help adding, "And to Chesty."

"To Chesty!" He growled back as we clinked our glasses and drank. He sighed, "Oh, that's great. I'm not usually one for beer, but that? That's good."

I grinned. "Glad you liked it."

Galaxy interrupted, "Chris was just telling me about how his plans for the Wild Hunt had been so far thwarted by his party in his previous work."

"Oh, awesome." I leaned forward and paused as he waited to continue. "Please, go on. I'd love to hear all about it."

"Well, things happen that the Hunt is delayed from getting to the group in time, and as they would have their quarry, one of the group summons the Queen of the Unseelie's attention with her name." He took another sip and continued. "After that, they're whisked away and the Hunt has no choice but to move on."

"I see." I hummed, and looked at Galaxy. "And what's the purpose of the Wild Hunt? I mean, in your book, it's to chase down the boys and kill them, if able to, right?"

"Right!" he agreed and tapped the table. "But that's not all. They protect the realm itself from intruders and lawbreakers. They fell under the control of the Seelie court for a while there and started hunting down specific kinds of creatures, those banished there or who made their way to the Fae Realm without being invited. But they were meant to be a force that protected the Fae and those who obeyed the laws."

"Were they always just a force for the Fae to use?" Galaxy asked curiously, but he shook his head. "Who else used them?"

"Well, in the history of my world, no one else has had the chance to use them that way in centuries, due to the Seelie controlling them." He took the time to think a bit. "But there's lore in all kinds of cultures here on Earth describing the Wild Hunt as a collection of monsters that comes in the night to ride down some terrible sinner or evil. Everything from faeries and demons to the souls of the dead having been used in the party to go after something. Though said something wasn't always described."

So this is *an opportunity to do some good,* I thought triumphantly. If we could get this mantle and get the power for ourselves, we could stop people like Ascal Qin Moira, or worse, from doing whatever the hell they wanted.

"Do you know how they get their powers?" Galaxy took a deep drink of her Old Fashioned and watched him.

"They relinquish them upon death to the next in line. A chosen, typically." He shrugged and seemed a little confused. "Is there a reason for the sudden interest in the Wild Hunt?"

"Yeah, we've got a wager on how you did it, and apparently I lost." I smiled at him and he relaxed a bit. "So, got a lot more planned for the series? I see only three are out so far?"

"Yeah, I have a lot planned for the world and the characters to come. Even more after." He grinned and leaned back a little. "Is there anything else you wanted to ask about?"

"Yes!" Galaxy spoke a little louder than she had meant to, and she offered a bashful smile. "Who is it that defends Maebe? I mean, other than herself, given how powerful she is."

"Well, you have her champion, then her guards." He smirked and added, "Then there are the various Fae creatures that she knows the true names of who answer to her."

"Oh?" She tilted her head. "And what would one of them be? Who are they?"

"Ancient ancestors that died in a horrible battle that the embodiment of their realm felt was… unjust. So they gave them the power to return in different forms." He smiled fondly as if recalling something. "The stronger they grow, the more of their original personality comes back."

"What are their names?" I asked, tracking her train of thought.

He laughed. "Well, those are going to be in the story!" He shook his head. "I want you to be surprised when it happens, but I will say that one would have you call him Servant."

I blinked at him and he took another drink. "What if he was real?"

He swallowed and looked at me as if I were crazy. "I mean, they talk to me in my head sometimes—my characters—but that doesn't mean anyone outside the main party is real."

"If you believed he was real, and you said his true name, do you think he would come?" I chuckled before taking a drink of my own.

"Don't I wish." He rolled his eyes, suddenly looking bashful and dejected. "Unfortunately, it's a made-up world that I used for selfish reasons."

"What if it wasn't?" Galaxy asked breathily, her eyes on his. "What if it was all real, and the voices you hear are memories that you can't forget?"

"That would make me crazier than I already am?" Chris chuckled uncertainly.

"Say the name with feeling then, Zeke." I flinched at the name and so did the author. "Be the king your memories tell you that you are."

He rolled his eyes and heaved a sigh. "If it will stop this weirdness, fine. Mil—"

Servant's dark figure rose up behind him and touched his shoulder. "King Zeke, do not say my name here in front of these people."

The author's eyes rolled up into the back of his head and he pitched forward onto the table with a loud crash.

Servant fixed us with his glowing eyes and growled, "What is your ploy?"

CHAPTER FOUR

I carried the hefty man up to Uncle Yen's office and put him in the chair while Galaxy and Servant whispered vehemently at each other behind me.

"Why would you trigger his memories and bring me out like this?" Servant hissed. "It is bad enough that he recalls his time in our world with my Queen in the way that he does, but this? Even after I had previously asked you to help me protect him. How can I do that now?"

He motioned to the still sleeping man in the chair, his rather noisy snoring bringing me back to my days as a lance and I *really* wanted to draw a mustache on his forehead.

"If he knows who he is and that you're here, we can protect him more effectively," Galaxy retorted with a roll of her eyes.

"That puts an even larger target on him!" The shadowy Fae hissed evilly. "Your gods hauled him back and repressed his memories, and now they are free to run rampant! They could kill him for this!"

"Do you truly think they would?" I asked, taking some of the attention from Galaxy. "We have the devil downstairs right now, likely on his third Manhattan, enough werewolves and other kinds of lycans that even a Van Helsing would shit their pants, and not to mention a few *very* protective and *highly* rowdy Oni. Do you think a god is going to try to come to a neutral place to kill one guy for his memories?"

"I do not just think it, I obsess over it," Servant snarled. "My whole duty is to protect him until such a time as he can either return home on his own, or dies after living his life here!"

"Why?" Galaxy asked in confusion. "You said that your queen loves this man and he loves her, shouldn't they be together?"

"I have already told you what happened, and cannot be bothered to explain again." He huffed and went over to check on his master. "He is so… pathetic here. Like a baby."

"Why don't we just kill him and allow him to go on to his home?" I asked, not really sure what to expect.

Servant turned on me and snarled, his form shifting into that of a great cat that bounded across the room at me. I ducked him and pulled my Oni blade.

"He returned home to be with his child here, anything that will take that from him is not something I will allow." Servant's teeth bared at me again as he paced around us to stand between myself and Chris.

"I won't kill him; it was just a thought." I shook my head and turned to Galaxy. *Are you sure we need this guy?*

He knows more about Queen Maebe than even Servant does. He will be useful even if it's only as a lore guy. She watched him as he slept on and frowned slightly. *It means that he might know something of me too.*

Okay. I glared at Servant for a moment and said, "We will honor a pact to protect him should either of you need us, but we're going to be away for a time. No, I don't know how long, just know that we're coming back if we can."

"Then how do you mean to protect him in the interim?" Servant shifted and took his shadowy elven form.

"He can come here to the High Table," I offered, texting Cassia to come upstairs real quick.

"And you think that enough?"

"It'll have to be, Servant." Chris coughed once and sat up a bit straighter in the chair. "I cannot believe this. It was all real. And here I am, on Earth, and everything is… not as it seems."

Servant turned and knelt in front of his king. "My king, forgive me for trying to keep you ignorant. I thought it the best way to keep you safe."

"I understand, but we have a lot to talk about." He put a hand on the Fae's shoulder. "A lot."

The other man nodded and stood, backing out of the way so that he could stand behind the chair his king sat in. "So does this mean we call you Chris, King Zeke? I don't know."

"Neither do I, but I'm not on Brindolla and King Zeke would be awkward." He smiled and shrugged. "Chris is fine, and thanks for agreeing to help him look after me. I don't know what he's promised you in return, but he will pay it."

"He's offered to help give us access to shadow and ice types of magic," Galaxy stated offhand. "This was not too long ago, so I trust you remember? But we could try to do more with a little information from you?"

"I'll help where I can, if only because it may make your lives easier." He smiled and pulled out his phone, opening it and tapping around on it. "Here, put your phone numbers in here for me and I'll answer anything I can via text or a meet up like this."

I entered my phone number, then texted myself and Galaxy did the same before passing his phone back to him.

She asked softly, "Did this Queen Maebe have a sister?"

He shook his head. "Not that she ever told me about, no. But I take it since you're asking that you could be a Celestial Elf like her?"

"That is correct, my king." Servant answered before she could. "She looks almost exactly like her."

Chris looked conflicted, like he wanted to ask her to change and show him, but there was a look of fear and worry in his gaze, then he shook his head. "I'll take your word for it, bud."

He stood up out of the chair, glancing back at Servant. "Uphold your end of the bargain and return to me in my car in the parking lot."

Servant nodded and waited as Chris stepped closer to us and shook our hands. "Thank you for helping with that. And more, likely. I'll come back sometime soon, and don't be a stranger. I'll be getting a grill soon and I want to have people over."

I grinned at him and said, "Of course, brother. What self-respecting Marine says no to a barbecue?"

"A dumber one than I know." He snickered back and we both shared a chuckle before he left the room and we turned back to Servant.

"How best do you learn magic?" he asked Galaxy as he crossed the room toward us.

"Usually just by having the magic done on him enough." She pointed to me. "But I can also just take some of your mana."

He frowned and pointed at me, a small shard of ice piercing my arm painfully.

"Ah, you motherf—"

More ice slammed into my arm and my legs began to freeze where they were. My blood started to feel like a slushy in my veins and I grew woozy.

"That's good," Galaxy blurted and the pain faded slightly. She reached out and absorbed some of the magic from the wounds and they healed a little faster than they would've with just my own healing abilities.

"And the shadows I will allow you to devour." He held his hand up and out to her with his head bowed like he was some kind of suitor.

She closed her eyes and a sucking sound ripped through me as she ate. His cheeks looked a bit gaunt to me, but she had finished and actually belched loudly before saying, "Thank you."

He nodded his head and faded from view without another word.

"He's gone." Cassia opened the door and tromped in as Galaxy spoke and looked at us strangely.

"Your human friend just left, and said you would be up here with his servant. What's going on?"

"He knows about the creature that had been in his dog now; apparently he was a king on another planet and plane and that had been hidden from him mentally. He thought it all a dream and we made him aware that it wasn't. So we're going to be providing him protection now." She stared at me uncertainly and I added. "He's one of ours now. If he comes here, he's to be treated like a patron as any Touched might be."

She perked right up. "Sure!" She texted something to someone on her phone and a second later there was a ping. "He's added to the index, and Yen will add him to the tome as soon as he can."

"Thank you." I looked over to Galaxy. "Can you get those spells to us? I still have points."

"The mana is more complex than I'm used to, but it feels… better?" She frowned. "No, that's not it. I'll get them into your systems as soon as I can relate them."

I nodded and turned to Cass. "I really meant for you to see him personally but he really wanted to leave."

"Well, I can imagine being outed to yourself like that has its setbacks mentally, and getting out of a noisy bar surrounded by things that you previously thought were myths would be necessary. It's like that for a lot of Normies." She shrugged as if it was the simplest thought ever. "It's almost time for people to start singing. You ready to pay the price your hubris allowed?"

I snorted. "I suppose so. Gonna need another couple drinks, though." I frowned. "Where's Merlin?"

"He's training with bubba Kenshi again." Cassia smiled, likely knowing I did *not* want him to see me singing.

"Good." I sighed and motioned for her and Galaxy to follow me out. "Let's get this show on the road."

———

"Luce, you're killing me." I groaned and the devil just grinned at me with all his pearly whites showing. "Are you seriously making me sing Britney Spears?"

"Toxic is one of *the* best songs I've ever heard and I have heard almost all of them!" He teased me with his wolfish grin growing only larger.

We'd felt bad having to turn people away, so I asked that Uncle Yen opened the bar to the patrons as a show of love and he had agreed, already deeper into his cups than I would have liked. Even Jolly stayed sober for him, which was saying something from what I'd heard.

Someone hollered, "Free Bird!"

Lucifer rolled his eyes, "Plebs."

So, I took the stage to cheers and applause; Lucifer had already selected my song and I started to sing Toxic. By now, I was about four Old Fashioneds in and had just polished off a rather tasty drink called a Comet, courtesy of Xerxes, that made me feel like I could actually pull this song off.

The music came on and suddenly I was more than happy to belt this song out, much to Lucifer's delight and the crowd's pleasure. I sang that tune like I owned it and had not a single fuck to give for it.

I was pretty sure that more than a couple of them were recording it, but it was what I owed, and for once I was happy. Were things perfect? Hell no. Was I about to risk my life? Yup.

But I was doing something. Something that now rivaled my service for the Marine Corps.

I hopped off the stage and let someone else sing an actually good song as I schmoozed and spoke to some of the patrons and folks who had well wishes for me and Cassia as well as anyone else going to Grestal.

Eventually, I'd had too much and everything got dark and blurry.

I woke up in a muddled state with Cassia spooning my foot

and light like stars whirling through the room. The messy grossness my hangover should have left me with was gone, replaced by fascination at the display above me.

Galaxy sat on the floor next to the bed, her gaze lifted to the sky and magical lights above her as tears streamed down her face. She looked like she was speaking to something, or about something, as I gently extracted my leg from Cassia's iron-like grip.

I leaned down once I was free and grabbed her into my arms. "Hey. You alright?"

She sniffed and wiped tears from her face. "Yes, I'll be fine. I just... Sometimes at night when all of you dream, your memories flood me, and I wonder what I could be. *Who* I could be. Why I don't have any memories past a few basic things."

I pulled her off the ground easily, a soft gasp escaping her throat as I turned with her so that she was between me and Cassia. I shook the larger woman and her eyes burst open red as she glared around.

"Cool it, Cass. Galaxy needs us right now," I warned her with a soft growl. Her gaze cleared of the crimson and she stared at the woman between us. "Make new memories here with us until we can get yours back, okay?"

Cassia wrapped her legs around Galaxy's and snuggled closer, muttering, "I like it when you sleep next to me, because you're soft and small and smell like ozone."

I had to fight not to laugh out loud at that last one, shaking my head and saying, "You smell like flowers; she's drunk and tired."

She laughed as well and let the larger woman hold her like a baby, though her hand raised and found my cheek, her palm warm and inviting. I pressed my cheek against it and was drawn into her. So inviting and encompassing.

It was hours before I woke and even then it was only because someone was beating on the door.

I went to rise and found Galaxy straddling my waist, then

getting up as if she hadn't been there at all to go and answer the door.

"What is it, Merlin?" she asked, her now-clothed body still in elven form.

"The Wardens arrived sooner than I thought and tracked me here; they're outside demanding that they either be allowed in, or I come with them." I was up and dressing after the first thought. "I still have that letter from Amelia that asked me to give it to them. But I don't know what else to do."

"We're responsible for you," I growled and pulled my shirt over my head. "I smell like a fucking bar."

"This is a bar." He smiled and muttered a few words, then suddenly I was cleaner and better smelling than I had been before. "Better?"

"Much." I frowned at the still-waking Cassia who smacked her lips and cast her gaze about the room. "Wardens have come to get Merlin; we're going to chat with them. Join us as soon as you can."

She nodded and flung herself off the bed with a massive thud as we headed out into the hall. I pulled Merlin to the front and muttered, "You go down there like nothing is wrong and like you could kill every motherfucker in that room, got me?"

He nodded and took a deep breath in and released it before stepping down the stairs into the main bar.

Someone snarled, "Finally!" A man in his mid-forties rolled his eyes and stood, his clothes a little tighter than they should have been, but it looked like he worked out. He crossed his arms and nodded to the door where a couple of robed figures stood waiting. "Let's go, I have shit to do."

"You would do well to mind your tongue, Warden Jetlo." An older, wiser-looking man sat next to Uncle Yen at one of the bars, the stool beneath him hidden behind his robes. "The boy belongs to me."

"Yeah, yeah, whatever." Jetlo spat and began to pace like a caged lion, eyes on Merlin, then flicking to us. "Who are these two?"

"My friends," Merlin stated simply. "Good to see you again, wise Master Xehano. I wish it were under better circumstances."

"As do I," the hooded man said with a tired sigh. "You were given orders to come to us, why didn't you?"

"I had other tasks that were important and I thought that it would take time for the Orders to come together." He bowed his head, then stepped closer. "I have word from the council of the High Table that Head Member Amelia asked me to give to you."

"Thank you." He took the envelope and as soon as he touched it, the milky-white object burst into a thousand pieces and left a note in the air. "Oh?"

As he spoke, the letter quivered and settled onto the table slowly before a magical hologram of Amelia's head appeared above it. "Hello, I hope this finds those of the three Orders well."

"A letter in magic? Quite interesting." Xehano frowned and paid closer attention.

"Stupid if you ask me." Jetlo sidled closer but kept us in his sight.

"No one did." I crossed my arms and turned back to the letter as he glared at me.

"As you'll likely be forced to come to the High Table due to it being relevant in the disappearance and death of Warden Varlin, I find myself in the precarious position of knowing enough, and yet far too little," Amelia stated vaguely, almost as if she expected this to cause a stir. It did. "Varlin is—as you are certain to have confirmed by now—dead. And his killers are those who work with the High Table."

"This is an outrage!" Jetlo howled, his closed fist slamming into his left palm and drawing a sword like some old-fashioned anime. "Who!"

"If this letter has reached you," Amelia spoke on chipperly. "You'll likely be in the presence of one of them. Our recently hired Marcus Bola, and the head of security for the Columbus High Table, the Oni Cassia."

As she said my name, I raised my hand and Cassia hopped down the steps with ease. "What'd I miss, Marcus?"

"We've been outed for having a part in Varlin's death." I rolled my eyes, wishing that I had been able to at least break the news myself in a more... controlled and less blasé manner. "They're mad."

"That's an understatement." Cassia glared at the man obviously from the Order of the Sword whose now-drawn weapon was up and aimed in our direction.

Amelia's tone darkened somewhat in the letter. "They are not to be harmed, as their reasoning for killing him was well-noted and I tasted no lies."

"How can we trust a dhampyr to tell the truth!" Jetlo growled and stared at us. "You probably did it on her command, didn't you? Admit it."

The older, wizened voice barked, "Quiet, fool!"

Jetlo's mouth snapped shut and Amelia spoke again, "The High Table stands with their statement, and as such, will afford them the protection necessary to sustain their employment and our ends. We, the Council of the Table, find their actions suitable and in accordance with the wishes of the High Table and in protecting our patrons—of which Warden Varlin threatened many and abused some. You know this to be true as well."

Her voice paused and the sword-wielding asshat muttered something under his breath murderously, but she continued speaking before I could challenge him to repeat himself.

"Varlin came to the High Table with the intent to harm one of our patrons that he had abused and hurt before, and did so while under the influence of a drug that ate away at his mind and mana to the point where he became a danger to himself and others." Amelia's voice took on a softer note as she said, "His death, orchestrated by Cassia and Marcus, was a mercy. Though I am certain his loss injures you both in pride and in saving face, please take the circumstances into account with his death."

"I say we kill them right now." Jetlo stomped forward with his sword raised, but Merlin suddenly stood in front of him with his own sword drawn.

Jetlo sliced his blade at Merlin to get him to move aside, but Merlin's sword blocked the blow as he shook his head. "No. They've done nothing wrong."

"Step aside, boy, now!" Jetlo roared and whipped around in a back kick aimed at the boy's chest, but Merlin just set his feet and caught the booted foot, sliding backward a couple feet. Begrudgingly impressed, Jetlo stood and looked to the older mage, "I thought you claimed him?"

"I did." Xehano's facial features except for his mouth were hidden from sight thanks to his hood, but his mouth formed a straight line. "What is the meaning of this, Merlin?"

"I've grown strong enough on my own to work differently." He squared his shoulders and bowed his head, lifting his sword in both hands. "I have found that I have developed an affinity for the Way of the Sword and would like to pursue it."

"That's impossible." Jetlo crossed his arms weirdly, the sword still somehow managing to be readily accessible and put into motion. "The Orders haven't had someone mix since the beginning."

"The Orders haven't seen someone like Merlin in millennia either," Xehano stated as he looked over Merlin. "What did you sacrifice and to who?"

"I sacrificed nothing, but was given everything." He spread his arms and let them see his new physique that matched his speed and strength. "With this new ability, I would like to audition for the right to become a member of the Order of the Sword, as well as retain my membership to the Staff."

"You would have yourself be a Chimera?" One of the cloaked figures at the door laughed, a younger man from the looks of him as he dropped his hood. He had black hair, dark red eyes, and a smile that made me wonder if he was a Warden at all. "This I have to see."

"Does this mean that the Order of the Heart gives permission for him to attempt it?" Xehano raised an eyebrow and Merlin frowned. "Forgive me. Theodorous decided that he would watch from the guise of a lesser Warden at the door rather than make his presence known."

"He's much too young to be an acting member of the Heart," Merlin stated, confusion evident in his tone.

"He would be, ordinarily, but much like you, Theodorous is a prodigy of sorts and now a member of this Judgement Tribunal," Xehano muttered with distaste that he tried to contain by sounding displeased as he spoke to Merlin. "You would waste yourself with the Sword?"

"I would see myself become something better." Merlin lifted his chin. "I wish to fight and protect the innocents of this world, and know that the staff is not the only viable weapon."

Jetlo snorted, grinning lopsidedly at the older Warden. "He has you there. Staff is for support and you know it." He looked over at Theodorous and raised an eyebrow. "Justice hasn't been decided. We still don't know what young trainee Merlin was doing. Or who his allegiance is to, now that he's mysteriously acquired this new power."

"My allegiance is to those who need me, my patron being my way of serving in a newer capacity." Merlin spoke again, a little more fanatical than I would have liked. "While I was training with Warden Varlin, he was apt to leave me alone for days on end and do what he liked. When we arrived here in Columbus, he disappeared again and I went on the required patrols to investigate the area and the deaths that had been occurring, as had been our orders from the Heart. While under his tutelage, Varlin became steadily more and more unhinged and started using a drug called 'Divinity' by its creators. By the time I figured this out, I had been saved from a junkie giantess who had been dealing the same substance by Cassia, Marcus, and another who is not here."

"What happened after that?" Theodorous asked, his smile still firmly in place.

"I reported in that things were normal, because they were, and then continued on with my investigation, knowing that these two had something to do with my trainer's disappearance —at this time he was still alive." Merlin took a deep breath in, then continued on. "Once I figured out that there was a chance that I would be recalled before completing our mission, and that it was the mission that had taken my trainer from me by way of the drug, I set about righting things with my rescuers."

"You worked hand in hand with a rogue Touched, an Oni, and whatever other filthy creature to solve this?" Jetlo roared his belittling question at the boy. "Warden business?"

I really want to kill him, I found myself thinking, hoping that he would swing that sword at Merlin or me once more so I had him dead to rights. Cassia must have sensed my bloodlust and grasped my shoulder, giving me the look that said she was right there with me.

"This 'Warden business' had already affected them here at the High Table, and I had no other leads." He shook his head and straightened himself out. "Arden isn't a filthy creature— she's a noble jinn and powerful beyond belief. With these peoples' help, I was able to assist in shutting down a threat that would have gone global before Christmas. It *killed* a Warden and would have enslaved countless others before we could have gotten a handle on it."

"If you had reported it, we would have been able to send more backup to assist you," Xehano retorted, refuting Merlin's logic, adding further, "If you had failed, you would have allowed the very thing that you had been working to stop. You were trained to put your faith in the Order, that the Order would provide and assist you in ways you could not on your own. Why did you fail in this?"

"Because he feared for his life," I interjected, Jetlo's sword falling to the ready again. "Shake that thing at me again, moth-erfucker, and I'll kill you."

His eyes widened as he smiled, taking a step forward until Theodorous barked, "Still!" Jetlo's eyes bulged and he froze as if placed in ice. Not a single muscle in his body moved other than what kept him alive. Theodorous turned to Merlin and barked, "Truth!"

Merlin grimaced and shook his head, fighting to the point that the veins in his neck bulged and he shook hard enough that I thought he was going to have a stroke, if not already having one. He grit his teeth and I stepped over to him. *Galaxy, eat whatever is affecting him if you can.*

Yes, Marcus. She answered and guided my hand to the back of his neck where her presence filtered into him, easing the discomfort almost immediately.

"Why do you resist me? All I want is the truth!" Theodorous grinned some more. "I said, *truth!*"

This time, he just sighed and looked over at him. "Marcus is correct. I worried that if you knew that I had allowed myself to work with what you all see as lesser beings outside your control, and had failed to bring Varlin's issues to your sight in a timely manner, you would restart my training or kill me."

"You think we would kill you?" Xehano hissed as if he had heard the worst kind of lies. "Merlin, I trained you personally for the last three years of your life. I have treated you as the son I always wished to have! I would never kill you."

"I would," Jetlo stated simply from where he still stood frozen. It came out all weird though, as if his mouth just couldn't move right.

I really fucking want to kill him. It doesn't help that they killed his parents and stole him either. My internal monologue must have bled into my face because Xehano flinched. "See why he was so worried? Any other Warden would have killed him. Hell, Varlin tried to drain him of his magic while he was dying from the drug. He was right to think that way."

"You have no stake in this matter, rogue." Xehano snorted as he glared at me. "Your masters at the High Table Council have all but absolved you of Varlin's death and have bought you your freedom from our wrath so far. You may leave."

"As long as you have my friend at your mercy, I think I'll stay." I crossed my arms and set my feet. "You are, after all, in my place of business."

"Then I think it time that we leave here and discuss things in a more secluded and private domain." Xehano stood up and made a motion with his hand, some sort of portal ripping to life in the middle of the bar room.

"No," Theodorous stated simply, as if he were in charge. The portal sputtered and stalled, then disappeared. Xehano turned to look at the younger man, speechless. "Here is fine. He thinks we would have killed him. We assure him that we won't, then when his friends state that they are going to stay and watch over his health, we get all secretive and want to go somewhere else—it's pointless and creates more unnecessary implications and misunderstandings."

He stepped between the two elder Wardens and said, "This tribunal is now in effect." He snapped his fingers and Jetlo unfroze. "Warden trainee Merlin, step forward and kneel for judgement in the failure to report."

Merlin did as he was told, his kneeling much the same as it had been with Kenshi.

"Orders, how do you find the subject before you on the matter of his failure to report, and, if guilty, what do you recommend as punishment?" Theodorous raised his voice.

"I find him guilty," Jetlo gleefully answered, his sword on his shoulder now, but he stared at the boy beside him. "His punishment should be the death he so feared as retribution."

Xehano frowned and stated, "I, too, find him guilty." He lifted his hand as the Sword Warden began to cackle. "However I think his punishment should be further training and counseling on how the Order works within the world."

Theodorous rubbed his hairless chin in consideration, and finally nodded. "Very well. I also feel that trainee Merlin failed in his duties, but will remand my sentence upon the completion of this tribunal."

Xehano turned to look at the boy. "That was the only thing that had been set to judgement, Theodorous! There was nothing else."

"False," the Order of the Heart representative stated dispassionately. "He asked to be permitted to join the Order of the Sword, did he not? This also takes a tribunal decision with a majority vote. We will vote now."

"I refuse," Xehano spat vehemently. "His talents would be wasted there, and he cannot be trusted until he is retrained."

Jetlo snorted. "I don't think he would cut it."

Theodorous smiled. "But that wasn't a *no* was it?"

"The only way I would approve is if he were to pass our rite of passage test, and there's no way he could." Jetlo shook his head.

"What does that entail?" Theodorous asked quietly.

"A trip to Grestal to hunt down a monster of at least tier six or above." He crossed his arms again and nodded toward Merlin. "He would have at least a few more years of training before he would be able to do it. And even then, there's a high mortality rate."

"Ah." Theodorous grinned. "Then my vote is yes, that he be allowed to attempt the rite of passage and become a fully-fledged member of your Order as his punishment. This satisfies both of your wishes."

He motioned to his right at Xehano. "If he succeeds, he will have been trained well enough to make it as a fully trained Warden." He motioned to his left at Jetlo. "And should he fail, it will be because he died. Is this an adequate agreement?"

The two elder Wardens nodded silently, both looking like they had swallowed something disgusting. "Good. Dismissed."

Jetlo swore beneath his breath, glaring at me and Cassia before turning and walking out of the bar, his sword disappearing as soon as he crossed the doorway.

Xehano looked like he wanted to speak to Merlin, but

Theodorous turned to look pointedly at him and said, "You are not permitted to interfere in my judgement, Warden Xehano. That means no contact with him until I say so, or he passes or fails his trial. *Dismissed.*"

The older Warden grimaced and snapped his fingers, disappearing from his spot instantly. Theodorous turned to Cassia and me. "If I understand correctly, you were being lenient in not killing Warden Jetlo as soon as he drew his sword, were you not?"

I would have attacked him on principle alone, but Cassia answered, "We can give someone a warning to leave or put it away, but yes, if we felt someone was sufficiently threatened, we could have. If you aren't staff and you have a weapon in here and draw it, your life is ours."

"I could have killed him for that?" I instantly felt cheated. "Fuck!"

"I appreciate your restraint." He smiled at me and chuckled. "Known or not."

He leaned down and touched Merlin on the shoulder and bid him, "Rise."

Merlin stood with the other man's hand on his shoulder and eyed him. "I know that your memories have been affected, otherwise you would not have been able to fight my command like that." He smiled and pointed at his chest. "The Heart runs everything, Merlin. We know all. I am disappointed that a young mage such as yourself chose not to come to our Order over the others to become a Chimera, but I understand the circumstances. Personally speaking, I think I would risk their wrath and death to produce results as well."

He patted Merlin's shoulder and turned to us. "Marcus Bola, Cassia the Oni, I believe I have you to thank for this potential nightmare being over with for now?" He held his hand out and neither of us moved to shake it, he just smiled more broadly and nodded to himself. "I understand, tensions high and all that. I am the new Ventricle here in Columbus— that's the leader of the Order within the city—and the outlying areas within the state now fall under my jurisdiction as well."

"How?" Merlin wondered at him, Theodorous turning to him to blink in his direction. "You can't be more than a year or two older than I am. How is that possible?"

"I am... as gifted as you are." Theodorous replied with a smile. "It is much to the chagrin of my peers and 'betters' that I attained this position so swiftly as I have, but I assure you that there will be no finer hand in this state than my own to control and manage the Wardens of Ohio."

He nodded to us and turned to his associate. "Oh, and one more thing!" He glanced back our way. "I see some promise in you, young Merlin. I expect great things—should you survive."

With a merry tune whistled into the air, he walked out of the bar with his associate going out behind him. Another one visible just on the other side of the door walking in front of him stepped into the street like a guard might before fading from sight.

"That was interesting," I muttered, but Cassia just went to Merlin and pulled him into a hug. "You okay, kiddo?"

He nodded, a bleak expression on his face. "What's wrong?"

"He has to kill a tier six creature or above in Grestal," Cassia hissed back.

"That doesn't sound too crazy." I shrugged. "Those junky Fae were pretty hard to kill, and that grass thing was pretty crazy, but it couldn't have been too high on the list."

"That creature was a tier ten, Marcus," Merlin whispered softly. "A tier four creature is something akin to say, the kraken. A dragon, tier two."

"Oni are tier ten. Jinn as well," Arden whispered from behind me. She looked distraught. "I thought I had the courage to say no, even with your offer to help me avenge and find my family. Now Merlin has to fight a tier six creature and win?"

"Oh," I muttered. "Well, he'll have us for it, so that's something, right?"

"About as useful as a pack of dogs trying to take down a

drake." Arden scowled and shook her head. "I have no choice now; I have to come with you."

"You'll always have a choice, Arden." I motioned to Merlin. "No one is going to force you to come with us."

I can. Galaxy's smile inside my head was spine tingling until her breath caught. *Oh, this is interesting.*

I blinked and suddenly saw that Arden was flush and looked really worried for some reason. *Spit it out, Galaxy.*

I never noticed it before, but now that I see it, it makes so much sense. She separated from me and stepped toward Merlin. "He's part jinn."

Merlin, Cassia, and I stilled and looked toward her before she and I asked, "He's *what?*"

CHAPTER FIVE

Merlin's surprise heritage had been enough to shock all of us into needing a drink, but it was Arden who looked the most distraught.

Merlin muttered, "How is that even possible? I thought jinn could only procreate with others of their kind?" He scratched his head and shook it as if trying to clear cobwebs away. "That's what we learned in all of our preternatural biology courses. Something about the differences in human DNA and the DNA of the supernatural party being too different to coexist."

That was almost how it had happened with Connell, I frowned and thought to myself. *He wasn't supposed to happen, but was elven and human DNA similar enough to allow it? Or was there something more?*

Still confused, I squinted. "I'm sorry, your what courses?" I was trying to wrap my brain around the fact that the Orders would teach something like that to their students, but then again, the Marine Corps taught Marines about the cultures they would be interacting with in country so… who was I to judge? "Sorry, just got really weirded out there."

"It shouldn't be possible." Arden sighed and ran her fingers through her hair. "Everything I've ever known said it shouldn't be possible. Jinn have been trying for years and it's never happened, yet here he is."

"Well, we'll be going to Grestal and going to the place where the jinn are, right?" I nodded when no one else said anything. "So maybe we can get some more information from someone there."

"It's likely that may be what has to happen," Galaxy advised, then looked at all four of us. "Are you finished preparing? You should bring food, something to camp with just in case, and less gun-related stuff since it's useless there."

I rolled my eyes. "Yeah, that's true." Turning to Cassia, I asked, "Do you think Kenshi will sell me a sword?"

"I know he will." She nodded and stood. "Leave your cells at home, and any other electronics too. The magic in Grestal is thick and tends to destroy modern technology."

Arden groaned and pulled out several small gaming devices. "I *hate* Grestal!"

———

A few hours later, we had the majority of what we would need, though no tent which was weird. Kenshi sold me a short sword, simple and unadorned like the one that Merlin had, that was treated with his blood. I had thought at first that he would only have katanas, but that was just my own misconceptions. He had everything from small knives to punch knives, and katanas to hefty bastard swords.

Which reminded me… "Kenshi, could you do me a solid? I'll pay you for it."

He raised an eyebrow at me and I pulled at my belt, he frowned and shook his head, "I will not fight you, bubba Marcus. Sissy Cass kill me."

I blinked at him, confused, then realized what he meant and blushed. "No!" I pulled the small punch knife from my belt and showed it to him. "I was going to see if you could make this an Oni weapon as well."

"Oh!" He looked relieved and though I had no interest, I was still a little insulted. He took the knife and ceremonially bathed it in his blood until he was satisfied, then cleaned it and handed it back to me. "Good luck in Grestal, bubba Marcus. Fight well. Remember Way of the Blade."

I nodded to him as he thumped my shoulder with the back of his hand and left me. I put the knife back into my belt and left for the parking lot where Cassia had loaded our stuff into the back of her SUV. "You ready?"

I nodded at her and she smiled. "We have a little bit of a drive ahead to get to the nearest entrance to Grestal."

"Where is it?" I raised an eyebrow at her. "Can you feel them? The entrances, that is."

She nodded. "Most creatures from there can sense them, but this is just one that I know of from Kenshi. He likes to explore and find them for us in case anything goes wrong and we need to go home quickly." She adjusted a pack and closed the trunk. "Are you familiar with Old Man's Cave?"

"Is that the one down in Logan? The cave system that a lot of humans visit?" I was concerned and she smiled. "Humans are going to be there, Cass, how can it be there?"

"Because most humans won't be brave enough to actually find it, and those who do, Grestal takes." She shrugged as if that were just the norm and she accepted it, so why shouldn't I. She must have seen my skeptical look, because she sighed and said, "Look, Grestal itself is just as predatory as the beings that live there. Our energy sustains it, gives it purpose. But occasionally it gets hungry and calls humans to it. Part of why the entrances are placed in dangerous areas, or hard to reach climates. A lot of the myths surrounding those areas are because we were there trying to protect the Normies from an even greater predator. We can't be held responsible for the ones who answer the call and die."

"Are there other places like that?" I wondered and she smiled. "It's going to be someplace ridiculous, isn't it?"

"Like Mt. Everest?" Her smile widened. "Why do you think

so few people survive it? It's not just the snow hiding all those failed climbers. There are many entrances there to Grestal, and it eats heartily there."

"Jesus." I closed my eyes and wondered how many times I had come close to an entrance to Grestal in my own life. Would I have known?

"Likely not." Galaxy's voice held a hint of a smile as she walked across the lot toward us. Her human figure mirrored her elven form, curvy and voluptuous, short shorts winding high on her waist with a tank top on, her hair parted and hanging over her shoulder and partially down her chest. She caught me staring at her, her lips parting as she prodded me mentally. *Do you find this physical form too much?*

No. I'm just... I couldn't find a word and she smirked. *You know damn well what I think and feel.*

I do. She chuckled to herself and winked at me before she bit her lower lip softly... and good God, what the hell was wrong with me? "How long is the ride? Do we need to stop and get snacks and whatnot?"

"Snacks?" I grunted and she just smiled. "You don't need to eat, do you?"

"No, but I like to." She motioned to Merlin as he joined us with Arden in tow. "Merlin told me of a drink, Doctor Salt?"

"Pepper," Merlin corrected her with a boyish grin.

"Yes, I want to try this drink and enjoy it with my friends." She stared at all of us. "It is the little things that make us enjoy life."

"Okay." I shook my head and she just clambered into the SUV as Cassia laughed and Arden rolled her eyes, piling in with us.

Galaxy and Merlin shared the back seat where they muttered and spoke to each other over the books that they had brought along with them. Arden sat in the middle section of the vehicle with her long legs up and a hand-held system in her hands that she tapped away at happily.

Cassia and I were up front with the directions and off we

went. Ten minutes in, Galaxy looked up from her book and stated, "There's a convenience store on this street, go there and collect snacks."

I just snorted and sure enough there was a green ring around the store on our minimap with an arrow pointing to it.

"How many you want?" I called back to her and she stared at me before consulting Merlin.

"I require one of each," she stated imperiously, then pointed to Merlin. "I also require one of each for Merlin. Also, get the raisins covered in chocolate, and a chocolate bar. Skittles. And pretzels."

"What the fu—you're going to shit your brains out on the way there." I growled at both of them. He was young, and she didn't know any better.

"Nonsense," she replied and smiled. "I'm not human."

I rolled my eyes and acquiesced, walking into the small store and grabbing a basket, with Arden coming along to help. "You sure you're okay with making this trip?"

"Yeah." She grabbed the pretzels and other snacks, adding some that she wanted too as I grabbed more pop than I had ever had in my life at one time. "I need answers for Merlin, and I also would love to kill the bastards who sold me and my family."

"If you make it there," someone muttered cheerily behind us and I turned to find a younger man, maybe twenty-one or so, with his hands in his pockets staring at us happily. He had a Mohawk and piercings in his nose and ears that made me think of a punk rocker.

"What'd you say?" I growled, not liking the way he was watching us.

"You won't make it to Grestal." He grinned at me and pointed to Arden with his spiked head. "Neither will the jinn, the Oni, or the traitor out there."

"Marcus—Wardens!" Arden snarled and whipped her arm up in time to swat aside a sword that sliced toward her neck.

Galaxy, get them ready! I growled, pissed that I had trusted them all enough not to listen to my instincts and bring at least one of my guns. I bellowed in frustrated sarcasm, "The space it takes up in your inventory could be useful, Marcus!"

"What?" The kid scoffed and I just cast Bolt at him, he hit the spell with his sword and cursed. "That was a weird little spell."

"Then you'll love this!" I grinned and cast Embodiment of Lightning, stepping out from behind him, then elbowed him in the back of the skull as hard as I could. His head snapped forward and he tumbled forward before another one came at me. People were screaming and running from the scene. Some of them had cell phones to their ears and others recording the fight.

Arden whipped her hands into a circle before spreading them and pressed down before a circle of flames erupted from her and flattened the two sword-wielding Wardens coming at her. "We've gotta go!"

I nodded and we booked it outside in time to watch Cassia toss a Warden onto the roof of the store. She looked at us and smiled. "Just what I needed before an annoying ride."

We piled into the SUV as they started to pour out of the store while I bellowed, "Gun it, Cassia!"

"Happily!" she roared back and punched the gas, squealing tires and the scent of burning rubber making my nose crinkle in disgust. Her actions sent us careening out of the lot and into oncoming traffic. Honks, more screeching tires, frustrated yells, and I was more than certain a few middle fingers saw us back into the right lane as we righted ourselves. "What the hell was that about?"

"Order of the Sword, was trying to kill us." I huffed as I turned around in my seat to see if we were being followed. "What the fuck."

There was no one behind us, but I could see a motorcycle leaving the lot we had just come from and heading in our direction. "We may have one on our six too."

"I can take care of that," Merlin grumbled, turning around

where he sat. I couldn't see him, but he poked his hand forward and the motorcyclist's front wheel locked into place and the rider flipped over the handles of the bike in a rather painful-looking manner.

I actually cringed, then grunted, "Oh, *shit*," as a car ran over his legs.

"Got what he deserved." Merlin smiled and turned back to face us.

Galaxy leaned forward and asked, "Where is our pop?"

I stared at her as if she were absolutely daft as I blinked at her, then at the baskets that Arden had managed to grab for us.

"Ah, excellent." She reached down and pulled out a Dr. Pepper and opened it. The fizz shot all over her, getting into her hair and face, Cassia laughing loudly as Galaxy just sat there angrily eyeing us both.

CHAPTER SIX

Half an hour into our drive, Galaxy had to change her clothes due to the pop exploding on her. She did it in a way that made it so no one could see her, including Merlin who sat next to her.

We stayed on vigil for anyone who could have been following us, taking a longer route in some respects just to throw them from our trail.

"Merlin, you have a way you can report to your handlers about your missions, so can't you tell them what's going on?" I leaned back and waited to hear his response, my eyes in the rear-view mirror for the umpteenth time.

I couldn't see anything but it made sense that I might not if there were cloaking spells and things out there.

"No go," Merlin snarled and threw his hands up. "They're not allowed to have contact with me per Ventricle Theodorous' orders. I'm on my own out here."

"Those bastards." I grumbled to myself more than anyone.

They are likely testing him in a way. Galaxy spoke softly, but I could tell that it annoyed her as well. *If he survives, he will be more welcome than any other, I should think.*

We hope, I mentally shot back. I was tired of driving already.

We rode on quietly, all attempts at conversation weighed down by a quagmire of uncertainty and awkwardness about what was coming.

"I'm excited to fight with you in Grestal, Marcus," Cassia casually uttered to me as she switched lanes. "This will be my second time to the place and I have only been to the demon portion of it."

"Demon portion? What's that mean?" I frowned at her and she chuckled. "I know. Ignorance and all."

"Grestal is broken into various sections that are treated as territories of sorts," Arden called over the seats to me. "Cassia's people are from the demonic and hellish territory, the majority of your fiends, demons, and nightmare creatures associated with a lot of myth and fantasy come from there."

"It's a really nice place if you like a lot of flayed corpses along the horizon line." Cassia smiled nervously at us. "The territories don't get too much overlap with each other due to the fact that when someone of a different race comes to another, it's either as a prisoner or as a hunter for someone else."

"That seems... weird at best?" I shook my head, then paused. "So this entrance we're going to, where does it lead, and how are we going to be okay if you guys are in places you shouldn't be?"

"Less that we shouldn't be, more that we will be suspected in," Arden corrected thoughtfully. "If we end up in Virani, you all will be my guests and will be treated as my responsibility. Same thing for Cassia if we end up in the demon city of Vel."

"Though other demons will likely try to buy you from me, so that will be riskier, all things considered," Cassia added and I saw her thinking. Likely about having to protect us all.

"What if we happen to arrive in the Mage's zone?" Merlin wondered and Arden looked back at him. "The Wardens have people deployed there to train and protect their interests. If we wind up there, there's a good chance we'll have to fight our way out."

"There is," Arden agreed and I just looked forward as we fell into silence once more.

A massive belch, almost enough to blow someone's hair back emanated from the back seat and I turned to find Galaxy grinning ear to ear. "If we have to fight, I will grow from it. Let them come."

"I'm glad you feel that way." I snorted and rolled my eyes. Though it was the truth, having to fight that many trained people was concerning. Especially in an unfamiliar area.

"Marcus, the Fae you fought before had you trumped in many ways, and you went toe to toe with them as if you were made to kill," Galaxy stated as if I wasn't aware of that fact. "This will be almost no different. Trust yourself."

I nodded and stayed quiet, thoughts still roiling through my head. Was I worthy of chasing down this mantle when everyone else had failed?

I also worried whether Galaxy was going to try to tell me I was being a big baby for thinking this as well, but she stayed quiet and allowed me my headspace for the remainder of the drive.

We pulled into a large parking lot after passing a sign for our destination and hopped out, taking some of our stuff out and putting it into our various inventories. Galaxy made all of the pop she and Merlin hadn't guzzled down disappear, leaving mainly what looked like a picnic basket behind.

"What's this for?" Arden blinked around at us.

Cassia grabbed it and handed it to Merlin. "It's so we will blend in and have an excuse for going off the beaten trail." She smiled. "No one ever thinks to stop people going for a picnic, right?"

I shrugged and we were on our way, all of us keeping an eye out for anyone who could be following us. The sky, overcast and slowly darkening, made me pause, wishing I had my phone to check the weather. But no, I left it at home in my room after sending Aeslyn an email that I was going to Grestal and to tell Connell I loved him.

No response, but I was pretty much used to that by now.

We hiked down the main trail a way, Cassia leading the way when she stopped and lifted her head toward a small waterfall. "The entrance moved from where I remember it."

"Is it underwater?" Arden asked quietly. "You know I don't swim very well."

"It's not *under* the water, I don't think." Cass knelt down and looked toward a small divot in the wall of the small waterfall and must have been able to see more than me. She touched her hand to the ground and began to hum softly to herself before opening her eyes and saying, "There looks to be a small underground cave system that just formed over there, and from the way it feels, the entrance is there. But that doesn't make sense."

"Why not?" I blinked at her and she frowned further. "You just told me that the entrances can change in the car. This one moved since the last time you were here, so what?"

"So." She motioned toward the road behind us by about ten minutes and muttered, "So what if it's a trap by the Wardens? We go into the water where Arden and me are weakest, and they attack us. We will be absolutely useless."

"What if we were to check the area that you were familiar with first?" Merlin suggested and the rest of us looked at him as if seeing him for the first time. "I mean, it's a tactic the Wardens would use. They want to attack and kill us, right?" We nodded; that was the way it seemed. "Then taking an entrance and cloaking it with something and placing another entrance might be something they would do to catch us."

He nodded to Cassia and Arden. "They may not know that Arden is a flame jinn other than because she uses fire magic so easily when others wouldn't be able to, and Oni have always been weak where water is concerned." He pointed to the water and smiled. "Oh, so pretty, can we get a photo?"

Is he having an aneurysm? I wondered to myself, but a couple in their forties had walked close enough to overhear us if they were quiet enough. "Yeah, come on, let's get one."

He flicked his wrist near his pocket and a cell phone

appeared. Arden took it since she was the tallest and we all posed like we were going to take a selfie together. She actually took one and Merlin took the phone back gratefully. "Didn't you tell me there was a huge cave here?"

Arden smiled. "Yup, let's go before it gets too crowded!"

We moved on, the couple smiling at us as if we were all just children to them before they stopped to appreciate the majesty of the scenery. I focused on them, trying to see if there was more to them than what appeared on the surface, but there was nothing. They were just civilians.

We walked for five minutes before Merlin sighed. "Close. Sorry, I figured asking that would be better than nothing and throw any suspicions off us."

"You did well." Galaxy smiled at him and he relaxed visibly. "Can you elaborate on your thoughts toward the Orders?"

"They would definitely do something like that, was what I was trying to say." He scratched his head. "Which means that they would have that entrance under alarm and watch. The one we're going to would likely be under heavier guard to protect whatever is dampening the call that you feel."

"Okay, so then we will go and look for the old one, but if it's moved, we need to figure out a way to get you to the entrance without severely weakening you." I glared around us, hoping that nothing was going to come and attack us out in the open. If that were to happen, the civilians here would be in as much danger as the ones in the store had been too. "Keep your heads on a swivel. Galaxy, can you fly ahead of us and be our overwatch?"

"Yes." Galaxy stepped back and closed her eyes before her body blinked out of existence and left a raven where she had been standing. Her black wings spread and she fluttered into the sky with a little hop of her legs.

She wasn't up there more than five minutes before she spoke in my head, *You have hikers and some runners coming up on you. I can't tell anything from this distance but they don't seem actively aggressive or like they're looking for anyone or thing.*

I nodded and looked at the others. "Can you make your-selves look different?"

"I can, but the Wardens will be able to see through my magic." Merlin waved his hand and stood a foot taller and a little thinner, his hair was blond and eyes brown, his features blander than they had been before.

Arden closed her eyes and did the same thing, making herself a little thicker and her hair shortening to the point that it was just about styled like the 'I want to see the manager' hair-cut. Her shirt filled out to the point where her blouse could have split from her bust. The way her face was made up changed slightly but she kept her facial features as they were. "Better?"

"You two could be mother and son," I whispered and she smiled at us. "Cass?"

"I don't want to hide." She lifted her chin. Her hair color changed to the platinum blonde it had been when we first met, but she added purple and red highlights to it to make it differ-ent. "But I will blend a little to give the illusion we are on a date with my family tagging along."

She laced her arm into mine and squared her shoulders. "Let's move on and get to Grestal—I want to kill something."

It took us about twenty more minutes walking at a decent pace to get to where we needed to cut off the trail.

Something is wrong, Galaxy muttered in our heads and I blinked up in her general direction. *The air feels different here. Cloying and sweet.*

"We're close, but she's right, something is off." Cassia sniffed around and looked to Arden. "Be ready for a fight."

"Always am." She nervously quirked her lips and took a deep breath to steady herself. "Don't burn any trees down, Arden."

I smiled at that; the old and gnarled trees here looked like they would burst into flame on their own at a glance, let alone a gout of heat from her. The loose, rocky soil below our feet was dry and almost like clay in consistency and color.

As we cautiously made our way toward our 'picnic' spot

west of the main trail, the hair on my arms and the back of my neck began to rise and goose flesh unfolded along my body. Something was wrong here, and it made the scared little monkey man in my brain want to run off and survive.

"There's a hollow tree up ahead, a hundred yards and at the bottom of a ravine, that's the marker for the entrance," Cassia whispered to us and turned toward the west. "We're going to be walking down a pathway with limited visibility once we get in, then into a small cave only large enough for a single file line before we come out into the ravine itself. Pay attention and if I stop—you stop."

We all nodded, I pulled my Oni blade from my inventory and left it concealed where the sheath was attached to my belt at my lower back, an empty sheath having been easier to conceal for humans than the knife too. I wished I could carry the sword the Kenshi had given me as well, but with that in hand, we would definitely give ourselves away if anyone was watching for suspicious activity.

"I have an idea," Arden muttered as we walked on. "Cassia, you take Marcus and go to the entrance like you're going to get frisky while we fake setting up for the picnic. If you need help, get us word through Galaxy, and we'll come running."

"I like that." Cassia grinned and squeezed my arm tighter. We walked for another ten minutes before the opening to the small cave was visible. The place was secluded enough that it did look ideal to enjoy lunch, so Arden made a show about collecting the basket from me.

She leaned over and opened the lid then flinched. "Cassia, there's a whole picnic set in here."

"Yeah, I packed it just in case." Cassia shrugged like it was the most normal thing in the world. She leaned forward and whispered, "If someone dropped it and it was empty, our cover was blown."

She grabbed my hand and pulled me toward the entrance to the cave with a grin on her face like we were about to do something truly bad.

Even knowing it was an act, my heart still thumped and thudded in my chest and butterflies flipped and fluttered around in my stomach like I was a schoolboy again.

She pulled me close and kissed me so deeply that my knees locked as she tugged my arms. I tripped and when I was regaining my balance, I caught a glimmer of something behind her.

I righted myself and muttered, "I want to fight you so badly."

Cassia's eyes lit up and she saw the quick flick of my gaze behind her right shoulder. "Yeah? You like my right hook, don't you?"

"Not nearly as much as your hammer fist." She moaned as my hand pressed against her right hip. "Especially as hard as you can go? Gets me really hot."

"I'm going to do it to you, you know," she whispered and pulled me closer so she could kiss my neck. I closed my eyes and she whispered, "Tap my hip again and I'll swing."

I growled and tapped her hip; her body reacted so fast that the wind from her movement blew back my hair. Her clenched fist slammed into whatever had been hiding against the rock wall behind her. The now-colorless and quickly losing shape humanoid sprawled out on the ground made me smile; it was definitely some sort of creature.

A mimic? Galaxy stepped out of me and unhinged her jaw before she slowly devoured the creature. It wasn't long before any and all drive to continue making out with Cassia was quashed and cold.

She finished and sighed contentedly before stepping back into my shadow and disappearing. *The mimic was here to conceal the real entrance. The one you were about to enter was a much larger version designed to devour travelers and keep the real entry to Grestal hidden.*

How do you know that? I blinked at her and she smiled inwardly at me.

I consumed it, Marcus. All of it. She purred and I could tell that meant just what I thought. She could eat its memories too. *Only the most recent ones. It was the Order of the Staff who captured it and its mate to try to devour anything traveling to Grestal.*

"Let's get going!" I turned and hollered back to the others. I turned back to Cassia. "Can you lead us in?"

Her head dipped once and she was into the entry and watching for any signs of someone joining us or coming up on us. Arden and Merlin had what little they had put out back in the basket and were heading toward us in a matter of seconds thanks to the jinn's speed.

I turned back and we were off once more, treading cautiously into the darkened cave-like entry into the ravine. The sharp incline was worrisome for a second, but I was glad I had my hiking boots on as the loose gravel beneath my feet scrabbled out of the way and rolled around.

The cave walls became smoother the longer we walked. Thirty feet into the space, the roof opened to the sky and on the other side and it made me pause. "Cassia, I know for damn sure it wasn't night when we walked into this place. Is this normal?"

She shook her head and motioned for me to be quiet, and to get low as we cautiously made our way further down the slope. Once again, I lamented not having my goddamn guns!

I closed my eyes and mentally prepared myself for what could possibly happen, then continued with the others, following closely behind Cassia.

We breached the ravine and sure enough, the stars above us shone with abandon, their light flickering above as if it were never day time here and never would be again.

This place is heavily inundated with magic, Galaxy whispered to all of us and we stilled as she paused. *Merlin says that he senses time magic of some flavor here, though I don't know what that means.*

He said it means that someone must have stopped or did something with this area of the world and he doesn't know what it is. I looked around as best I could, wishing I had the lycanthropic senses along with their healing, but beggars and choosers, right?

I crept further out of the cave and looked back above me.

The wall of the ravine entrance wound up and into the darkness, but luckily there was nothing that I could see.

I turned my focus to the path ahead of us and slid further ahead with my Oni blade bared and at the ready. Muttering from closer to the wall drew my attention and I saw something similar to a fire and someone with their back turned.

I snuck closer and watched as the figure raised something in his left hand and slid a stick down his arm.

Stop them! Galaxy howled and my body moved almost of its own accord, the knife in my hand whirling into his back just above his hips. Cassia hopped over me and slammed down onto his head and snarled as magic roared around us, voices raising all around.

"Ard, get 'em!" I closed my eyes as she flashed her flames brightly and blinded a couple of them, but I doubted that it worked on everyone as something cold crashed into my hip and tossed me backward six feet.

Frozen Stone – Devoured – Ice magic path opened slightly.

I grit my teeth, glad that I had gotten something out of it and stood painfully to my feet before I had to throw myself to the right to avoid another glacial projectile.

"Could really use my fucking guns right now!" I snarled in frustration.

"Just fucking kill them!" Cassia shot back as she lifted a mage and threw them into another one casting a spell her way, the projectile crashing into his friend as he collided with him.

I grimaced and cast Embodiment of Lightning, moving to the original caster to grab the blade I had thrown, the random Bolt flit from my chest to a mage who cried out in pain and began to convulse on the ground. I windmilled around, my arms tight then lashing out to slice a mage on my right before my fingers clawed at his eyes.

His nose broke and there were gashes in his face as he fell to Galaxy who climbed out of my shadow in cat form to bite him and begin draining him of his mana and life force. His body began to wilt before my eyes, but I couldn't dwell on that.

I still had Embodiment active and could cast my next Bolt at half mana, so I did, slinging the electrical energy at the woman making ever-increasingly broad motions. A blue shield burst into existence before her and the spell fizzled out before it could reach her and a studious-looking man stepped forward to block my path to her.

He made a sign with his hand and tossed something that looked like powder at me. The air before him solidified and rushed at me, in what looked like a ram. It hit me in the stomach and flattened me.

The woman spoke three words that escaped my mind and went to speak again when a clear shot rang out in the air and her head rocked back. The building amber magic that she had been weaving in the air between her hands sort of sucked in and imploded, dragging her corpse and the mage that had defended her toward a small black hole.

He shouted a phrase and a glowing sphere of light burst into life around the hole like a container and it fizzled out; his body stopped moving. Another shot rang out and his body jumped as he cried out.

I cast Wisp at him and he rolled out of the way in time for Cassia to stomp on his head, crushing it instantly. She lifted her club in defiance and roared, "Who's next?"

The mages that survived turned to run toward the cave to leave the ravine, but Galaxy stood in their way, making all of them pause until one of them tried to leave and she hissed at them, sounding like a panther.

"We'll leave!" one of them cried out as the force that held me down dissipated and I could get up.

"No," Merlin growled, surprising me. He had the gun that I had bought him in hand and I couldn't tell if I was upset that he was armed or proud of him for having the forethought to ignore them advising against it. "What kind of spell were you doing?"

"It was an impermanence spell of Cory's design!" the same one said. He held up his hands as if to show he was no threat. "It was meant to shut the entrance to Grestal here. Please, don't kill us!"

As he said this last thing, he muttered something under his breath and Merlin shot him in the stomach, the spell slashing the rocky ground in front of him. "Anyone else tries any magic, and we kill all of you."

They looked at me as I spoke, punctuating my threat by casting Blade and throwing it into his chest, his dying wheezes scaring the rest of them badly enough that one of them had a puddle forming at their feet.

"Why close it?" Cassia growled at them as she positioned herself next to Galaxy.

"So we could capture all of you," a voice spoke off to our right, which made me frown. Xehano walked out of a vortex that I got the distinct portal type vibe from. "I have to say, Merlin, I expected so much better of you. You'll be good as new with some retraining. Better even."

He made a motion with his hand and Merlin fell to a knee, grunting and holding his head, the gun in his grasp clattered to the ground noisily and a barrier formed around him as Xehano ordered, "Kill them."

Not waiting to be done in, I cast Embodiment of Lightning once more, moving so fast that the spells aimed at me whizzed through the air where I had been and flew toward the elder mage. His hands slid from their robed sheathes and a shimmering blue orb of arcane power encompassed him.

And me crouched behind him.

Casting Blade once more, I slid the magical sword into his right thigh hoping he didn't know any healing magic, but knew damned well he probably did. My random Bolt spell scorched the back of his robes and he grunted but it didn't put him down like I had hoped.

Get to the fucking entrance now! I snarled to Galaxy so the others would start moving.

I twisted the blade in my hands and went for the other leg but he reached back and an unseen force rammed me into the wall of his shield as he winced and growled at the pain in his leg.

"I should have struck you down at the High Table." He seethed as he started to turn toward me.

"You should've been a blowjob," I spat at his head and grinned as I cast Embodiment of Lightning to get in front of him this time. He cast his arm behind him and I grinned, stabbing my spell forward toward his heart.

He snarled a word and I was blown backward into something solid and soft all at the same time.

"You have such a way of pissing off powerful people," Cassia shook her head as she ran with me in her grasp.

"Merlin?" I gasped as the pain started to recede in my rib cage.

"Arden got him. They went through." She rushed forward and jumped over something I couldn't see and it felt like we were falling up.

The sensation of it built and built until it felt like I was going to hurl, then it stopped and Cassia threw me onto the ground where I did toss my cookies.

I looked up at our surroundings and gasped.

Cassia's tone held a hint of her grinning as she said, "Welcome to Grestal, Marcus."

CHAPTER SEVEN

The sky that I stared up at was a distinct kind of blue that I had never really seen before, outside of art. The same sort of blue that made you truly feel that the word encompassed and perfectly described the visual before your eyes.

Clouds of a silvery build billowed above in broad waves that shadowed the land below in cool darkness as they passed overhead, dimming the vivid green grass of the hill we exited from.

Someone grabbed my shoulder and I realized it was Arden. "Yes, it's beautiful here, but we don't have time to enjoy the scenery. It could only be a matter of seconds before they come after us."

"There's a slight time difference, so we don't *have* to sprint to get away from them, but I would recommend that we do." Cassia grinned at us before she looked around, pointing to what could only be considered easterly if my mini-map was to be trusted. "Let's go."

We took off at a dead sprint, none of us able to keep up with Arden as she quite literally zoomed ahead of us for a good ten minutes before we needed to rest a little. No matter how good our Physiques were, ten minutes at full tilt would put anyone on their ass. We rested on a gently sloping hillside with a tree standing centrally in the area. It wasn't the only one in the area, but it was one of the largest and looked like it would offer a decent place to rest out of the sun.

"Where are we?" I huffed for a moment before my lungs seemed to catch enough air to keep things good for me.

"It looks like we're in the Animal Plains, if memory serves." Cassia grunted as she put her boot back on. "Which means that finding their city and a way to the other realms of Grestal is going to be interesting."

"Can't we just walk to the other places?" I raised an eyebrow at her before looking to Arden. "We need to get to Virani, if I recall the letter I got from our informant—whoever that is."

"The lands here are all connected but... not," Merlin began cautiously, glancing at the others for help but they were content to let him explain. "Each is separated by the Bones of the Grestal."

"I'm sorry, the what?" I looked around at them and Galaxy separated herself from my shadow and stretched languorously next to me before taking her elven shape. "Did you know this?"

"What little I know of Grestal is what I have gleaned from Merlin and the others, but I am highly interested to hear what more they can tell us." She smiled and hit Merlin with a pointed look. "Continue, please?"

"As was said before—Grestal is a living, breathing being," Merlin explained softly so as not to draw attention from anyone who could be in the area, namely other Wardens. "It separates the creatures within into areas designed best for their comfort and needs. More predatory creatures like vampires and whatnot need victims so it sends the occasional stray human there for those who can't go to Earth themselves. The elemental plains are vast with rolling hills of various elemental types and seas floating in the air, volcanoes, plus other ecosystems that make truly no sense."

"That's a lot to take in, I'll level with you." I tried to piece it all together in my mind, but that just wasn't working the way I wanted.

"The important part is that you know the place we are is as alive as you and me and is as dedicated to consuming as Galaxy is." Arden sighed, interrupting Merlin as he was about to speak. "The Bones of Grestal are like massive mountains, or vast oceans that separate everything here except the Forest of Fel Tidings."

"Why is that?" I stood and brushed myself off, tired of sitting already, but more so that the ground being a living being weirded me the fuck out. "And what's with the weird name?"

"That's where the creatures that are too feral to exist among the sentient creatures are held and contained." Cassia spoke softly too, but more out of reverence or fear than anything that I could see. "It's called that because going in there is nearly suicide. The creatures there are savage and powerful. That's where Merlin will likely have to hunt."

"Well, that's going to be fun then," I groused, then looked at all of them. "So we have to find a city to move from one—what are they? Zones?—zone to another?"

"Realms," Merlin corrected me quickly. "And yes, unless you want to move through the Forest of Fel Tidings, which would be an ignorant move. Those who go in there and die are basically food for Grestal itself."

"So if this thing is so intent on killing and eating, why does it have countless magical and mythical beings living on it?" I looked directly at Arden and Cassia. "You know this thing is dangerous and yet this is home, why?"

"Grestal needs us to survive—we need Grestal to survive." Arden explained. "With us on it, Grestal has a line of defense against anything that would seek to kill it and claim its power. With Grestal, we are protected from those who would seek to kill us—namely humans and Wardens."

"What was it before, and what could possibly threaten a creature like this?" It was hard to keep the skepticism out of my voice but Merlin whistled. I looked his way and he pointed behind me and motioned for me to get low. "What?"

"Someone is nearby!" he hissed as we all crouched where we were and started crowding closer to the tree for cover. I poked my head out from behind the gnarled brown bark to find a woman covered in cheetah-print-like fur pacing through the grass at a swift pace.

She didn't look like she was running from anyone, just like she was searching for something.

Galaxy, ask Arden and Cassia what we should do.

They say that we should keep our distance, but that we could follow her and get to her city. Her answer made sense, but at the same time, who knew if she was going there in the first place?

A soft hissing drew my attention and I looked up in time to find some sort of brown snake with an angular head flicking its tongue at me. I kicked Merlin out of the way and cast Embodiment of Lightning to step six feet back, just avoiding the serpent's striking at me. The random Bolt that cast on its own zipped toward it and stunned the reptile, dropping its long body to the ground where Cassia grabbed it by the neck with her left hand and grabbed a section a half-a-foot behind that before she took her Oni form and bit it.

Her teeth pierced the writhing snake's scaled flesh and tore a hole in it large enough for her to pull the head from the body and throw the former far from us.

We all looked about to see if we had been discovered by the cheetah woman, only to find her watching us with a smile on her face as she leaned against the tree. "Don't meet many of your kind around here, though I suppose you would be why I felt the entrance fluctuating as if someone had come in."

All of us blinked at her and she smiled, her teeth—pointed and animalistic—flashed in the light as she spoke again. "I guess you'll be heading toward the Mirage?"

"What's the Mirage?" I asked before I could stop myself. The others looked deflated.

She smiled wider as she flicked her discerning gaze to me. "A newbie, huh? Planning to sacrifice him to Grestal?"

"No, we just need to get to Malarna and then we'll be on our way to Virani," Arden explained and stepped in front of me like she was trying to protect me.

"Well, Malarna is difficult to find without the help of the Mirage and its transportation." The cheetah woman shifted her weight and came to full height as she stepped past us, her clawed hands brushing the dust of traveling off her brown, soft-looking leather dress. "Come with me and I'll show you the way. My Matron will want to know who it was that came through the portal anyway."

"What do you get out of it?" Cassia asked carefully.

"My Matron off my back." She smiled as she passed us and moved on. "That and there is no small amount of safety in numbers. Especially with the Wardens that just came through the entrance to Grestal hunting for someone."

The way she said that last bit was just a little too well-knowing for my comfort. She had likely guessed we were on the run from them, but not the why.

The why likely means very little to her, as she gets what she wants as well. Galaxy sighed heavily as her spectral eyes inside me opened wide to regard the new strange woman. *We will simply need to maintain a cautious watch for her and others who might seek to devour us here.*

What is it with you and food metaphors? She remained quiet despite mental prodding from me and we carried on, following the woman.

"What's your name?" Merlin asked quietly as we walked, breaking the already tense silence.

"I am called much, but you may call me what my Matron chose for me—Amabala." She called over her shoulder, "Don't lag behind too much, dangerous creatures have begun to roam this place in search of food, and the creatures from the Fel are much more at home in the open in our realm than in yours for some unknown reason."

She took us toward the sun for a time, stopping occasionally to scent at something or to check tracks, then her tail stood up and she looked back toward where we had come from. "Just how many are crossing over?"

Cassia looked at Amabala and quirked her head to the side, then a look of understanding dawned on her face. "You're a seeker, aren't you?"

The cheetah woman blinked and glanced at Cass before correcting her, "My people call us Keepers, and I am not the only one. My entire litter are Keepers, and we keep our lands and people safe."

Galaxy interrupted me before I could launch into a question. *Before you show how ignorant you are, I will explain thanks to Arden and Merlin's knowledge, yes?*

I begrudgingly agreed and her smile inside my mana sea almost made me roll my eyes.

Keepers, or seekers, are those who are attuned to Grestal and its many entrances and exits to and from each of the realms and to Earth. Galaxy's explanation seemed hurried as we moved on, but I realized it was likely due to the fact that she was siphoning knowledge from all three of them to explain to me. I had to smile, because learning this way was so much more interesting than reading a book. *They acquire this attunement by spending a great deal of their formative years in close proximity to the portals Grestal makes. They learn much from the fluctuations between realms and as such can tell when someone uses a portal near them and when there is one too.*

Can we do that? I asked softly, watching Amabala almost jealously. It would be a good thing to be able to know when someone was just popping in on you. Or opening portals in the area.

"Are Keepers as celebrated here as they are in other realms?" Cassia wondered aloud as we continued our trek.

Amabala paused and sniffed the air before looking behind us. "We are treated as hunters would be. No differently, as it should be, because we provide all the same."

"You keep your people safe, how isn't that different from a

hunter?" Arden snorted and looked at the cheetah woman as if she were being humble.

The ground began to quake and rumbling drew our attention as Amabala dropped into a crouch and hissed, "Because our hunters defy the Fel. Prepare yourselves for combat!"

Massive antlers cleared the horizon line followed by a huge elephantine trunk, with spikes adorning it like a mace, raised in the air, that trumpeted a war cry that chilled my blood. Green eyes with no irises filled with pure animal fury and rage so potent that the killing intent from the creature was just a flood that filled the air until there was hardly any oxygen left to breathe.

Marcus! Get your ass in gear, this thing is a tier eight from what Cassia is warning.

I took a few shallow breaths to jump start my adrenaline and get my heart rate up before I roared a challenging call back at the thirty-foot-tall pachyderm. It reared and charged toward us, almost within a hundred feet.

Amabala turned toward me in time for me to cast Embodiment of Lightning and propelled myself onto the creature's back, my random Bolt doing precious little to it. My feet screamed as I landed on small spikes, but I used the pain to cut through the fear within me and called the Oni sword from the inventory ring on my right hand.

"*Raaaaaaaargh!*" I slammed the weapon into the spiky shell of a back and a trumpeting cry of anger served as a sign I'd hurt it, but I couldn't tell how much.

Cassia surged forward with a battle cry of her own as she pulled her spiked club out of her own inventory. Arden whipped her hands out to her sides and brought them together with a sonorous clap that echoed out around her and a bubble of pure flame singed the grass around her, Merlin, and Amabala.

I couldn't see Merlin, but I knew the kid wouldn't let us have all the fun and that he was likely planning something big.

I pulled my sword out and snarled as I stabbed and slashed again and again to little avail. The elephant reared again and my healing feet were torn from the spikes beneath my feet, tossing me back toward the ground and likely a very painful trampling.

We would need to hit this thing in a vital place. Somewhere without this hardened, spiked shell to protect it.

Someone caught me as I was about to cast Embodiment again, clawed fingers lightly piercing my arms but it was nothing compared to the massive foot that crushed the ground I should have landed on.

"That was foolish—but brave," Amabala muttered in my ear as she moved a little further away from the fight to put me down.

I grinned at her before I turned back to the battle. Cassia fought the thing as best as she could, but it was gaining ground and those spikes on its trunk were painted with her blood. Clouds built just above them, darkening as Merlin appeared out of the flaming barrier Arden had made.

He made a symbol with his hands and a thick bolt of lightning cracked down onto the antlered head and put it onto its stomach. Cassia smashed her mace onto it and one of the antlers cracked but it looked like the creature was about to get back up.

Two flaming spears appeared in its shoulder and it trumpeted its rage as it collapsed once more. If I was going to make use of the opportunity of it being on the ground and vulnerable, now was the time.

I still had the majority of my mana, so I cast Embodiment of Lightning once more and appeared in front of the massive monster, casting Fireblast in its mouth as it tried to swing at Cassia. I booked it back out of there, tackling Cassia and narrowly avoiding the trunk's backswing.

A *whompf,* then a burst of flame burned at my back; Cassia tossed me off her and stood to see what the damage was.

She sneered at the creature, then fixed me with her gaze. "I had it right where I wanted it, you know."

I grinned up at her. "I know you did."

"And you know I'm hardier than you?"

I grinned wider. "How could I not? You show me that all the time."

She knelt next to me, staring me in the eyes. "Then why did you push me out of the way?"

"Because I protect who I care about." She frowned at my statement for a moment before I added, "I don't think you're weak. I know that you are capable and can defend yourself, but I want to protect you if I can. To show you that I care."

Her eyes narrowed at me. "This is a human ideal, isn't it?"

I chuckled at her statement. "Yeah. Kind of like you picking fights with all of us to make sure we're up to your standards of being capable in a fight."

She brightened immediately. "Ah! I see." She reached down and grabbed me, lifting me from the ground easily. "I don't quite get it, but if it is how you wish to show me affection, then so be it. As long as you know I am capable and don't make too much of a habit of doing that."

"I make no promises." I winked at her and turned to our kill. "What the hell is this thing?"

"A Felaphant?" Arden quipped and I snorted.

"They're called Quilladerms, and they are usually found closer to the Fel. I do not know why this one is so far from its herd, but that you killed it is impressive. Very impressive." Amabala stared at all of us with a look of shocked wonder, then narrowed her eyes at us. "Two mages, an Oni, and a jinn mage? What kind of monsters are you?"

Cassia chuckled at that last statement, ignoring it, but said, "Something like that." Cassia grunted as she moved closer to the creature to inspect it, lifting its trunk and looking it over intently.

I want to eat it, Galaxy said hungrily. I could feel my own stomach growling as she salivated in me for the meal that this creature would make. *Think of what it could possibly give us!*

I turned over to Amabala as she continued to look at us all

anew in the light of an actual threat now. "What do you usually do with these things?"

"If it were a smaller creature, we would take it back to the forest and give it back to the Grestal if it wasn't edible." She motioned to the Quilladerm. "This is not edible, and it is much too large. Grestal will have to reclaim it over time on its own."

You stay behind and devour it once we leave. Cassia perked up and nodded to herself as I said, "Well, let's move on and let that happen."

We all turned to move away when I heard a snap and a grunt.

I looked back to find the Oni woman grinning ear to ear as she carried the broken antler. "What the hell is that for?"

"Kill trophy." She shrugged happily and headed toward us as we all laughed.

CHAPTER EIGHT

It took another couple hours walking at a stiff pace to get to the oasis, but cresting the hill to it was like stepping into yet another world.

The grass here took on an even deeper hue of green while the shrubs and trees were huge and healthy with a myriad of smaller animals scattered around in the shade provided by the monumental trees.

"Welcome to the Mirage." Amabala smiled at our various looks of wonder. "This is where we will find the portal to Malarna, then you can meet my Matron and from there—be on your way to somewhere else."

I was excited to be able to see a Grestallan city for the first time, but this was happening faster than I'd expected, and Galaxy hadn't come back yet.

Galaxy, you almost done? When there was no reply for a moment, I called again. *Galaxy!*

Can I not enjoy a delicious meal? she fired back irritably. *Eating this thing is what is getting you experience because it has no soul.*

How much longer will you be? We're less than a twenty-minute walk from the Mirage.

Not long, stall her so I can finish this.

I rolled my eyes and pretended like I saw something concerning. "Let's take our time going down there, just in case another creature is lurking about."

Amabala eyed me suspiciously, but seemed to decide that was acceptable, adding, "Fine." She offered me, then all of the rest of us, a smile before saying, "Far be it for me to refute the experience and instincts of a hunter."

I found the sudden deference to be a little irritating, and alarming, but if that meant we would be going it slower, then so be it.

As we walked, I had to ask, "What's Malarna like?"

"It is an ever-growing caravan of my people and many others." She smiled wistfully as she paused and listened for something, then moved on into a copse of trees and bushes. "Within it, there are hundreds of thousands of my kind, and shifters who work together to ensure that the caravan and its people are safe and secure."

"How can a caravan hold that many people?" I tried to wrap my head around that thought as the sheer amount of space needed would be mind-blowing. "I mean, it would have to be miles and miles long!"

"Something to that effect, maybe?" She answered with a shrug, then grinned and showed off her sharp teeth. "I don't wish to ruin the surprise though."

She kept us moving reasonably slowly for a few more minutes before she stilled and closed her eyes, taking a deep breath in before her nose crinkled. "It's near, come."

Amabala led us under a tree and pushed a small branch aside before a massive crystalline lake, the sandy shore of it still and picturesque.

"Where does the water come from?"

"I would say that the Grestal provides, but we learned long ago that the waters here came from underground canals and rivers that well up here due to some sort of spell that was cast in the area long ago." Amabala's explanation was succinct, but did well to show me that I knew dog shit about magic and had just scratched the surface.

Maybe it's time to read that book that Uncle Yen gave me? I wondered to myself just before a fluttering caught my attention and a black feathered raven landed on my shoulder.

"Where did this bird come from?" Amabala asked quietly, curiosity dripping from her tone. "I did not see it before."

A little lax in your hiding, Galaxy, I mentally chided her but she just pecked my head and I offered, "My familiar. I had her scouting for us."

"Familiar?" She stepped toward us and Galaxy melted into my body as easily as water dripping into a sink. "Oh my, so she's a part of you? Human mages are so different."

"Do you have many mages among your people?" Merlin wondered aloud and blinked at her hungrily. "I find all forms of magic fascinating, forgive me if it seems an odd question."

"We have many witch-doctors and shamans among us, some priests of the Grestal too." She thought a moment longer then shrugged. "A few Touched among the shifters too, though not many."

I found that news interesting; lycanthropes couldn't be Touched unless they had been born a lycanthrope, and even then, they were rare. Rarer than human Touched by a long shot.

With Galaxy here at long last, we could move on to Malarna, and then on from there. "So where is the portal?"

"In front of us." Amabala grinned and pointed to the sand not twenty feet from us where I—of course—saw nothing. "Come along, it is almost time that the caravan will stop for the night. You don't want to miss this."

She moved to the beach and stepped onto the sand, then disappeared from sight.

"Be very careful when we go here," Cassia advised as she stepped in front of us. "Mind your P's and Q's, and do nothing that could seem aggressive unless absolutely necessary."

Galaxy stepped out of me and added, "And see if we can keep Amabala or if I can devour her."

"I'm sorry, what?" I blinked at her and the others looked equally shocked.

"Having the ability to know when there are portals around you is an unmistakable advantage and if we can take her with us, it would be better," Galaxy explained curtly, then added, "But if we can't—I will eat her or a couple of her siblings to ensure we have at least someone who can sense portals. Also, you all leveled up from that fight."

"Can we get a notification for that next time?" Cassia groused, then threw her hands up defensively as Galaxy turned a reproachful eye her way. "I'm not trying to sound ungrateful, just wanted some consistency, you know?"

"Fine." Galaxy growled, looking at all of us. "The air here is ripe with mana and I find it easier to gather it as well. It should be easier to make things here. But work on getting her to come with us."

We all nodded as she faded back into me and turned to see Amabala walk back through the portal. "Are you coming?"

"Yup!" I grinned at her and walked forward toward the gate, then through it.

When I blinked and opened my eyes again, I found myself in a sort of dark place with lanterns strung up in the corners of the room. It was difficult to make out any sort of real shape to the place, but I needed to move so the others could come through without plowing into me. I stepped out of the way as Amabala came through, followed shortly by Cassia, Arden, and finally Merlin.

A door opened over on my right and another cheetah person poked their head in. "Ah, sister, I see you bring company as you had initially said. The Matron is still busy, but will be with you in the quest room within a few moments. Please, take our guests with you and refreshments will be brought along."

"Thank you, Jabari." Amabala nodded to who I assumed was her brother, then looked at us. "Come with me, please."

She had us follow her out of the door and then onto some kind of firm, wooden walkway with wooden rails above a truly mind-blowing view.

We were inside a large, domed place with what could have passed for a small city or large village below us. Homes of wood and other kinds of materials were piled on top of one another with wooden walkways and paths leading to and from. Ladders and slides could be found on each one like some kind of weird matrix of alleyways and method of travel. Pulley systems and thick ropes where figures glided and zip-lined across vast distances or short ones alike crisscrossed the 'sky' in a chaotic display.

"Welcome to Malarna. This is Sahen, the first of the five Malarna tortoises." She waved her hand at the massive dome above us, some of the shell missing pieces here and there that provided plenty of light to those within. "If you would follow me?"

We wordlessly followed her to a slide that had guard rails on the side that we slid down, the wood having been long sanded and worn to prevent splintering. She shepherded us into a room with cushions on the floor and a low table that we could sit at with a tea set in the center. But along one of the walls was a panel that she pressed and muttered a single word. It became clear and showed us the outside. There were perhaps a few hours of sunlight left at this point from what I could feel, but the sun was already beginning to fall in the sky, purple and orange fire spreading slowly, but it wasn't the sunset that she had wanted us to see.

No. It was the other portions of the city. Amabala smiled and announced, "These are the other Malarna tortoises, Sahen's mate Akupara, his younger sister Morla, his daughter Danu, and his son Kiko."

The other tortoises slowly tapered off in size but each was larger than three destroyer-class vessels end to end, and even taller than that. Their shells were covered in crystalline structures that looked like precious gemstones that jutted out all over the place, though the smallest one, Kiko's, all faced forward like horns meant to ram and pierce. His neck was long and he swung it from side to side like he was on watch for predators.

"What's going on with the small one?" Arden asked with an edge of concern to her voice.

"Kiko is a warrior." Amabala grinned and motioned to the little guy. "He protects the other tortoises while they sleep, and only needs a little rest himself."

"That's wild," Cassia whispered more to herself than to anyone else. "This whole place is so interesting. Have you ever been to the other realms, Amabala?"

"Only when necessary to bring back someone who should not have gone, and then when I was younger to get a better feel for the portals. Why?"

"We were wondering if you would help be our guide," I asked hopefully. More because I hoped that Galaxy wouldn't have to put us all at risk to eat someone to get the ability. Especially if she didn't get it the first time.

You act as though you wouldn't condone it, she grumped at me internally, almost like she was hurt.

I would rather not have to make more enemies than we have at present, thank you. I could feel her rolling her eyes at me from within and mentally growled at her. "I feel like we could benefit from having an expert of your caliber with us."

"As much as I would like to travel the realms with strangers, I think I would have to pass on that." She smiled and stepped toward me. "Though I appreciate the thought of a brave hunter such as you."

I glanced up and over at Cassia who watched Amabala with interest, but glanced at me and made certain she had my gaze, Galaxy passing her thoughts to me, *If you can get her interested in coming with us, Marcus, do it. But I will not allow her to touch you. Galaxy I can understand, as she is a part of you. I am comfortable with Arden, though I don't know how she feels about you other than thinking your butt looks good. But I will not tolerate her touching you. Not right now.*

I blinked at her and blushed before straightening myself out and leveling a disappointed gaze at the animal woman. "That's too bad, I'm sure a brave woman like you could have kept us safe as we hunted for the treasure."

She perked up, but didn't have time to ask her question as the door opened and several large, burly men carrying platters of food and exquisite smelling drinks and soups flooded the room. They set their various dishes and delicacies on the table in the center before stepping to the side of the room and bowing their heads in unison.

A tall, cheetah-skinned woman strutted into the room as if she owned everything in it and everyone in the city.

"Honored Matron, I bring guests from the portal."

"I have been warned, thank you, Keeper Amabala." The woman spoke with her head tilted up and back so that she could look down her nose at all of us. "Why do I smell magic on them?"

"Two of them are Touched, an oni, and a jinn mage." She took a knee when speaking this time. "They fought and killed a Quilladerm as I was leading them to the Mirage to see you. The battle was fierce, but they won handily."

The Matron stepped closer, finally allowing her chin to fall so that she could look at each of us in turn. As she came to me, she took a deep whiff and her nose wrinkled slightly. "You did not say that you brought a shifter."

"Because I'm not, I just smell like one." I smiled at her and she frowned, her arm moving so fast that I barely saw it until three lines of fire danced down my right cheek.

Cassia was up and out of her cushion so fast that the table would have flipped if it hadn't been for the meat slabs that appeared and held it down before grabbing her to move her away.

"I will not be called a liar," the Matron hissed as she stared at me. "I could have you flogged with silver for such."

I lifted an eyebrow at her and shook my head. "I'm not from here, so forgive me for not knowing your laws, but I don't appreciate being struck by someone I don't know." I glared at her as my face became a perfect mask of stoic bearing meant to conceal my slowly rising ire. "I don't care who you are here; if you touch me or mine again, I'll do the same to you."

"You threaten me?" She scoffed and I saw her shoulder flinch, casting Embodiment of Lightning so that I stood behind her, the random Bolt lashing out at one of the goons holding Cassia. He dropped to his knees as I put a hand on her shoulder.

"I don't make threats," I whispered softly in her ear. "I don't want any trouble here, and neither do you, right?"

"You don't know what I want," she yowled back, her tail flicking between her feet.

"I have a good idea with the way that you've treated us so far—you want someone to bully and show your power off to." I shook my head, looking at the stoic but telling faces of the men around the room. They all looked defeated. As if this was their lot in life.

I gather what you mean, Marcus, Galaxy whispered through me. *It does seem like she came in here with the intent to be offended. Though I don't know why one would do so without knowing the full breadth of their enemies' capabilities. Seems a waste of a potential ally to me.*

"So, here's what's going to happen." I flicked my gaze to the man still struggling to hold Cassia. "He's going to let her go, and we're going to leave here. We aren't a threat to you or yours. All we want is to leave this realm and move on. Okay? Do that, and no hard feelings."

"And what if I do not allow you your way?" She laughed, a low and throaty chortle of a thing. "I rule here, second only to the council of Malarna, and they do not even know you exist here. I could take and break all of you."

"Because the second you try to give the order for that, I'll kill you, and then everyone in this room that I don't like." I made sure to keep my voice even and almost amicable as I said it. I wanted her to know that I was serious, and saying it as a threat would just make it seem like I was nervous, or uncertain.

I said it with the certainty of the cold graves all these people would be lying in if they were a threat to us. Glaring at all of them, their auras began to bloom around them, all of them some flavor of lycanthrope.

"Do you really think that you can take on so many of my people?" The Matron sounded sure of herself, but there was a small thread of worry at the end that I knew could be used to my advantage.

"Does the answer matter to a dead woman?" I smiled with no teeth and squeezed the hand on her shoulder. "I won't ask you to let my friends and I go—I'm telling you to." Before I lifted my hand from her shoulder, I added, "And if you promise to behave, we can all go back to being amicable. Okay?"

My hand fell to my side and I watched her for any sort of indication that she was going to attack or give the command to kill us, but she remained calm and sighed. "Let her go, and stand down."

The goon struggling with Cassia let go and she overcorrected, almost falling onto her ass on top of the man still laying on the ground. Someone caught her, allowing her to catch her balance and she stood perfectly straight, saying a strained, "Thanks."

The Matron turned and glared at Amabala. "We will discuss this later." She turned back to us. "Are any of you a threat to this city, our tortoises, or way of life?"

"No," we answered together, but Cassia added, "So long as you leave us alone, we will do the same. Don't tempt us."

The Matron's eyes narrowed. "I see." She looked at us again and asked, "And do any of you have contraband you wish to declare?"

I blinked at that and looked around at the rest of us before saying, "No?"

She looked to Amabala who just dropped her gaze, then the Matron turned to leave, speaking as she walked. "Eat, drink, and rest, but you will leave within two hours."

She stopped at the doorway and pointed to Amabala. "Come."

Amabala's shoulders and tail drooped and she trudged forward toward the door. I touched her shoulder and she flinched, moving back from me. I whispered as low as I could, "You needn't fear forever. Come back to us. We can help you."

She stared into my eyes for a second that felt like an eternity, then blinked and the connection was gone, her gaze falling once more as she fled the room.

Once all of the men were clear of the room, Arden released a pent-up breath in a whoosh and stared at me. "What the hell caused you to threaten someone you just met like that?"

"She threatened us first?" I answered with a shrug, then motioned to the drying blood that replaced the cuts on my skin. After that, I stared longingly at the food. It looked good, but I couldn't trust it after what had just taken place.

"And your first thought is to threaten her? Someone powerful that we *just* met?" Arden rolled her eyes as I offered her an unapologetic grin. She glared off in the distance and I looked back to the food that made my stomach grumble sadly.

At least until Merlin waved his hands over it and muttered a phrase that made the room seem fuzzy for a moment before everything cleared. "Food is clean. Don't drink the water though, it's not good."

"How so?" I frowned at him as he grabbed some of the rolls and started to make a sandwich.

"Is it rainwater?" Cassia asked and he nodded. "Ugh, it's basically a neurotoxin in some of the Realms, in others it's acidic or poisonous to those who can't stomach it. Many of the creatures in the Fel thrive on it, so it can be a little crazy out there when it's raining."

"Oh." I thought, *Galaxy, you think you want to try it?*

No. Her answer was quick, almost too quick. *This stuff is toxic, even to me. I can smell it from here. We would do well to leave it alone.*

If it was that bad, how come they offered it to us? I said as much and they looked to each other for a moment before shrugging, Merlin offering, "Maybe as a test?"

"Tests fucking suck," I growled and snatched up a roll. I took a bite. It was good but sort of bland too.

Looking back out at the Malarna tortoises, they had all circled together tightly and looked to have begun a slow retreat into their shells for the night. Or however long it would be before they got up again.

We stayed together, eating quietly, just in case we could be listened in on and chatted through Galaxy, which she found more annoying than we found her reading our minds.

After an hour and a half, the door opened and we watched, some of us more annoyed than the others, as a beaten and bloodied Amabala rejoined us.

Her Matron walked in behind her sporting bloodied knuckles and a sly grin like she had won some kind of award, four of her boy-toys in tow. She motioned to us. "Take them to the portal to wherever they are going, then return to your duties in the outer regions. You disgust me."

Amabala just stood there with her chin nearly touching her chest as she waited for the other woman and her entourage to leave.

Cassia stepped forward and lifted the other woman's chin so that she could stare her in the eyes. "I do not like this Matron." As she spoke, the wounds on the cheetah-woman's face closed and the bruises faded slightly until they looked a few days old. "You would be so much more appreciated elsewhere."

She looked at us and muttered, "If you would please, follow me."

All attempts to speak to her were quashed by the heavy silence and stoic refusal to meet our questing gazes and glances. Finally, we just spoke to the air itself as we trekked up and down ladders, across the cavernous shell to the other side of Sahen to a guarded room with a crystal reinforced door. The guards, more cheetah people, sneered at Amabala, one of them muttering, "Weakling," as she entered through the door and closed it behind us.

We just stared at her as she stood and pointed to the blank space at the other side of the room.

I sighed and accepted defeat, knowing that Galaxy would likely consume her before saying, "I wish you the best of luck in whatever you're going to be doing for these people who treat you like garbage. You don't deserve that."

Droplets of something splattered against the ground before she finally looked up at us, tears flooding from her eyes. "Did you say something about treasure?"

I grinned, holding out my hand to beckon her to us, Merlin, Arden, and Cassia all smiling as she stepped closer. "I sure did. Why don't you step into my office over here and we can discuss that a little further?"

CHAPTER NINE

The other side of the portal was breezy and cool, the land that we stood on covered in gravel and deep brown grooves.

"I recognize this place," Arden whispered softly. "We aren't far from Virani, just on the outskirts of the air plane where the wind jinn rule. This is the earthen plane where the earth jinn grow what little food our people need to eat to survive."

"You're home." Amabala sniffed as she wiped her eyes. "Shouldn't you feel a little more at ease?"

"Being here for me is about as exciting as you being alone with your Matron." Arden huffed, visibly trying to collect herself. "I was bottled last time I was here, and haven't returned since."

"I am so sorry." Amabala ducked her head and I couldn't blame her for feeling bad. It was one thing to say something out of ignorance, something else completely to project yourself and your own misgivings along with it onto someone.

Never know what someone else is going through, I reminded myself, thinking about all the times my Marines had been having shitty days and I'd had to get a little in their asses to dig their heads out. On top of having to deal with my own issues. It was why it was so important for me to try to be firm but fair.

The sky here was the same deep blue hue as before and that gave me pause. "Is time different from realm to realm?"

Arden glanced my direction before looking up into the sky. "It is for some of them. No one has ever really broken down the time differential between realms, because it's never been necessary. Each realm typically works and operates as if it were its own world away from the others, except for the Fae realms. There are two, but they connect in a weird way."

"That's so cool." I smiled to myself, despite the fact that I was hopelessly overwhelmed by the constant influx of new information that seemed so rudimentary and readily available to the others, as I was happy to be learning about it all. "So what is it that we all need to be aware of here, Arden?"

"Much like the other realms, each place here—rather, plane—has elemental creatures that roam within." She looked around us cautiously. "We're on the earthen plane now, so we could be attacked by any earth-type creature who wanders close. We should move."

We nodded, though Cassia took out her mace to have it in hand just in case as we made the trek in whatever direction Arden felt compelled to take us. Each step for her looked to weigh on her, as if she had taken a thousand and the air just kept on getting thinner and thinner for her.

"Arden, are you okay?" I asked softly, knowing that the others likely heard every word, but I wanted to at least try to be delicate.

"No, I'm not," she hissed back, but the determined set of her jaw said more than she did—she would keep moving forward.

All she can think about is revenge, and possibly finding her family. Galaxy's voice echoed through me and I nodded as if just to myself.

"Hey, Amabala?" The cheetah woman glanced at me and

raised her eyebrows questioningly. "What the hell was your Matron's problem with us?"

She looked uncomfortable for a time, then answered, "She hates outsiders almost as much as she hates weakness, and since I'm not much of a fighter, she hates me almost as much as that."

"So it was the fact that you brought outsiders to the city?" Merlin asked and tilted his head to the side.

"That and the fact that you all could have been a threat that we weren't prepared to neutralize." Amabala sighed, looking around. "She failed at poisoning you with the food because she takes offense to anything and everything, especially that someone questioned her, or made her out to be anything less than perfect."

"So she's a narcissist?" I raised a brow and Amabala nodded, a little amusement flickering across her face. "Got it. What could she have done to us?"

"She would have tried to kill or enslave you," Amabala stated matter of fact. "But now that I'm with you, she will kill you just to bring me back and put me in my place."

She fell silent and so we all did the same, walking on for the better part of twenty minutes before there was any sign of life, and the signs were magnificent.

Buffalo-like creatures with fur the color and shape of grass ate the brown dirt beneath their cloven hooves then lifted their heads to chew their meal and watch us cautiously.

Animals and other types of winged creatures soared, dipped, dived, ducked and dodged each other in a playful game above us in the sky so far away that I couldn't tell what they were.

"Harpies," Arden called back to the rest of us as she trudged on, pointing to a flock that adorned a cliff growing off to our right with more than a score of the same kinds of creatures but larger, watching protectively. "If one of them flies down here, don't do anything that could be misconstrued as an attack. Ignore them unless they touch you."

"What happens if they touch us?" Merlin asked quietly, so as to not tip off the ones watching to our notice.

"Run like hell," Arden answered simply and pressed on.

A couple of the juvenile harpies dropped down to watch us curiously. Their child-like size would make them somewhat cute if it hadn't been for the wickedly-sharp talons curling from their bird-like feet. Their arms were large eagles' wings, and their mouths were pinched and beak-like, opening to reveal that they were serrated on the sides like saw blades.

Almost makes you wonder what the parents look like, Galaxy's tone was plainly sarcastic and made me snort.

One of the braver ones dropped down onto the ground in front of us, cawing and speaking in an airy way that made Arden grimace. We tried to walk around it, but it persisted until a loud, shrill, whistling cry made it flinch and fly into the air quickly. All of the children above us fluttered back toward the rocks, one of the larger adults standing on the top-most point of the cliff with their wings spread wide as if to welcome them, watching us like a hawk.

"I don't know if that's good or bad, but whatever you do— don't run," Arden muttered, confusing me.

"I thought you said *to* run?" I whispered to her and she shook her head. "I'm confused."

"This place is confusing, get over it," she snarled back in a harsh whisper. "If we run now, we look weak. The elemental planes are *not* the place to make yourself look scared, got it? We walk on as if we're unbothered, and if they fuck with us, we nuke them."

I nodded and just went with it. If the rules of engagement were that they had to strike first, at least I knew where I stood.

As we continued on, I kept noticing the scent of salt and sulfur on the breeze, until I finally figured out why. Floating in the sky ahead of us was a massive monument to magic if I could have ever chosen one.

"Welcome to Virani, everyone." Arden's tone was bleak, tears forming in her eyes as she beheld the city with us.

Truly intuitively created buildings and monuments aloft in the air made of so many different materials and in so many different shapes and states that it was almost impossible for my mind to truly comprehend the sheer skill and magical chutzpah it would take to do one section of the city, let alone several. Each one—earth, water, fire, and air—mixed and melded and even created other zones where the magics intertwined and aligned in the most natural ways.

"Oh my God," I whispered despite the flatlining going on inside my brain. The simple majesty of it almost made me a drooling simpleton for a minute until I got a rather vicious mental kick from Galaxy.

Don't get too worked up, I'm helping you understand it all right now—but you need to remember that this place is dangerous and one of your friends was basically sold into slavery here. Her tone wasn't exactly venomous but it was damned-near close to it. *As you are so fond of saying to yourself, get your shit together, Marine.*

Aye, ma'am! I gave her a mental growl on par with any I'd give a senior staff non-commissioned officer and fucked off over to Arden. "We'll find your family. Let's get the information on the ruins we need to go visit and ask around about them before we leave. If at any time you want to get the fuck out of here, we're gone, okay?"

She nodded a few times, sniffling and obviously not trusting herself to speak, but turned toward Merlin and he nodded back as if understanding and said, "Yeah, I guess we could find some answers about what I am here."

"We will have to be cautious," Cassia stated and looked to the city with concern. "You're not supposed to exist at all, Merlin, and the fact that you do is going to make people uncomfortable."

I sighed, knowing what she was alluding to. "And people are dangerous when uncomfortable and scared of something. I don't know if jinn are the same way, but you can imagine what it would be like to learn that there's a half-jinn running around somewhere out there that shouldn't be possible."

A gasp drew our attention to Amabala, her clawed hands covering her cheetah snout like a child having just figured out a big secret, her eyes massive as she stared at the boy mage. "You're... But... How...?"

Her eyes darted from him to all of us as we grimaced in her direction. I had honestly forgotten that she was there and now the cat was out of the bag. If only we knew if the cat would get her tongue and keep it from wagging.

She must have sensed the building tension in all of us as she put her hands up. "I won't say anything! I'm on the run now basically too, so if I did, you could kill me and be on your way. I need you to stay safe."

"Can you not fight?" Merlin asked with a frown on his face.

"I can, but I'm not very good at it. I'm better at running away since I'm the smallest in my litter." She looked forlornly at the ground. "All of my siblings are better trackers than me too, so if they figure out that I'm gone—I won't be safe."

"She'll keep his secret." Cassia spoke calmly, drawing all of our attention, even Amabala. "She needs us, and we want her with us. She'll keep it. Let's get this show on the road. I need to get back to the High Table at some point."

"Do you not trust that they will be okay?" Merlin raised an eyebrow at her, but joined our jinn at the front of the group to walk on.

"I do, but I still want to be there with my family and friends just in case." She shrugged. "I've been at the High Table for a while and I like it there. Though this isn't the sort of vacation I envisioned."

"Oh, we are still going to Japan, my friend," Arden growled, throwing a look over her shoulder. "We are *not* missing out on the promised land of nerds and weebs."

I snorted while Cassia laughed outright, leaving Merlin and Amabala both confused. As we closed the distance between us and the city, I found myself wondering how we would get up there. There was no stationary device of transport, no conveyor, no steps. Nothing.

I decided to save my questions for when we got closer and let Arden handle getting us into the city. It wasn't like she wouldn't be able to, right? She was born here.

As we trod into the shadow of the behemoth magical marvel, Arden gasped and held her hand out to make us stop as a figure about four feet tall separated itself from some larger boulders and rocks covered in moss. It loped toward us then sat there stoically watching us.

She says that this is very rare, and has only heard of it happening in myths, Galaxy explained in a low whisper, as if the sound of her voice in our minds might startle the creature away. *This is a fox golem, a spirit that fused with the stones of an earth elemental's corpse and made a new creature.*

As soon as she said it, I began to be able to make out the real shape of the figure. It wasn't the fur that was gray like the rocks—it was actually pure stone. It was cracked and piled in places that looked like joints that should have made a grinding noise when it moved, but it was perfectly silent. Its vulpine statue-like face stared at us, pointed stone ears covered at the tips by bristly looking moss that resembled fur as you glanced at it, but they weren't attached to the head, just floating there. As it watched us, two fluffy moss tails fanned out behind it and moved slowly back and forth in the air.

It slowly edged closer until it stood no less than ten feet from us and we could finally see its eyes. Beautiful gemstones of amber and yellow reflected some of the ambient light that happened into the shade here and there, but what was truly bewitching about the experience was the magnitude of intelligence behind those eyes.

And all of that intellect bore directly toward Merlin.

"It's staring at me, what do I do?" Merlin whispered softly, unable to look away from the creature. His arm flopped in the air as he groped for Arden to get her attention.

"If it's staring at you, go talk to it." Cassia grunted and nudged the boy forward. "Even a yokai like me knows that a fox spirit isn't to be ignored. A nogitsune is something you don't want to deal with."

Merlin took a deep breath and took a cautious step forward, and when the creature didn't react took another one. The next two steps the fox golem mirrored until they stood in front of each other.

Merlin tilted his head to the side and the fox did the same, copying his movements and mannerisms. Finally, Merlin grew bold and held his hand out like he wanted to touch the fox, and it shied away just a bit. He was about to take his hand back, a sadness overtaking his features when the fox's head shot forward into his palm and a muted *whompf* noise popped my ears.

Amber-yellow light spread from the fox to Merlin's palm and radiated around him.

Galaxy stepped out of me in her human form and moved closer to Merlin, entranced by what was happening. The fox stared past the boy and sat back down as she approached.

"He's become my familiar?" Merlin spoke softly, but in confusion. His eyes raised to look at Galaxy. "What does this mean?"

"It means that you must be of relation to earth jinn?" She answered as best she could, but a flash of uncertainty across her features gave her thoughts away. Even she wasn't sure.

"It was bad enough that we were going into the city with so many non-jinn but now we have a fox coming with us as well?" Arden chuckled, her hands raising to cover her face for a moment before they dropped and her shoulders shook with laughter. A smile on her face for the first time since we had come to this realm of elements. "If I had to come back, I'd never thought it would be like this. I'm glad it is."

Cassia grabbed her shoulder. "So am I." She grinned and her teeth were sharper than normal. "Let's go find these assholes and kill them for you."

Arden just shook her head and looked up to Virani and muttered, "One true daughter of flame and her guests seek passage to the city."

A bright light flooded around us and suddenly we were standing in a very metropolitan area, a luscious green park surrounding us with buildings of red and orange hues.

"Welcome again to Virani," Arden whispered as several people turned toward us and came closer to investigate.

CHAPTER TEN

Those closing in around us had pointed ears and varying features, but there was one thing that remained the same—the colors of their skin and hair deeply reflected their elemental affinities.

Children with blue and brown hair inched closer to check us out as various adults did the same. None of them had any weapons, so they weren't a threat in that manner, but I still felt like a bit of a freak for standing out and being scrutinized like this.

A wash of heat flared from next to me and I watched as Arden's body lifted off the ground slightly, her skin turning a slight shade of green, though her hair set ablaze. Her eyes shimmered red as well, her gaze searching the faces of the people around her for something. Anything.

"Ardent Flame?" someone in the back called out. An older woman, hunched over and moving slowly through the crowd of onlookers and nosy residents, coming towards us. When she made her way fully through, she fixed Arden with a knowing look and threw her arms out. "I'd recognize that powerful aura anywhere. Come see Gammy Nums."

"Gammy?" Arden whispered a heartbeat before she launched herself at the woman. She lifted her in a massive hug, the woman's back adjusting with the force of it. She cried out and Arden flinched and let her down. "Are you okay?"

"Never been better!" The woman actually stood straighter than she had and grinned to the point that her smile could have swallowed her face. "I'll never forget one of my babies—don't matter that I'm pushing twenty-three thousand!"

Her triumphant demeanor made me want to laugh. "You know Arden?"

"Since the day her momma birthed her." She nodded and looked at me. "Human? Huh, strange company you keep, dearest, but I don't mind. Come to Gammy Nums and sit a while. I'd love to hear more about the time you've been gone."

Arden looked to us, and Cassia looked straight at me and Galaxy.

I shrugged. "We're here for Arden as much as anything else. We can chat with Gammy."

The old woman didn't have to take us far, her home was the equivalent to a condo in the middle of a busy city, but everywhere she went, the people around her were courteous and looked to pay her a special sort of eye. Whether it was out of respect for her, her age, or that she was someone special, I couldn't tell, but they did it and it made me wonder just who and what she was.

Even as I stared at her while she walked through her door, I could hardly see a thing.

Because she's what could be considered much too powerful for you to truly gaze at, Galaxy whispered to me mentally, grasping my wrist to pull me into the older woman's home so she could close the door. *She's older than so many things and the people here give her a wide berth. I would behave with her.*

I gave her a slight head tilt to say I got it and watched as the older woman waved her hands and a tea set materialized on a table in the middle of her living room. The table hadn't been there before and I could have sworn the room was smaller than the thirty feet square it was now.

I realized that part of the reason for the stares could have been the fox, but when I went to look for it, it was gone. Merlin must have noticed me looking for it, because he motioned to his left wrist where a stone bracelet now took up a good four or five inches of his forearm. He winked and I relaxed, resigning to talk to him later about it.

She snapped her fingers and several larger chairs and couches burst from the floor with a whoosh and she motioned for us to be seated while she tinkered with the tea on the table. She lit a flame before setting a metal stand over it then settling the teapot on it to boil. She settled herself into what could have been a rocking chair, but it was so deeply covered in furs that I couldn't make out anything about it.

She sighed and looked expectantly over at Arden. "What have you been up to, dear?"

"I've been on Earth for the majority of my life, I was… bottled and sold while I was still young." I could have sworn as Arden spoke, I heard a crack of thunder as Gammy listened, her face serene but a steely glint in her eyes. "Part of why I've returned was to see if I couldn't figure out who did it, and try to find my family."

"Your brother is here." Arden stilled, and stared at her as she added, "Has been for more than four thousand years. Though, like the rest of your family, he disappeared for a while too."

"Where is he?" she asked excitedly, her eyes wide and her lip between her teeth as she waited. "Is he okay?"

I thought he was dead? I muttered to Galaxy, her head bobbed once and I looked at Cassia. The Oni woman stared at Arden carefully, then looked to Gammy Nums.

"He's seemed perfectly fine, though he does lament that he misses his lost family." Gammy Nums paused as the teakettle whistled, added the tea in a small metal tube that she put into the top of the kettle and stirred exactly three times before leaving it in to steep. "Works closely with the air jinn who run the city. He's one of the only flame jinn that they will work with and has been basically acting as a sort of mayor for your people, though there's no true position."

Arden looked so… odd just then. She seemed conflicted and didn't look to be able to decide.

"Gammy, what's your actual name?" Cassia blurted and Arden actually snorted at that. "It can't be Nums."

The elderly woman laughed, her wizened voice filled with delight as she answered, "No, it isn't, but Nums is easier for the babies to say, rather than the much more difficult Numarialos." She turned her gaze to Arden as she poured all of us a cup. "It's okay to not know how to feel, my love. It's okay to feel confused. It's okay to feel hurt, or numb. What is not okay is hiding it from your Gammy. Come to me, child."

Arden stood up and walked around the dark wood table to kneel down and hug the old woman, her shoulders shaking as she sobbed. It was so awkward to sit there and just watch as she poured her soul, her anguish, and millennia of torment out in one large push.

The tea was good though.

Marcus! Galaxy's head whipped toward me, her eyes narrowing. I sagged a bit and muttered an apology to her mentally before just letting myself fade out of the moment.

———

It was a good two hours later that we made our way toward the library in the city to research the ruins north of the city. Gammy Nums had been kind enough to let us know that she would get Arden's brother to join us at her place in a little while.

The further into the city we went, the more I realized that the population wasn't as diverse here. They all looked gray and had various kinds of gray to white or silver hair. The buildings looked like they were made of some kind of cloud-like material that was supple but sturdy. It was weird and I didn't like it.

I also didn't like how some of them stared openly at Arden as if she didn't belong here.

"What's with all the weird looks, Arden?" Merlin asked softly, and I was relieved that I wasn't the only one who had been dying to know.

"Air jinn are more numerous, and since they have the most population, the city is basically run by them." She glared at one of the ones staring a little more brazenly at her and scowled as they scoffed and walked away. "That gives them a sense of entitlement that drives the other jinn nuts."

"So why are they so numerous?" I asked softly.

"The sky is massive and full of mana, so much so that it creates them regularly and their birth rates are higher," Cassia answered, which surprised me a little. "I studied jinn so I would know how to best fight with Arden. It's what made her eventually agree to fight me."

"And here I thought it was you throwing the first ten punches," Arden retorted whimsically. Moments after that, we arrived at a small building that had to be the library. "I guess this is it?"

We walked in and immediately came back out. The library inside was truly massive, but the reason we had to leave actually had the balls to follow us out the door.

"I will not have your kind in a place of fabled knowledge!" The air jinn with glasses sneered, crossing his arms. "You'll burn the place down when you can't find what you want and I won't be held responsible."

Keep him distracted. Galaxy sighed and faded into my shadow while he glared at Arden who looked like she was ready to blow the hell up.

"Maybe you would be kind enough to let one of *us* in?" I asked politely as if it would work.

"Humans won't understand our language." He actually smiled as if he had it all figured out.

Cassia spoke in a language that sounded like pure flames crackling from a log and the jinn just stared at her in disgust, and she grimaced. "Was my pronunciation off?" She shrugged and started to speak in a language that sounded like rushing wind and breezes over leaves.

"Stop that at once!" The man screeched as if he were dying from what she said alone. "How dare you!"

"All I did was call you a dickhead," Cassia said innocently, but her smirk said it all—if she could swing on him, he'd die.

"If you don't leave here right now, I will be forced to summon the guard." He stood with his hands close together like he was about to clap his hands.

"How about you bless us with some of that famous air jinn knowledge, eh?" Merlin tried with a smile. "See, you know a lot more than we do about *everything,* and I bet you know where we would have to look to find information on the local archeological finds?"

"The local what?" Cassia grunted and the jinn rolled his eyes.

"The study of past cultures, and we don't have those here." He just shook his head. "This city was made countless eons ago, there's nothing to find out there but monsters, elemental creatures, and death. Good day."

He turned and left us without a return glance and I just shrugged before we moved away from the doorway and toward the side of the small building. Half an hour of loitering and furtive glances from passersby paid off when Galaxy returned to my shadow.

I've got the goods—let's get out of here. She sounded a little winded but I motioned the others away and we began walking back to the district of the city that was Gammy's.

What did you get? I peered around cautiously for anyone who could be following us, just to be safe, and didn't find anything.

Information and some goodies that I think some of our more magically inclined folks will enjoy.

I grinned at that answer and decided to just keep a lookout until we were back at Gammy's.

We walked for a little longer, Arden taking us down an alley to get to the district that belonged to what she called the 'Outcast jinn' when a group of air jinn blocked off the exit.

"What the hell are you doing?" Arden raised her voice menacingly. "Move."

"I don't think you understand who's in charge here." One of them sneered, a look of disgust on his face as he crossed his arms over his chest.

All three of them were well-dressed in ren-faire-style clothes that made me think they were trying too hard even if they could be considered classically good looking, but their apparent disdain just colored them ugly.

"I don't give a shit who you think is in charge, either you move, or I move you," Arden growled, her fiery hair starting to flicker and start to move like an actual flame. "I won't tell you again—get the fuck out of my way."

"You clearly need to learn your place." The apparent leader seethed, just a second before his two buddies raised their open palms toward her. "Let's show her."

The air around us was suddenly depleted somehow, like it was that much harder to take a full breath. Arden's flames guttered and suddenly Cassia lunged forward and grabbed the jinn on the right by his face and whipped him into the wall with a roar, shouting something in the airy language they spoke that drew the other two goons' attention.

I was about to attack one of them myself when Arden snarled and thrust her hand out. A wave of her aura unleashed before her, colliding into the last two standing jinn, sending them ass over teakettle into the street behind them, where people walking by screamed and took off in fear.

They struggled to stand up, but Merlin stepped past me, his hands moving until he could clench his fists and bring them down next to him like a kid beating a desk. Except every time he brought them down, both of the jinn on the ground cried out in pain and coughed up blood.

Where the hell did he learn that? I gasped to myself as I watched him pull both of them in with a motion of his hands.

He's always known how to do this, but without my interference and your influence, could never bring himself to use the full extent of his magical strength in brute force like this. There was an edge of pure pride in Galaxy's tone as he continued to drag them toward himself.

She stepped out of me in her cat form and opened her mouth wide, the bones in her jaw cracking and shifting as the maw opened wider and wider. She consumed one in a second and locked her eyes hungrily on the leader.

Her fur rose, spiking in the air like a feral beast and the man's eyes widened. "Wait! Please—no!"

She pounced, her mouth working over his kicking feet. "We were told to come here and take care of you all! We were just following orders!"

"How many times have we heard that excuse?" I growled, remembering all the people we had interrogated overseas, always placing the blame on someone else so they might be spared. "Who sent you?"

"We don't know!" He screamed, her teeth grazing his right arm painfully. "They used magic to hide themselves from us. We couldn't see their faces or anything. Please—*please!*"

"Not good enough, give me a name!" I spat in his face with a grimace as a gleeful wash of hunger almost consumed me, Galaxy's delight spilling through me so hard that I almost didn't want him to give me the information.

"No, please!" He continued to beg as her throat constricted and her jaws clamped down; a rush of blood fountained onto the ground. I looked away, some of the hot liquid splattering against my back and shoulder just as I did.

I glanced over at Cassia and found that the jinn she held no longer struggled and laid on the ground in a heap with the back of his head caved in on one side.

Cassia stared over at Arden. "You are much sturdier than the others of your kind."

Arden scowled at her and just rolled her eyes, attention falling out to possible onlookers. "We need to get somewhere, quickly. The guards have likely been summoned."

"Can't you do the hazy heat thing to make people see something else?" I followed her gaze and found that people were coming back en masse to investigate.

"It works well on humans, but not on other jinn." She grimaced and closed her eyes, before shaking her head. "I can't think of a way for us to get out of here without being seen. We need to get out of the city."

"What about your brother?" Cassia stepped closer to Arden and touched her shoulder. "You're so close to seeing him—you thought he was dead and gone!"

"I know that better than anyone else!" she cried, throwing her arms into the air. "Don't you think I want to see him? Someone here wants us dead, and if the guards get ahold of us, we might be better off having died. So let's leave and wait until the heat dies down before we come back."

She didn't wait, and neither had Galaxy, the third body having disappeared and her decidedly happy kitty grin confirming the evidence was almost all gone.

We followed behind Arden as she walked toward the street once more. When she stepped foot into the cloudy roadway, she whispered something and the road lowered, "Come on!"

She hopped down into the hole, followed quickly by Merlin and Cassia, then me with Galaxy riding on my shoulder. Amabala dropped like a stone, having been silently observing the rest of us this whole time; she looked either pensive or perturbed but kept her thoughts to herself.

We landed on the cloud with soft *thunks* and lowered down toward the ground faster and faster until we landed with a resounding fluffy *crack*, which made no sense.

"Move!" Arden growled and ran us away from the city as quickly as we could manage, her and Amabala in the lead.

Amabala motioned farther ahead of us. "There's a portal that way!"

"We need to get to somewhere out of sight of the city, not to a portal, our goal for now is here," I called, hoping that was what Arden had in mind.

"The water plane is ahead. It'll be uncomfortable for me, but it should be the last place they think to check for us." She huffed as the wind picked up, her gaze flying upward. "Let's *go!*"

We soldiered on, sprinting for as long as our bodies would hold out. Just when I started to believe that my legs would no longer carry me any farther without rest, we broke through a barrier of some kind and stood on a beach. Soft sand crunched beneath our footfalls, but threw my balance hard enough that I slid a few feet and almost tumbled to the ground.

I managed to land on a knee, but I knew I was done for now. "Let's—" *Huff, wheeze.* "—Rest. Here. Galaxy."

She knew what I wanted before I had put together the thought and hopped off my shoulder onto the sand, landing in her human form with a book in her hand. "Arden, this is for you."

The jinn turned and glared at it before taking it. She opened the pages and her breathing quickened. "Is this…?"

"Yes, a spell book of jinn design." She grinned. "They hid it, but I was able to find it because most physical barriers cannot contain me."

"Speaking of containment, Merlin, that fox turned into a bracelet?" I watched the boy nod and shrug. "That doesn't bother you, or seem freaky?"

"I can sense it, like you sense Galaxy." He held it up in front of his face for a time and shrugged again. "It just feels right."

That thing is nothing like me, though it is powerful. Galaxy almost sounded curmudgeonly about it, like she was jealous. Her head whipped over toward me and she glared at me. "You think I would be jealous of something like that? I gave him life again."

I was about to fire back a retort when someone cleared their throat and I turned to see Amabala raising her hand. "I don't know what kind of dynamic this is, but she seems to come and go from you unlike any familiar I've ever heard of. If I'm going to travel with you guys, I need answers."

"Then start asking questions." Cassia crossed her arms and

stared at the cheetah woman expectantly. "We can't just assume what you want to know."

"Who are all of you, and what are all of you?" She looked directly at Galaxy when she said the last bit, her cat eyes narrowing curiously.

Galaxy smiled. "I don't know who I am, but I'm not someone to be trifled with. You've seen what I can do, at least some of it." She pointed out the rest of us each in turn as she said, "They. Are. All. Mine. I give them power and strength, and the ability to become more than they ever could have been on their own."

"Can you do the same for me?" Amabala asked softly, her voice almost a whine as she held her left arm with her right hand across her stomach.

"In time, if you prove yourself useful to us all." Galaxy shrugged and stretched, producing another smaller book. "In the meantime, rest at ease knowing that so long as you are with us, we will protect you. Because you've already begun to prove your worth to me."

"You want to know when there are portals near you, is that it?" She looked almost hurt as she stared at Galaxy.

"Yes," Galaxy replied simply, Amabala flinching at her directness. "You'll have to forgive me. I'm a little drunk on power, and feeling stronger than I should. I'll get used to it, I think. You seem to me, Amabala, an intelligent woman who can survive. All of us are survivors and warriors here in some way or another. Don't see a simple use as all you're worth, know that you can be more—like us."

"I'll think on that a time, thank you," she muttered softly and walked toward the water on her own as the rest of us watched.

"Is it okay for her to know that?" Merlin asked cautiously. "What if she's spying on us for her Matron?"

"I will know if I ever decide to bless her, but she would find out more than we wanted her to regardless when we start to truly look for the mantle of the Huntsman." She waved the book in her hand. "I know languages of old, but this confuses me. Merlin, is there something you can do about that?"

He caught the book as she tossed it to him and opened it readily, poring over the contents. He sat on the ground and pulled out another book with a flick of his wrist that I was minutely jealous of.

"Marcus?" Amabala spoke softly so as not to disturb the others, but she wrung her hands as she stared at me. I turned and gave a nod to Cassia who sat watching the way we had come from protectively before giving me the go ahead to walk away from the group.

We moved about forty feet away along the sandy shore, and stood in relative silence while she worked up the nerve to speak. Which she still hadn't managed to do on her own, so I said, "If you're worried about us hurting you, we could have at any time while we were with you so far. We haven't, and personally speaking—I don't want to. You seem like you have a good head on your shoulders, and can take care of yourself."

"Yeah, when I'm not being bullied by my family." She snorted and rolled her eyes. "I know that you all could have killed me. I just didn't realize the depth of the danger I was in until those jinn attacked us and you guys put them down so handily. No, what I wanted to talk about was what your end goal is, and how I can help you achieve it."

I arched an eyebrow at her forward statement, gathering she got the gall from Galaxy, but asked anyway. *No use hiding it from her, right?*

No, we need to know whether she will stay with us or not, Galaxy answered as she knelt down next to Merlin.

I nodded as if I was deciding on my own and answered, "We're going to be searching for an artifact called the Huntsman's Mantle. We mean to bring back the Wild Hunt, and I will be taking the role of the Huntsman." Her jaw dropped, her eyes widening as I chuckled. "Yeah, surprising, right?"

"Surprising? More like suicidal—no one has heard anything about the Hunt outside the kind of nursery tales that mothers tell naughty children to make them mind." She snorted and almost doubled over while laughing. "You're going to go hunting for one of the most powerful non-god-touched artifacts in Grestallan history? Are you crazy?"

"Yes." I smiled at her and she rolled her eyes. "I spent some time with Uncle Sam's misguided children, and I know it's a long shot, but I wasn't trained to back down. The High Table Council gave me this task as a way to prove that I wanted to keep our patrons safe, and since I'm new to all this, I want to do it."

"Why?" She frowned at me. "I know what the High Table is, and I know that it cares only about neutrality—why would they need the Hunt?"

"Because times change and there are those who seek to take over in places?" I shrugged. "We had to deal with this Seelie asshole who tried to take over Columbus with a drug that ate the magic of the user, and he was going to go world-wide with it. If we have the power of the Hunt, we can keep assholes like him in check."

"You hope." She folded her arms over her chest and eyed me. "There's always someone stronger, Marcus. The dragons stood toe to toe with the Huntsman and the full might of a centuries-old and thousand body-strong Hunt and almost won. They are weaker now, but still, not something to be taken lightly. Should they find out the Hunt has returned, they may seek you out."

"Almost won?" I frowned, ignoring that last part and she nodded. "Sorry, the Cull wasn't something I'd heard about until very recently and have had a shit time getting myself to research anything. How did they not win?"

"The Huntsman sacrificed himself and every life in his care to take them down, and even then, some survive to this day. Those who chose not to fight, or those strong enough to just be severely weakened." She frowned, her whiskers dipping as she stared out over the vast, blue waves. "From what my Matron always told our litter when we were younger, the Huntsman's true strength was in numbers. That he could call the souls of his riders to him and use them to empower himself, but he had never used the ability to that level before and it cost him everything. After he died, people searched for the mantle to take up his cause, but no one ever returned from trying to find it."

"Thanks for the cautionary tale." I grinned at her and she just stared at me in disbelief. "It bothers you that I'm not scared or concerned?" She nodded silently. "I've fought Fae, met gods, killed nephilim, and literally danced with the devil. I'm not the most well-informed, but I've started to grasp that the world I knew is gone, and that I need to adapt to the one I've entered, quickly, or I'm going to get eaten alive by it. I'm trying to stop letting it bother me, so I'll take the criticisms and being called crazy in stride, so long as I survive and my friends are okay."

"That may be so, but this is the mantle. You have to be crazy to search for it," Amabala insisted.

"Aren't we all?" I asked her quietly and she seemed confused. "You just met us today, and yet here you are with us on the run from your abusive family. Some would call you crazy."

"Some might be right," she growled back, then sighed, closing her eyes. "What did you get yourself into, runt?"

"Don't call yourself that," I snarled, unable to stop myself. She opened her eyes to stare at me in surprise. "You're letting them keep owning you by questioning yourself like they would. You're braver than them, and you know that."

She smiled, her whiskers twitching. "Sure."

"Amabala, we're all a little crazy." I smiled and just watched her. "We need you. We need your skills, and if you're useful to us, we may be able to do some more for you. Stick with us."

She was quiet and pensive for a time before Merlin growled, "Ah-*ha*!"

We both whipped around to face him as he stood. "I've figured out the encryption!"

"So where do we go?" Cassia asked excitedly, bouncing to her feet and walking closer to him. "Are we close?"

"I have no idea!" He grinned and she looked like she was ready to strangle him. "But with that, I can start decoding it and reading it."

She rolled her eyes, plopping back down onto the sand with a huff. "May as well just spend the night here on the beach then. Give him time to study that, and us the time to rest."

"Do we have camping gear?" Merlin looked up.

"We do, and I brought you a bedroll as well." Arden absently produced one from her inventory and tossed it to him.

"What about a tent?" I asked looking up at the sky. It wasn't dark or anything like it was going to rain, but you never knew.

"There are no bugs here in the elemental portion of Grestal unless you go far out into the water part," Arden explained in a muttering tone as she continued to read the book Galaxy had brought her. "A tent would just inhibit our ability to fight back quickly if we were attacked."

I shrugged, begrudgingly understanding. It wasn't like I *needed* a tent to sleep. Shit, I had slept in foxholes in the field for training, I could sleep on a beach just fine. Dig myself a little hole and cuddle right in.

I walked over to Cassia and sat down beside her. "How you doing?"

"Good. A little irritated we can't just be on our way, but I'll live." She glanced at me and smiled. "How about you?"

"I'm alright. Glad I have you all here to learn from and keep my feet on the ground." I rolled out the sleeping bag I had and slid the insert in the bottom to make it a little firmer on the bottom. "This place is pretty damn wild."

"Yeah, it is." She watched me as I set myself up next to her. "You know I won't be sleeping, right?"

"Uh huh." I smiled back at her and winked. "I remember that cat nap you had in the bar. You telling me that Oni don't need to sleep as much as the rest of us, especially you because you're so tough."

She smirked. "Damn right I am."

"So I'll just keep you company." I unzipped the bag and

took my boots off to get in it and lay back. "You okay with that?"

She touched my chest. "Of course I am." She grinned, looking around before leaning down to give me a kiss. "I wish we were alone."

"I do too, but having everyone here is a good thing." She frowned at me. "What?"

"I wish to scrap."

Arden sighed loudly. "You two act like bunnies!"

I laughed at that and looked back at her from where I lay on the ground, having to tilt my head until she was upside down to me. "I mean, she's an Oni and I'm a guy—can you blame us?"

"Yes?" She raised an eyebrow back. "I've never met someone with such an active... Shut the fuck up and let me read, damn it."

She continued to huff and be nearly insufferable for a little bit, but I just laughed. I didn't think that Cassia and I were all that bad, though with how curiously Amabala watched the two of us, she seemed jealous or concerned.

I closed my eyes that night to a starry, watery-looking sky, and didn't dream.

CHAPTER ELEVEN

We woke up to some pre-packed breakfast food that Arden had brought along, eating gratefully. Even Amabala had some, though she was like a child about it.

She opened one of the silver packets and took the small, blocky pastry out to observe it. The frosted side with sprinkles made her tilt her head. I watched her as she bit into it and laughed as she realized that it had fruity filling. She asked for more, but Arden didn't budge.

I decided that while the others ate, I'd go over the leveling that I had neglected and check out my new spells and spell paths.

Level 9
Stats
Brawn: 14
Dexterity: 13
Physique: 12
Mana: 20
Charisma: 10
Points to spend: 10
Spells Known

Wisp 1/6
Physical Buff 1/6
Bolt 3/6
Blade 2/6
Embodiment*
Fire Blast 5/8

That was quite the number of points to use and I was happy to have them, along with the six points to spend on spells, and upgrading the ones I had.

I opened my spell matrix and smiled, glad to finally see that I had access to the ice spells Galaxy had promised me. I frowned. *Shouldn't there be some shadow ones in here as well?*

Yes, if I had the time to fully process them and relate them to you, but I haven't and I don't know when I will, so relax. Galaxy yawned and stared at me defiantly. *The shadow magic he gave me was... more intricate than the ice, and I don't know how best to give it to you without literally blowing up your mind.*

Oh, thanks for that, then. I blinked at her as she watched me and stared at the spell options I had.

Chill – Rapidly cool whatever it is that you touch. 2 mana per second.

"Oh, that's really interesting!" I grinned at all the applications that could possibly have and considered buying it outright, but opted to look at the others first.

Frigid Lance – Summon and use a long icicle as a weapon to attack or throw. 25 mana.

Slick – Freeze the ground in a ten-foot diameter around a point of your choosing. 15 mana.

Snow Cone – Cast a single cone of frost at targets within sixty feet. 10 mana.

That last one was interesting too, but with my other spells, it wouldn't work that well, or be as good. Slick would be good for crowd control, but it was situational and with how quickly and hands on we all were, it was just not as useful for the fights we would be getting into.

The Lance and Chill were the best, but if I had to pick one

to give me the most bang for my buck, I'd have to go with Chill. It had so much more use than just to attack, and that would be better, at least in my mind.

I chose the spell and checked out the stats for it and saw that it already had two points in it. "Galaxy, what's this?"

She closed her eyes and frowned before looking back at me. "You have an affinity for the cold, it seems." She frowned further and blinked in disbelief. "More so than even I do."

"Is that good?" I wondered, glad that I had a boost to how much the spell would freeze per use.

"Your ice spells will be stronger for it, and you might be a little more resistant to cold, but I don't know why." She scratched her head and stepped closer to me. "We will figure ourselves out."

I grinned. "I had no doubt." I added the next four points into the spell.

Congratulations on fully investing in a spell. Here is your fully upgraded and realized spell.

Congratulations, your spell has evolved into the stronger version: Frost.

Frost – Your control over the cold encompasses you, and you can freeze things within five feet of you. 3 mana per second.

Your grin is threatening to swallow your head, Marcus, Galaxy teased and I just laughed as I opened the upgrades.

Upgrades*

While active, your Frost is equivalent to your will, and responds to your thoughts. You have a heightened chance of slowing those affected by it by more than half and can even freeze lesser enemies solid given enough time. The strength of your Frost can be added to by increased levels of Mana and Charisma.

I frowned. *And here I thought Charisma would just be a dump stat for me.*

Shrugging, I pulled my stats back up and began to plot out

the additions to my stats. One to Brawn; two to Dexterity, Physique, and Charisma; and finally three to Mana.

Level 9
Stats
Brawn: 15
Dexterity: 15
Physique: 14
Mana: 23
Charisma: 12
Points to spend: 0
Spells Known
Wisp 1/6
Physical Buff 1/6
Bolt 3/6
Blade 2/6
Embodiment*
Fire Blast 5/8
Frost 2/8

Instantly my muscles bulged, then got leaner. I felt more alive than before, for certain. I noted that there was no asterisk at the end of Frost and frowned, that had to mean that it wasn't finished growing, right?

I rolled my head back and forth from side to side, then shrugged my shoulders to relax a little more, before I shook out and rolled up my sleeping bag to put into my inventory.

No birds sang overhead, the only noise to break up the sounds of the soft conversation in the small camp were the waves slowly breaking on the shoreline.

Cold enveloped me as I moved close enough to the water to affect the waves. A patch of thin ice thickened in front of me as I willed the Frost spell to increase its output near my feet. I stood on a thick strand of ice on the water and grinned like I had just discovered the coolest thing—because I had.

And for only working five seconds, I was only out 15 of my 230 mana. "This spell is going to be so nice."

"Yes, it is, and we will need it too." Merlin grunted at me from where he stood behind me on the sand.

"What makes you say that?" I frowned at him and blinked in surprise as my mini-map went from a fuzzy blur to crystalline clarity with a green arrow pointing straight out to sea.

"Do we need a boat of some sort?" I raised an eyebrow at him, worried that we would be shit out of luck with Arden being a flame jinn in water.

"I brought one." Arden sighed, already looking seasick. "At least this way I can practice my new elemental spells."

"Wind?"

I couldn't help my boyish smile, but she hit me with one of her own as she said, "Water."

————

Four hours and at least six haphazard attempts to keep all the vomit spewing from Amabala and Cassia out of the inflatable raft and from hitting me or the captain in the face later, we were still uncertain as to how long we had to ride in the inflatable.

"Are we there yet?" Cassia groaned, her skin a little green against the ever-growing light.

Merlin snorted and rolled his eyes. "No, and if you wouldn't have puked on me, I'd offer to try to help with that motion sickness again."

"I said I was sorr—*regh.*" She gagged and flung her head over the side of the raft, water spritzing her face as she came up miserably.

"The book says that we head straight along the border to the plane of earth, and travel until the sky gives way." Merlin huffed and sat back. "When respects are paid, the ruins will appear. We aren't close for right now. Just focus on breathing and trying to get used to the motion."

The surly-looking boy tried to close his eyes to rest but Amabala loudly retched and yowled pitiably.

We carried on, the two miserable women eventually passing

out from the stress of the continued vomiting, and with a little help from Merlin's spells.

I worked on trying to affect and cool the air around us with Frost and eventually my stomach gurgled loudly enough that I had to break into the nutrition bars that I had brought with me to replenish my mana.

Finally, darkness fell and the stars flickered into being far above. It was so nice to be able to really see the stars without all the light pollution on Earth.

"They're pretty," Arden whispered, my head bobbing as I agreed with her.

Merlin stirred next to Arden and sat up, fumbling for the book that had fallen from his lap onto the bottom of the raft. He lifted it and a small globe of light burst into light behind his left shoulder. "The sky gives way. The sky giving way could be interpreted as nightfall—Arden, stop!"

"But the arrow on our minimap says to keep going," she reasoned, but when he continued to glare at her to stop, she released the magic that she had been getting good at all day and we floated for about a hundred feet or so before coming to a stop. "Now what?"

"We wait for the ruin to present itself after we pay our respects." He thumped the book happily, then his mouth opened and closed. "How do we pay our respects?"

"Doesn't it say in the book?" Galaxy yawned and stretched as much as she could before sitting up to stare at him.

He shook his head, then frowned at the scenery around him. "We're in the realm of the elements. The jinn. Arden, what would someone do to show their respects to someone they've never met before?"

"I mean, I wouldn't really know, but in order for us to be free of our enslavement in the bottle, we require the 'respect' of a blood sacrifice." She shook her head and beat me to speaking. "No, not someone's life. Just blood."

Merlin took the knife that he kept attached to his belt now and sliced his forearm. "I pay my respects." Blood droplets plopped against the oceanic waters and when nothing happened for a while he sighed and looked at the rest of us. "Maybe it requires some from all of us?"

"Can't hurt to do it." I shrugged and slit my forearm a little to offer some blood. Cassia came up ready to fight and almost tipped us all over in the water, but when she realized what was going on, she acquiesced. Amabala didn't like it, but she did so. Finally, that left Galaxy and she shrugged, so I said, "What?"

"I don't know if I even have blood." Her sincerity and almost-embarrassed discomfort made me want to hug her.

"Only one way to find out." I took Merlin's knife and handed it to her. She took a steadying breath and brought the blade's edge along the outside of her forearm. Dark blood pooled there for a long heartbeat, then three drops splattered onto the water, and we all stilled.

The blood circulated and faded from view, moments before large shadows danced beneath the surface of the already-dark water.

"I swear to whatever god may or may not be listening, if we summoned some kind of super jaws—I'll just freak the fuck out!" I growled and readied myself for a fight.

"Wait!" Merlin cried, his hands flying up. "This is it!"

"What?" Arden growled and gripped his shirt, yanking him closer as the raft started rocking precariously.

The water around us began to slowly swirl and build speed as the shadow continued to ascend from the untold depths.

Merlin shouted, "It's the ruins!"

The hair on the back of my neck stood on end as something dark and massive separated itself from the large shadow below us. "And something else—brace yourselves!"

The shadow did nothing for us as that something launched itself at the bottom of our raft. Arden wasn't a punk and whipped us out of the way.

A massive angular head with scarred and jagged spike-like protrusions growing from the back like a ridge dripped water as it lifted from the depths with a glare of primal hatred centered on us. Whipping tentacle whiskers floated in the air below it from the chin, writhing and seeking in the air as the creature turned its head to one side to stare at us with one yellow-gold slitted eye as it hissed menacingly.

Large, fin-like protrusions decorated its back, greenish on the outside and purple on the inside but what was so interesting about them was that they looked like they were sharp enough to slice the water in half.

"If this thing was the Loch Ness monster, I'd shit myself," I muttered more to myself than anyone else as I fought the lump in my throat to swallow.

Two huge paddles lifted from the water and swung forward to launch it at us, the wave it flicked behind its body like a tidal wave as it moved forward.

"Shit!" Merlin roared and clapped his hands together, a massive bolt of lightning arcing into the creature's chin. "We can't kill that thing; we need to run until the island can fully rise!"

"Fuck!" I roared and went through my options. Fire? *Nope, it's in water, Marcus.* Ice? *Fucking really, devil?* All I had was my sword and lightning. They would have to do.

The creature had to be less than seventy feet from us and gaining fast, despite Merlin helping Arden maneuver the raft around the rising ruins.

I growled to myself and looked back at the others. "I'm gonna do something really fucking dumb!"

"You better come back!" Cassia tried to be okay, but the motion won out over her rage and she got sick all over the side of the raft.

I summoned the short sword from my inventory and mentally psyched myself up like I would before going through a nasty obstacle course. This was going to be dangerous, but the potential payout was too great to ignore.

Roaring in defiance, I cast Embodiment of Lightning and threw myself forward and up, flashing up to the slight ridge above the creature's eye. A sickening odor of fish and musky death washed over me, but I spat and scrabbled along the skin until I almost fell off. My right arm swung over the ridge, the sword held with the pommel near my thumb so I could stab it straight into the beast's eye as I took a gamble and cast Physical Buff on myself.

The sword had been treated with Kenshi's blood, so I expected it to be able to do at least some damage. Instead, it bounced off the eye and the creature just roared and flung its head to the side, shaking me violently and tossing me into the air above the water.

I grimaced and realized that there was no way to get out of hitting the water from a good eighty feet up without using even more of my mana, and it was going to hurt like a motherfucker.

As fast as I was going, it would be really dangerous to hit the water without something to hit it first to disperse the impact, so I cast Embodiment one more time and reappeared back on top of the head and stabbed for anything I could reach as the beast tried to get to my friends.

The sword did little more than scrape at the flesh beneath my feet and I grew steadily more frustrated, until the creature plummeted in the water and my stomach flew up into my throat as my platform was gone. "Woah!"

I crossed my arms and legs, hoping that my legs would be okay hitting the water like this, then plugged my nose with my left hand as I put my sword back into my ring.

I hit the water, the freezing impact of it almost enough to make me take a deep breath under the surface, but I gritted my teeth and spread myself out to start swimming for the surface.

Something grabbed me and yanked me backward violently, the air rushing from my lungs as I fought, then something sharp cut my right leg and I lashed out with Frost. The water around me froze swiftly and my travel slowed, but Galaxy shouted in my mind, *Stop that, fool! Arden is trying to pull you from the beast's maw!*

I canceled the spell and the water rushed past me again

before I landed on something solid and fought for air, gasping and sputtering water.

"Stop doing stupid things!" Arden howled as she threw globules of flame at the beast where it rose from the water.

I looked around and realized we were on the beach of something floating in the water and started to rise as the creature gathered air loudly.

"That ain't good!" Cassia roared and grabbed the back of my shirt, hauling me to my feet so we could start to book it to cover. "Move!"

Even as weak and worn as I suddenly felt, my legs pumped harder than they ever had. I glanced back over my shoulder, water building as the beast's jaws widened and its eyes bulged.

"Water shot, get down!" Amabala cried as Merlin swiped with one hand and growled a single word. He shoved her into the large swath of ground he had just magically slashed away and dove on top of the cheetah woman protectively. I fell in next to them with Arden and Cassia tripping into the hole as well.

"God damn it!" Arden hissed and lifted her hand. "Eyes closed!"

I just barely got my eyes closed when a blast of light washed over us, the rushing sound of spraying water shot overhead and covered us in mist as the beast screamed in pain.

"Get inside—now!" Cassia gasped as if in shock and shoved me and Arden away from the monstrous sea creature.

She ran off as we landed and shouted a challenge, "Come and get me, you slime-covered bastard!"

An echoing return shook the ground before a rushed intake of water nearly drew my attention from the stony entrance to the ruins only fifteen feet away from us.

The thought to turn around and rush after Cassia was almost overwhelming, but Galaxy lashed out at me mentally. *She's told me that if you do, she will beat you nearly to death and then heal you.*

That's not so bad, I fired back, starting to slow and turn.

Then she will beat you again and feed you to Kenshi.

"Not turning around!" I growled back and grit my teeth, my feet moving quicker as I fought to get inside with the others.

A loud crashing *bang* rattled us hard enough that it made my teeth chatter, but we were inside and out of harm's way for now. A moment later, Cassia ran in, blood dripping from her arm, but her grin triumphant as we all stared at the entrance pointedly looking for the creature. "Lost it near the beach by throwing a rock into the water. Good idea blinding it, Arden."

Arden just nodded once and sighed in relief, but the sound of water rushing around us was concerning.

Merlin glanced outside for a moment before sprinting back toward us. "Go deeper in!"

"What?" Amabala yowled in complaint, her eyes disbelieving as the young Warden-in-training flew past her.

Water rose up to our ankles and the creature roared outside. "Gogogogo!" I waved the women off to follow Merlin and used Frost to freeze the water in front of me and cover the entrance as much as I could.

It was about halfway and the water still rose as I spotted a monstrous eye glaring in from behind.

Rather than waiting for the beast to see me, I turned and high-tailed it out of there to find my friends.

Straight down the stairs on the right of the corridor in the back, Galaxy coached me as my body reacted to her instructions. *Take the second left and jump as high as you can with your arms up.*

I had enough time to think, *The fuck?* when a gaping maw of a hole appeared in front of me. My legs coiled and I shot as far into the air as I could. Something grabbed me and pulled me up by my arms, I glanced up to see Merlin straining with his hands out toward me and an invisible force lifting me.

"How the hell did you know about this?" I griped, breathing heavily due to the fear of being suddenly cast into the dark depths below if Merlin lost control of his spell more than any kind of physical exertion.

"The fox golem told me about it." He lifted his wrist and

stared at the stony bracelet in wonder and confusion. "It talks to me, whispers softly to me what will keep me safe."

I don't know what it is, but I do not hear it speaking to him when he says it is, Galaxy whispered to me and I could feel her staring at the fox bracelet as if accusing it of keeping secrets. *I find it very vexing.*

Can you blame it? We've kept you somewhat a secret, but not the best that we could've, if I'm being honest. What the hell is going on?

"We're waiting as the ruin entrance falls back to the rest of it down below," Merlin muttered to the rest of us as silence prevailed. The sound of water continuing to flood into the entrance made the hair on the back of my neck stand on end.

"We're below the surface now, and I hate that the book mentioned a protector, but there was nothing about that thing." Merlin's light flickered into life over his shoulder as he flicked through the pages. "'The guardian here takes its duty to heart, the thrill of the chase and defense of its base is more an art. Beware the darkness and the depth of the water at your feet, or the end of your life and the reaper you'll meet.'"

"Was that a poem?" I raised an eyebrow at him and he shook his head. "Then what was it?"

A warning. Galaxy sighed. *It means that there's something else in the ruins that could be even more of a monster than that thing that came at us first.*

Great, I growled to myself and rolled my eyes.

We waited for a brief time as the sensation of falling continued, then worsened to the point where it felt like we would fall toward the ceiling of the entrance.

We rested for a short while until the falling stopped and we came to a halt. I glanced over the ledge and noticed that instead of the massive pit below us, there was a stone staircase that swirled downward into the darkness.

"That's the true entrance," Merlin warned, hopping down off the ledge and onto the center platform of the stairs. "Once we go down there, we're going to be subjected to some kind of tests? I don't know, this is the extent of what the author knows about this place, and doesn't devolve into theories and guesses as to what could have been down here."

"What do they think?" Cassia wondered aloud. Her curious gaze on Merlin's shadowed outline.

"They think this was a place where the Huntsman made a base, or that he used this place to test the souls of those who would join him." Merlin's answer was more than a little cryptic, but I was more worried because of the fact that there would be a test of sorts.

"I hate tests," I grumbled and hopped down to join Merlin, the others doing the same.

"This won't be multiple choice, I don't think." Arden huffed and rolled her shoulders, then started down the stairs. "Let's go. The sooner we end this, the better."

I watched as she went stoically into the darkness below, then did the same.

CHAPTER TWELVE

Cool currents of air brushing against my body almost made me shiver, but it was too hard to pay attention to that now.

The stairs below my feet were uneven enough that it took all of my focus to keep my footing.

There was no telling how far that we had walked down those stairs, but by the time my feet touched the ground on a landing or on the bottom, my stomach was grumbling and loudly.

I pulled a snack bar from my inventory and gobbled it up before turning and saying, "Anyone else want a snack bar?"

No one else is here, Marcus. Galaxy's voice sounded hollow to me, but it was still her voice.

"Where are they?" I tried to control my voice, the discomfort at being alone down here threatening to overcome me even as I tamped down my emotions.

They all take their tests as we speak. Her voice sent shivers down my spine. *My apologies for mimicking this creature's voice so that I can speak with you in a manner that won't break your mind. I do the same thing to all of the others.*

"Then who are you and what do you want?"

I am the spirit of the first Huntsman—I am the spirit of the Wild Hunt. The voice grew deeper, colder. The weight of it reached out toward me from within and grabbed my heart in cold clutches. *I am the test for those who wish to join in the search for my mantle. Those who find it without passing my test die.*

"I thought the majority of those who search for it die?"

Yes. And this would be one of the many reasons for those failures.

I smiled. "Good to know." My lungs inflated and a hefty sigh passed through my lips. "So then, what's this test?"

You and I are going to play a little game, would-be Huntsman. The voice sounded like it was grinning at me. *There's a creature down here who feeds on those who take my tests. It gets a tad annoying to be in the middle of finding someone's worth, only for them to become a snack for the clever little thing.*

"You want me to kill it?" I had to fight to keep from rolling my eyes at the request. How RPG of him.

No. I blinked in surprise. *I want you to tame it, and use it to leave here.*

"What?" I growled, looking around and trying to peer into the darkness around me.

You heard me, hunted. Go forth.

I still peered around and there was nothing to find before the voice returned. *I would hurry, if I were you. Your companions are in danger.*

I growled and focused my senses on the world around me, trying to send my senses into the shadows as my hands followed suit in search of something solid that I could use as a guide. Anything at all. Finally I found a stone wall of sorts, the solid feel of it crumbling slightly beneath my fingertips and more than a little slimy to the touch. I hadn't wanted to do this, but I couldn't waste any more time. If the thing hunting us saw me, at least it wasn't near my friends.

I summoned a Wisp in my hand, not throwing it but just using it as a light. All it did was confirm my proctor's words—I was in a room by myself and there was only one way out before me and there really was something down here with us.

Bones—some shattered and some whole, but all of them gnawed on—littered the ground at my feet. Skulls that were caved in and staring without sight at the ceiling made my skin crawl and the terror of all the bodies I had seen in the desert came back to me in a wave. I had to take deep breaths to fight through the urge to fall into a fit, and I only barely won out as I returned my attention to the rest of my surroundings.

The darkness only fled from the flames for a few feet in front of and around me, and as I moved toward the singular doorway it inched back in as if it were as alive as I was.

Calling out to them aloud may attract this thing's attention to me and bring it to me, or it could frighten it and make it hunt faster. My feet moved on their own as I wondered what I should do. *I could always call to Galaxy, but could she hear me during her own test? Why is this my test? Shouldn't I have to go through the same things they are?*

I shook my head and perished the thoughts roiling there. They wouldn't serve the purpose I needed for now. I had a mission and a task at hand that needed handling and my hands would be full with it.

Too much hand talk, Marcus. Let's go. I closed my eyes for the briefest second I could allow, and refocused myself to think on the fly and get shit done.

I took a glance at my mana and saw that I was still good, the spell didn't need to be thrown from what I could see, though how long it would last like this would be a good experiment.

I crouched and observed the floor as best I could, the shadows there melting away from the Wisp still in my hand, finding that there were long gashes from something like claws. Hundreds of them in the area and they led in two different directions—left and right. So I didn't need to waste too much time worrying about whether or not this was a large room that I had just walked into, but more of a hall of sorts.

I held the Wisp forward and sure enough, there was a wall with similar grooves on it, but lesser in number to those on the floor. I took the human way of things and went with my instincts to go left first, staying in a middling crouch so that I didn't make too much noise as I moved.

I took my time walking, stopping often to see if there was any noise other than the nearly-deafening sound of my own heart and breathing. I did everything I could to keep my pulse from racing, but in this ever-present darkness, it was nearly impossible not to stop and wonder at every noise. If it was the creature coming to end me.

I took out the short sword that I had and it went a long way toward easing my mind. I held it like I would a knife, the blade of the weapon behind me to keep the reflection of the light from giving my position to anything that could be in front of me.

Keeping my wits about me was hard, but I pushed on and pressed myself to listen and try to pick through the sounds that mattered and the ones that didn't. My breathing and heartbeat? Fuck 'em. My footsteps? Mildly annoying, but necessary to watch and pay attention to. The sound of running water? Fuck it.

Wait, running water? I pushed my luck a little and trod forward toward the sound and was rewarded with the sight of a massive cavernous room with a pool of water at the bottom with a shimmering beacon in the center of it. Ripples of water from a small waterfall opposite me obscured it from sight a little more. *Weird. What could be down there?*

The beacon bobbed for a little bit before I took my eyes off it and let the Wisp in my hand go, flying into the darkness to reveal a dangerous-looking pathway that led down toward the water. Looked like a set of stairs or stalactites that had fallen down but remained upright as a means of getting down to the white sand and water below.

Did I even want to go down there? What if the water was like the neurotoxin that had been offered to us in Virani?

I tried to look down at the light and found that it was too hard to see from this high up, so I would need to try to get closer than my spot above. I could use Embodiment to get closer to it, but that would eat more of my mana and that wasn't smart. Of course, neither was leaping headfirst into the darkness with who knew how many dangerous variables in this room alone.

You've taken less sure bets, Marine, I growled at myself and took a deep breath. The first set of stalactite steps was about ten to thirteen feet away from what I could tell, and given my Brawn and Dexterity, it would be easier to overshoot them than to fall short. With that in mind I took a step back and then launched myself forward with a soft, "*Hup!*"

My legs cycled through the air as the wind rushed by me, then the first step came too soon and I skittered across the top of it and barely came to a stop in time to avoid falling off.

Careful, Marcus. I sighed to myself and jumped to the next, the amount of space between jumps progressively lessening as the ground grew closer. Eventually, I just hopped softly from one stalactite step to the other as if I were skipping.

Two from the bottom, the stalactite shifted and pitched backward toward the previous step I had used. "Woah!" I hissed and launched myself forward, the clattering crash of the stone on stone tumbling down below me made me wince enough that my grasp missed a ledge on top of my target landing.

The landing was still a good forty feet below me and my instincts kicked in. I shoved the sword still in my right hand into the stone where I could and ground to a halt. My feet dangled in the air and I glanced below me, the rocks from the crumbling steps still falling and crushing whatever was beneath them. Other stones, fungus—previous victims?

It was hard to see from up here, but I got a distinct feeling that those bits of white sand and stone were bone fragments.

Oh, this place is not safe. My internal grumbling did nothing for my piece of mind and nothing for my situation. *Nothing for your friends, either—get a fucking move on.*

I stomped down my sudden adrenaline rush at the prospect of them being in danger and worked on getting myself down.

I focused Frost on my left hand and froze the sweat on my

palms and fingertips until they were basically claws and jagged climbing equipment. I experimented a bit with grasping the rock in front of me. At first, they wouldn't grasp because they were too brittle, but I poured more of my mana into them and made the ice colder. Stronger. Thicker.

The ice on my palms grew and got heavier but the cold was somehow comforting to me. My claws pressed into the stone and dug deep this time. Deep enough that I could use the same process on the toes of my boots so that I could get down.

I yanked the sword out and put it back into my inventory before making my way down. It was easy enough with ice claws, thankfully. The sound of running water was louder now, and looking into it, the beacon appeared to be something small floating in the water.

Something that looked like it was curled into a ball.

Something that looked like Arden!

Fuck. I took a couple steps forward, leaping and diving into the water toward her. The water wasn't anything special aside from boiling hot, enough so that my skin immediately felt like it was going to slough off my body to make some kind of twisted stew.

My body ached, but I pushed on and started to fight back with Frost, super-cooling the water as much as I could. It was hard, swimming and willing the spell to cool the water around me just enough to keep it liquid and nice enough to not cook me. My mana dropped faster and faster and I still needed to get to her.

I pushed my body to new limits and sent wave after wave of Frost into the water around me until I was close enough to grab her and pull her to me. The heat ramped up and my mana was damn close to bottoming out.

I grimaced and strained, pushing myself further. All I had to do was get out of the water. I glanced around and saw the rocks that had fallen into the water and paddled for them. My lungs burned, my muscles ached and spasmed as if I were about to cramp up.

Come the fuck on! Roaring at myself the way my drill instructors used to helped spur me on just a little more. I could feel the veins in my neck and arms popping to the surface of my skin with the strain until finally I came up for air.

I took such a deep, coughing breath that it was so hard not to swallow water.

I half dragged and lifted Arden out of the water as my chest rose and fell rapidly, but I couldn't lay down and rest like I wanted to. She didn't look to be breathing right. Or at all.

I put her on her back, her clothes were gone now that I could really look at her, but no time to dwell.

I got up onto my knees and clasped my hands together so that my left hand was behind my right and interlocked my fingers and began compressions like they had taught me in the Marine Corps for basic first aid. After thirty compressions, I tilted her chin back, plugged her nose and gave her two deep breaths before returning to the compressions.

I seethed, hissing, "Come on, God damn it!" Two more breaths, third round of compressions. "You better wake the fuck up, Arden!"

Hacking coughs racked her body as she spat water from her mouth. I rolled her onto her side so she could get it all out. She sputtered more water out of her lungs before finally huffing and falling onto her back.

I collapsed next to her, my fatigue catching up to me. I didn't hate swimming. I was a great swimmer and I'd nearly gone to school to be a Marine Corps swim instructor, but this kind of shit?

Would take it out of you. Hard.

As I lay there next to her, warmth washed over me, my shivering in the cold darkness beginning to abate slowly.

Movement drew my attention to Arden as she sat up and moved closer to me, her eyes on mine. She leaned over me and pulled me close, another wash of heat passed over me and her hands grasped my face. "You're welcom—*mmf!*"

My mouth was covered, her lips pressed to mine in a way

that I hadn't expected at all and with a need that I didn't understand.

Light began to trail down my throat until I could have stood up and ran a marathon backward, then beat the hell out of Godzilla.

She finally let me go, and I muttered, "Cassia is going to fucking kill us."

"I'll worry about her, but that was more for you to recover than anything untoward." She grinned at me and looked down. "Wow, that's really weak for me to say naked."

I couldn't help the soft laughter that burst from me as I stood and averted my gaze. "You happen to have fresh clothes in your inventory?"

"Yup, already getting dressed. Where are the others?"

I glared into the darkness and silently dared whatever it was out there that could be patrolling this place to come out and attack me before I answered, "I don't know. But something hunts whoever is taking the Hunt's test, and they're in danger. We need to get to them quickly, but this place is pretty dark, and won't let magic light pass more than a few feet."

"That won't be too much of a problem with both of us here with it." She lifted her hand and made a petting motion before a watery globule lifted from the lake behind her and settled in her palm.

Light like a torch built inside it until she narrowed her eyes and the water shifted, the light within focusing into a beam of light that cut into the darkness like an LED flashlight.

"Oh, that's too awesome." I muttered and blinked at her. "We don't have time, and I don't trust whatever is hunting us to be kind enough to allow conversation. So what is that?"

"My test gave me a lot; being able to work through my trauma was part of it, but it was very… *enlightening.*" She grinned and it may as well have been no smile at all. It was more predatory than joyful. "Let's find our friends."

I nodded and summoned my sword once more from my inventory and took the lead as she shined her light over my shoulder. The warmth of it radiated into my body as it scared off the darkness.

We moved down the tunnel in front of us and followed claw marks that decorated the ground and walls. Once more, my senses were thrown forward to see if anything was amiss. If there was anything I could hear, smell, or see that could give me any clue as to how far away my friends were.

There were rooms, dark and empty save for the decrepit remains of previous victims. How many had fallen before we got here?

The chill that rolled down my spine like the red carpet of fear was colder than anything I'd ever experienced before in my entire life.

And the damn thing is supposed to be able to be tamed? I rolled my eyes. *Sure. Fuck.*

Sssss. I blinked and stopped as another soft hiss of movement over the stone near us drew my attention again. I motioned back to Arden to point her light away for a second, then crept forward with my sword in my hand pointed toward the sound.

I moved as quickly and quietly as I could until I was about to round a corner, then stopped as a soft chuffing noise made the hair on my arms stand straight up.

It's scenting for something. I glanced down and got the distinct sense of motion as dust sprinkled my boot. *And it's facing toward us.*

I held my sword out like it was a mirror and used some of the light Arden was still shining near her feet to try to get a glimpse of it.

A beak-like snout covered in scales and dried gore came into view, serrated teeth inside the beak with chunks of rotting meat stuck inside flashed before the beak clacked shut and the creature lowered its head until it could gaze at itself with piercing blue eyes.

It growled appreciatively at itself and began toward the

sword, moving forward enough that it touched the blade and moved it back swiftly.

Enough that Arden could see it and gasp, "Run!" The creature reared up and cocked its head but Arden grabbed me, and shouted, "Basilisk—run!"

I didn't question her and sprinted with her, her grip tightening on my wrist so that she could run us into the room with the water and stalactite stairs.

She glanced around and pointed up, "Get up there, and whatever you do, don't look at it directly."

"Why?"

She shoved me and jumped straight up. "Move!"

I rolled my eyes and cast Embodiment of Lightning, moving straight up the stalactite in front of me. "You have to talk to me, Arden."

"Not until that thing is far away from us!" As if to punctuate her statement, a hissing squelch of something hit the stone on my left and an acrid scent wafted toward me.

Sizzling pops made my skin crawl. "Acid spit?" She didn't answer me as she sprinted further away.

I growled and took a couple steps back before I bolted forward and leaped as hard as I could. More globs of spit flew at me but missed as I landed on the last stalactite and flung myself into the tunnel behind Arden.

She waited for me in the hall beyond the tunnel and huffed, "They can turn you to stone if you look directly at them, like a Gorgon. Their bite is ten times deadlier than a Komodo dragon's and, as you can see, they spit acid like a king cobra—not to be fucked with lightly."

"Great, and I'm supposed to *tame* that fucking thing?" I swore deeply and quickly before looking at Arden, finding her staring at me in confusion. "My test is stopping it from killing all of you, and taming it because we will need it to get out of here."

"Then we need to find the others, fast." She turned and motioned for me to move ahead. "This thing knows this place better than we do, and we have the disadvantage of not being able to move freely because of that."

"So I use the sword like a mirror to check for it around corners?" I moved ahead and kept the sword raised and pointed in front of me.

"And if you see it, you run the other way." She shook her head at me as I tried to make an argument for a plan of attack. "This thing is too strong to take on by ourselves and without Galaxy to consume its magic. It's a tier seven creature."

A tier weaker than what Merlin needs to hunt down, shit. I grimaced and began to move toward the hall I hadn't taken earlier.

We passed where I had first come to with a quick check and then moved on a little quicker than I would have liked, but now the basilisk knew it had prey down here and it would be hunting for it.

There was no time to waste.

CHAPTER THIRTEEN

We passed the fourth room in a long line of open doorways and by now my nerves should have been raw.

Each time we passed a door, and scanned a room for signs of Cassia, Galaxy, Merlin or Amabala, there was nothing but bone dust and claw marks that appeared ageless to me. That alone was unnerving, but coupled with the fact that a single glance at those baby blues would end me was enough to really rustle my jimmies.

I grimaced and passed my smaller Oni blade to Arden. I hated giving it up, but there were rooms on both sides of this hallway and we needed to be quicker about this.

She didn't need me to tell her what to do, just diffused her light so it was more of a glow than a beam and went to search the other side of the hall.

We took turns looking so neither of us truly had to give our backs to a room, and I was grateful for that. Twelve rooms down, several more to go, and that was only if there wasn't something lurking in the shadows.

"*Pst!*" Arden hissed behind me after the third door I'd checked, and I lifted my sword, ready to strike at whatever it was that she was going to point me at, regardless of her warning. Rather than finding the basilisk, she pointed at a figure laying on the ground in the room she checked.

We rushed in and found a gored man, elven from what it looked like, with his entrails strewn onto the floor, one of his legs missing. But I think the worst part of the scene was that his eyes were open with a look of pained fear frozen and etched into his features.

"We need to hurry," I whispered and checked behind us with my sword and found the coast clear.

We checked the hall; Arden cleared her side and I cleared mine with a nod before we stepped out into the open and began to look with renewed vigor.

Six more rooms came and went before we were into the next hall with nothing else having been found but either more petrified remains or rotting corpses that hadn't had a chance to become stone.

We checked the first room on the right and both of us gasped, "Merlin!"

He stood in the middle of the room facing the wall with his hands at his sides. I rushed into the room and touched his shoulder.

He immediately lashed out with a yelp of surprise, his hand slapping his hip and flicking toward my face. I had the good sense to dodge his attempt at killing me, but just barely avoided losing an eye.

"What the hell is wrong with you, sneaking up on me like that!" he snarled, and Arden covered his mouth with her palm as he continued to seethe.

"Basilisk in the ruins," she whispered softly and he stiffened, eyes wide. "Keep noise to a minimum, 'kay?"

He nodded and slid his blade back into the sheath on his hip with a mouthed *sorry* and an apologetic shrug.

I shook my head and just motioned for him to come with us. He fell in line behind me and Arden; we checked the hallway for any kind of reflection and found a set of blue eyes coming from where we should have been going.

Arden gave me a nod as my eyes widened and I shook my head, withdrawing my sword. I nodded to the other side of the door and pressed Merlin back against my side with a finger to my lips.

The soft hissing rasp of scaled hide sliding across the stone ground outside the room made me shiver in anticipation of a fight that I wasn't sure I'd win, for once. The other fights I'd gone into intent to kill as many as I could before I went down myself, though I figured I would still at least survive. There was a peace to that thought and belief.

But this? This thing would fuck me up and I couldn't touch it, and that unnerved me. Just like the big ass Nessy wannabe outside the ruins. I hated that I couldn't even do enough damage to warrant more than a head flick from the bastard.

The basilisk paused outside the room and Merlin leaned over my shoulder with a hand cupped to his mouth. My instant urge was to elbow him but he mouthed a word and blew threw his lips before a sharp whistle echoed down the hall from the direction it was already walking.

A low hissed growl made my bowels tighten before the rasp of scales on stone signaled the creature moving on to hunt down whatever made that sound.

I shook my head and held up a thumb in the universal sign that what he'd done was okay by me and thumped his shoulder with my fist.

I owe him a damn drink for that. I grinned and stuck my sword out the doorway just to be safe. We confirmed it was gone and moved along as quickly as we could.

Now that it had heard something nearby, it wasn't exactly quiet about stalking and there was a crashing sound followed by what could have been angry cries of impotence around ten minutes after we had moved on.

"Must've figured out it was duped somehow." Merlin spat

on the ground and looked around. "We need to find them faster. I know a spell but I don't know if it will work. Want me to try?"

Arden and I both nodded, irritated that he hadn't done so to begin with.

At first it was nothing to worry about, but then there was a golden bar of light that appeared in front of him, which began to pulsate and hum quietly.

"It worked!" he whispered quietly and I was more than pissed now. "Let's go!"

"This thing will draw it to us!" I hissed at him and he nodded. "You knew it might be like this? Cancel it!"

A low growl echoed down the hall toward us. Arden watched as we stepped into the hall and the bar moved toward the opposite direction of the noise. "Too late. Merlin, go."

We sprinted down the hall and into a larger room that reminded me of a dining area. Old and ruined tables, splintered wooden boards and stone chairs clustered together in various mounds that looked reminiscent of a nest of sorts against the far wall.

Six halls and one larger tunnel opened around the room but there was a hole in the center of the floor that the golden bar in front of Merlin guided us toward.

"We gotta go down that," he whispered, clearing dreading it. "There's no way, it's like a trash chute or something right? It probably goes out into the ocean, or a spelled incinerator. No way."

"Who's that spell for?" I grabbed his shoulder when he didn't answer me as we closed the distance to the dark hole. Looking into the depths of it, I knew who it was likely for—Galaxy. "Come on."

I jumped into the hole without thinking and cast Wisp as air rushed by me hard enough to tug at my clothes and make them flap like cloth wings.

Sure enough, it was a chute that led down into a truly massive open-air area. The chute, stone that could have been metal for how smooth it was, swirled down in a wide circle toward whatever was at the bottom. I knew Arden and Merlin were behind me because I could hear the latter nearly hyperventilating over the wind.

The light I cast reflected off something in the middle of the room and I attempted to figure out what it was, but couldn't get close enough to get a good enough look.

"Can you see what that is?" I called back to the others but I worried that the words were drowned out by the wind. I tried to point to it, but putting my hand outside of the chute soon became dangerous as something shadowy and painful lashed out at me. "Is there something else fucking down here?"

I cradled my bloodied hand to my chest and glared into the darkness but found nothing.

Eventually the chute opened up to a wide trough of sorts and I skidded painfully to a halt, Arden and Merlin doing the same seconds after. The spell was still active and led further into the darkness in front of the trough, opposite the chute.

"Where did this spell come from?" I questioned the boy softly, worried that there was a way that the basilisk might be able to follow us down here, or that whatever had lashed out at me on the chute would hear us. "Have you always known it? Why didn't you use it to find Varlin?"

"It's something I learned during my test." He looked at Arden, his voice shaking. "I had to find you. I had to find all of you. And each time I found you, you were dead."

"Why?" He shrugged at my continued line of questioning and didn't seem keen to share too much more.

Arden had learned to control her water magic better during the test. Merlin had learned to track better. Were the others learning as well?

Which begged the question—what was I learning?

"Merlin, you're going to be my A-driver, you walk just behind me and mutter where we're going to me so I can protect us." My gaze flicked to Arden. "You're right next to him on my other side, lighting this place up as best you can with minimal mana expenditure."

"You know that I can recharge my mana super-fast here, right?" She eyed me with a sly grin. "I mean, I recharged yours, did I not?"

Thinking about it made me stammer a bit, then I ground my teeth and whispered, "Just keep it simple and cheap, okay?"

She actually laughed at that and rolled her eyes. "Leave it to a man to tell a lady how much to, and not to, spend."

My mouth opened and Merlin just shook his head in a manner that almost made me laugh if it wasn't for the knowing look on Arden's face. I did an about face and stalked forward, my sword at my side ready to kill anything that was in our way, if I could.

Or at the very least, try.

We moved surely into the darkness as Arden's light sliced through it. The tendrils of darkness recoiled from the contact with the golden beam as if in pain, which was concerning, but I could do nothing about it, so I focused on what I could control.

Eventually, Merlin had to slow down, the vibrations and pulsing from the spell in front of him too much to bear. He grit his teeth and tried to soldier on, but I could tell from the look of pain on his face, and the veins bulging in his neck and forearms, that it was getting to be a lot for him.

"Merlin, cancel the spell." He ignored my order at first, but I tapped his shoulder and made him look at me. "I know you want to find her—so do I. Cancel it."

He dropped the spell and immediately fell to his knees in relief from the strain, panting as if he was trying to recover from some serious pain. "I don't know—" *Huff… Huff…* "—what it was, but something…" He took a shuddering breath and swallowed heavily. "…was pushing back. It doesn't want us to try to find her."

"It's the shadows," I muttered, and both my friends looked at me in confusion. "Think about it. The shadows around this place are so thick and impenetrable that they can withstand magical light. They obscure *everything* from us. And while you guys were learning something from the tests you were in—this one was mine."

"And?" Arden shrugged, confused.

"The proctor, the original Huntsman, sounded like Galaxy. It knows us well enough to know that she can consume magic." I looked at the shadows around us. "What if he's trying to keep us from finding her because he's trying to do the same to her, and she worked through him to give you both advantages against him? What if he summoned that basilisk here to kill me, or us? Or distract us?"

"That seems like a stretch, but it could be possible." Merlin scratched his head. "I don't know why the Huntsman would keep me from continuing on after getting so close instead of trying to confuse me, or kill me outright."

"Because he's busier elsewhere." I growled low and looked around into the ever-present shadows. "Aren't you, you old fucker?"

Nothing answered, but I had my suspicions, and it was time to act on them. "Arden? Light this whole fucking room up. No shadows anywhere."

She grinned at me and rolled her shoulders. "Better cover your eyes with both hands then."

The ball of light floating in the water floated toward her hand and she lifted it like a volleyball player about to serve the ball, then tossed it into the air and her arm flew back.

I closed my eyes and hid them behind both my palms and the light *still* managed to filter through. The skin on my hands, arms, and face felt tight, like I'd been in the California sun all day on a working party. I took my hands from my face and searched around with my eyes narrowed. Sure enough, two figures laid on the ground a hundred feet from us, the larger of the two crawling slowly toward the smaller figure.

I cast Embodiment of Lightning and appeared next to it, the random casting of Bolt striking the crawling, blackened figure and making it squeal in pain.

My eyes flicked to Galaxy in her human form on the ground

unconscious. I touched her and *pulled* with my will, trying desperately to call her into my mana sea. It didn't happen at first, but at my touch, the grimace on her face lessened until she looked at least a little more peaceful. "Come on, Galaxy."

My whispered request must have been enough, because she faded into my shadow and I could tell that she was there in me.

"What are you doing?" The other figure wheezed, reaching out toward me. "You stopped me from eliminating the threat!"

"I stopped you from eliminating my friend," I corrected him, rage boiling my blood as it flowed through my breast. My arms were hot, my legs heavier than lead, and all the while I stared down at the shadowy figure at my feet. "I stopped you from killing someone I care about—and passed your test."

Coughing laughter made my skin crawl as he looked up at me, his eyes gray pits. "She's a monster, and needs to be stopped. You cannot possess the mantle while she resides in you." Teeth flashed in his mouth as he smiled. "I will not pass you so long as she lives."

I crouched down so that I could more easily stare into his eyes as I spoke in a monotone voice, suddenly cold with surety. "She's not the monster—we are." I lifted my sword and stabbed it straight through his too-thin neck, then twisted it with a savage grunt. "And your death means there's no one to prove that I'm worthy to."

You did the right thing, Marcus, Galaxy whispered tiredly. *He was going to consume me, and use our bond to take control of your body to rebuild the Hunt in his image.*

I spoke out loud so the others would hear me, mainly because I wasn't sure if she had said anything to them or not. "No one kills my friends. And he can't do that dead. Let's go find the others. Merlin?"

He closed his eyes and did the same spell as he had before, but Galaxy tugged at my mind, *They are likely awake already. I did what I could to prepare Cassia, Arden, and Merlin, but I couldn't touch Amabala, I am afraid.*

That's okay, we'll find them. My reassurance was terse out of necessity. The more active she was, the less focused on recovering she was. She knew we could talk later once we were all safe.

"You ready to track them down, Merlin?" He nodded just as there was a monumental crash above us and something screeched inhumanly before an outraged cry met it, then another *boom*!

"Cassia's awake and that could have been the basilisk." Arden ran toward the chute as dust and debris clattered onto the floor. "I swear to God, if she gets herself petrified, I'll kill her!"

A resounding crack and crushing echo burst above us as Cassia let out another bellow of absolute rage and a portion of the ceiling fell.

"Move!"

My call to the others wasn't enough and I shoved Merlin as far away as I could before I cast Embodiment of Lightning on myself and got the hell out of the way.

The ruin shook beneath our feet hard enough that I lost my balance and ended up finding a seat, rather painfully, on my ass. Cassia snarled savagely and battered the basilisk with her fists, but what caught my eye about it was the fact that she was covered in red spikes that had burst from her skin.

"What the fuck is that?" I gasped to myself and clambered to my feet.

Yin form, Galaxy explained softly. *Oni thing that she unlocked in that farce of a test with a little prodding from me. She needs help—go.*

I shook myself out and sprang forward. "Heavy spells in three, two—now!"

Arden came to her senses after Merlin slung his hand forward and conjured a screen in front of Cassia that she roared at and started to pound on. Her eyes glimmered with rage so powerful that her normally red eyes had gone completely white with black irises.

The basilisk hissed and stared at itself before a massive watery hammer appeared above it and walloped it over the head, drawing its attention upward. It recoiled from the water, the liquid rolling over its scales, which gave me an idea.

"Arden, douse it!" My eyes averted as the basilisk turned toward me and reached again. "Do it now!"

A loud *sploosh* and a wash of water crashed over my foot before I risked a glance into my sword toward the basilisk and lashed out with Frost.

A slow, pained hiss came from the creature and I felt something flick across my left shoulder. The basilisk was closer now, standing near me and close enough that it could attack and I wouldn't be able to do shit.

Galaxy, you got my back?

She frowned inside me, and gathered what I would try to do. *This is reckless, but I think I can manage it if I pull mana from the surroundings, Merlin, and Arden. Be fast.*

I covered my head in a thin bowl of ice and roared, "Look at me, you big lizard bastard!"

The lizard hissed, the beaky muzzle lifting toward me and the blue eyes leveled with mine.

Merlin cried out and Arden dropped the wall behind her as she fell to her knees, drained.

It's too much! Galaxy strained inside me and my mana began to fall as well, plummeting faster as I used Frost to supercool the basilisk in front of me. It started forward, fore leg lifting slowly only to stop in the air as my nose started to bleed and the blood froze to my skin instantly.

I grunted and gasped as I kept pushing my body to cool the air around the lizard until its eyes closed and it stilled completely.

My legs crumpled and Cassia roared as she lifted her massive club over her head and jumped into the air, bringing the weapon down on the frozen basilisk's head.

The basilisk's head burst on one side, the front of the body and some of the ground beneath shattering like ice cubes at the force of the attack.

That was stupid, Galaxy groaned and I could feel a headache beginning to knock at the back of my head.

I blinked and looked around. Cassia stood over her prey and eyed the rest of us, her breathing slowing over the silent seconds until her eyes returned to their more natural glowing red and the spikes along her skin retreated.

She sighed. "That's an unpleasant feeling."

"I can imagine." I grinned at her and laid back on the ground. "How was your test?"

"I don't know if I passed or failed because, as I was about to finish, the proctor left and I was in a room on my own." She shook herself then motioned to the corpse at her feet. "Then this guy showed up and tried to attack me. Luckily, I know how to fight basilisks."

"You've fought them before?" Merlin grunted and sat up as if it pained him.

She nodded happily and pointed to the stomach and back leg portions of the body that were still intact. "And eaten them before too—they make great steaks."

Galaxy popped out of my shadow in cat form and sprang onto the body, her teeth digging into the semi-frozen flesh with wet and meaty sounds as she consumed.

Cassia immediately went to work cutting slabs of meat off with a practiced hand before glancing at Arden. "Can you make us a fire?"

Arden stared at her, blushing, and Galaxy stopped eating so that she could turn to me, *You... Arden...*

It was a necessity and she came on to me, I retorted and growled as I sat up, staring at her with a hint of warning in my glare. *She was giving me mana.*

That's all? Galaxy's smile was evident in her tone.

I'll tell Cass. Don't make it weird, please?

Arden feels that you should tell her together, was all Galaxy said in return as she returned to her meal.

I glanced to Arden and she nodded once as she cast a fire onto the floor, Cassia pulling out a spit to roast the meat over.

"Merlin? Think you can try to find Amabala for us?" He blinked at me and nodded quietly before standing and wandering out of the room in a random-seeming direction.

Arden scooted closer to Cassia and I stood up, suddenly sore and uncertain. "Cassia, we need to talk."

She looked up from the meat she was cutting as the slab on the spit cooked over the flames, "What's up?"

Arden ripped the bandaid off, which I could respect. "I kissed Marcus after he saved me."

The knife in her hand stilled and she lifted her gaze to us, glancing from me to Arden.

"I know you find him attractive, we've discussed that, but why did you kiss him when you know I have claim to him?" There was a softness to her tone and she looked genuinely confused.

"It was more of an instant reaction, and through the kiss, I was able to give him mana." Arden frowned and blinked. "I've never been able to do that before and I don't know what to think about it. But I didn't want to hide it from you."

She means that, Galaxy added, earning a glare from me.

"It didn't mean anything," Arden continued as Cassia glared thoughtfully at the cooking basilisk meat in front of her.

She didn't mean that.

I glared at Galaxy some more and she just continued to eat until finally she sighed. *Cassia knows she's lying, and she wants to know how you felt about it.*

Cassia turned and there was hurt in her eyes as she stared into my eyes. All I could say was, "I keep being told that I'm a healthy man, and that I feel certain ways. That I'm excited by both of you, and that if given the opportunity to do it, I'd uh... scrap with you both."

Cassia blinked and started to turn away, but I crossed the distance and put a hand on her shoulder. "But she isn't you."

She looked back up at me, and I finished the thought on my mind. "I'm attracted to Arden—she's beautiful. I'd have to be out of my mind not to be, and you know that's true because you've commented on it before. Hell, Galaxy outed me to you both."

"It's one thing to think a thing and another to act on it." She turned to glare at Arden. "It didn't bother me that you thought he was good looking. It didn't bother me that you were flattered he felt that way. What gets to me is the fact that you did it and it was as instinctive to you as wanting to fight is for me. You did it and didn't think of the consequences."

She stood up and dusted herself off before stepping closer to Arden, almost to the point where they could touch as Cassia loomed over the other woman. "You're my oldest and best friend, Ardent Flame. I trust you with my life. I might not love Marcus, but that still hurt that I couldn't trust you with him."

"I'm sorry," Arden whispered. "I won't do it again."

Cassia raised her voice. "And what pisses me off even more is that I can't blame you for it!" She screamed, long and deep, her anguish and sorrow mixing and rising like a howl, her back arched as she let it all go until finally she was hunched forward. Her shoulders shook with angry tears as she spoke bitterly. "I watched as all of my loved ones were ripped away from me in that test because I wasn't strong enough to save you all. And I woke up *alone*. Marcus found *you* first, and not me. I woke up to that basilisk coming to end me and I had no other choice but to act."

She looked back at me, and all I felt was like I had failed her. "I know you did your best. Galaxy showed me everything, but it would have been nice for you to come and rescue me for once."

I walked over to her and smiled up at her. "It would have been nice to be able to." I gripped her chin between my thumb and forefinger and pulled her down toward me. "But I know how strong you are. So while Merlin searches for Amabala, let's fight."

She blinked at me, but I already threw the meanest left cross I think I'd ever thrown and her head rocked back.

Her head popped back up as I grinned. "I couldn't rescue

you, so the best thing I can offer to make it up to you is to make sure that you're capable in a fight, right? Isn't that how an Oni does it?"

She offered me a small smile before she pulled me close and kissed me, her tusk-like teeth grinding into my lips in a familiar way. When she stopped, she whispered, "Yes, it is, Marcus. Yes, it is."

She leaned her head back then slammed her forehead into my nose so hard that the crunch of it rang my bell. I flew out of her grip and landed twenty feet away as she bellowed, "You aren't getting out of this, Ardent Flame. You owe me for taking away my being treated like a damsel in distress!"

"Who the hell wants to be one of those?" Arden snorted, then screeched as Cassia fell on her and started to pummel her with her fists. A wave of heat hit me and Cassia was flung away, landing near me.

Arden floated a foot off the ground and rolled her eyes. "I suppose if I have to, I will. But only if you'll forgive me."

Cassia groaned and sat up, her chest singed slightly and just shook herself out before shrugging. "I might if you can beat me."

"Team up?" I called and Cassia looked at me as if I had fouled the air with the suggestion.

Arden cracked her knuckles. "Oh yeah."

CHAPTER FOURTEEN

It took Merlin two hours to come back with Amabala and she looked highly freaked out, even more so with both Arden and I laying gasping on the floor with Cassia offering pointers to us as she stood between us.

We were all battered and bruised, sure, but now Cassia, Arden, and me were in the clear. No hard feelings that we were aware of.

Though I was still uncertain as to what was going on emotionally for both of them.

And no—nosy whiskers—I don't want you to tell me. Galaxy just flicked her tail at me as she continued to snack on the basilisk meat. *Any luck leveling up at all?*

Why do you think I consume this thing? Remember, experience here comes from me consuming what you kill.

I grimaced and left her to her devices. We ate the meat Cassia prepared, though Amabala was reticent about it. Her nose scrunched up as she took a delicate bite, Cassia watching her. She made a placating sound and rubbed her stomach like an adult might mime to a child and Cassia just snorted and turned back to her own food.

I took a bite of the meat in my hand and hissed, the heat of it a little more than what I had thought it would be.

Basilisk – Devoured – Your consumption of the basilisk's body permanently altered the makeup of your body. Physique increased by 1, and resistance to poison and venom increased.

I grinned at that and continued to eat the food, and judging by the others' reactions, they were getting similar messages.

I thought about it for a minute and reached out to the frozen chunks, grabbing a chunk that could mean something. I had resistance to venom, right? The most it could do was make me sick. What if I ate a tooth? Or some of the venom directly?

The globe of ice helped keep you from being petrified right away, and the fact that the cold made it sleepy gave me enough time to counteract the petrification process, Galaxy yowled at me in her cat form. *Do not try the venom!*

"Yes, ma'am." I sighed and Cassia looked at me strangely. "Eating certain things has a chance of giving me extra perks. Like the Bite of the Wolf having given me accelerated healing."

She perked up and began to sift through the chunks of ice near her. She grabbed a piece and held up what looked like an eye. I tried to tell her to stop, but she popped it into her mouth like a gory popsicle before she bit down on it.

She chewed it and swallowed then stilled, and grinned widely. "It says that my gaze can petrify people who are weaker than me for a mana cost!"

"You gotta be careful with that!" I hissed at her as she went for another one, but paused at my reprimand. "There can be harmful effects too, like my slight allergy to silver."

"Interesting," Merlin muttered as he ate, a contemplative look on his face. "So, theoretically, we could eat magical creatures and gain abilities and stats from it and grow uber powerful. Like a lottery of sorts."

Exactly, Galaxy purred from where she stood, having decided to stop playing with her food and finish it in a massive snake-like gulp.

She finished and belched surprisingly loudly for a cat. It made the rest of us laugh.

She sauntered over to the first Huntsman's charred corpse and devoured it as well.

She sat and closed her eyes for a time, then opened them and took her human form. "We have a problem."

Her voice was solemn as she glanced up at us. "The mantle was last found to have been within the Forest of Fel Tidings, somewhere near the human realm."

Human realm? I blinked and stared at the others, gauging their reactions and from the looks of them? This news was shit.

"What's wrong with that?" I asked, then remembered. Humans. "That means there are likely Wardens there, aren't there?"

Merlin, Cass, and Arden nodded, and I just growled, "Shit."

"I know of a way to get there if we can get back to Virani," Arden whispered, but the pensive look on her face almost creeped me out.

"What's going through your mind?" My question startled her and she stared at me. "You want to see your brother?"

She winced. "Yes, more than anything now."

"Why is that?" Cassia asked as she helped shovel frozen bits of basilisk into Galaxy's gullet.

"Because I think he had a hand in bottling my family."

Cassia audibly gasped and Galaxy nearly choked as the Oni's fist ended up flying into her throat at Arden's revelation.

"Seriously?" I whispered and Merlin just blinked at her like he wasn't surprised. "You got something to say?"

"The one human thing I did when I was a child was read books," Merlin explained patiently, his gaze alighting on Arden's face. "My favorite types were mysteries. Typically, when one goes through something the way you did, there are events that lead up to and foreshadow certain other happenings. I first suspected something was amiss when Gammy stated that the brother you thought had died was *alive* and a well-respected and powerful figure among your kind."

He stood up and brushed himself off before continuing to theorize, "I then suspected further when Gammy sent him word you were back and we were attacked by those miscreants before you could see him."

"Okay, Warlock Holmes, calm it down a smidge and put the booger sugar away." He snorted and rolled his eyes at me while I turned to watch Arden. "You know what you want to do with him? Do you want revenge? Want to take him down? Whatever you want, we're in."

"We have to go get the mantle." Arden rubbed her forehead, her gaze at her feet. "We're here on a mission. I never should have come back and now I know he was involved."

"Isn't knowing he was involved better than not?" Amabala asked quietly, all eyes flicking to her. "I know I don't know all of you well, but it seems to be that this could be advantageous to you finding those answers you desire, Arden."

She stepped closer and spoke low, but reassuringly. "If he is like any would-be politician I know, he will likely keep tabs on those who could unmake him and that would mean he keeps a detailed list either in his care, home, or possession. Find it, and it could be of use to you, no?"

Arden's jaw hung open and even Merlin looked surprised as the cheetah woman smiled at our friend.

Cassia closed the distance between her and Amabala and nodded at the smaller woman. "I may not have been certain about you, but I am now. We could use someone like you in our group of friends, you're useful and devious. Would you like to fight?"

Amabala blinked at her then glanced at all of us. "Is this normal?"

"For her?" I raised an eyebrow and smiled. "Yeah. It just means she likes you now. It's her way of making sure that you're capable of defending yourself."

"I don't know how to fight very well," Amabala muttered and backed down, her whiskers falling.

"I will teach you," Cassia stated, then looked over at Galaxy. "Can you make her yours?"

Galaxy paused and began to think on it. "I can, if I take all the experience I've just gained and was about to give to you all to her?" She smiled as Amabala looked confused. "This will be very foreign for you, but I assure you that we will get through it and that you will learn."

"Learn what?" Amabala asked quietly.

"How best you can be useful, to us and for yourself," Galaxy answered with a larger smile. "See, you know enough about our dynamic to know that I can make them stronger. But I only do this for people who can be useful. I don't know how you can grow, and it will be limited, but if you serve us, you will become more than you are now. Do you wish to serve?"

"I wish to be able to stand on my own." She affirmed and squared her shoulders. The look that I had been searching for in her before when we first discussed her joining us was finally in her gaze, but it wasn't favorable this time. "I was forced to serve my family and Matron. I will serve no more."

"I think what Galaxy means is, do you wish to be a part of something bigger than yourself?" I spoke softly as I approached her with Galaxy on my left. "All of us have a purpose. Cassia is strong and an amazing fighter, Arden is fast and can burn the absolute shit out of our enemies. Merlin is super intelligent and a spell-casting cannon."

"In training with the sword," he added with his arms crossed and an easy smile on his face.

I rolled my eyes and he just chuckled as I spoke on. "We all have our quirks and talents, but we contribute to the group. See what I mean?"

"So then, other than being a handsome container for Galaxy, what purpose do you serve?" Amabala raised an eyebrow at me, and I heard Cassia's breathing deepen.

"I'm the one who kills indiscriminately and has no problem being viewed as evil." I smiled at her, then added, "I also make one *hell* of a bartender."

"You tried to reach for that butler line *real* hard, Marcus—I respect that." Arden laughed openly at my confusion, which made Cassia snort. "Listen, Amabala, things with Galaxy and Marcus will always be weird, but he's with Cassia and from the way things seem, you wouldn't be the first in line to get with him."

Cassia raised a brow at the jinn, but she kept speaking. "Come with us. Be useful and prove to yourself that you're better than what your label has been for your whole life." She pointed to me and I smiled as she explained, "He's one of the most capable killers that I've met in quite some time, and I used to live in the Middle East when Rome ran rampant."

"I've always wondered—was Alexander really so great?" Merlin's question made me laugh, and Cassia just rolled her eyes.

"He was a bit of a prat and took the glory for his generals' victories, but he was an excellent strategist when he wasn't trying to screw anything that breathed." Arden's answer was dismissive. "Achilles? That guy was a beast. Fair, and a little less than level headed at times, but he was a natural-born killer. Is Marcus at that level? No, but he could get there."

"Honestly, I'm not even insulted at that comparison, thank you." It was a real treat to know that I could someday be as deadly as a demigod. Amabala was less amused and more confused but I just said, "Want to join us? We have fun."

"I would like that, thank you." Galaxy stepped up to her and held her hand out. "Is that all I must do?"

"No, but it's a start." Once the cheetah woman clasped Galaxy's hand, her breath caught as Galaxy stared her in the eyes. Galaxy brought Amabala's hand to her lips and bit her, slowly at first, then truly drew blood and the new member of the party gasped.

Where her tan and black spotted fur had once been, there was a star-shaped spot that glowed with a celestial energy.

"Welcome aboard, Amabala." Galaxy smiled at the cheetah woman and the rest of us clapped politely. "Now, can you find us a way out of here without us having to go back out there to fight that thing?"

"I can try, but I don't feel any portals nearby." Galaxy closed her eyes and Amabala's clouded over as information swept over her. I was only privy to some of it because Galaxy and I were now so much closer thanks to recovering her. "What is this status business, and how am I to know what to place these… *points* in to?"

"I'll help you!" Cassia and Arden cried before grinning at each other, rushing to join the newest member of the group and help her allocate her stats.

Galaxy stood off to the side quietly and watched the other woman, her gaze flickering as if she was reading something and she smiled before turning to me. *If she spends her stat points and spell points right, she can create portals.*

I'm kind of surprised Merlin can't do that already, what with him pulling magical hat tricks out like he did to find you. I watched the boy as he pulled out a few of the small vials that the dwarven smiths had given him and stored ambient magic into them.

It was wild to see how far he had come in the short time that I'd known him.

Is that jealousy I feel? Galaxy's teasing tone made me grin as she answered for me. *A little?*

I nodded, then shook my head as Cass and Arden began to bicker over the appropriate use of Amabala's efforts and I just sighed. *You got me. Why don't you just tell them that she should go with mana and that she can get that sort of spell?*

Because that would negate her being able to grow in a manner that feels satisfying to her. Galaxy closed the distance between us and grasped my arm softly, like a loved one reaching out to reassure someone they cared for. "I allow all of you the choice to grow as you see fit, all I do is reap the rewards of that growth."

I chuckled. "You sure do." She continued to hold my arm and I was okay with it. "Do you have a problem with what Arden did?"

Galaxy blinked up at me. "Me? No. I'm a part of you. Even

after we had been slightly separated, I felt what happened. That gave me the strength I needed to offer the others more power." She squeezed lightly. "Personally speaking, I think you would benefit from having all three of them."

My pulse quickened, my cheeks burning. "What?"

"Think about it." She tilted her head toward the three women. "If all three of them were as enamored with you as Cassia is currently, you would gain much. Their loyalty would be to you and you alone. Not to mention the fringe benefits."

"What's that supposed to mean?" I growled and she just laughed. "You act like I'm some kind of horn dog and it's a little grating."

"Marcus Bola." Galaxy's voice took on a deeper, chiding tone. "You forget that I know your mind better than even you do. You would happily accept all of them if you could, and the fringe benefits I spoke of would quite potentially be greater power. Every time you and Cassia 'scrap,' as you so affectionately have deemed the term, you gain a slight bit of experience with her. The two of you are slightly stronger than Arden, and more so than both Merlin and Amabala. Though they can catch up to you if you aren't careful."

"Why do you give us experience for sex?" My voice was low but it must have carried farther because the girls all stopped and glanced my way. I raised my voice and waved. "What does she need in Dex?"

Arden raised a brow and snorted. "Nothing, hers is almost as high as mine. Keep it down over there, we got this."

I just grinned placatingly and turned my back on them to glare at Galaxy expectantly.

It has to do with getting to know their ins and outs. Learning about them, not to mention the swapping of saliva and other… things. My cheeks should have been glowing maroon with the bits of indignant embarrassment and anger at having just now found this out.

So you're telling me that I have to have what… some kind of harem?

She snorted at me and shook her head. *I'm not telling you that you have to do anything, Marcus. I'm simply giving you all the information that I have available to me so that you can do with it what you will. I can tell you right now, Amabala would take you. Cassia would be angry, but the experience gained would be nice, and I could change Cassia's disposition on it if I was certain you wanted it. Arden? Well, you know deep down that she wouldn't say no to you either.*

What about Masonai? I almost felt ill. *Arden really likes him; she was thinking of dating him before all of this, although I don't know how serious she was.*

She was considering it. Galaxy glanced over my shoulder and smiled. *The time for idle chit chat is up. Talk to them and see what they think, if my word isn't enough. And no, Marcus, I won't go 'tinkering' with anyone's emotions and dispositions without consulting you.*

I muttered a soft, "Thanks," then turned to the ladies. "We up and running? How's she divvying her stats?"

"A couple points to Brawn to help her fight, and the rest of it to Mana so she can make us a portal to a place she's been before," Cassia explained as she closed the distance between us. Her hands gripped my waist and pulled me out of Galaxy's grasp as she hugged me, whispering, "Thank you for trying to come to my rescue with the basilisk."

I floundered; had that been what I was doing?

Arden shot a glare at me as if she knew what I was thinking and nodded once before I said, "Yeah, of course. I knew you could handle it, but I'm not going to just sit out of a fight."

She squeezed just a bit before kissing me and putting me back onto the ground. "So since she's been to Virani before, she can take us there and we can hunt down your asshat brother, right, Arden?"

"Yes, and we will need to find where he lives, though that shouldn't be an issue." Arden grinned and looked thoughtfully at Merlin. "Merlin, what do you need for that spell of yours to track someone?"

"I need to know what they look like currently." He thought

for a moment, then shrugged. "Or something that belonged to them at some point."

Arden pulled a small brush out of her pocket, charred and somewhat metallic-looking in the light that still hung in the room above us. "This was his. I took it the morning that we were betrayed."

"That should work." He reached for it, then looked her in the face. "Have you always carried that? Why?"

Her face fell, her voice a mutter, "Gryn was my hero when we were kids. The other jinn children would bully us for being 'hot heads,' and come for me and my sister." She stared at the brush as a glower overtook her features, distaste all we could see and hear in her tone. "He was so vain back then, but he would always come to defend us and run the other kids off. He left this out the morning we were supposed to start schooling and I nabbed it because I thought it might help me be brave like him."

Despite her growing unease and rising anger, tears still wet her cheeks as she sniffed and spoke on. "I tried to save him when they had him in their grasp and they bottled us." She wiped her eyes with her palm and spat. "The sword fell as I was pulled into the darkness of the bottle to sleep until I awoke thirty years later on Earth in the desert to some kid rubbing my lamp. I never even saw him die."

I grabbed her shoulder and she narrowed her gaze at me. "We'll avenge you."

"She's still alive, Marcus, that makes it revenge." Merlin snickered and winked at me.

A heavy palm plopped onto my shoulder and Cassia growled, "I don't think there's too much of a difference between either word other than that this bastard will pay for hurting my friend." She glanced down at me and looked to the others before adding, "And potentially tried to hurt more people I hold dear."

"I think I can do it now!" Amabala sounded excited, like she was a child with a new toy. "It won't last long, but I can make a portal!"

"Then let's go!" Arden's savage smile was enough to jump-start my adrenaline as Amabala held out her hands and focused.

A tear opened in front of us and she nodded. "Me last, go!"

This was going to be fun.

CHAPTER FIFTEEN

The portal opened up right into the middle of the square that we had entered the city in before, though there were significantly less people now, as night had fallen in Virani.

I squared my shoulders and pointed toward Amabala and Merlin. "Amabala, you're going to be our wheels. We'll need a getaway and your portals are it. Stick to Cass and she will keep you safe. Merlin, is there anything you can do to make that spell of yours a lot less conspicuous?"

"It's pretty much just what it is, it glows golden and that's all we can do about it." He frowned and opened his book. "I can tinker with spells but it will take more time than we have if we want to avoid suspicion and have the cover of darkness on our side."

Fuck. "Okay, we all gather around Merlin and shield his spell from view as much as we can. He will give directions to Galaxy and she will pass them to all of us." No one seemed to take umbrage with my plan, but I turned to Arden. "This is your home, your vendetta. We will listen to you. What do you need?"

"To find him and know why he did it," she answered quietly. "Let's move."

"I have a question," Amabala stated tentatively. We all looked at her expectantly given the situation we were in currently. "What do you mean by Galaxy will pass the directions to us? He's right here and I can hear him just fine."

I rolled my eyes due to the sheer stupidity on my part. Of course she wouldn't have known that we were basically all connected to Galaxy within our minds. She had *so* much to learn. "The short of it is that, since Galaxy is a part of all of us, she can communicate with us through our thoughts."

Her eyes widened as she made a small O with her mouth and nodded in apparent disbelief.

Merlin took her brother's brush from Arden and cast the spell with a few muttered words as we gathered around him.

He says go forward down this roadway and hang a right. We moved according to his directions, rewarded with open curiosity from those who were out this late, but nothing more. This was a great opportunity for Galaxy to kind of fill her in on some of the aspects of what it meant to now be a part of her and our group, as well as get used to Galaxy being in her head. What a trip that must have been.

We walked for nearly ten minutes before Merlin's voice stopped us with a hiss. "Here!"

We stood in front of an iron gate, a metal fence on either side that wrapped around and had stone pillars every ten feet. Behind the fence was a largish yard decorated sparsely by a bench under a tree opposite a water fountain. All that led to the front door was a brick pathway.

The house was three stories and the lights were on inside, their glow to the outside festive and welcoming, but also a sign of wealth somehow. As if the nice and expertly crafted windows painted to match the rest of the trim were more than anyone else in this area got, and you should be able to see them at all times.

"There are wards to protect and warn those inside of the gate being opened." Merlin blinked at the offending obstruction as he dropped his locating spell.

Stand back, Galaxy ordered and stepped out of my shadow. "All of you step back from the gate and leave it to me. Keep an eye out for anyone watching."

We did as she said, taking cover in the shadows of stoops and alleys in the area surrounding the open plot of land in an otherwise densely populated and more apartment-ladened area. My eyes scanned the windows of the homes around us; some motion, but never much more than a silhouette that moved by too quickly to take notice of the goings on below them.

Galaxy passed her hands over the gate, then pulled toward the center of herself and began to feed on the magic of the wards and alarms.

Won't that alert them?

She continued what she was doing until there was an electric pull, like I was a magnet and her the metal.

Not now, it won't. She turned and hit me with a radiant smile and all of us moved together toward her and stopped at the gate. She took her raven form and winged it up to the nearest window and glanced inside. *From what it looks like, there's a dinner of some kind going on. I see at least six people, including a flame jinn that bears a striking resemblance to our friend Arden.*

"That'll be Gryn," Arden whispered, she took a calming breath and refocused. "Six people?"

Galaxy's bird head bobbed after she landed on my shoulder.

"Okay. We sneak in and take out those we can quickly and leave him for last." She stood up from where she'd knelt by the gate and walked along the brick path to the door and we followed.

Personally, I'd have waited until they were gone and took him as soon as the last one left to give the city law enforcement someone to look at aside from us, but if these guys had some part in his scheme, they would get theirs.

Or Arden's. I was just a tool to carry out her justice and I was okay with being that tool for once.

I cannot believe you willingly called yourself a tool, Marcus, Galaxy teased and I just rolled my eyes and thought at her hard. She laughed again. *Very well*, meatsuit, *I see your point. Pay attention.*

A mental snap from her focused my gaze on the door as Cassia stood next to me. "You okay?"

I nodded and glanced down to see her holding a mangled doorknob, then back up to see her grinning before giving me a wink while she opened the door.

The voices inside were of a typical volume that one might expect for a get together among friends and associates. There was laughter and talking, cutlery being used, and even soft music playing from somewhere.

"So who was it that ran off after that errand you sent them on?" one of the deeper voices asked as we piled into the small room behind the door. It was lavishly decorated with art and racks with coats and other things for guests. Swanky, even.

"Oh, some kids from my political party, no one important enough to matter for my upcoming campaign." The voice sounded confident, sophisticated—almost like a boot Second Lieutenant trying to sound like he wasn't still a boot in the company of higher-ranking officers for drinks.

"Speaking of," another guest raised his voice as Arden listened, stunned into stillness. "How does your work with the other flame jinn go? I take it they look up to you, but is there anyone else they would consider backing against you?"

"Not to my knowledge, since the majority of them adore me," Gryn answered surely, then added, "If only my dear, lost family were here to see me ascend the ashes of tragedy."

There was a pointed silence for a moment and I could see Arden's jawline harden as my own anger flared, but the sweeping laughter in the other room said it all.

They knew everything.

She nodded to Cassia and me as we both straightened up and turned toward the doorway. I made the motion of ladies first just before her eyes bled white and her irises turned black as pitch, her skin bursting as red spikes grew out of her flesh.

In a heartbeat, we stole around the corner into the dining

room and Cassia had the nearest jinn snatched up by the head and crushed it like a child crushing Play-Doh.

My knuckles cracked against his buddy's skull and pitched him forward loudly onto the table with a *bang*.

"What is the meaning of this!" one of them roared and lifted a fist full of something that crackled toward us. A shield burst in front of me as Cassia flipped the table in front of herself protectively.

Amabala shouted, "Someone's yelling outside!"

"Okay," I called back and moved behind Cass. I dove behind a glass case and cast Bolt at the jinn who sent the last spell at us, but he fell back in his chair when the guy opposite him burst into flames.

Arden stepped through the doorway and Gryn froze where he was and stared in horror as she sneered. "Your campaign helpers couldn't quite do the job. Then again, neither could you, Gryn."

"You were supposed to be dead!" her brother shouted, visibly trying to collect himself. "I had no idea what was going on! Thank goodness you're here."

I spoke in a low growl, "If only my dear, lost family were here…" His eyes darted to me. "She's here, but not to watch you ascend anything."

"Who are these people, Gryn?" The jinn on the ground whined as I stepped closer to him. "Stay away from me!"

Gryn stuttered and stammered as his sister made her way around the ruined table to close the distance between them, but she offered the answer to his question. "We are justice. We're the judges, jury, and executioners."

I stepped forward and slowly squared down so that I'd be closer to my soon-to-be victim and whispered, grinning cruelly, "And you've been found guilty by association."

I cast Blade and whipped it into his throat. Blood splattered against my face and clothes.

"More voices and shouting closing in!" Amabala warned. "Door's closed and I can do another portal."

"Not yet," Arden called back and turned to her brother, a soft and pained smile on her face. "You sold us into bondage and slavery. You faked your death and used your 'loss' to rise to some semblance of power in a place where the majority see you as lesser. Why?"

Gryn held his hands out like he was trying to hug her, then ward her off. "I was only doing what I was told to, otherwise they would have killed me and I didn't want to die. Ardent, plea—"

Arden hit him with a fist wreathed in water, and he screamed pitiably like it had been acid.

"Don't you *dare* try to lie to me, you filthy thief!" Her eyes flooded with tears as her voice broke. "You stole a whole life from me and now I have to take it back. Where is our family?"

"I don't know." He seethed through his teeth, his face blackened and crusty-looking. Any resemblance he'd had to Arden was gone now.

"Liar," Cassia roared and stomped toward him, crushing the body of the suspiciously only remaining dead jinn in the room. I spotted a dark tail waving in the air and the body began to move in jerky, sliding motions.

"I don't know!" he asserted as he stared at Arden. "They're gone. We're all we have left. Arden, stop this."

She punched him again and even as blood hungry as I was, the sound of the impact made me wince and recoil. Her snarled response, "Never say that name again! You only cared about yourself. Your image." She grasped him by his hair and pulled him closer for another strike, punctuated by her cry of, "You!"

She let him fall to the ground and sobbed. "You only care about yourself. If you won't help us of your own will, you can be a stepping stone on my path to recovering the family you don't deserve." She wiped her face and sniffed. "Galaxy."

Galaxy stepped forward and began to grow until she was almost the size of a cougar, her jaws hanging open, ready to strike.

Don't make it easy, Galaxy, I muttered to her through our bond. *Make him suffer.*

He will. She battered him with her forepaws and he screamed loudly. *For eternity.*

He continued to shriek and shout as Cassia moved to Arden's side. Footsteps rang out down the hall as Merlin huffed into the room. "Got books. Guards all over... Gotta go."

Shouting outside made Amabala jump, but Arden muttered, "Open the portal as soon as Galaxy is done."

"I'm done," Galaxy cheerily called and dabbed her cheeks with her shirt in human form. "Let's get to somewhere safe and rest for the night. I'm feeling a bit tired."

Amabala complied and opened a portal for us and we ended up back in the ruins beneath the ocean.

"Why are we back here?" I wondered at her, but she collapsed on the floor and began to snore loudly. "She alright?"

"The strain of a portal is unique and using them so closely together is hard on the body," Merlin explained and sat down on the ground. "As to why here? It's secluded and somewhere her siblings can't follow if they're hunting her."

"How do you know that?" Cassia asked as her body began to revert once more, the bags under her eyes a little concerning.

"It makes the most sense, logically speaking. If she has the ability to feel when a portal is used around her, so do they." He pulled out a stack of books and began to look at them. "I found these in his house, though I had to run from room to room. I hope one of these is his journal or something."

"I'll help you look," Arden muttered and he just waved her off, much to her surprise. "Listen boy, you may be able to lift weights and swing a sword now, but I'm older than you, so give me a goddamn book!"

"You need to remove yourself from this and rest." Merlin stared up at her from over a book. "You've been through a lot today. You don't need all this too."

I took one and opened it, glancing through and finding I

understood not a damn thing. "He's got a point. You just relived a lot of past shit tonight, Arden. You should rest a little."

Arden glared at me coldly. "You don't own me, Marcus."

I chuckled. "I dare say I don't. I sure as fuck hope I never do—but that's not the point." My gaze softened; she was tired and it looked to be taking everything in her to just stay strong and up right. "The point is, as a friend, I'm asking you to trust us to help you."

"That's what you tried to teach me years ago, Arden," Cassia, in her shorter human form, muttered with her arms circling the taller woman from the side so she could stare up at her. "Took me a while to trust you, and here we are. Trust us all and let us work for you and with you. Let your chosen family help you find your real one with you."

Arden's cheeks shimmered with tears as light poured from behind Merlin. She snorted. "I doubt that I could say I chose *all* of you. Cassia, you forced me to like you, and Merlin reminds me of one of my children from a past life. Marcus is just... well, him."

Amabala cleared her throat, she looked exhausted and about to fall back over, but Arden turned toward her as the cheetah woman yawned. "I chose you." She blearily looked at us all. "You treat me better than my family ever has."

That made the jinn's lips twitch and she nodded. "You did, didn't you?" She looked back to Merlin. "Fine, but if you find anything, you have to tell me okay?"

"Only if you promise to buy me a Nintendo Switch after this is all over." Merlin grinned but yelped as both Cassia and Arden gasped and all but tackled the poor boy in pure joy.

They'd made him a gamer after all.

CHAPTER SIXTEEN

We woke up and ate a meal before deciding to plan a little bit, though Galaxy had been a little quieter in this aspect of our journey than she had before.

"We're going to leave in ten minutes," Amabala explained finally. "I don't know where exactly we will be coming into the city at, but my siblings will know we're there immediately, and will be coming to investigate."

"So we kill them." Cassia punched her left palm with her right fist, a savage grin on her face until Amabala affixed her with a withering glare. "Or injure them really badly?"

Amabala's sharp teeth flashed. "Better. You'll need to stick close to me for this to work because as soon as they get to this area we come into, they'll find my scent and be able to track me."

"So we just have to be faster than them—got it." Arden nodded to herself, stretched, and then went off to the other side of the cave to do whatever it was she was going to do.

I turned my sights inward. *What's going on with you? Normally you would have come in on that kind of planning session.*

There wasn't an answer so much as a sort of awareness that

brushed up against mine. I closed my eyes and dove into myself and opened them again as I stood inside my mana sea with Galaxy sitting on top of the energy within me, looking lost.

"Galaxy?"

My voice barely reached her as she stared down into the dark liquid beneath us, somehow unseeing but flicking back and forth as if watching something in minute detail. "I was a goddess."

"We figured as much." I tried to tease, but her eyes lifted to mine and tears fell from her chin. Her elven form radiated a darkness that was new to me, and even as I stood there and watched her, it was hard to make out where the shadows started and she began.

"I was there at the beginning of this universe, Marcus." She waved her hand and the stars above us burst into motion creating what I could only assume was a Big-Bang-level event. Stars raced across the universes and in the center of it she stood —the silent composer to an orchestra of sights and sounds so monumental and inconsequential at the same time. Where her will flowed, so did the blood and body of the cosmos.

In a flash, worlds popped into existence and began to twirl like ballerinas in orbit, never ceasing their celestial swirling.

"With every new planet, a new set of gods rose from the beliefs of the life that was there." She stared at all of them lovingly. "I was there. And I remember no more for a long time, other than the brief touching of other gods' minds. Probing and questioning me about creation. I can't even recall what I told them."

"Then wait, how does that make sense?" I tried to wrap my mind around it but stopped and just continued the thought I had. "You said you recalled that numbers, the status screens, were how you had done it in the past. You had to remember something right? If you were the ultimate creator, how could you have known that and associated with mortals?"

Her lips trembled as she whispered, "I don't know." Her head fell forward, shoulders shaking as tears splashed against the mana below her feet. She lifted her hands to hide her embarrassment at being so lost in the storm of emotions and questions that whirled inside her. "There's still so much I don't know!"

She felt jabbing agony at being so close to knowing more about herself and yet so far away. Why had she, a goddess who could birth an entire universe, been brought so low as this? To end up this broken thing?

All these thoughts assailed her and all I could offer her was to hold her and be there. We stood there for what felt like forever until I felt something on my shoulder.

I glanced back, the light of the cavernous ruin making me wince as Cassia asked, "You ready to go?"

I blinked at her and nodded quietly. "Yeah, let's get to it. Quicker we go, the quicker we get back to home."

"I'd like that." Cassia smiled, but it appeared she suspected something was wrong as she frowned at me. "You okay? You were staring at nothing for a while."

"Galaxy thing," I muttered in return and I tried to act a little more chipper than I felt. "She learned a little more about her past, but it's not sitting well with her."

She paused and stared at me before saying, "She will sleep with us tonight."

She turned away and walked to where the others waited patiently for me. I followed after taking inventory of myself and watched as, once more, Amabala summoned her portal.

The transition for this one was a little rougher. A barely-lived-in small room, hardly large enough to fully stand in, was where I came out and I tried to open the door, but someone crashed into my back and I thudded into the wooden object and had to stay there until all of us stood in this cramped space.

"Where are we?" Arden hissed and grunted. "Ouch! What was that I just stepped on? What's this bed made of?"

"My old room, and that was likely some crystal my siblings put there as a prank." Someone touched my thigh and I jumped as the hand groped pretty far north until the pressure was gone and the door opened outward. "We must leave now."

Voices in the distance greeted my ears and I growled. "Get behind me, and tell me which way to go." I grabbed her as she started to move, forcing her to look me in the eye. "I don't plan to kill them, but I will defend myself and you. Don't interfere."

She looked like she wanted to argue but the voices rose and I whipped around to shoulder my way through the hallway before me. The doors opened in front of me to admit the people in the rooms they barred but I slammed them shut.

I heard bending and groaning metal and cast a questioning glance over my shoulder to see Cassia and Arden bending and superheating knobs to keep the doors from being opened as easily.

I owe them a drink for that. Head forward, I pushed on. One of her brothers had made it into the hall and brandished a bow at me with an arrow notched and aimed.

My fist rocketed out and Bolt leaped from my knuckles to him. The arrow shot wide and buried itself into the wall to my right and someone inside bellowed, "Hey!"

The cheetah-man on the ground was still shaking and convulsing violently when I came upon him. My hands were in his clothes, twisting and yanking him up into the air with ease as we moved on.

Once we were in the open, I tossed him at the wave of guards that came toward us on the one bridge there leading straight at us. Three guards were down, one knocked off completely, and the other two had the sense to back up and try to scrabble over their friends.

"Take this ladder, go three flights up!" Amabala grunted as she push-kicked a man who had tried to rush her from the rope on our right that came up from a lower level. The man screamed as he fell, but she turned back to me and ordered, "Then turn right."

"Got it." I launched myself up the ladder on the left of the platform and punched an armored guard in the kneecap, then push-kicked him into the netting behind him. He gnashed his teeth and growled at me in futility, I narrowed my gaze at him and snarled, "Stay there and be a good boy."

"I'll kill you!" he roared back but went limp as Cassia came up onto the floor in her Oni form.

"What I thought." she rumbled and turned to me. "Go."

We were up and onto the next ladder by the time some kind of bell began to ring through the area, calling attention to us.

"Faster!" Arden called from the rear of the little line up the taller ladder we were on.

I started to pump my arms and legs as fast as I could but it felt like the ladder just wouldn't end. There was no sense of motion.

I glanced up and glared at a figure that looked to be touching the ladder. *He's enchanting the ladder to become endless until they can wear us down and trap us.*

Will Embodiment work?

Galaxy shook her head inside me and I grimaced as she said, *No, you're out of range by about eighty feet.*

I wondered to myself, *If range is an issue, I can solve that.* I growled and looked down between myself and the ladder. "Cassia, throw me as hard as you can straight up."

"What?" she growled.

I didn't give her the chance to comprehend and dropped down toward her.

"Marcus!"

She hooked her hands in mine and I grinned as she let her arm drop, then launched me up with a roaring, "Graaaaaa!"

The wind battered my cheeks, but as soon as I was within range by Galaxy's standards, I used Embodiment of Lightning to land on the fucker.

He cried out as my fist collided with his chin and snapped his head to the left. The ladder stopped moving and soon the others were with me on the platform.

Cassia eyed me angrily and muttered, "Stop making me throw you, damn it. What if I missed?"

"Then you would have missed and I would have caught myself on the ladder." I touched her forearm and grinned again. "Or you would have caught me like the powerful Oni you are."

"Can we cut the bull and get the hell out of here!" Arden howled and turned to fire a spell at someone who had shot an arrow directly in front of her path. Someone in the distance screamed loudly and she smiled. "That'll teach them."

We turned to go into the area Amabala had said to and came face to face with a mob of guards.

"Can we kill them?" Cassia rumbled, her body thickening as spikes grew from her.

"Disable, don't kill." I sighed, knowing this was going to be difficult to say the least. "If you have to protect someone else, though—don't hesitate."

"Good." Cassia's voice dropped an octave and we both darted forward into the line that waited for us.

I covered my forearms with Frost and pulled out my Oni sword just before we clashed. My sword rang as it crashed against a guard's club and I twisted to elbow his friend who reached around him.

Ice formed on his nose, blood turning to crystal as I shoved him aside and slid my sword into the shoulder of the guard to my left.

Sharp pain erupted in my right leg and I growled, glancing down to see a spearhead being pulled back, slick with my blood, but it looked off somehow. "Fuck, I wish I had my guns!"

"*Graaaaaargh!*" Cassia bellowed in return as she tossed four of the guards aside so she could get to the one holding the spear.

Suddenly, Merlin stood next to me and slashed with his sword, a wave of earthen energy fanning out and slashing someone's arm off at the elbow.

I hissed, "Oh, shit."

He growled and snarled at the guards that came after the others, his sword weaving patterns of amber-colored energy that stabbed and slashed at our opponents until it ran out. "Shit!"

Arden rushed out from behind him, whirling in front of a guard about to stab forward with a rapier of some kind. The blade met a rush of water which transformed into a wall of water that bent the metal, then Arden shoved her right hand into it and the wall surged forward in a wave that washed the guards before us to the side of the entrance.

Arden glanced back. "Come on!"

We moved forward, my sparing use of Frost depleting my mana reserves but just enough to keep the guards there slightly frozen to the floor.

"Straight through!" Amabala urged us as we must have arrived at our destination.

My body jerked forward as Cassia shoved me and Merlin grabbed my shoulder to help me hobble forward; the pain had gotten to the point where my leg nearly felt like I should just lop it off.

The familiar feeling of traversing a portal washed over us as Merlin continued to drag me forward. "Come on, Marcus, we're almost there!"

"What the fuck is going on with my leg?" I gasped as a wave of pain so gnarly that I vomited slightly in my mouth hit me. Spitting it out, I growled, "Fuck!"

He sat me on the ground and whipped around as someone yelled something I couldn't quite make out as my vision grew blurry.

Galax... Gal, what's gon on? My muddled mind desperately fought to string words together but all I could manage was that.

Her response evaded me.

CHAPTER SEVENTEEN

Marcus.

My eyes opened and I found myself sitting across from a shadowy Galaxy. Her figure was cloaked in darkness, yet I could see her for what she was. *Who* she was.

A goddess, timeless and immortal, who had the power to grant life and take it just as easily. She watched me as the ebon mass around her shifted and waved in the air.

That darkness was the cloak of the beginning. The shroud of something to create and craft with. The blanket that fostered countless planets and lives but also snuffed out the stars and entire solar systems.

Why is this coming to me now?

Because, Marcus. Something spoke that made me frown. It was Galaxy's mouth moving, but not her voice at all. *Something within you has awakened. Something ancient in its own right, and it recognizes her.*

A pinprick of light opened, popping into existence next to my head. Then another.

This memory can remain your own if you so wish it. We can teach you much.

The voice echoed to the point that it sounded like just a whisper, then I was lifted out of the darkened realm and into the light of the world.

"Where am I?" I groaned and covered my eyes as the bright light lanced through me, even through my eyelids. "What happened?"

"You were poisoned by something," Galaxy muttered as she leaned over my head, her body helping to shade my eyes to the point that I could slightly open them to look at her.

Concern warped her features, and it was so hard to not see her silhouetted by the goddess-like glory that she had been. That I had seen. *We need to talk, but I want you to take a look at my memories and see what I remember first. See if you can make something of it.*

She nodded once and closed her eyes for the barest of seconds. Her connection with me snapped back into place stronger than it had ever been.

This is… concerning, Marcus. She huffed and held my head tighter where it laid against her thighs. *That's what I used to look like? What awakened?*

I don't know, but it was trying to say it could teach *me things. Like it was trying to lure me away from you.*

Her grip tightened more and her heart rate spiked nervously. I lifted my hand and put it against her cheek before whispering, "Not going to happen."

"He's awake!" Cassia's voice crashed through me a heart-beat before her hand was on my chest and her face floated into view. Her hair was a bright orange color and styled in a crew cut now that she was back in human form. "How do you feel?"

Blinking, I took an inventory of my body. "Like shit, but only slightly worse than after a fight with you?"

"Ah, so you're more likely to make it." Her smile was infectious and even Galaxy snorted at her response.

"I take it higher resistance to venom and poison meant fuck all to whatever was on that spear?" I looked at Galaxy and she confirmed it for me mentally. "We didn't get anything from it?"

She shook her head and remained pensive.

"What happened?" I tried to sit up, but both women looked at me and held me down. "Why can't I get up?"

"You're going to want to stay laying down for this, Marcus." Cassia had to look away for a moment but when she looked back, she offered me a softer look than I had ever seen.

"I swear to Odin, if one of you says I lost that leg, I'm going back to Virani and I'm murdering the whole fucking guard." My heart raced as I continued to try to sit up.

"We couldn't get the venom all out in time and there were some other complications," Galaxy offered somberly, the pressure she put on my head getting annoying. "You didn't lose anything but a sizable chunk of the leg and we're working on fixing it, but you need to be still."

"Cass, is that true?" My heart raced along with Galaxy's and she rolled her eyes, knowing damned well she had no reason to lie to me.

"Yes—we saved the leg, but it's not pretty and if you panic, it will be harder to heal." She frowned and then sighed. "Even with your lycanthropic healing, it's taking much longer than it should."

"That poison is rare, and meant to attack the enhanced metabolism and healing rate of shifters." Amabala groaned and sat up as if she was hungover. "Did you have to take so much of my mana so quickly?"

Galaxy smiled. "I can always take more."

Amabala held up a hand and shook it. "No, that was fine."

"Where're Merlin and Arden?" I tried to relax but not being able to really move fucking sucked. It was like being back in the hospital after the attacks that killed my Marines.

"They went to see if they could get some help, or some medicine to help you, in one of the cities nearby." Cassia's head floated out of my vision and my leg began to ache terribly.

"Won't they be recognized and followed here by Wardens if they aren't careful? Fuck, even if they are?" I glanced up at

Amabala. "And what's to stop those assholes from coming through the portal after us?"

"I ate the portal." Galaxy grinned at me wolfishly, much to my stunned confusion. "Through Amabala, I discovered a means of doing so. It was good, but I had to use the majority of that power to keep the poison suppressed and confined to that part of your leg. Then a little more from her so that I could keep you unconscious for the worst of that."

"How long have they been gone?" My stomach was starting to grumble angrily and I had to summon something to eat or I worried that I'd pass out from hunger.

I munched while Galaxy and Cassia conferred silently before Cass answered, "A day and a half."

"*What!*" I launched myself up, Galaxy not able to hold me, and nearly passed out from the rush of blood to my head. She steadied me and as she lowered me, I got a glance of my leg.

The meat there looked rotten and sickly, an open wound that festered and refused to heal, with red and black streaks in the skin around it. There was no smell, thankfully, but the sight of it managed to turn my stomach and send chills down my spine all on its own. The hole was about six inches and jagged, like something had bitten a chunk out of my flesh and muscle deep enough to show me bone.

"Oh?" I tried for levity but failed miserably and we all knew it. "That's all it is?"

"Be quiet and try to finish the bar you have in your hand." Cassia pressed the bar toward my face. I complied, but it may as well have been dirt for all it did for my palette.

I finished the bar, then another one, and gave another to the others.

"I'm worried about the others." I stared at Galaxy pointedly but she was avoiding my gaze. "Galaxy, can you go and find them?"

"I won't leave you like this," she said simply, from the set of her jaw, I was certain she meant it.

I closed my eyes and let myself rest, focusing my mind on my injury to try to see if it would heal it at all.

... at the very least I can cool the injury down to keep it from being so inflamed, right?

That would help with the inflammation, yes, but not the infection, Galaxy advised sagely. *While putting mana into the area isn't a bad idea, unaspected mana like yours might do more harm than good.*

Fuck. I hated just sitting here and doing nothing like this.

"Why don't you get some more rest while Cassia tries another round of healing on you?" She stroked my cheek softly. "That should help a little."

I tried to lay down and sleep. It came fitfully after a while, though my treatment from Cass was wildly itchy and frustrating.

After hours of nothing, a piercing whistle rent the air and my eyes flew open. I sat up slowly as Arden and Merlin sprinted into view, arms waving wildly.

"Where the *hell* have you been?" I called to them, but something looked off. Then I felt an electricity in the air, a heartbeat before a gargantuan bird flew over head.

It had to be as big as a bus from wing tip to wing tip and it was magnificent. But I couldn't make out more than a yellowish hue before its storm gray eyes lit upon me and my body went cold.

It screeched, wings flaring out as Merlin bellowed, "Run!" He threw his right hand up, sword appearing and watery energy rocketing from it as he moved toward us. "Ruuuun!"

Cassia lifted me in her arms and began to sprint away from the bird. "Where are we going!"

"Trees ahead!" Arden howled and shot flames at the bird, making it veer to the right slightly to get away from the blast.

Thunder crashed above us and lightning fried the ground six feet to Cassia's right, the hair on my body rising as the current swept toward us.

"Fuck!" The pain of the electrical charge hitting my leg stole my breath as Cassia grunted and sprinted on.

We had to be around two hundred feet from the trees and there was no way we were going to make it before this thing attacked again.

Until something launched itself out of the forest and up at the bird, roaring hard enough that it shook the ground.

Arden was ahead of us in an instant as the two beasts clashed, electrical snapping and guttural growling and snarling covering any and all possible noise we could make.

"What the fuck is that!" I cried, my eyes widening as the intruding monster bit into the bird's neck with an alligator shaped mouth and sort of hung there for a second before shaking its whole body for added measure. The bird screeched and the scent of ozone was so overpowering my head swam and the overwhelming urge to wipe my nose came over me.

I did so and saw that I was bleeding and not by a little. Cassia had a small trickle of blood on her lip as well, but it just looked to fuel her as she ran on. Merlin caught up to us and eventually we crashed into the tree line and kept moving until the sounds of pitched combat were well behind us and fading slowly.

"Slow down." Cassia huffed and started to flag; her endurance was impressive, but that long a distance and all of that on top of it? Wasn't easy. "Be careful. This place is dangerous."

"We know." Merlin put his hands on his knees and bent over, his panting almost asthmatically with how hard he was breathing. "Keep an eye out."

I glanced around cautiously and counted our party. Me, Arden, Cass, and Merlin. Galaxy was in me. Where was Amabala?

A piercing scream echoed through the air and I clawed my way out of Cassia's shocked grasp. Hitting the ground hurt like hell, but I was able to get onto my remaining working leg and hopped toward the sound of the scream.

"Marcus, wait!" Arden's voice was just a blip to me as I fought my way through the brush and forest of flora.

Marcus, please wait, Galaxy pleaded, but I knew if I didn't do something—*anything*—she was going to die. I couldn't go through that again.

No Marine left behind! I bellowed mentally and urged myself on.

The scene unfolding before me was enough to make my blood boil. The green-scaled creature that had attacked the bird crouched before Amabala, staring at her with blood dribbling from jagged yellowed teeth. It looked like some kind of dragon or something, but the whole time I could only see that its eyes were on her.

A thick tongue lapped the blood on its lip before it roared a challenge that made the cheetah woman fall to the ground, likely having fainted.

I held up my hand, voices that I didn't recognize whispering instructions in my ear. Channeling my mana from my mana sea to finger with a swirling motion in mind, I cast Fireblast. A small, bullet-like shot of red burst from my index finger and toward the beast's chin, the head flicking to the left to observe. It took the beam and stilled.

There wasn't the concussive *boom* that I had expected, but instead more of a piercing. The creature's head reared back, blood spilling from the hole that my attack left behind.

A thunderous blast of force slammed down onto it and the creature fled with a hiss at me. As if to say that this wasn't over.

The bloodied bird landed on the ground in front of me, wings torn and breast bleeding as it stared at me hatefully.

I snarled, "You want some too, tweety-bird?" I likely sounded more menacing than I felt. That spell had taken the majority of my mana and I had enough to cast Wisp or Bolt and that was about it.

My sword in my grasp, I squared off at the creature, my injured leg creaking ominously as I tried to settle my weight onto it somewhat.

A shadow sailed over me, Cassia and Arden crashing into the bird, weapons flashing. I didn't trust myself to move forward anymore, so I settled for throwing my sword at the bird's breast.

The sword sliced a few feathers off, but otherwise it was the ladies who did the majority of the work putting the bird down.

I collapsed onto my ass with a pained grunt as my leg cramped and burned.

The bird fell and I muttered, "Get what you want to keep off it, because Galaxy needs to eat that thing." I nudged her, angry as she was at me, and she separated herself from me to go and eat the bird. "What in the fuck was that other thing?"

"A drake, or some other brutish kind of reptile—a lesser, much more animalistic and brutal kind of dragon-kin," Arden panted. She had twelve large feathers, three talons and what looked like an entire leg of meat. "Very. Fucking. Dangerous. Marcus."

Each of her words was punctuated by a menacing step toward me and uttered through her grit teeth. She stared down at me. "This isn't *Monster Hunter*, Marcus. You don't go up against a nasty creature like this halfcocked and injured. That was a boss fight, motherfucker. You could have *died.*"

"I'm glad I didn't." I hissed as the pain in my leg grew to an unbearable level before I shot a glare up at her. "I'm not going to leave a party member hanging out to dry like that. We need her. She committed herself to us. We owe her the same."

"You owed me nothing," Amabala hissed at me from where she sat up, but the look on her face was one of gratitude. "Though I will never forget this kindness."

I nodded once in her direction and stared up at Arden. "You better have something stronger than Motrin and foot powder for this, or I'm going to have to cut this shit off."

She rolled her eyes and dropped a slightly partitioned tablet into my hand. "Break it in half. Crumble one half of it up and sprinkle it into the wound, then shove the other half up your ass."

I chuckled at her surly humor, then looked to Merlin who watched us stoically. "What a kidder," I probed, but he just watched me quietly for a moment too long. "Merlin, please tell me she wasn't serious."

He turned and walked away and I couldn't tell if his shoulders were shaking from laughing or if he was shrugging off his responsibility to pass on proper procedure.

Fuck, this was about to be a lot less pleasant.

CHAPTER EIGHTEEN

My leg felt better almost immediately, though I was more than a little stiff and… upset at the outcome of things.

Serves you right. Galaxy was sulking, having eaten the massive bird as quickly as she could. We weren't going to go into the forest without some serious goodies, and in order to get those, we needed to visit a city.

Specifically, the city that Merlin and Arden had just come back from.

We would be discussing that soon, but we had each stopped talking so that Cassia could cook Arden's giant chicken leg and we could allocate our points from leveling up.

Turned out that surviving a tier six creature attack, that of a drake, doled out a good amount of experience points even if she didn't manage to eat any of it. It was hard for Galaxy to explain to us how it happened, but we got something and that was nice. Add that to the dead bird Galaxy devoured, and we had managed to grow quite a good bit. According to Galaxy, I was close to getting to eleven.

With that in mind, I decided that keeping things generally even keeled for now would be better than not. So I raised my

Mana by two and Charisma by three. That made all my stats save for Mana fifteen. Nice.

Was that okay for now? For now. Later on, I would up things a little less evenly, but I needed to be a little more likable if we were going to be going into a city full of Talented people and mages.

"So what the hell took you so long?" Cassia finally asked, not caring that Arden still had her stat screen open in front of her.

"Finding the medicine wasn't easy, and the city wasn't small either." Merlin answered for Arden and took a swig from a bottle of pop that he'd had stored somewhere, likely in his inventory but that robe had its own of sorts and I didn't know for certain. Galaxy turned within me to stare at the bottle lustfully and I snorted.

Imagine, a goddess with a caffeine addiction.

She scowled at me and I just grinned wider as Merlin spoke again. "The place is crawling with Wardens and they have signs up asking for information and sightings of us."

"So then we need to go somewhere else?" I raised a brow at him but he shook his head. "Why not?"

"This place has a good population of goblins and their magic weapons and gear are too good to pass up if we're going into that place," Arden answered this time, but she looked considerably less happy about needing to go there. "And I know that we could go talk to the goblins back in Columbus, but the Wardens will be watching for us everywhere."

"Then I say we go in there and start killing them all." I crossed my arms and Merlin hit me with a look that was all kinds of dirty. "I'm serious. They started this. We've done nothing wrong and they're interfering with your ability to do what needs doing. They've earned it."

"I don't want to be the Warden who attacked his people and killed them." He had a point. If he did that, his people wouldn't trust him. They'd treat him like a pariah, even if we did the killing.

"Goddamnit, I hate this!" I started to pace back and forth slowly. "Those assholes can interfere with you and our mission, and there's nothing we can do?"

"I'm not saying that they can't have their asses handed to them." Merlin grinned and that made me stop. "I'm tired of being picked on too. They called me weak in their flyers, and all of the Wardens they sent on all sides were younger ones. I'm not going to stand for it, and we need the extra firepower. I say we go get what we need and take them down a peg or two."

My mouth widened and I flexed my still healing leg muscles before deciding. "Then let's go play."

———

It wasn't long before we found ourselves on the outskirts of the city; the place was huge, and made one of the Malarna turtles seem small.

Wood and metal buildings rose to the heights of small city buildings, ten to eleven stories tall with glass windows that shimmered with different colors as the light shone on them. People walked the streets busily, their paths to their next destination slightly crowded as they fought to get to those destinations.

"Where are the goblins?" I asked softly as people milled about near us, waiting to gain entry into the city through a magical barrier of sorts.

"On this side, I think, but getting to them is going to take some ingenuity on my part." Merlin rolled his shoulders and nodded to Arden, then rolled up his sleeves. "Rocky."

Shimmering heat scorched the grass around us and it was a little hard to breathe for a moment while the stones on Merlin's wrist flexed and dropped onto the ground, growing until the stone fox shook itself out and looked up at him as if waiting for orders.

"We're digging our way into the city, Rocky." Merlin spoke softly but intently, until someone snickered and he looked up. "What?"

"You named a fox golem made of stone 'Rocky' and you expect us not to laugh?" Cassia raised an eyebrow at him in challenge and delight, which the boy just rolled his eyes at. "Carry on."

The earth in front of us caved in as the fox turned toward it, silently tunneling into the ground at an angle we could follow.

All of us moved to follow him and Merlin stayed until he was the last one outside the hole, the darkness falling over us as Merlin closed the hole. I used Wisp to light the tunnel for us as much as I could, but Arden snatched the flames out of my hand and snuffed them, muttering, "Oxygen use."

I mouthed, *Oh, good catch*, before realizing she probably couldn't see it. So we continued on down the hole as quickly as Rocky could dig us down.

It took a few minutes, but once we broke into an open area, we could breathe a little easier. Small, ghostly flames flickered inside glass globes glued to the walls a little higher than head height, casting shadows deeply all around us.

"This is as far as I can get us," Merlin muttered, the fox golem latching onto his wrist to become a bracelet of stone once more. "I figured out how far down the barrier went, and on which side the goblins would be, but I don't know much else unfortunately."

"You did well." I grasped his shoulder and smiled at him. "We really need to go over naming conventions though."

"Says the guy who named a goddess with stars all over her skin 'Galaxy,'" Arden teased, then quickly added, "No offense, Galaxy."

None taken, though I think it's a cute name. Her soft chuckle made me smile.

"She's okay with it," I grumbled, scratching my head. "I'll be honest, I have no idea what we're doing here."

"Think about this like visiting a city with the gear you need to move on to the new area on the map in a game," Arden explained with a grin. "Just before exploring, you need to gear up and make sure you've got the right shit. Goblins are some of the *best* creators of magical items in the worlds. You can't go wrong with their work."

"I could use a new staff." Merlin smiled wistfully.

"What about money, do they take cards?" I was trying to be only *slightly* sarcastic, but Cassia just chortled and pulled something out of her pocket that did—in fact—look like a card. "No fucking way, seriously?"

"It works differently than a normal card, but yeah, they take them." She rolled her eyes. "It's a magstripe card to get into my place in Japan. Of course they don't take cards. They like precious jewels and stones, plus other odds and ends that vary based on the goblin."

"And we have *plenty* of those from over the years." Arden grinned and laughed with her friend at my ignorance and just took it on the chin. I really would have to fix that sometime.

I knew that, but you didn't ask. Galaxy's smugness truly wasn't helpful.

Take this as an invitation to just tell me this shit whenever you think it pertinent to the situation at hand, okay?

Yes, mister surly-pants.

I rolled my eyes at her sassy attitude and just growled. "Let's get this over with. We need to get the mantle and get back to Earth so we can protect our people and keep Merlin safe from the Wardens." I glared down the tunnels and sighed. "Galaxy, can you map the tunnels for us?"

The cat that was Galaxy hopped out of my shadow and yowled long and hard for a few seconds before listening. When she was done, my map blurred and there was an outline of tunnels.

She took human form with a sigh and held her head. "That was a little rougher than I had planned." She shook herself a bit and muttered, "Once you close on a shop, you'll know based on a symbol what kind it will be. Merlin, I will be draining you often to restore myself and keep growing. Arden, you too. Keep drawing mana into yourselves and if you need mana, let me know so I can stop."

"Yes ma'am." Merlin bowed his head and turned left to begin walking off. "I think I smell them this way."

"That's a distracting scent, it misleads," Amabala offered quietly, then pointed the opposite way. "The scent is strongest this way."

He blinked at her distrusting, then snorted when she tapped her crinkled nose and winked at him. "Okay. Yes."

She walked us down the tunnel to the right, her ears flicking occasionally as she took deep breaths near the earthen walls. We hooked a left down a tunnel that turned into a set of stairs with a railway next to them on the right side and followed it down to an almost equally busy area beneath the earth as it had been above it.

There was a large circle above us about three hundred feet up that gave off a dim sort of light like a cloudy day, as well as a post with the same ghostly light bulbs every dozen feet or so. The place was crowded and lively, and it was easy to see that this was a melting pot of societies.

There were humans, dwarves, elves and even some other creatures here and there, yet there were cloaked figures moving through the crowds, people moving out of their way like they were riddled with the plague.

Merlin says those are Wardens, we need to be careful of them.

I nodded at Galaxy's warning before we made our way into the large underground trade district.

Several kinds of symbols popped into view and I gasped; a sword over a shield appeared over a stall in the distance. Not on my map, but physically above them in my sight.

"Anyone else seeing that?" I whispered to the others and they all nodded. "I'm giving you all kinds of burgers when we get back, Galaxy. You want pop, you fucking got it."

Her smug smile was triumphant and even Merlin grinned about that as we made our way forward.

Clothing popped into view off to my right, then something that looked like a ring after that. A staff or something on my left and further in. The displays coming into my view were wild.

"We should probably go look at clothes to hide ourselves," Arden suggested, heading toward the coat that hung above a building a little more than twenty feet away from us now.

I gave a brief tilt of my head and we moved through the crowd to the entrance and made our way inside. The store was well lit with the ghostly lights, and the colors of the clothes stood out in stark contrast to the light that was truly there.

"An enchantment on the table allows the viewer to see the colors as they are meant to be seen." A grave-sounding voice slithered across the room; a goblin strode toward all of us with a smile on his face. "Something similar to ward off on-lookers outside who might be curious or searching for someone whose faces adorn the walls outside this shop."

He held up a green hand as Arden opened her mouth. "I hold no love for the Wardens, their laws, or their wanted information. All I care for is this…" He held up one of the many cloaks draped on his tables, then the other hand where the thumb and a finger rubbed together in the universal sign for money. "And this. Provided you have the latter or something of equivalent value, I keep my trap shut, and you out of theirs, agreeable?"

"And who do we have the pleasure of being agreeable with?" Cassia asked softly, her eyes on our surroundings as opposed to the one she spoke to.

"I am Krixik, purveyor of pomp and protection for those wealthy enough to afford it." He grinned and added, "Among other things."

"We need clothes that will help us blend in, as well as some gear that will protect us from the Fel." Krixik's jaw dropped, making me frown. "What's wrong?"

"The first I can do without issue, but why would one want to go in *there*?" He stared at all of us for a moment, but when we didn't answer or offer any information, his disbelief only grew and then became a knowing scowl. "Fine, keep your secrets. I have some things, but they would be more suited toward hiding and blending in rather than true protection. You'll want Flippet's Fine Fancies for trinkets that can protect you. Or armor from Mortet's Portents of Protection if you're feeling especially rich and under prepared."

The name of the last one was odd, but that was still okay.

"Blending in would be nice for now." I nodded at him, his ears waggling as he nodded his head and began to sift through some of his wares before piling clothes onto the counter behind him.

"These will manage for that, standing still allows you to blend with your surroundings and even while moving you'll be much harder to notice, and it nullifies all but the briefest inter-actions with your scent." He pointed as if counting to each of us. "That will run you about thirty pieces."

Arden flew into a fit of haggling like nothing I had ever seen before. She pulled him down to twenty-five but that was as low as he would go for her.

I don't understand why you don't just steal what you need, but having all of the goblins on your side, or at least amicable, would be good. Galaxy's observation was true. Would there be something that I could take if we couldn't afford it?

I resolved to keep an eye out; stealing wasn't honest, but this guy wasn't either and gear adrift was a gift in the Marine Corps. So fuck this guy.

We ended up getting the cloaks, then put them on before we left, as Krixik explained, "The hood has to be up and covering your face to work its magic and it wears off after an hour and will recharge on its own."

Arden looked like she was about to explode, but he just pointed to a sign that stated, "All sales final."

I grimaced and looked at her as she muttered, "We should have gotten them for even less if that was the case. A normal one would be about that much, but last six hours before needing to recharge."

"So he fucked us?" She nodded and I turned around, only to walk into Merlin who smiled at me. "What? I'm going back to get our money's worth."

He held up the sack that had held our money in front of him so it wasn't visible to anyone but us. "You mean this?"

I punched his shoulder. "Good man!"

He winked and I turned around to head with him into the accessories shop. Arden spoke to the small goblin woman who nodded and waved us to the back of the shop. The whole place could have been a store on Earth for all it seemed to me. Mannequins and fake hands and necks held and displayed jewelry of all shapes, sizes, and varieties.

The items on display in front of you are all garbage, enchanted sure, but the good stuff is in the display behind you. The others will distract her while you move; I'll point out some items I think you'll like.

I backed up and acted like I was interested in a pendant as the others filled the gap in and distracted the woman. Once they were there, I stepped over to the display that wasn't nearly as glamorous.

"I see that you know the real deal when you see it," a soft voice said.

I glanced up and on the other side of the case leaned the same goblin woman with soft purple hair.

The others were still talking to someone and she chuckled throatily. "That's a simulacrum that I made, helps me test people."

"Why test people and waste their time?"

Her counter: "Why not test them so I don't waste mine?" She smiled as I let my own soft smirk take over my face. "I see you know what I mean. Tell me, what is it you need?"

"I don't rightly know, but we will be going into the Forest of the Fel."

She gasped softly, eyes wide as she stared at me. She tilted her head and narrowed her gaze. "Hunting?"

I nodded, happy to let her think what she wanted. She nodded to herself and pulled out several accessories that made me frown. The rings looked normal enough, but from Galaxy's intake of them by touching them herself, it was apparent that they were far from it.

"This ring will give a Touched access to more mana." She tapped one with a small skull on it. "This one will keep you safe from dying, just once. These glasses will let you pierce the dense vegetation."

"Anything that will increase the damage of a spell?" She shook her head at me and I frowned. *That sucks. Though increased mana would be nice.* "You going to make me haggle for a good price on the mana ring?"

"No, I hate haggling. My price is thirty pieces for it." I whistled low and she nodded sagely. "I guarantee that you will not be dissatisfied."

"Would you mind if I tried it on?" She motioned that I could and I slipped it on my pinky finger. Immediately, my Mana shot up from 25 to 30, giving me 300 mana to sling spells with. "Oh, that's very nice indeed."

"I told you so is never far from my tongue." She grinned and her sharp teeth unsettled me slightly. "The death ward is triple that and the glasses I could part with for… five pieces?"

Merlin wordlessly joined me, passing me the pieces we saved from not having paid Krixik, and said, "For the mana ring."

She took the bag and smiled. "You want something to make your magic stronger?"

I could drain her here and now and we could have it all. Unleash me, Marcus. Galaxy's urgency made me grimace.

We aren't murderhobos, Galaxy, we don't just kill at random. I stared at the woman. "What did you have in mind?"

"There's a man who sells wands, staves, and scepters behind my shop." She glanced at my friends and stared intently. "I know that a few of them are magic users, not uncommon for some of them, especially the Wardenling there, but the Oni? Very odd."

"And you would take us to this man?" I raised an eyebrow at her and she smiled.

"He's my husband, of course I would, though discretion is an absolute must." I sent a call through Galaxy to the others to turn around and join us. The goblin's eyes widened. "Are you all connected somehow?"

"Something like that." I grinned at her and she just motioned for the simulacrum to mind the store.

She led us through the small entry to the storage room in back and then beyond that to a rather large alley where there was a workshop with wood all over the place around us.

"Obrin?" the goblin seller called and one of the piles of wood shifted, a larger goblin sitting up from beneath it. "You fell asleep again?"

"You keep me enchanting incessantly, woman!" he hissed at her, squinting. "Who are these assholes?"

I blinked. *I like this guy.* "We're potential customers."

"I don't take *potential customers*, human." He turned to glare at his wife. "Zilda, you promised to only bring serious mages here, and not interrupt my sleep. Do you want a divorce, woman?"

"You can sleep anytime, you little troll!" She actually threw a thick board at him, hitting him in the head and making him sit up straighter as she pointed to me and Merlin. "These two are Touched with mana above their tier, and the boy is stronger than the other. They would benefit from your work."

He looked disinterested still, but then she added, "They're going to the Fel too."

He blinked and stood up, throwing his hands into the air. "Why didn't you say so to begin with, you old biddy!"

She hefted a branch twice her size and stalked toward him only to be stopped by an invisible wall.

"Don't bother me, woman, I'm working!"

"I'll work *you!*" she howled in return and began to bang on the wall with the branch as Cassia watched and chuckled appreciatively. She tired herself out as her husband gathered his tools and tossed the branch aside. "See if you get any dinner tonight, you... you...!"

She threw her hands up in the air and turned to walk away

as he shouted, "I'm an asshole!" She turned and nodded at him. "I'm a hungry asshole. Can we have tuna casserole?"

She tapped her finger on her chin and finally said, "No," then stormed off.

Obrin grinned, and pumped his arm excitedly, whispering, "Yes!"

"I heard that!" she shouted back, and he swore mercilessly before turning his emerald gaze on us. "You two, mages. What kind of weapons were you looking for?"

"I'm partial to a staff, but have begun to take training with the sword, so a smaller scepter would work," Merlin answered with a curious glance at the area around him, the workshop in a state of having never really been built in the first place.

I couldn't even find a work bench.

The goblin reached out and touched the boy's hand, taking it in both of his before he grunted. "Sword and staff? Bah, kids these days—so indecisive!"

Merlin just sputtered noiselessly as the goblin sifted through piles of what looked like junk wood and sticks until he pulled something out and lifted it high into the air. "There we go."

Obrin turned and brought the three-foot stick to Merlin and held it out to him. "Touch it, and give it a *little* juice. If it don't work at first stop."

Merlin did as Obrin asked, closing his eyes as he grasped the wood. A soft amber glow emanated from the top and the goblin frowned. "Nope, not it."

"It felt great!" Merlin protested and Obrin just waved him away. "Seriously, it did!"

"Of course it did!" Obrin snapped and shook the item at him. "You gave it a trickle and it glowed amber. Imagine if you fed it a real spell? It would be like shoving a watermelon into a garden hose. Some goes in, the hose gets clogged—you get dead and magic shrapnel in your friends. You done telling me how to do my damn job, kid?"

"Hey, woah," I growled and stepped forward. "He doesn't know any better."

"And neither do you, so shut your trap, unless you want to pay more or not get anything." He eyed me for a moment. "Muscles, calluses on the hands and the knives on your person, you're a fighter too. Let me guess, you want a scepter?"

"I don't know what I want, other than for you to not be as surly with us as you are with your wife." I crossed my arms and stared at him evenly.

He laughed, a coughing sound of sorts, then slapped his knee. "You're funny, kid. I like you. That stuff with Zilda? That was just us sweet talking each other. Gimme a minute, and just let me do my job, okay?"

He turned to Merlin. "Amber glow at a trickle is like a steam gauge in the red when a machine is off. It ain't good, feel me? So giving you that because it felt good, would kill you. Ease it down, I've forgotten about more magic items than you've ever held, got it?"

Merlin nodded once and the goblin turned toward another pile, rooting around in it for a minute before throwing a long, gnarled piece of staff toward me, then went to another pile and started digging. I stepped closer to look at the weapon and found myself reaching for it, when Obrin called, "You touch that, and I'll kick you so hard, your babies'll be prettier."

I snorted and he chuckled and I stood back up from where I was. *I really like this guy.*

You are so weird. Galaxy sighed and rolled her eyes in my head.

Eventually the goblin found what he was looking for and when Merlin used mana to charge the scepter, the glow was green and dull. "Good. That's what we want. Good color on that one there."

"What's the point of the staves, scepters, and wands, again?" Amabala asked politely.

The goblin stepped closer to me as I stood there and spoke in a low tone as he grabbed my hand. "They're meant to act as a focus, channeling power and magic through their cores and the runes on them to enhance spells or the caster's intent."

He held out a hand and a muted pop made us all flinch as a thick stump at the end of the alley rose into the air and began to sway forward slowly.

"Without a focus, I waste precious mana on keeping the stump steady and moving slowly toward me." He stopped and the stump crashed to the ground. He produced a staff nearly twice his height and tipped it slightly toward the same stump.

This time it rocketed toward him and stopped, as if time itself couldn't have been bothered to register for the thing.

He grinned, his long, pointed ears reddening a little from the attention. "I used a little more than I should have for that, but you get the idea, right?"

Amabala nodded silently and watched as he went back to examining me. "You look like you're used to different kinds of weapons. Got calluses alright, but the way you carry yourself is different. Soldierly, even."

"I'm a Marine." I offered to him and he just snorted. "Got a problem with that?"

"My old man was a goblin who fought with the allies in World War One on naval vessels. Kept them tip top and firing magic ammo, not that he would've been celebrated, but the Navy is where my loyalties lay." He grinned up at me and I just hit with one of my own. "Glad to meet another of your kind, boy. Let's get you something nice, huh?"

He spent some time looking through piles of things before finally deciding on two scepters and a staff.

The staff took my mana easily and a soft green glow emanated from it, which made him smile. "Good fit. Better than the kid's scepter. Try these on for size."

He held out the first scepter and I fed a little mana into it and it glowed red. "Jesus, kid, throw it!"

I did as he ordered and both he and Merlin whipped their magical instruments into position just as the scepter cracked and burst.

A muffled *whoomph* came from inside a small barrier, that shattered only to be caught against the inside of a slightly larger one. Obrin glanced sideways at Merlin. "Good thinking, for a Wardenling."

"I'll take that compliment." Merlin grinned back cheerfully and stared at his new scepter, no doubt appreciating the strength it allowed him.

Obrin turned back to me and carefully offered me the remaining scepter. This one glowed amber and he snatched it out of my hand as I muttered, "Think I'll stick to the staff."

He nodded and glanced at the ladies behind us. "I sense magic from one of you—all of you, really—but it isn't necessarily battle magic that will translate well to what I do, I'm sorry."

"Can you make weapons that will take an enchantment?" Cassia asked politely. "I know that you can enchant things. What if you made it so that my stick would transfer a spell, or convey elemental damage for me?"

He scratched his green chin before saying, "I could try for a minor spell, maybe. But you would have to demonstrate it, and the weapon would need to be of a decent quality."

"It's Oni-made, it's of fantastic quality." She pulled out the long mace she carried and set it in front of her. "And the spell is called Earth Spike."

She held her hand out in front of her and a spike of pure stone shot from her body and into the ground between her feet, where the projectile pierced the street and crumbled to dust.

"Interesting spell for an Oni to have." Obrin frowned at her for a moment, then shrugged and shook his head. "I suppose I could do something like that. Give me a minute to get the item engraved and we can take a look at anything else."

It took him half an hour to get the engravings just right, then he had Cassia help him embed the spell within it. Not so that the spell would be cast by the weapon itself, but through it. It would cost her a little more mana to use Earth Spike through the massive weapon.

I could imagine it would suck on the receiving end of that attack though.

Obrin wiped some sweat off his forehead and grinned, shoving the weapon toward her. "Done. Gonna cost a pretty penny." He held up three fingers and winked. "Two hundred."

Merlin frowned. "That's insanely steep." Even Cassia and Arden nodded their heads in agreement. "I doubt we have that on hand."

"I'm not my wife, I'll haggle, but you better be good, because it can go up to three hundred." He crossed his arms as if daring us to challenge him.

"You do a military discount?" I tried with a goofy smile and he snickered.

"Yeah, okay." He closed his eyes and muttered something before saying, "One eighty."

I snorted, "Ten percent, gotcha." Shaking my head, I glanced at him and asked politely, "Take about another ten off if I give you something nice?"

"We'll see if I like it or not." He still had his arms crossed as I stepped closer to Merlin.

The young mage watched me curiously but I just said, "Going to need a bottle of pop."

"What?" His sudden change in volume made the others close in on us. "Marcus, come on, I only have like, five left! And who knows how long we'll be here?"

"Galaxy won't give me any of hers, I can just feel it, and we don't want to spend that much scratch, do we?" I held my hand out and he just snarled before pressing a bottle of Pepsi into my palm. "Thank you."

I turned around and offered Obrin the bottle, he stared at it skeptically and sneered. "You offering me shit water, Devil?"

I snorted. "Nothing from Twenty-Nine Palms here, Obrin." I twisted the top and passed the drink under his nose.

"It smells... spicy." I raised an eyebrow at him and he just snatched it out of my hand to smell again. He leered at us distrustfully before taking a small sip, closing his eyes. "It tastes like liquid lightning, what *is* this?"

He could barely keep his eyes off the bottle, muttering the

word "Peepsee" under his breath before he went absolutely wild. He tipped the bottle into his gullet and swallowed the contents greedily before he closed his eyes. "Yummy."

"We can tell you where to get more of it, big gallon bottles of the stuff, if you'll give us a good deal." I spoke sweetly, but he was still ingesting the caffeine of it all. He opened his eyes, the irises huge like a cat's in the dark, then sprang toward a massive pile of wood and began to work on creating something.

We tried in vain to get his attention but he was hyper focused on what he was making until finally he fit the empty bottle into a wood receptacle. He carved a few symbols around it and spoke a word and the bottle began to refill on its own!

Merlin gasped in awe and damn-near shouted, "You have to teach me that!"

Obrin whipped around. "Fool! It only works so many times. I need more."

Great, Marcus, you've created an addict of your own, Galaxy purred at me ironically.

If you could drink Dr. Pepper where you are inside me, you would, so who are you to speak about addictions? I heard the distinct hiss of a bottle being opened and rolled my eyes. *Of course.*

"So, we have a deal, Obrin?" It was so hard to keep my voice and face neutral.

He scowled at me and stalked toward me until his chin was nearly poking into my navel. "You tell me where to find more, or bring me more yourself, and I'll do miracles for you, boy."

I reached down and offered him my hand, pulling it back as he was about to clasp it, adding, "With a good discount today for the gear?"

"Drive a hard bargain, but yes." He snatched my hand and shook it as he said, "A hundred pieces."

"Done," Cassia barked and smiled, a purse appearing in her grasp. She shifted it a few times and tossed it to the goblin.

He turned toward the bottle still in the receptacle and touched it nearly lovingly. "No one can tell my wife of this."

"She'll drink it, won't she?"

He nodded then froze, turning to find his wife having been the one to say the last sentence. "Don't drink it, my love."

"I think I'm entitled to a taste, seeing as though your work is being given nearly for half." She stepped closer and Obrin just placed himself in the middle.

Galaxy, you might need to share some of your pop to keep the peace. I watched as Zilda closed the distance between her and her husband's prize slowly.

I think not. They can share. I rolled my eyes and vowed that her pop drinking days were numbered. *I can let you die, you know.*

You wouldn't, you love me too much.

She stilled in me and remained quiet but the couple before us had begun to really bicker and argue.

"Merlin, gimme another bottle." He gave me a pained look that said I was killing him and he just handed me a Sprite. I raised an eyebrow at him and he just shook his head and moved away from me, lest I take his soul or something. Poor kid.

"Zilda, here, a gift for you." I offered her the bottle of Sprite and she took it, smelling it as her husband had. I noticed the look of jealousy that ranged over his face as she removed the lid and tasted it.

"Ah, yes, lemon and something... *more*. Refreshing." She sighed and belched loudly enough that it made her husband nearly fall over with laughter. "That's odd."

"Carbonation is like that." I smiled and she nodded as if I had offered sage advice. "I think we should probably take our leave before the Wardens realize that we're here."

Obrin turned and stared at me. "No time frame, but we have a deal that I expect to be honored, understand?"

I nodded once and he nodded back. We would keep our word.

He pulled out a smaller stick and tossed it to me. I caught it and it began to glow a steady green. The goblin waved his hand over it and a candle appeared on his desk—which was really just an overturned trash can—the flame of it burning a deep green to match the glow at the tip. "You keep that on you, and if anything happens, the candle will go out. That way I know if you're in trouble, or worse."

"You going to send in the cavalry?" I raised an eyebrow at him and he just snorted. "Then what's it for?"

"To know if I have to find a way to get more peepshee myself or not, boy." His toothy grin made me snort, so I reached down and shook his hand one last time before we walked through the back door and into the shop.

Someone was picking through some of the accessories in front of the simulacrum, who waved to us as we left. I couldn't tell who they were due to a cloak of their own, but they seemed only minutely interested in the wares.

We walked out into the crowded walkways and watched as the people around us seemed to step away for a few seconds, then back in. Weird.

We put up our hoods and marched with the crowd until we got to the point where we could take an elevator of sorts that lifted onto a street in the sunlight. The warmth of the rays hitting the cloak nearly made me want to take off my hood, but it was Arden who stopped me. "We're being followed."

I blinked at her, and just said, "And?" She seemed surprised. "The guy looking through stuff in the store wasn't all that subtle about leaving mid-sentence to follow behind us, and isn't exactly the best tail either. Some of the kids in theater were better at it than they are."

I turned and casually glanced back at our pursuer who made no effort to hide that they were coming after us, shoving people aside and walking faster and faster. I turned back to Arden and said, "I'd be more surprised if he wasn't a plant to make us try to lose him only to walk into a trap."

"So what should we do?" Merlin asked quietly as we continued on.

"Ignore him and anyone else until we get out of the city for now. Keep an eye out for anyone suspicious and if you see anything, say something." I cast my gaze around, for the first time really taking in the aspects of the city as they should have been.

The buildings were all made of stone and well built. Some of them were squat and seemed stacked on top of each other rather closely, but when the majority of the population was capable of using magic to some degree, the idea that a fire might run rampant just wasn't a major concern for anyone in particular.

People tried to sell all sorts of things, from trinkets to full on animals that made Galaxy salivate within me. I was half tempted to buy one of the fiery-looking birds but figured something that hot wouldn't agree with me.

We came to the exit of the city and found that there was a line to get out. "That's one way to limit our escape route," Cassia grumbled as she looked around the line to the guards checking people at the gate before they left. "Checking everyone; they must have been tipped off."

"I was wondering when you would see that I was trying to get your attention," a soft voice growled behind us.

I turned and grabbed the speaker by their cloak, hauling them bodily into the alley near where we stood and spoke quietly, but with force, "So this was what you wanted, to lure us into a trap?"

He pulled his hood down and revealed that he wasn't human at all. His face was furred and looked like that of an ape, his brown eyes seemed spiteful, but not in a way that meant harm. "You're pulling my fur, and I'd appreciate you letting go."

I let go, but the others fanned out around us, Amabala leaning up against the wall next to the entrance to the alley where she faced outward as a watcher.

"I was trying to catch up to you without calling out. I was sent here to guide you out of the city if the Wardens or other parties got too heavily involved." The monkey person sighed heavily and glanced toward the other end of the alley. "And they're all on the move."

"Who are these 'other parties'?" Cassia growled low, her teeth starting to lengthen.

"Parties interested in obtaining the power of the Huntsman." He looked up and began to scent the air.

"How did you know that we would be here?" Arden asked as she stared at him.

He shook his head. "We didn't. We're everywhere, and our boss is highly connected. We go where they tell us to, and we watch for what they tell us to."

"How did you find us then?" He didn't answer me, but rather looked directly at me. "So you're tracking me? How?"

He didn't mind the fact that I was closer to him now, but he just took the time to take a deep whiff of the skin near my neck. "Scent. My kind are bounty hunters who use magic to augment their tracking abilities."

"That's not something that you would want someone who is an enemy to know," Amabala purred back toward us. "I should know."

"I don't care if you trust me or not." He paused as his ears twitched, then he sighed. "I'm here to fulfill a contract, so if you'll follow me, I'll get you out of the city."

"We don't even know who you are," Merlin hissed, his sword leveled at the monkey-man's neck.

"And you'll continue to be in the dark, because I don't care—follow me." He moved out from under the blade in a motion that was hard to follow, then walked us down the alley opposite where we had come into it.

We stuck close to him, but not so close to him that we couldn't get away if needed. He led us out and down another alley across the street, then into a larger building that could have been a warehouse.

What is it with my life recently that leads me into so many damned warehouses and old factories? I complained to myself.

Seems like magic has a way of drawing the best out of those places. Galaxy stretched within me and made her presence known in my mind once more. *Plus, they're a good place to hide things in plain sight.*

We moved through the towering piles of goods, some of the boxes wooden and thick, the others cardboard, but the cool thing was that in the center of the room was a circle one would expect to see in some kind of occult film.

"Walk through this, and it will make you invisible to the barrier." The monkey man stepped through it and though I couldn't really see what happened, I could focus and see that the aura that had been glowing a slight orange around him before was now completely clear.

I can't see his aura, I told Galaxy so that she would let the others know, then stepped through the circle.

It was like stepping through some kind of aural car wash; the warmth of it radiated around me, then through my aura and I felt pure. Which was weird for some reason.

"It takes getting used to, and doesn't last too long, so if we could move along?" Monkey-man tapped his wrist like a guy late for a meeting.

The others piled through the circle and we were on our way once more, through a doorway into a closed alley where we moved a massive box then opened a hatch that led us down about twelve feet into a dimly lit corridor.

"This leads us outside?" I asked skeptically, thinking of using Wisp to burn away some of the cobwebs that hung in the corners near my head.

"Straight through the barrier, yeah." He turned and whispered, "Whatever you do, don't use magic. It will muddy your aura and make it so the barrier can see you."

Galaxy whispered for me, *Those don't sound like the famous last words of the guy who's leading us into a trap or anything.*

I had to fight not to laugh at that. It was so much worse when I could feel how proud she was that she had made a funny, and I snorted a little bit.

The monkey man turned and eyed me. "Something funny?"

"Just trying to make sure spiders don't shit on me." I tried to make it seem earnest but he wasn't convinced and just growled as he moved on.

We walked for ten minutes before coming to a hollow in the earth where the barrier dipped down and inward like a bubble. The barrier was thick and while we watched, our guide stepped through it. Nothing happened to him, so I guessed that it was okay to do the same. I passed through, getting the sensation of walking through cellophane but it wasn't any more uncomfortable than that.

On the other side, I watched as the others crossed over, their apparent discomfort more comforting than my own had been. After that, he led us on down the earthen tunnel until there was a slow rise that led us to an opening in the ground that he propped up. Once he was outside, he held it open for us, so we could get out without hitting our heads.

Once all of us were free of the hole in the earth, he dropped the opening's lid and turned to us. "My job is done." He turned back, opened the door, and shouted, "Have fun!"

With that, we turned toward the Forest of Fel Tidings in the distance and started off.

Or at least we wanted to, but the dozen or so people who stripped cloaks of invisibility of some sort off themselves kind of stood in our way.

"Hey, criminals." One of the younger ones that I recognized from the convenience store greeted me. His Mohawk was green now and he leaned on his sword like it was a cane. He grabbed his neck and cracked it like it was stiff. "You know, that sneaky shit wasn't nice last time. You know that, right?"

CHAPTER NINETEEN

For the first time in a while, I felt like I was alive as I sneered back. "You know that sneaky shit last time was so that we wouldn't kill you, right?"

He lifted an eyebrow and allowed his head to tilt to the point that his ear could have rested on his free shoulder. His sword was a thick thing at the base that slowly tapered up to a box point four feet later. It looked more like a greatsword than any other kind of sword, but it was pretty to him it seemed. "You were worried about killing us?"

"I wasn't—no, not me." I jerked my thumb to where Merlin stood, his sword in his right hand and left hand open in front of him at the ready. "He was. See, he seems to have this idea that if he seriously injures, maims, or kills one of you, the others won't want to have him in their Orders at all."

The Wardens all chuckled darkly, one of them even going so far as to say, "That's why you don't belong with us in the first place—Sword only cares about strength and being the best."

Merlin actually sighed and called to him, "You really shouldn't have said that." The guy laughed, but by then it was already far too late.

Cassia reared up from behind him like the ghost of past mistakes, a leviathan of hatred and violence from the depths of having been told to take it easy on these punkasses.

And she had just been released.

Cassia snarled and swiped her mace at the kid's head, knocking the now-flying thing into the Warden next to him.

"Merlin, you heard them—make us proud." I had to fight to keep the grim joy out of my tone, but I knew the Mohawk kid would likely come at me. I didn't bother calling my Oni sword out of my inventory for this, opting to just cast Blade and move forward to meet his sword as it crashed toward me.

We collided and rather than just taking the brunt of the attack, I allowed it to slide down my spell sword and twisted my body so I could swing my elbow at his head.

He ducked it and laughed. "Not too bad, old man!"

"I'm barely thirty, you little shit." I growled and twisted the sword in my grasp and stabbed at his stomach, but he threw himself backward and away from me.

One of his friends roared and tried to rush me, but Amabala was suddenly there and tackled him, her claws sliding into his flesh painfully as Merlin loomed over her with his sword slashing down at her struggling victim.

Cassia and Arden kept the others more than busy and it was purely because they just didn't have the experience to take on an overpowered Oni and a pissed off jinn whose spells were hopelessly stronger than theirs.

I pulled my Oni blade out, having been a little more used to fighting with it and kept it in my left hand, then cast Embodiment of Lightning on myself to rush Mohawk. To his credit, he reacted instantly, turning in a one-eighty to lash out with his sword, but I didn't stay standing tall. I ducked low and whipped my small blade up into his guard toward his stomach.

He dropped his elbow and took the knife to the forearm before he twisted his wrist and brought his sword's razor edge toward my knees. I rolled backward, hopping up onto my feet and lunging forward with my sword held straight.

He parried that easily but I just grinned as his sword chopped toward my shoulder. I twisted at the waist and hopped into a spinning back kick that should have caught him in the chest and shoulder, then took a boot straight to the back of the head.

The kid laughed as I spat out grass, not even bothering to take advantage of his apparent opportunity. He took my blade from his forearm and tossed it to the ground as he stared at me. "I learn from my mistakes, old man, not that you will."

I rolled my eyes and climbed to my feet. "Fine. You want me to learn from my mistakes? Got it."

My body blurred as I cast Embodiment once more, the little bastard whipping his sword under his arm to slash upward and not even bothering to turn around. Instead of popping out behind him, I stood in front of him and the random Bolt hit him in the chest the same time I used Frost to cover my fingers in sharp claws to slash him with. His skin split under my attack, his body jerking with the bolt.

He recovered quickly and I piled on the Frost. I froze his feet to the ground and continued to slash at him, his body shivering as I attacked with my mana and raw rage. My Blade lashed out and blood splattered against his feet, freezing and adding to the ice around his ankles as he fell backward.

I kicked him in the face twice, his head bouncing off the ground as I fell into the little area of cold and went to finish things. His sword came up toward me and I slapped it aside with my frozen palm, then slid the Blade in my right hand into his stomach. The blood froze against the raw mana and solidified it slightly. If I wasn't so focused on teaching the kid a lesson, I'd have been interested in it.

But he needed to learn something in his final moments.

Cold drifted off me in waves, but I was fine. His teeth chattered, clacking as the fear and realization set in. Good.

Anyone still alive in the area that was with him would see his fall and we would rise victorious.

We? I blinked and shook my head. That wasn't right.

I hesitated long enough that the kid was able to break one of his earrings with his fist and disappeared into a rift. I snarled angrily and stabbed the ground with my sword, then realized that he had left something. Something that I was certain the little fucker would miss.

I took the hilt of his sword into my hand and lifted it easily. Despite being massive, it was lighter than I expected. I put it into my inventory and just sighed, upset.

"That was more fruitful than I had imagined it would be." Cassia exhaled, clapping her hands as if trying to get the dirt off them. "Where's their little leader?"

"He got away, teleported." Amabala watched me carefully. "You hesitated for a moment, and I've seen you do some brutal things. You okay?"

I nodded, uncertain as to how to voice my concern without sounding insane. *So that you know, I wasn't privy to that thought. I think something else is at work here, and I will help you figure out what it is.*

Thanks, Galaxy. I turned to the aftermath of the fight. Three of the Wardens hung from six-foot-tall spikes that rose from the ground in various painful ways. Four were burnt and smoking on the ground. The others lay on the ground in a few differing states of dismemberment and disembowelment.

I blinked at them and felt numb. "Take what you can from their corpses, rings, everything that could be used to identify them. Galaxy will take care of the evidence."

I walked away from the group as they worked, Galaxy having stepped from my shadow in cat form to begin her work. I stood alone and stared into the plains between us and the forest in the distance. Surprisingly, it wasn't too far. We could reach the tree line likely by this evening if we hoofed it at a good click.

"He's going to come after you, you know." Merlin spoke to me in a low tone of voice that I didn't find grating, wrecking my solace.

"I figured, seeing as I have his sword." I bent down to

collect my discarded blade, wiping it on the grass before sheathing it. I'd clean it better later.

"That's not it," Merlin corrected me, so I glanced over at him. He was bleeding a little from a cut under his right eye, and had a few slices on his arms from defending himself. "You kicked his ass. You had him dead to rights and all he could do was watch as you were about to kill him. He's seen nothing like you before, and he's going to hunt you down and kill you so he can feel safe again."

I blinked at him, uncertain how to take that information or how he had come up with it in the first place, but his steady gaze eye to eye with me gave me some insight.

Merlin felt the same way. "You want to kill all of them, despite having to work with them to achieve your goals." He nodded once, jaw set. "And now that the flood gates have been opened, you don't know if you'll be safe stopping."

He grimaced and looked away before saying, "I worry that if I stop, the Staff will come down on me and I'll be retrained. That if I do continue to work with them, they'll get to me when I'm not with the rest of you, and try to put me back under their thumb."

"That ain't gonna happen, kiddo." I grasped his shoulder and smiled at him comfortingly. "You'll be way too strong for them to deal with."

Cassia, Arden, and Amabala came back with a small haul of swords, slightly magicked rings, and even a nice earring that I was certain might be of a similar make to the one that Mohawk used. "Anything good?"

They shook their heads but Amabala held up two small, wickedly curved knives. "Can I have these?"

"Absolutely, you can." Cassia smiled and patted her on the shoulder with a grin on her face. "I saw you fighting back there, that was something. We need to fight sometime soon."

I blinked at her and watched the joy on Amabala's face grow. "You think so?"

"I know so." Cassia patted her again, a little harder this

time, rough enough to make the smaller woman stumble a bit. "You'll be a very capable fighter by the time I finish with you."

"Or she'll be dead. Either way." Arden snickered and Cass just grinned, Amabala's joy fading as she tried to figure out what was going on.

"Once Galaxy is finished with the bodies, we need to get moving." I peered behind us toward the city and found what I had dreaded to really think about happening. Bodies poured out of the entrance, high-tailing it toward us. "Scratch that—we're going now."

"This had to have been a set up!" Cassia growled as she readied herself to fight.

Arden locked her left arm around the Oni's throat and snarled, "It likely was, but we can't take on fifty fucking Wardens or trainees—we have to go now!" She twisted and turned so that she faced the forest and began to move as Cass struggled.

I grabbed her arm and said, "Now's not the time to be heroic, there's likely more coming."

We hadn't made it far when the first volley of spells came hurtling through the air at us. The ground exploded slightly to my left, a crater forming instantly and I had to fight to keep my footing.

"I have the shield, but we need to stick close!" Merlin grabbed my shoulder and looked back in time to catch a fireball on his shield spell.

"Arden, cover fire for us if you can!" I turned my sights forward and focused on keeping Merlin moving steadily forward. Cassia had nothing she could do at this distance but keep moving as well, and I could tell it pissed her off to no end.

"I knew I should have learned to wield the bow!" She gnashed her teeth, a bolt of lightning crashing into the ground, clipping her as she ran by. "Damn it, come here, Merlin."

She didn't wait, turning to grab the boy mage, cradling him to her chest so that his legs almost wrapped around her massive waist. "Keep that shield steady!"

She ducked her head under his arm so she could see well enough not to trip. A wave of roiling heat left us cold for a moment as the oxygen in our immediate vicinity burned away, Arden having sent a gout of flame flying back at the enemy.

A resounding crash and the screams of Wardens dying made me smile grimly. At least it worked.

And since they have souls, I'm collecting experience for you all too.

"Even better," I muttered out loud. The others didn't bother trying to figure out what I had said and just kept running.

We sprinted all out for as long as we could without a break, leaving the majority of the Wardens well and truly far behind, but there was no way we could rest without at least some of them catching up to us. We had to push on.

"What I wouldn't give to be back at the High Table with a few dozen shots of something strong and some music!" Arden screamed and launched another nuke of a fireball. The screams this time weren't as numerous but it was still nice to know she wasn't tiring herself for no reason.

"Same!" I bellowed and jumped over a small log where a little snake hid. "Fucking snakes!"

This one reared and somehow a Warden sprang out of nowhere and tried to whack me with a staff. "How the fu—" His staff missed my shoulder by a centimeter yet my left arm immediately went numb.

He would have said something, but instead he yelped and glanced down at the snake that bit his ankle and slowly grew to a much less manageable size as the kid yelled, "Mommy!"

"What the hell is with this place and snakes!" I spat angrily, my eyes scanning the ground before my feet as carefully as I dared allow.

"That was a little titan, and they are not to be trifled with!" Amabala explained from where she ran ahead of us. "They can grow to almost indeterminate sizes to consume their prey."

"So, what, that thing could eat a dragon?" I huffed and she just nodded. "Fuck!"

"Shut your mouths and run!" Cassia howled and tried to

move faster, only to fall with Merlin windmilling from her as she went down.

We all skidded to a halt around her, turning to be sure there was no danger apparent to us. Nothing reached out to grab us, and the majority of the Wardens were too distracted by the little titan snake to care about us.

We had to act fast. "Arden, throw up a wide haze in front of us." I turned to Merlin. "And you, dig us a little grotto or hole we can hide in."

"What about them?" Merlin waved to the Wardens as they fought the snake. "They won't believe that we are gone without a reason."

"They'll have one." I pointed to Amabala. "Once we're underground, Arden is going to make it look like we're going into a portal that she makes."

"That's a waste of a portal," Cassia hissed as she sat up, her ankle twisted the wrong way. "That's not good."

"Exactly." I clapped twice and set about helping Merlin move dirt out of the way by hand.

Once we were good and had a decent hole in the ground, we put Cass down in it and we all joined her. "Cover us with enough earth up top to make the ground stable enough for about six people or so to stand on. Use pillars to support it if you have to."

"You have no intention of hiding, do you?" Cassia muttered with a careful look on her face.

I shook my head. "No. They tried to kill us and they need to pay. Plus, we can't be constantly worrying about those assholes in the forest when we will have everything in there trying to kill and eat us."

She grabbed my chin and pulled me close, butting her forehead and horn against my head affectionately. "You would make a terrible and powerful Oni, Marcus Massacre."

I grinned at her and whispered, "Thank you?"

She nodded. "It was a compliment." She kissed me softly before adding, "We will scrap later."

I chuckled darkly and winked at her before I pulled my Oni sword out, then decided that I wanted to try wielding Mohawk's sword too.

I put the old sword in my left hand and worked on getting used to the feel of both of them, then decided that I would need to be stealthier for this. Back into inventory they went, my Oni blade in my hand once more. Familiar, tried and true.

"Galaxy, put the enemies that Merlin and Rocky can feel above us on my mini map." I heard her assent and stared upward in the dark as I waited.

Checking my mana, I still had *211/300,* and I could see that my mana had recovered a point. Nice.

Running and regaining mana on the go like that is hard, and a lot of creatures cannot manage it. Even Merlin and Arden cannot. That you got a single point is odd.

I sniffed and watched as a soft drizzle of dirt dropped in front of my face, the ground sort of bowing above.

A small pillar of earth and stone rose to support the ground above our hole, then another. And another. Finally, a fourth shot from the ground and I grabbed the lip of it to rise along with it. Once I was almost to the ceiling, I slammed my free hand, blade and all, into the earth and pushed against the pillar toward one of the orange dots that had been above us.

My arms wrapped around their waist, the force of my accidental tackle knocking them to the ground as my blade slid home in their chest.

"There!" someone shouted before they began working their way through an incantation of some kind.

I rolled as something thudded into the body where I had been, and oriented myself as something small burst from the ground where I had come from. Amabala spread out and as soon as her feet touched the grass, she was a blur.

Her wicked daggers lashed out, slashing and stabbing at the Warden's arms and legs, anything she could reach. She was moving too fast to do substantial damage, so I moved in on my next target.

Bolt crossed the distance between us the same time that I broke into a sprint, the hooded figure flailing like a fish on the ground as the spell worked itself through them. I stopped long enough to slash their throat and took a boot to the hip. Luckily for me, the person who kicked me was weak as hell and I just popped back up and stabbed them in the arm.

They slid their hand over the blood and put the hand out toward me, muttering a word that sent the crimson stuff at me like a splash. My legs moved on their own as I flung myself to the side, narrowly avoiding the liquid attack. A faint sizzle threw my adrenaline into overdrive as the blood sank into the ground like acid.

You need to kill her now, that acid will be hard to heal. Gritting my teeth, I stomped forward once and cast Embodiment of Lightning and crossed the distance between us in a heartbeat, slipping my blade into her neck as I stepped around her. An acrid-smelling gurgle made a chill run down my spine, so I let go of the blade in time to avoid a gout of sizzling gore.

My knife bent and snapped, the hilt falling uselessly to the ground as acidic blood bubbled from her throat and mouth. I could see her face now—pain wracked her, but she had at least taken my weapon from me.

A sharp twinge in my back drew a growl from my lips as I whipped around and cast Wisp at the perpetrator. They swatted the spell aside with a small barrier and lifted their hands to cast a spell of their own when Amabala slashed into the sides of their hood and killed them. The body dropped to the ground and she was gone again with a wild whooping cry.

There was no one immediately in my vicinity, and the ones who had survived the encounter and avoided the majority of Amabala's strafing strikes were able to run away, or at least limp quickly. It was those ones that I chose to pick on this time. There were at least six of them running back toward the city and the slower Wardens who came with them.

"Let them go, Amabala, the cowards," I called, the group of them probably feeling more secure. Or at least confident enough to group together and move with each other with little separation.

Bad tactics, that.

So I did what I had to and cast Fireblast into the spot just in front of them. The beam of mana shot forward and detonated with a cacophonous *boom* that shook the ground and made me smile. The majority of them were flailing on the ground, trying to move weakly and smack out the flames—magic forgotten— while the lone survivor limped on. It was one of the ones in the back who had erected a shield in front of himself, but hadn't fully covered his body in time. One of his legs burned as he moved and I took pity on him, casting Embodiment one last time and appearing next to him.

He flinched away, but couldn't raise his hands fast enough to ward away my right hook, or the Bolt that slammed into him from my spell. He landed on the ground and my booted foot came up in an arc, then dropped with all the force I could muster in an axe kick that executed him. His crushed head and gray matter on the ground were enough to make someone nearby vomit.

I turned to my left and found the cheetah warrior on the ground on all fours, retching and tossing up everything, so I called out, "You alright?"

Her tail flicked to the side and she vomited again. "No!" Then she spat and looked away. "That was so gross!"

CHAPTER TWENTY

"I can't believe you both did as well as you did." Arden crossed her arms and stared at the carnage on the ground around her as the others worked on getting Cassia out of the hole.

I shrugged and dug through one of the Warden of the Staff's pockets, finding nothing of interest. I moved on as Galaxy came in behind me and devoured the ones we moved through. We found some staffs and other magic items that Merlin tucked away for us and then some small gems and precious stones that we pulled from some pockets and purses.

All of you have leveled up, and Marcus you've got a few notifications that I thought of keeping to myself for the time. But now seems as good a time as any because you're about to head into the forest. She was quiet for a moment then, with excitement in her tone, she added, *For making it to level ten, I can also give you more spell points!*

Thank you, Galaxy. Lay it on me. I cracked my neck and opened my eyes to find system messages from her. I began to walk toward the forest slowly as I peered through my messages and options.

+1 points to Wisp, Bolt, Fireblast.
+2 to Frost and Blade.

That gave me a few options with my spell points. If I wanted to, I could spend the four points left over from leveling up, and the bonus three, on some good stuff. I could completely level up Fireblast for two points, Blade for one, and Frost for four. It would take all of the points I had, but that would be three spells that I had fully leveled up to add to Embodiment of Lightning.

As much as I would have loved to fully level up Wisp, that would just be ignorant with having Fireblast. But what if there was a new spell after that?

Why not level up one or two of them to see if it's worth it? Then if there's a spell you want after that, get it, and use the points as you see fit. She chuckled and muttered, *Cassia and Arden aren't watching you like they watch Merlin, so just do as you please—optimization be damned.*

I laughed to myself and shook my head. She was right.

Of course I am. Her purr through my mind made me roll my eyes as I paid the one point for Blade.

Congratulations on fully investing in a spell. Here is your fully upgraded and realized spell.

Mana Blade – Spine of mana and honed sharp enough to carve even the most fearsome foes, this sword will now stay summoned until dismissed or an hour passes. 20 mana.

I grinned and pressed the upgrades portion to see if there was anything else about it that was cool.

Upgrades*

While the sword is summoned, your reach is that of a normal long sword, but you will find that non-magical armor and materials are easier to bypass, and even some magical ones may fail before your blade.

Arcane Infusion – Sacrifice the casting of an elemental spell to infuse this spell with an elemental effect.

Oh, that was so fucking cool! I glanced at it and saw that it cost a point to buy though. It wasn't like it was a spell, it was just an add on *to* the spell. But with that, I could do aspected damage to something. And that was awesome.

Thinking about it, I could always do Fireblast later, since I would likely not be using it in the forest if I could help it. Due to all the wood around and also the likelihood the noise would draw unwanted attention. *I'll see what happens when I level up Frost all the way.*

I added four points to Frost and a similar message congratulating me popped into view, but it was the other messages that made me even more giddy.

Hoarfrost – Your control over the cold encompasses you, and you can freeze things within sixty feet of you. 3 mana per second with an added point of mana consumed per ten feet.

Upgrades*

Your will is the frozen winds and chill of death – Hoarfrost can lance through the body of an enemy and slow them with nothing more than a whim. The strength of your cold can be added to by increased levels of Mana and Charisma.

Icy Forge – With your ingenuity, you've created instruments of tool-like quality and deadly use, and now given your budding expertise, you can create more with little more than your will and intent.

"God damn, that's cool as hell!" My grin only widened as I realized that Galaxy's sage advice had been right. I spent the points for both Icy Forge and Arcane Infusion.

That left me with one last duty and that was to spend my attribute points. I shook my head, finally deciding and added two to both Brawn and Physique, and adding one to Charisma.

I pulled out one of my meal bars and bit into it angrily, my stomach protesting all the mana I had used. Despite the one-point gain while moving, I still needed to figure out how to regenerate it like Merlin and Arden did. That would take actual knowhow though. Or meditation. I wasn't too good at that last one unless I had a gun to clean.

Cassia sauntered over and grinned at me. "How was your level up?"

"Fantastic. Yours?"

"I gained a new form like the one that I can take, and I got some more healing abilities." Her arm passed through mine and she held onto me quietly for a time. "Are you interested in the other women?"

I coughed, nearly choking on the bite that I had taken, before managing, "What?"

"Arden kissed you, Amabala seems to like you for some weird reason and flirts with you by killing people for you, and Galaxy is... well, she's herself." She frowned at the ground, which was unlike her.

Galaxy started to rear her head for a sarcastic or witty addition, but she could sense the air of warning I adopted toward her and her presence quieted and quelled.

I continued walking with Cassia in silence for a minute before I finally said, "Yeah, I'm interested in them." Her arm stiffened and she tried to school her face to exude curiosity rather than the hurt that she initially displayed. "But not like that."

She looked up at me with confusion in her eyes. "How do you mean, then?"

"Arden is beautiful, sure. No denying that." I shrugged. "Yeah, she kissed me and it was a spur of the moment thing, but I don't get butterflies in my stomach when I think about it. Just the recall of power. She's an amazing person, but I think she would make a better friend."

She frowned again and nodded. "And Amabala?"

I chuckled. "She might be flirting by killing someone for me, but that someone *was* trying to kill me." It was hard to really think about her in a sexual manner too because she was a cat, didn't really matter how good she might look. "I don't think we would be compatible in a lot of ways. She's nice and all, but not really for me, I don't think."

And what about me, Marcus? Galaxy asked quietly, her tone flaccid, almost like she was worried about what I might say.

I thought about it and I finally just said, "I don't know about Galaxy, honestly." Cassia raised an eyebrow and smiled. "What?"

"She said I should punch you for that." Cassia snorted and shook her head. "She said to hit you with the old cock shot."

"Now, that hardly seems fair," I groused, but smirked. "I don't know about Galaxy, because she's a mystery to me. She's smart, funny, brutal, beautiful, and has all the qualities I would look for in a woman. All the same qualities you have. And she's a part of me. She knows me better than anyone likely ever has, or will."

I scratched my head. "I would be lying if I said that I wasn't attracted to her. And we both know that she knows how I feel and how you feel about her."

Cassia nodded and surprisingly, so did Galaxy, so I continued, "But she's never tried anything other than to encourage me and be there for me. I think if she wanted me, she could have me, and would likely take you too." My frown just deepened. "I kind of wish I knew what to say to you about it all."

I grabbed her closer, tugging her arm so that the line of her body was up against mine. "I do know that when you kiss me, my stomach still flips from it. I get excited at the prospect of seeing you and being with you. You're caring in your own way, brave, smart, funny, loyal, gorgeous. You're a lot of woman, Cass, and I like you a lot."

She grinned and said, "You forgot powerful."

"Did I?" I asked playfully and poked her shoulder. "I'm pretty sure I said something about that, or was it that strong people don't have to say they're strong?"

She grabbed my stomach and I yelped, the touch tickling me slightly so I bucked and tried to free myself of her grasp as she teased me. "Okay!" I bellowed. "Please, have mercy on this poor pitiful man, Cassia the All Powerful!"

"God, you two make me want to hurl," Arden complained

loudly. "I just want to throw lightning at you, is that so much to ask?"

"Yes, seeing as though you don't have that kind of magic yet," Merlin teased her in return.

"Who's fucking side are you on?" Arden hissed at him angrily and he just laughed. Arden turned her attentions elsewhere and called, "You okay, Amabala? Not going to puke again?"

"Will I ever live that down?" the tired-sounding cheetah woman mewled.

We all paused for a moment then Arden said, "Not likely, no." She laughed a little and added, "Though it does get easier."

———

It took us the whole of the day to get to the forest with breaks to rest and recover ourselves. Having fought as hard as we had, we were all tired and our strength was beginning to wane. Even Cassia, who could stay up for days at a time with little repercussion, had begun to nod off.

"You all rest and sleep for a little bit." I looked over the others and watched them considering to bicker with me over the watch. I shook my head and pointed to the ground. "Merlin, get us all underground again, buddy. We'll need holes for airflow but this'll be a good way to stay hidden."

He nodded and got to work, opting to do so just inside the forest itself rather than out in the open, that way we could hide ourselves among some of the roots. Short work for Merlin and his new spellcraft, and with Rocky's help there was no way for us to be spotted, though we made the hole smaller and a little bit thicker in case something truly massive made its way through the area, like that drake or that massive bird.

Stone pillars supported the roof alongside some of the roots and the others covered themselves up with blankets and fell asleep swiftly.

I would have nodded off too if it hadn't been for Galaxy joining me, her body pressed close to mine in elven form.

"Hey, you," I whispered to her softly. "How're you doing?"

"I'm confused." She sighed and leaned a little further back as I stared at her. "Thinking of Cassia's questions earlier has me thinking about what you all mean to me as well."

I lifted my chin. "Ah."

"The others are my blessed, out of choice, most, and necessity some, but they have their roles." She pointed to all of the others except me. "They are the pawns by which I should be regaining my strength and they bring me many morsels with which I feed on. However…"

She was quiet for a short amount of time before she whispered, "However, I feel like that's not enough. I like them all, though I'm still figuring things out with Amabala, she seems like a good girl. She has a lot going on in her head."

She glanced over at where Arden and Merlin slept near each other. "I feel affection for both of them. Merlin is a reliable tool, and Arden is a powerful mage. Both of them work hard and are very loyal. I want to reward that loyalty."

"You're their friend, you're worthy of that loyalty." She frowned some, so I added, "Sure, there's some give and take from all of us. But that doesn't mean that they can't like you, or you them."

"And what of Cassia?" She reached down and touched the Oni woman's face as she slumbered noisily.

"She seems to like you too." I shrugged, uncertain as to what she was searching for with all this. "Are you okay?"

She smiled at me then. "No." She held Cassia's face for a time quietly as her thoughts consumed her. "I don't know what it's like to love. I don't remember what it was to feel affection for someone outside of what a human might feel for a pet. I remember my blessed, but they were merely subjects. Tools. Pawns in the games that the gods played against each other."

"So you don't know how or why you're feeling the way you are, or if those feelings are true to you?" I raised an eyebrow at her and she just nodded, a tear falling down her face as she stared forward. I reached out and grabbed her, pulling her up into my lap to hold her. "It's okay to be confused. You've been asleep for who knows how long, and know almost nothing about yourself. You have a right to feel the way you're feeling."

"What does love feel like?" Her sudden, blurted question took me by surprise.

I frowned. "You've been inside my head, seen my memories and how I felt about Aeslyn. I loved her. I think a part of me still does, buried deep down somewhere in my bitter, jaded heart."

She snorted. "You? Jaded?" I raised an eyebrow at her and smirked. "You've found yourself someone new to love."

"Have I?" I looked down at Cassia. I did really enjoy myself with her. She was strong, and loyal. She didn't have the same hang ups that Aeslyn did, racially, I didn't think. I was content to just be with her. We had fun. "I don't know that I would call it love. But I'm not against the idea."

"Do you think you could love someone who doesn't know themselves?" That question made me tilt my head at her as she looked up at me with her head down low, her eyes all that I could see.

"Do you think you could love yourself?" My soft rebuttal took her by surprise. "You know me better than anyone, Galaxy. You and I are inseparable. One. Even Cassia doesn't know what we are. Though I know that if anything were to happen to you, I would be distraught."

"When you were taken from me during that farce of a test, I was sure I would either die, or be left alone again." Galaxy's voice had been so soft that I'd have been lucky to have heard it if she wasn't on my lap.

"I'm not going to let anything come between us like that again," I growled and leaned closer to her, my forehead touching the side of hers just above her ear. "Not you, those voices, or anyone else, is going to stop us finding out more about you, okay?"

"Why would I stop you?" She raised an eyebrow at me as if I had said something absolutely insane.

"Because sometimes learning about ourselves can be hard, and I don't want you getting cold feet about it." I smiled at her and winked, which made her smile back, so I brushed her hair away from her face and behind her long ear. "You feeling better?"

She nodded and stared deeply into my eyes for a long moment that seemed to span an immeasurable amount of time. Her face so close to mine, button nose almost pressed to mine, then she blinked those big eyes at me and time resumed, though my heart hammered in my chest.

She put her hands on my chest and continued to look at me as she moved, straddling my lap carefully so as not to hurt me. Her breath was warm against my chest, but her gaze was intense, "I don't know what I'm doing."

I laughed softly. "Neither do I."

She smacked my bicep lightly. "No, I mean, I don't know what I'm doing right now." She looked down at herself and then back up at me. "Any of this. It scares me, but… it's exciting too."

She closed her eyes and tilted her head as if she were remembering something, then opened them and stared back at me, my breath catching. "Cassia already thinks of our connection as a bond she can't compete with, and she knows that there's almost no separation between us."

"It sounds like you're trying to justify something to yourself and anyone who might see what you have in mind," I teased her lightly, wondering what she was talking about. "What're you on about?"

"This." She leaned forward and claimed my mouth with hers, lips soft, but somehow shaking and uncertain. Then she grabbed my shoulder and pulled me closer and it was all I could do to continue breathing. It was like the air had been sucked out of the hole we hid in and everything was on fire. My body burned and everywhere her hands and body touched mine was cool solace.

She broke away from me, my lips still scorched from the contact and I just stared at her wordlessly, until finally I could manage, "Wha—"

She placed a finger on my lips to hush me and melted into my mind and body.

I needed to know what I felt, she whispered through my head, my body somehow hollow right that second. *When Cassia spoke of me earlier with you, I wondered if the ache inside me at how you felt toward Aeslyn and the way you are with Cassia was for me as well. It didn't just have to be because you're healthy and virile and like beautiful women...*

She was quiet for a small amount of time as I fought to process what she was trying to say, before she added, *It just had to be you. I feel crazy about you, and the more I get to know you, from the past, and present, the more I know I cannot be away from you. Or deny myself the chance that I could experience something even more new to me with you.*

And you're okay with all of this? I had to admit, I was skeptical to say the least. *I mean, this is the second time in just a few days that someone other than Cass has kissed me, and I have to admit it makes me feel like a bit of a floozy.*

Cassia trusts you and me both, but she also isn't certain of us either. I frowned, not comforted by that and she damn well knew it. *I'll talk to her.*

I held up a hand and warned her, *Do not play with her mind or her emotions. I want you to give it to her straight, and without tampering. Am I perfectly clear?*

Crystal. She seemed almost giddy as her mind fled from mine. Cassia snored louder and for once, Arden woke up on her own and stared at me blearily. I raised an eyebrow at her and she just pointed to me, then my sleeping bag.

I got the message and let her take over for the night. I still felt the kiss on my lips and I wondered what the next day would hold for us.

I slumbered after that, fitfully for a time, but at least it was rest.

Something that smelled delicious caught my attention from deep within a dream that I couldn't understand in any way, shape, or form. Something about the day of time or some such other shit. But this? This I could smell well.

It smelled like bacon.

My eyes crashed open and I sat up like one of those sleepy cartoon characters in the old TV shows on Saturday mornings, drawn by the scent of delicious food that took on a life of its own.

Everyone was gathered by a cooking pan with Arden heating it with her palm. "Good morning, sleepyhead."

I grunted something inarticulate at her and stared at the bacon longingly. "Where'd this come from?"

"I hunted it." Cassia spoke softly behind me, scaring me a little bit. I turned to look at her, the bacon almost forgotten. She seemed sullen and I had to admit my heart fell. Seeing her pouting like this was worrisome.

"Hey, did Galaxy talk to you?" She nodded and looked straight ahead. I didn't see that as a good sign. "Can we talk about it?"

She nodded and pointed toward the other side of the root system that we had used, a small entrance to the outside was readily available as if she had made it to get out.

I followed her up into the light of the morning sun, having to use the roots almost like a ladder to get up.

She stood there waiting for me, Galaxy seated on the half-eaten body of a boar the size of a horse. "Morning." She waved at me with a smile and I nodded back, looking back to Cassia.

She had her arms crossed under her chest and stared at me, trying to find something. "I don't want to be angry."

"I don't want you to be either."

She scowled. "Galaxy told me how she felt about you. What she did."

I stayed quiet, not ashamed somehow, but still thinking of how it could have hurt her.

"Did you know something like this would happen? Did you suspect how she felt?"

I shook my head. "Not until after she kissed me." I held my hands up as she took a menacing step forward. "I've always been attracted to her, but like you, I never thought about it coming to be more. Not that I can actively recall."

Cassia stared at me, frowning, seething silently. "I don't know what to do," she muttered angrily. Almost as if she was more upset with herself than with me. "I never planned on any of this."

I watched as she reached up and covered her face with her hands, clearly frustrated. "I don't know what to say."

"Do you even care!" she bellowed, the veins in her neck bulging as she eyed me, her skin slowly coloring until she was in her Oni form, her anger apparent.

I sighed, frowning before I looked up at her and took off my cloak, throwing it to the side near the roots. Cassia stood up, confused as I took off my boots and tossed them aside. "What are you doing?"

I just ignored her and took my socks off, tossing them onto my boots as both women watched me curiously. I took my shirt off and then my belt; they went on the boots too.

Now I was angry. I may have been confused and I knew she was upset, but now she was questioning whether I cared about her or not? "Marcus, don't ignore me," Cassia pressed as I stood up straight, a growl in her tone. "I'm already upset enough as it is."

I stared at her. "You want to know something?"

She crossed her arms a little tighter before she spat, "What?"

I cast Embodiment of Lightning and appeared in front of her, throwing my whole body behind an elbow to her stomach that sent her flying into and through a small tree behind her. As she sat up from the blow, I spread my arms wide. "I'm just going to show you how much I fucking care about you." I pointed at her using the Marine Corps' patented knife hand. "Oni style."

She frowned, but I just started tromping through the forest after her, deeper in and further from the safety of our little underground camp.

"Oni show affection and that they care by ensuring the people they care about are capable in a fight, and it's been a little bit since you and I had it out, so let's see it." I growled at her, leaping over the stomp that her foot had made to try to punch her. She caught me in the stomach with her foot and shoved me above her head into a tree that was thick enough to stop me from flying through.

She roared loudly enough that some of the leaves shook above me, my breath slowly returning as she clambered to her feet. "You think a cheap shot like that is going to show you care?"

"I thought you liked my cheap shots?" I wheezed and ducked out of the way of the four-foot-long branch she whipped at me like a damn spear. The wood slapped against my shoulder as it shuddered near the end and I ignored it to dodge the round kick to my midsection.

No longer the one to speak, she just tried to kill me. Every time she swung at me, the wind would whip at my bare skin, stinging and raising welts. How strong had she become?

Or how much had she been holding back until the end, in our first fight? I blinked for a heartbeat too long and her fist connected with my stomach, lifting me from my feet into the air.

Ten feet, fifteen, twenty. Branches battered against my shoulders and the back of my neck until I finally had the good sense to reach out and grab something to stop my ascent.

Cassia watched me from below and I just scowled. *Okay. No more mister nice guy. You want caring?*

I took a deep breath and whipped myself up and over the branch I was on until my feet were on it before I cast Embodiment again.

She stayed completely still but it wasn't behind or in front of her that I wanted to go to, it was beside her. I hopped up onto her side, barring one of her arms from moving as I rubbed my forehead against hers. "Of course I fucking care. You mean a lot to me, and I hunted for you when I thought you were in danger."

"You found them first!" she cried, her anger palpable as the spikes began to grow from her body, her eyes beginning to pale.

"Because they were weaker than you!" I roared back, holding onto her, my right knee in her stomach. "I trust you with my life, and I trust you to take care of yourself until I can be with you."

"I've always been stronger, taking care of myself." She seethed, her teeth clenched as she stared at me. "I don't need anyone!"

That's not her saying that, something is wrong, Galaxy warned me, her presence instantly soothing to me.

Cassia shifted her stance and twisted viciously, her spine cracking as she threw me away from her. The wind screeching by my ears was deafening but the crash that came from me slamming through one tree into another was just as loud. My ribs were broken, at least two of them, and they would hurt like a bitch.

I've summoned the others to assist you. Galaxy sounded scared, but I grunted at her and she frowned inside me. *You can't be serious.*

Deadly serious. I wheezed. *I have to be the one to stop her. Or she's never going to be able to trust me.*

I hope you know what an idiot you're being, Galaxy muttered darkly.

"Course I do." I grunted and tried to take a decent breath, but it was hard. "Ouch. That hurts. When I'm ready, you better be able to get whatever is fucking with her head out of her, got me?"

I didn't have time to wait for the answer; Cassia had already started crashing her way toward me. I settled myself against the tree that was helping me stand and prepared myself. I had the majority of my mana. So I was about to dump it all at her.

As soon as she was within twenty feet, the freezing cold within me crept outward in a steady flow. Three seconds later, she'd crossed into the ten-foot zone and I really laid it on thick. She was hot blooded, that was for sure, but even as strong as she was, Hoarfrost sapped the strength from her for every minute movement of her body.

She snarled and growled as she made her way toward me, her arm rising as wracking shivers threatened to overtake her. I held my hand out and a cold snap made the air smell harsh, manacles of ice now forming around her feet and growing toward the ground.

The more I worked the cold, the more at home I felt. Like this was where I belonged. Her teeth began to chatter as she eyed me hatefully, the ice at her feet beginning to crack as her eyes began to glow anew.

Not enough time to revel in the power I had. Oh well.

My feet crunched over the now-dead and frozen grass, a soft smattering of snow beneath my feet now as I put my hand on her shoulder and climbed up her leg to stand on it. She stared at me with her teeth clattering together and all I could do was feel the omen of my cold press upon her.

I reached down and pressed my lips against her lips, her chattering teeth slowing. Galaxy quested through her body, slowly sucking Cassia's strength from her, likely as the best way to clear out whatever or whoever it was trying to turn her against us.

Her teeth stilled fully and I stopped my spell. I kissed her for all I was worth and more as I used the dregs of my mana to cast Wisp and help thaw her as quickly as I could.

She kissed me back, her tongue dancing with mine until finally she was free and there was nothing left for Galaxy to drain, it seemed. She collapsed against me, both of us breathing raggedly. My ribs hurt like hell and not breathing hadn't helped in the slightest.

Cassia's lips worked as if she was trying to say something, but I just grunted and put a hand on her cheek. "You're the strongest among all of us, but I'll never stop fighting for you. I know this is all a lot to handle, and you've taken it in stride—but you don't have to carry the burden alone."

Her breath caught and for the first time, a tear fell down her face as she smiled at me. "Thank you."

I tapped her face playfully and she sniffed before touching my ribs, which made my knees give out.

"You really are pretty fragile." She touched my cheek and leaned down toward me. "I think I'll have to stick around for you."

I grinned up at her, pained but happy. "Think so?"

She rumbled at me, "Know so." She thought for a moment, then leaned closer and stared me in the eyes. "I can see why Galaxy is so attached. And I think Aeslyn was stupid. I could fall in love with you too, I think."

My blood drained from my face and I felt faint, but that was good, right?

I think it is. Galaxy purred inside me as the Oni woman carried me back toward Arden and Merlin who stared at us with looks of resignation on their faces. It was Amabala who watched us as if we had screws loose and threatened to burst any moment.

"What the hell is wrong with the two of you?" Her whisper reached me and I grinned tiredly.

I winked at her and answered, "We like each other a whole lot, and I think I won for once."

"I let you win," Cassia grunted affectionately.

I turned toward her and growled, "Can't you just let me fucking have this?"

She laughed, and I started to, but my ribs ached fiercely and all I wanted to was to nap and eat bacon.

Maybe not in that order.

CHAPTER TWENTY-ONE

"Three fucking goddamn days we've been in this fucking hell hole!" I raged for the second time since I'd woken up this morning, then kicked a small root that slowly grew upward like a spike.

True to what I had said, we'd trekked through this forest, deeper into the darkness and mysteries of the Forest of Fel Tidings. We'd dodged countless attacks by just being crafty enough to avoid detection, relying on our camouflaging cloaks when we needed to, and generally traveling slowly.

It also didn't help that the forest seemed to be as alive as we were and was almost constantly trying to consume us. Small roots would wriggle from the ground and snake toward us, tree limbs would slowly lower as if they were trying to grab us.

It had gotten so bad after a while, it was all we could do to travel in the places where it seemed like the forest was trying to eat us *less*.

"This whole place is carnivorous," Arden muttered, burning an insistent root that kept tapping at her foot like it was trying to stab her.

The sky above us was almost constantly and consistently

flashing through the limbs as if there was a storm above us that would never end, but there was no accompanying rain. Just flashes of lightning.

I sighed and we continued on, Galaxy pulling in information about our surroundings as best she could so that our maps would update and we could see what we were walking into. We rounded a rather large tree trunk and ran nearly smack into a city built of stone and gold.

"Is this the lost city of El Dorado or some shit?" I whispered to Cassia.

She rolled her eyes. "Don't be dense. That's in Florida beneath Disney." She pulled out her mace and watched our surroundings uneasily. "Place this big shouldn't be so quiet."

"There's nothing of any kind of barrier either," Merlin grumbled softly, his sword bare and ready. I cracked my neck and pulled out my staff, more curious about using it for once than I likely had any right to be, though if I was going to train with it, no better time than the present.

Setting things on fire with it had been pretty easy and swift, but now I'd need to figure out how to use it to the best effect.

We made our way into the city, the shadows deeper here than in the other places within the forest, as if the shadows were as alive as they had been in the ruins.

The grass here wasn't grasping at our heels when we didn't pay enough attention. There was nothing lunging out of the darkness to try to snack on us. Just a quiet area. We followed the road that we found, noticing more that connected in a web-like structure, but they all funneled toward the center of the city.

"Should we check inside some of the places?" Amabala whispered to us as she crept forward. I managed to grab her before she made it too far. "Should I have waited?"

I nodded pointedly at her and motioned for her to step back to us. She complied and I explained, "You're squishy. You get hit, you get hurt. Cassia and I are a tankier sort. You let us investigate and if it's safe, we will call you in."

I smiled at her and kept my hand on her shoulder as I

stepped beyond her to investigate the home. There was bedding, for sure, a mat that could have been filled with almost anything soft enough to sleep on, likely leaves. There was a table with stools around it, all of them small and wooden with woven grass cushions. There was a fire pit in the center of the room with a green pot that looked to be made of bone hanging over it, soup boiling in it.

"Is it all clear?" Cassia muttered from the door and made me jump.

"No, this place is lived in and there's someone here." I joined her and the others and continued to explain. "Something is wrong. There's a fire in there with food cooking and no one to tend it."

"That's not a good sign." Merlin frowned and scratched his head, looking around curiously.

A huge roar of lifted voices echoed through the city toward us, like a crowd cheering, then a chant built up. Saying the same words over and over in a tongue that I likely had no damn business hearing.

"Sounds like it's coming from the center of the city." Arden tried to stand a little taller to see if there was anything she could see from where we were, but to no avail.

"Because why wouldn't it be?" I snarled quietly, hyper aware that we were probably walking into the B-est list trap in the fucking movie world and there was nothing we could do because we needed to find the Huntsman's mantle.

You could always give up the quest and hunt things here for a time to amass power, Galaxy offered softly, knowing I was in a shitty mood. *I believe the saying being, there's more than one way to skin a cat?*

Terrible thing, that—you know, coming from a cat and all? She laughed at my poor attempt at a joke, the sound calming me a little. *As much as I would like to, I need something really good if I'm going to be truly useful to you and my friends. The mantle is a way for me to make sure no more assholes like Qin Moira can show their ugly fucking mugs the way he did before. And if they do, we can put them down and keep innocent people on both sides safe.*

The way it should be, she added for me and I nodded.

Sighing, I muttered, "Let's go investigate."

The others seemed to catch on to my ire and just shook their heads as I trudged past them. Cassia caught up to me easily and ducked her head down to get my attention. "I thought you would be enjoying this? Is this not what you and your Marines are used to?"

"We had guns and weren't stuck in a B-grade plot hook for a bad thriller or horror movie." She blinked, clearly confused, so I tried to offer an example. "You know how in a lot of straight-to-TV movies they have these characters that don't pay any attention to the warning signs around them and walk straight into some really bad shit?"

She thought on it for a moment, then a bright look crossed her face as she smiled and nodded. "Like all those times you watch the Friday night horror movies in October on the Syfy channel and yell, 'No bitch, he's in there!'?"

I pointed at her and said, "Yup!"

She stomped her foot with a soft thud on the ground as she grunted, "Shit. This is bad."

I threw my hands up. "Finally."

"We just need to be cautious then." She looked back at the others and hissed, "Eyes on the shadows, see something speak up, and I swear to God if you see a little man asking about his stolen gold, you fucking run!"

"Are you seriously scared of leprechauns?" I raised an eyebrow at her as Merlin nearly snapped his neck trying to look around for the imagined little creatures.

"Yes!" She groaned. "The one in the movies was surprisingly accurate."

"Wait, they're real?"

Arden grabbed us both and pulled us against the side of a building. "There are people coming and you want to talk about the little folk?" She flicked my nose, annoyed. "Shut the hell up."

A stream of heat burst from her as she put the haze in front of where we stood on the side of the stone home, small people who looked entirely like little cat people walked by. Their bodies could have been toddlers' if it hadn't been for the fact that each one had fur, a tail, and ears like that of a cat.

I mouthed, *What the entire fuck?* And blinked at my friends who had clearly never seen this shit before either.

One of them walked near the wall and stopped, dropping into a low stance before sniffing the air. It turned and hissed at us, a surprisingly deep yowl coming from it.

Fuck! Galaxy bellowed a heartbeat before something dropped onto my shoulder and something sharp pressed into my skin, a meowing I didn't understand reaching my ears from where the little cat person perched. I touched the ring to my staff and it disappeared into my inventory, earning me a yowl.

I chanced a glance at the others and saw similar situations. Cat people crouched on shoulders and heads, claws poised next to our jugular veins as more flooded the area.

"Goddamn B-list shit!" I snarled and the cat's claws sank in menacingly.

Several of the little people had spears trained on us, small vicious-looking arrows nocked in bows that they looked competent with aimed our way. The one who had spotted us pointed at us and then motioned for us to follow them.

"Are they going to eat us?" Merlin whispered to Amabala, who just shrugged. "Don't you understand them?"

"Not all cats speak the same language, human!" Amabala seethed, her tail flicking violently. The cat on her shoulders yowled and punched her ear, more for effect than damage, but it made me want to lash out.

Something prodded my leg and I heard more growling behind me. "Better move along with them for now, and find a way to escape if we can."

We followed them, amassing more and more onlookers and witnesses as we traveled toward the center of the city. It looked like we had attracted almost every resident and they were not as unopposed to us being there as I had thought at first.

A lot of them looked really happy to see us and I didn't know whether that was good or not, but either way, the claws drawing blood at my neck annoyed the ever-loving hell out of me.

My mini map unfocused and refocused, a large gray hole opening like a yawning mouth in front of where we walked toward.

"Oh, that's fucking huge," Cassia muttered as we closed in on it. "Of course there's a fucking ziggurat in the center of it."

"Oh, ziggurats are *never* good!" Arden spat vehemently. "Last time I ran into a ziggurat, this dude Jesus was tearing it apart for blasphemy or something or another."

"That was a temple, I thought." She seemed to just chuckle at my confusion.

"Really? I wasn't there or anything." I blinked at her sarcasm and she shrugged, pointing with her chin at the truly breath-taking black stone building below. "They have temples on top of them sometimes, it's a status thing for the god or creature they're worshiping, and I've *never* seen one that big."

Had I seen something like this before? The only building I had any sort of reference for was the temple that I had found Galaxy's necklace in.

It's bigger than that as well, Galaxy explained softly, a sense of awe in her words as we both beheld the marvel below.

In a pit bottomed with white sand and stone, stood a massive, black-stoned building, with three sets of stairs closest to us. One stout, low set that led to the base of the monumental building, then two that circled up and out from that and up to the temple above in a display of grandeur that only the richest people might have in their homes.

The temple had banners of blackened silk that had nothing on them, waving like ghostly tendrils in the wind that worked below.

I could have sworn I saw something moving near the back of the temple, but I couldn't place it, even with my peripheral vision. Nothing appeared and nothing returned. It had vanished for all I knew.

"Welcome, our sacrifices, to the home of the Death Shroud," a woman's voice greeted us from our left.

She stood cloaked in black with a veil over her face, but her eyes were a milky white so bright they could have been glowing. "Your lives will keep the Shroud pleased for many moons, enough time for us to recover from its displeasure of late."

"Death Shroud?" I raised an eyebrow and she nodded once. "What does it want?"

"To be complete," she answered cryptically, before smiling. "It consumes, because it is not consumed. It hungers for flesh and freedom, but we guard it and keep it safe, and the rest of Grestal with it."

She motioned and the cats on our shoulders backed off, kicking us forward. The fall was much too high to be safe whatsoever, but she waved her hands and stomped her foot, a metallic clanking rang out around us as the ground shook. Black stairs of the same stone as that of the building below slowly crawled from below until there was a path down more than halfway.

There was no way that we would be able to come back.

Amabala says that we should play along and that once we're safe, she can get us out of here with one of her portals.

Grateful for Galaxy's interruption into my thoughts, I nodded and stepped forward.

"Our first willing sacrifice!" the woman called, raising her arms until they were out to the side and above her head as if she was beseeching someone to look down upon her and her flock. "Go forth and feed our god."

I rolled my eyes and slowly made my way down the stairs as the others followed my lead, the crowds chanting voices rising once more in the language I had no business hearing. It set my teeth on edge and I very much wanted to go back up there and start killing them all.

We had about twenty-five feet left to descend when the stairs stopped and dropped off.

"Suppose we just hop off and get the fuck out of here?" Arden grinned, jumping down, with me following her closely behind.

The others joined us, though Cassia caught Amabala with ease before setting her on the ground.

Amabala closed her eyes and stretched out her hands, muttering something beneath her breath before she flinched and the portal was supposed to appear.

"Something wrong?"

She stared down at her palms, numbly. "I forgot how to make a portal." She frowned to herself and blinked. "I have my mana, still. But when I reach for the spell itself, I can't grasp it."

"So we're stuck here?" She shook her head at Cassia as the larger woman stared at her. "What do you mean?"

"There's a portal here somewhere." She grimaced and held her head. "But it's like it doesn't want to be found. The more I try to focus on it, the more my head hurts."

"Stop trying to find it and pinpoint it." I grabbed her shoulder and looked her in the eyes. "Give us a direction."

She turned her whole body toward the ziggurat and said, "That way."

A soft growl escaped my throat as the thought of going in there made my skin crawl, but there was a time for fear—and it wasn't now. "Then it looks like we're going inside."

CHAPTER TWENTY-TWO

Dull, thunking footsteps echoed throughout the hole we were in as we ascended the staircase to the bottom portion of the structure.

The stairs that led to the top and the temple were covered in bones of all kinds of sizes, some of them crushed or snapped like twigs, others still parts of skeletons.

Merlin shuddered and muttered, "Not going up that way, there's no telling what could be here and all those corpses were going up those stairs."

"Hadn't planned to go up to a potential death deity's temple in the first place, buddy." I winked at him even though the adrenaline in my body made every nerve a fucking live wire. The shadows looked thick enough to hide a full platoon of fighters from us and there wouldn't be a damn thing for us to do about them other than get fucking shot.

We pressed on the door to get inside the bottom of the ziggurat and it slid open, a hushed *whoosh* and the grinding of stone preceded the scent of death, decay, and copper.

Galaxy, tell them to all be on high alert. She nodded within me and I felt the others around me stiffening as they stared into the ebony void barring our sight.

I closed my eyes, called to my staff, and pulled it out, casting Wisp through it. The mana swirled from me into the staff where my hand was just before a ball of flames swirled into life above the knob at the end of it. Light fought against the darkness that just seemed to morph and ebb around it before giving way slightly.

More bones decorated the floor of this room and it was all I could do to keep from crying out as I saw one of the little cat people struggling forward out of the shadows, mewling as it crawled hand over hand until it was doused fully in light.

The scent of copper grew stronger, and my stomach flipped as I stared down at the creature who reached out to me with only the upper half of its body remaining. It dragged its lower intestines through the gore-soaked detritus and cried out pitiably before a huge, black-taloned claw reached out and grabbed it, slowly dragging it back into the darkness where the mewling reached a pitch and suddenly fell silent, replaced by a rolling hiss and nasty swallowing sound.

Merlin and Arden both raised their hands and I covered my face with my arm as light burst from both of them. The creature screeched and I recognized it, my heart nearly dropping out of my ass, as I opened my eyes to see a black-scaled drake rearing back to try to save its vision.

There was no chance we could take this creature without being able to see where all of this thing was. I bellowed, "Flash, Arden! Then out." They weren't moving fast enough, so I roared again, "*Out!*"

The thing had to be some kind of drake, though it was slightly different, with a beak-like nose over sharp teeth stained red by its meal. I couldn't see its eyes but small, nubby horns decorated the top of its head, sweeping back toward its bulky, black-scaled body.

It swiped toward my friends as they still lingered in fright, but the temporary blindness, coupled with having just been rearing up, drew the strike short and dropped it onto its shoulder with a booming crash. The door had started to close behind them, but Cassia had it open and held that way, grasping Merlin and flinging him out the door as the drake snarled savagely.

Cassia bumped the door with her hip and grabbed me, pulling me through and jumping as something splintered the stones she had stood on and clashed with the door, slamming it shut.

She huffed, "Up, go up."

"But the death thing!" Amabala cried even as she moved to the stairs.

"It's better to have the high ground on an enemy—go!" I spat and got up, lifting Cassia with me as she limped forward. I glanced down and there was a sliver of stone stuck in her leg just below the knee. "If I pull it, can you heal yourself?"

She nodded once, so I reached down and yanked the piece out of her with a grunt of effort. She hissed at the pain, but her knee began to knit itself back together almost immediately. "Thanks."

"Yup," I gasped, the sharp edges having cut me as I pulled, but my lycan-gifted healing closed the wounds quickly enough. But it had stung fiercely.

My legs churned, sending me up the stairs next to Cassia just as the doors downstairs bowed outward impossibly before one of them gave way and shattered as the monster trapped within made its way outside.

The people above had weirdly kept chanting, but now stopped, some of them meowing in concern and in ever-growing frequency until the sound was nearly as deafening as the frightful roar of challenge the drake loosed into the air.

The cat people screeched nearly in unison when the drake leaped into the air and scrambled up the side of the lower stone wall. Its eyes blazed before it turned toward them and roared again, then back at us. The others were further behind Cassia and I at this point and we would truly be the only physical line of defense, Merlin being better off at casting those big spells.

"Merlin, you light that fucker up with me!" Arden raised her voice even as she started to gather water in her hands to cast her spell. "Lightning if you got it."

He grimaced and pulled out his scepter silently as he focused on the beast before us. There was a sort of scuffling noise just before something flew over the lip of the hole we were in toward us, a great shadow becoming something of an issue as we stood ready.

Another drake, but this one was green and had a bloodied eye and a mass of missing scales around it.

It barked, an echoing call toward the black drake, then turned its head toward us and barked again. Like some kind of fucking lizard dolphin. "This isn't good."

The green heard me and reared, spitting a globule of disgusting yellowish phlegm toward us. Cassia shoved me back and stepped to the side as the green rushed her. The phlegm hit the stone and began to spew noxious fumes into the air that Cassia just ignored and dodged the first strike from her attacker, only to be whacked on the follow through by its tail.

She slid back and gasped, hitting her head on a stone something hard enough to daze her. Amabala rushed forward to stand over her protectively, even though the hands holding her daggers shook like leaves in the wind.

Galaxy, go pull Cassia back with Amabala, she's not strong enough on her own.

She didn't argue, launching herself from me in cat form just before taking human form and pulling, growling, "Help me, damn it!"

They started to drag her away from the drakes and toward Merlin, who launched an arc of lightning thicker than my forearm at the green. The drake flattened itself, avoiding the spell, and rushed forward at me. I dodged it easily, kicking it in the nose on the way by, but it was just going for Merlin and the girls straight on without stopping.

The boy mage threw up a shield in front of the girls by about thirty feet and rolled behind it with them, but the beast just speared straight through it like a dog through loose cellophane. It opened its mouth almost like it was victorious, but I cast Embodiment and stepped to the side of the others, shoving them all out of the way as far as I could toward Arden.

Water slapped against the drake's face, kicking it away from us just in time for the black one to spring from where it had followed the green. Its head slammed into me, rocketing me backward into the dark and cold of somewhere.

My back and body ached painfully as I fought to sit up.

Ah, another morsel, something hissed at the edge of my mind, the roaring and shouts outside almost enough to drown it out. *Another ignorant meal as so many were before.*

CHAPTER TWENTY-THREE

There was no sign of breathing or movement in the shadows that I could detect.

"I'm not getting eaten by a damn thing." I grunted and sat up, something sticky on my back, probably blood. "Least of all you, or those scaly bitches out there."

A tone of surprise crept into the whisper. *You can hear me?*

I tried to stand and my sense of equilibrium shifted and I pitched forward before I caught myself on something that jabbed painfully into my palm before snorting. "You're hardly the first to speak to me in my head."

The voice was silent long enough for me to think it had gone, then asked, *You are not... broken are you?*

"Clean bill of health, thanks to a few nurses' tender mercies." I put weight on my legs and they started to work, then gave out on me. "Fuck."

The drakes roared as a gout of flame washed over them, and Cassia bellowed tiredly. Things weren't going well out there.

They will die, morsel, the voice whispered, and for some reason, the voice sounded more familiar this time.

"Listen, death shroud, or shroud of doom—whatever the fuck you are—I'm going out there to keep my friends alive, so fuck off with the negatives." I winced as I tried to stand and my lower back popped audibly. Power rushed back into my legs and I could stand but it hurt like hell.

I saw the way you moved in front of them like that. Brave, it whispered, sickly sweet. *Foolish, and brave. You would save the dying?*

"I would save as many as I can, now *shut. Up.*" My snarled last words had drawn the attention of one of the drakes, the green one, its ruined eye trying to search for me.

I like that, and I can see that you met my former master.

A chill ran down my spine at the realization. This wasn't the shroud of death or whatever the hell those things up there were worshipping—this was the Huntsman's mantle.

"I killed him."

The voice just snickered. *He was dead already, though I could sense him growing stronger for a short time until he was truly gone. Likely for the better. He tried to steal the bodies of those who ventured here, but never could.*

"You going to offer me some kind of deal or something?" It was quiet for a few seconds too long and I growled, watching as Cassia tried to wrest her mace from the mouth of the black drake and the green slowly closed on where I hid. "Fine then, be that way."

I rolled my neck and cast Mana Blade. "Be back for you in a minute."

Repeat after me, it encouraged me as the green drake lifted its nose to the air no more than fifty feet from me.

In my head I growled, *There's no time!*

Blackest night, brightest day, let evil fear my way.

I muttered softly, hoping the scaled fucker outside was deaf too. "Blackest night, brightest day, let evil fear my way."

Boiling clouds my traveled road, sound the horn my coming bode.

I repeated the words as the drake's alligator lips rose and its head turned toward me.

Where I walk be hallowed grounds—

The drake charged toward me as I raised my voice to repeat the phrase.

Almost as one, the voice and I screamed the last verse, "I am the Huntsman, release the hounds!"

The shadows in the temple I was in waned and dragged toward me, collecting on my back. Through the mantle, I knew they were gathering to me, the once-dark stone of the temple and ziggurat drained toward me like I was a massive leech.

I am weakened from millennia unused, but I have enough strength to assist you, the mantle whispered and suddenly the shadows lifted the Mana Blade from my hand, twisting around it until it was about a foot and a half above me and made a sort of makeshift scythe. *It is not perfect, but it only needs to function.*

"Time to put up or shut up." I put both hands on the haft of my new scythe and bolted forward, feeling stronger than I ever had.

Shadows slithered along the ground toward me, then propelled me forward as the green drake loomed closer. As soon as it was close enough, shadows wrapped around the blade of my weapon and I swung it as hard as I could toward its injured side.

I got lucky and it started lifting its leg, but not high enough, and the shadow-encrusted blade sliced through the scales and bones like a warm knife through a cream pie. The drake screamed loudly, my ears ringing from it, but I stepped closer as it listed to the right and twirled my scythe until the blade made a windmill and slashed upward.

The blade erupted from the drake's skull and the shadows helped me tug the weapon free of the corpse.

My friends watched, enraptured for some reason as even the black drake hesitated to come at me.

You will need a mount to make our bond closer to complete, the mantle whispered. *You can select nearly anything and if it will bow to you, then I can make it yours.*

I blinked and stared at the black drake. Massive as it was, it watched me stepping toward it in an almost primal fashion. As if it wasn't sure whether I was predator or prey, but that uncertainty made it still.

I stepped closer, my shoulders squared and my head and chin high. It was larger than me but I would be damned it if it was going to think I was intimidated at all.

"Bow to me, and live." My voice was modulated, sounding sort of hollow and deep, like I was a specter given a voice. I kind of liked it. Sweeping my scythe back toward the dead drake behind me, I finished the ultimatum, "Or end up like that thing."

It blinked at me, lids on the inside of its eye sweeping from the inside out, then up and down as it watched me. *I do not think it understood you.*

See if it understands this then. I banged the shadowy butt of my scythe down and bellowed for all I was worth, all the fury the Marine Corps had taught me to call upon on command mixing with the slowly budding rage at events out of my control. I was tired, sore, hungry, and I wanted a drink so fucking bad I would even drink tequila straight. This thing was *not* going to stand in our way.

It lifted its head high and for a second I was sure it was going to lash out, so I tightened my grip on the scythe in my right hand.

To my surprised delight, the drake's head lowered until it nearly touched the ground.

My hand lifted and I put it on the middle of its forehead and the shadows around me and that made up the scythe I had transferred to the drake, binding it in chains of pure ebon energy. It tried to raise its head, but I pressed my hand down and muttered, "Easy now, I don't think this will hurt you."

It roared, low and piteous, before it collapsed onto the ground in a huff. The chains lifted from the ground and slammed into me so hard that I lost my footing and fell onto my ass.

Pain, soul deep and all-encompassing for entirely too long,

seared me as the chains clanked against my chest as they reeled into my body.

The pain was unbearable and even the drake cried out as the spectral shadow chains dragged it closer to me.

Almost through. Try to relax, the binding is rather painful, the mantle explained, voice softening as I snarled and glared up into the sky. Fighting my own reactions and knee jerk need to fight the pain and escape was nearly impossible.

I might as well have been trying to climb Everest with lead shoes and a dinosaur standing on my shoulders.

"Marcus!" someone shouted and I opened my eyes as my chest heaved; I couldn't catch my breath. Galaxy and Cassia floated into view and I had to be hallucinating, because there were small hearts floating over their shoulders.

Cassia tried to grab the chains and pull them out of me, but she screamed and let go, blood dripping from her palms onto my chest.

Something within me snapped and I grit my teeth, reaching out and grasping the chains in my hands before yanking them into myself. The cold, iron-like material slapped against my chest and disappeared as it should have.

The drake pulled back, skittering claws trying to get away from the source of its pain. The poor beast. I hated seeing it in pain the way it was more than I hated the pain I felt. I'd fought a corporal in Afghanistan for trying to get rid of one of the dogs that I had been giving snacks and stuff from my MRE's. He'd hated dogs and had tried to kill it so he wouldn't have to worry about it attacking him or begging for scraps.

That dog's whining while he had been poised over it with his rifle was so close to how the drake sounded right now that I had to act.

I grabbed the chains once more and yanked, the drake's pulling back tugging me to my feet where I swayed slowly. One grueling step forward was all I could manage before the pain was so unbearable that I had to cry out again just to stay focused enough to stand. Spittle ran down my chin as I snarled and growled at the pain and took another step, my hands guiding me along the chain like a dying man pulling himself to land.

My muscles strained and jumped, twitching as the length of chain shortened and the drake whined ceaselessly. So I tried to comfort it. "It's okay, li'l guy… Gah." My body bucked as the pain worsened tremendously, but I had to push on. "Come on, almost there."

Hands on my back helped to guide me forward, Galaxy pressed against my mind, but there was nothing that she could do to get in, the pain was so intense.

After three more steps, the drake finally stopped trying to pull away and its head shot forward into my hand.

The mantle cried, *It is done!*

The chains faded away and the drake and I stood closer together than I would have liked a few minutes ago. It stared down at me, with eyes that I could now see were as close to a true golden color as anything I had ever seen in my life.

The drake's head dipped closer to mine entirely too fast for comfort, but he didn't mean any harm. Wait, *he?* Looking up at him, I just knew that he was a male.

"What should we call you, buddy?" I muttered as he snuffed at my shoulder and the back of my head like a giant dog.

"Are you talking to that thing?" Amabala whispered harshly as I reached up to stroke his muzzle. We both turned to look at her and she fell over with a cry of fear. "What the hells was that?"

Confused, I blinked at her and she frowned. "It's gone?"

"What is?" Cassia asked and stepped into view once more, the small heart still floating over her shoulder. She turned back and obscured my vision of it before I could focus too much on it.

"Something dark slid across his eyes, made him look like a predator." Amabala stared at me and I started to see something floating above her right shoulder too.

Am I losing my mind?

The mantle snickered and answered, *No. That would be a perk of your new power. I thrive and grow from the bonds of those to the Huntsman. The better the bond with the people who ride with you, the stronger your bonds. The stronger the bonds are, the stronger I become.*

"I thought you fed on souls." I thought I had heard something of that.

The mantle was quiet for a time, then said, *I used to, but it's not something that you'll have to worry about for a long time. So focus on the bonds you can create and then we will worry about it, alright?*

It was quiet a time then said, *The dark one... What's her name?*

Galaxy? I blinked at her as she stared at me, hard.

She keeps trying to tear me aside like a veil so that she can peer within you. He sounded angry about that. *You think I should kill her?*

NO! The fury in my voice was palpable and even the others must have seen something on my face because they all started. *She's a part of me. Let her in.*

She growled and took a step forward then blinked in shock. "Oh." She faded from view and I could once more feel her within me, thinking. *Oh, so this is the mantle then?*

She talks to you too? The mantle gasped and I just laughed.

You and I need to have a little discussion, mister mantle, Galaxy purred predatorily.

"Don't eat it, Galaxy." I warned her out loud and she pouted. "We have our goal done here; we can return home soon."

I glanced up at the drake who sat there staring at me and the others, "Uh... what do I do with him?"

He can travel with you. The First used to make his horse turn into a cat.

No more cats, Galaxy yowled and I laughed.

Can I turn him into something other? I asked politely and then watched as the drake seemed to understand something I didn't.

He can do pretty much anything you want, honestly. He can hitchhike in your shadow for all I care. Turn him into a dog, a crow, something befitting your new station. The mantle grunted, sighing, *Manny? ...Sure. Call me Manny.*

Cool, thanks Manny. I grinned and thought about it for a moment before asking the drake, "What do you call yourself?"

The creature reared his head up and roared, snuffling after the initial blast of noise, then growled slightly. I nodded, "Yeah, no, that's a great name. How about we call you Kane? You know, cause you tried to eat us and all that, but you're cool now."

The drake huffed and looked away, much to the surprise and delight of the girls. "Look, it's either that, Chesty, Chongo, or Devilnuts."

If the drake could frown, it would have been just then. It whined.

"A compromise?" I threw my hands up. "Fine! I'll let the ladies decide on some options, how's that?"

Arden offered, "Newt!" Her grin was something else, but she didn't appear to be completely afraid of the massive beast. Until he growled low at her and narrowed his eyes. "Not a fan?"

"Seems small," I offered on his behalf before glancing at Amabala. She shook her head, her eyes locked on the drake with his teeth glimmering in the light. "Fair."

"I like Mako," Cassia offered, and I smiled. So did I. Casting my gaze up at the giant drake turned puppy dog, he was nodding his head in agreement.

"Mako it is." I reached out and willed him to take a place on my left forearm like a tattoo. He whined at first, I could hear him clear as day in my head. I smiled to myself and patted where he was with a finger. He growled and I nodded. "Okay, I won't tickle you."

"This is getting weird," Amabala whispered and I just chuckled.

"No kidding," Merlin grumbled, but he touched the drake I had killed and shook his head. "We can't return yet."

"Why not?" Amabala stared at him as if he was a demon.

"We need to hunt something for Merlin, but he needs to be the one to kill it." Cassia frowned, staring at the fallen drake. "I have never seen so many drakes in one place. They are fiercely territorial and known to fight over meals, but these two teamed up."

"Mako said that it was because the green one had blood debt to repay, and all dragonkind will allow those with them priority, sometimes even assisting them." I blinked... *How the hell had he put that in my head so quickly?* "The only reason it came at all was because Mako made the call of a challenge. Anything of a certain level or higher within a few miles would have heard it and come running, usually another drake."

"I... see." Cassia turned so that she was staring at Merlin. "Do you think that spell of yours could be used to track a certain tier of beast?"

"I might be able to, but it would be hard without knowing them, or having something of theirs." Merlin scratched his head, then Arden whistled to get his attention and slapped the dead drake.

"This baby carries so many scales." She waggled her eyebrows at the boy pointedly and his palm rocketed to his forehead. "I thought you would get it."

He took a moment to pull a scale and a fang from the corpse and walked well away from it. He muttered the spell as I ate some of the leftover bacon we had to let my mana replenish. Cassia and Arden had already begun to pull scales from the corpse and some of the fangs as well before Galaxy went to work devouring our prize.

Merlin's spell arced to life, then failed to eat the scale that he had, his voice hissing out a soft, "Damn."

He tried again, the manner in which he muttered the words changing slightly. The spell burst into life and then fizzled out just as swiftly as it had come to life. Merlin snarled, "Damn it!"

"It's okay!" I comforted him softly; he just huffed and nodded. "Don't give up. There's a lot that we could do in our time here, but we need to kill something quickly, so we can get back home, right?"

He nodded without a word.

"So then all we have to do is call something to us."

I grinned at him as the realization dawned on him. "You mean to call something here? With all those people above us?"

I laughed probably more harshly than I meant to. "You mean the cat people who tried to sacrifice us to their deity?" I shook my head at him and patted his shoulder. "They'll be fine if they get stepped on, I'm sure. They deserve it too."

He grinned back at me and laughed too. "Then how do we do it?"

I glanced around, feeling the wind that dived deep into the hole we were in, gathering and blowing around the now-pale gray stone ziggurat we stood on.

"I think that we're going to have our new friend make a call for us." I stared down at the hyper-realistic drake tattoo crouching on my forearm.

CHAPTER TWENTY-FOUR

"Everyone in position?" I called down to the others as they waited in their various shadows and hidey holes.

Merlin and Mako stood in the center of the temple level of the ziggurat, waiting patiently for the signal to begin. I heard all of them yell back affirmatives and willed Mako to make the call.

Like a wolf howling to his brothers and sisters of the moon, Mako's head started low, slowly rising as he roared a challenge for all to hear.

I'm surprised that nothing else has come to investigate the previous call, but with this? I have no doubt that something will come. Galaxy sounded like she was smiling as she spoke. *If I hadn't needed to shore up a wall inside you to keep myself from Manny, all of you would have been able to level up.*

Sorry that you had to do it. I watched the tree line, where I could see no movement other than some of the cat people watching curiously from above us. *If I thought you could devour it and still give me all the power, I would allow it.*

Her retort was catty, if anything, but very much her. *If I thought I could do the same, I wouldn't need your allowance.* She stared out of my eyes with me and frowned. *What do you suppose those things are above everyone's shoulders?*

I have no clue, but once things really calm down, I plan to have a real long talk with our resident Wild Hunt expert about it all.

A roar echoed through the air, birds of differing shapes and sizes scattering from the trees behind me, flying overhead as I turned to watch for signs of our prey. There was nothing for a moment or two, then a humongous rotten-looking creature rolled over the trees like it was a damn tank. The trees that had to be hundreds of years old only stood to its chest and they stood no chance against its strength. It reached down and grabbed one, then flung it across the hole at our spectators, their screams exciting it as it stared down at us. It had arms covered in spiked and rotten flesh, some of the bone inside the chest and legs visible, and the stench was nearly enough to make me vomit where I was.

That would be a Rot King, and they are about tier four to four and a half, depending on their age, Galaxy whispered to me.

I didn't even care where she had gotten the knowledge from. The creature stared down at us with burning, sickly green eyes, half of its face missing and all the bone showing.

"Did we just bite off more than we could chew?" I hung my head and muttered to myself just a heartbeat before another call echoed through the area.

A thunderous boom echoed on the other side of the hole from the Rot King and trees burst into flame. A smaller creature, maybe thirty feet tall and covered in green fur along the shoulders and legs, looked like it was made of roots or moss of some sort. It had tree-like antlers that butted from its head, and bark-like skin on its chest that could well have been armor. It screeched in a whistling hiss that sounded like winds whipping through tree branches.

An Elder Dryad, this one is supposed to still be asleep, according to Amabala and the rumors that she's heard. Galaxy sounded like she was choking on something. *We can't take these things. We need to run!*

Fair! I cast Embodiment of Lightning and stepped down to

where Merlin and Mako stood, glued to the spot as the two behemoths eyed each other like they were about to start fighting just that second. The others made their way to us and I whispered, "Amabala, we need a quick way the hell out of here, get us up out of here and into the city, or back to the city where the Wardens are."

She nodded and began to cast her spell when the ground shook and she lost her balance, falling onto her ass. The spell was gone and the fight was on.

The Rot King had jumped down into the hole with us and tore the roof off the temple to throw at the Elder Dryad with a screeching cry. The Dryad ducked under it and lifted a wooded hand, roots screaming into existence just under it as stone cracked and splintered. The roots wrapped around one of the King's legs and distracted it long enough that the Dryad was able to make a bridge of roots to run down toward its enemy.

As it closed in, the whooshing cry whispered through again and it leapt forward, a flying elbow of leaves and gnarled branches slammed into the Rot King's face and collar bone with a solid smack. It looked like a child play-wrestling with an adult, but the skin that slipped from the bone causing more fresh grossness turned my stomach and made it less endearing.

"What if we help the Dryad kill this thing?" Cassia asked over the crashing, her voice raised so that she was almost screaming. We all stared at her as if she were daft. "Think about it, with our help, the Dryad can take it!"

"Think about all the experience!" she continued to urge, a manic grin on her face.

"And what about when one is dead?" Arden countered, pointing up at the battle. "They kill the other, and the victor has unobscured access to the rest of us. We don't get experience until Galaxy consumes the body, and yet you want to sit here and try to distract the winner long enough to allow that?"

"Well, it's better than running away!" Cassia shot back.

"Guys?" Merlin spoke softly at first, the two women continuing to bicker as the crashing of the fight continued. Finally, he turned around and yelled, "Shut up!"

We all turned to stare at him as he motioned wildly to the lip of the hole where the Rot King had come through. Where now a snake with the body of a woman watched the proceeding fight with little interest, then turned her gaze toward us.

Merlin snarled, turning back to us. "That… is a tier six Gorgana, and we can kill that. How about it?"

Judging by how little interest she had in the other fighting monsters, it was easy to assume she wouldn't be coming to us.

"Fine." I glanced at him. "Any chance it has the ability to turn us to stone or some shit?"

"Not really, they're just hard to kill and can cast spells." He thought about it for a moment. "It might have some lesser followers, thralls or snakes or something."

"Let's get up there to it then." I tried to think of a way up there, but got nothing. "Merlin, can you get us a set of stairs going or something with Rocky?"

He frowned and closed his eyes. "We can try something, but that will tire us both out." He pointed to me with his chin. "The Hunt is supposed to be able to ride into battle with steeds that can fly, can't you and Mako fly us out?"

That is a no in my weakened state, Marcus, sorry. Manny grunted and I sighed, shaking my head to let the others know. *If you were to kill something and let me have it, or flex the power of some of your bonds, I would be able to do something for you.*

How do I do that then?

I could hear a smile in the mantle's tone. *Some of the people here are really close to having some drastically strong emotions for you, child. Harvest those emotions, and I could probably offer you enough juice to get all of you up there.*

"How do I even do that!" I growled my frustration and stared around me. All of the people around me had something over their shoulders. Cassia had a heart over her shoulder, Arden and Amabala too, but Merlin had a plus symbol, which was weird.

Focusing on each of them made them grow until I could get a good look at them. Inside each symbol was a sort of growth, like a gauge, that showed how highly they thought of me. When I focused on Amabala's I saw that it said **curious**.

But it wasn't filled very high at all, so that must not have been who it was that Manny was speaking about.

Merlin's plus said **trusted** and branched into two different categories, **friend** and **mentor**. It looked like it was high enough that I could push it over the edge to one of them. But which one?

There you go, Manny encouraged. *This is the Huntsman's Bond at work. Through these bonds, you will be able to gauge other's feelings about you, and with those insights, control how your bond develops in new and better ways. Depending on how the various members of your Hunt grow, they can acquire new titles and powers through me as well.*

Then how do I grow them? And step on the explanation pedal, we have things to kill and surviving to do.

If the mantle had eyes, it would have rolled them. *You're close enough now that you can choose an interaction. Basically, talk to him and let him know what he's already trying to decide. At this point, you can become either to him, all you must do—is choose.*

"Why are you staring at me like that?" Merlin raised an eyebrow, then looked down at himself. "Is there blood on me?"

I shook my head and reached out to him, my hand landing on his shoulder before I played my hunch. "No. I'm just trying to figure out when it was that you got so damn strong."

He snorted and rolled his eyes, pointing to the monsters that had managed to fight themselves into a corner. "Kind of on a time crunch here, boss."

I winked at him. "And don't you forget who the boss is, kid." He stared at me to see if I was joking, but I just smiled. "I'll teach you everything I know, and I'll need you to help me grow accustomed to all of this. Think you'd be okay with guiding each other some?"

He laughed, smiling for the first time in a little while despite the danger. "Yeah, now let's find a way up there to kick some ass."

With that, the thing floating over his shoulder became a star with the bar at the bottom of **trusted friend**.

I turned over to look at the others, but it was Cassia who surprised me. She grinned at me with her Oni smile, and over her shoulder her heart icon read **Love**.

That's what I needed! Manny roared, Mako jumping off my arm as the shadows around us deepened and flung toward us. *As you get ready to ride, don't forget to shout: Commence the Hunt.*

Shadows slithered up Mako's sides until there was a colorless saddle on his back that looked like it was perfect for me. He laid down on the ground so I could jump up and into the saddle before I looked back at the others who watched me in shock. I faced forward and kicked Mako in the sides as I bellowed, "Commence the Hunt!"

Shadows burst from me and covered Mako's scales as he launched himself forward and up, his feet touching nothing but finding purchase in the air itself as he rose.

I chanced a glance back at the others and all I saw were hazy dark figures mounted on horses the color of midnight, their muzzles exuding puffs of shadow as opposed to gusts of air. The riders were as formless and without feature as a normal shadow might be, the outline of a person, but without depth or detail.

The horses trod behind us on a trail of shadows and nothingness, but what truly made this all surreal was the distance we covered was nothing like what it should have been. The enemy we chased after had to have been more than two hundred yards from us and yet we had covered half that distance and surmounted the cliff-like wall surrounding the ziggurat in the mere seconds since having taken those first few steps.

It was impossible to keep the grin from my face as I howled in delight. Wind whipped past us and Mako touched ground on the side of the cliff and surged forward until the others were on solid ground as well. Once the last rider was with us, the shadows faded from us all. It was disappointing, but we were here and the Gorgana wasn't far from us.

"Arden and Amabala, get over there and distract her while the rest of us catch up," I ordered and both of them took off.

"Can't you get to her with a couple castings of Embodiment of Lighting?" Cassia asked softly as we started to run forward.

"Yeah, but that takes mana and I want to save it for now." I rode on top of Mako still and held out a hand for Cassia and Merlin to hop aboard. "Merlin, what kind of magic does that thing have?"

"Usually, they excel at poison and binding things in place, kind of like a paralysis, but nothing turns to stone." He grunted as the drake jumped and it jostled him violently. "Damn, this thing is a rough ride."

Mako growled menacingly and the mage's mouth snapped shut audibly.

"Something else is out there just beyond her." Cassia hissed and prepared to launch herself forward, but my hand snaked out and grasped her shoulder. "The girls are about to be over-run; they need me."

"They do, but I have a better idea." I reached back from where I was seated high on Mako's shoulder blades and grabbed Merlin. "We're going to make a magical battering ram so that thing has no chance against us."

"What?" Merlin yelped and I just smiled at him.

A second later, my heartbeat and the thrumming of Mako's muscles were all I could hear and feel until the resounding *crash* of Merlin's stone-reinforced barrier slammed into the snake, a puff of gaseous poison wafting into the air beneath it as we rode over the Gorgana.

Cassia had leaped high into the air with her fists clasped together to smash her skull, but the creature's snake tail lashed out and whipped her into the closest tree like a foul ball into a fence. Shambling dead walked into view while the writhing Gorgana screamed in frustration as the others waded closer to compensate.

Arden stabbed down at the Gorgana with spears of flame and Amabala tried to dance closer to slash at her enemy with her knives but the tail struck the ground in front of her. The hissing monster spat venom at Arden and hurled itself away from a rampaging Mako, a green-tinged aura rippling around her hands.

Merlin appeared next to her, his sword slicing at her wrist with an amber wave erupting from the tip to sail through her forearm. Blood sprayed and she screeched as the limb fell away, but her tail shot forward and slapped him into Mako's shoulder.

"Mako, back off and go after the undead!" I ordered and launched myself off his back as he careened away. "Merlin, you good?"

"Ow!" the boy groaned and sat up from where he had fallen, nursing his shoulder as if it hurt.

The Gorgana hissed again and a burst of light flashed behind her as humanoid creatures flooded into view. Six of them with limbs reminiscent of snakes and other misshapen appendages threw themselves at us as their supposed master tried to back away.

Cassia exploded into the group of them with her spiked limbs lashing out in all directions, her voice raised in a bout of laughter as the dead began to pile up and their shadows rose around them.

I will be going to consume the dead as there are more of them, so long as Mako doesn't eat them first. Galaxy sounded less than thrilled about the turn of events but I knew, and she knew, that we couldn't afford to let any of it go to waste.

I couldn't tell if it was Manny consuming the corpses or if it was Galaxy, and I almost didn't care who it was so long as we were stronger for it.

Merlin, Arden, and I converged on the Gorgana as Cass, Amabala, and Mako fought together to rid us of the new arrivals.

The serpent woman hissed a few words and a weak barrier slid out of the air in front of her that Arden seared and washed away in a baptism of flame. Merlin's sword radiated the red of flames and he leapt forward with it raised.

Her tail lashed forward once more, but this time I stood there and cast Physical Buff. My body density shifted and suddenly I may as well have been rooted to the spot, arms raised and ready to catch the tail rocketing toward my young friend. I managed to stop it and a wash of heat and a spray of blood splattered against my face as Merlin's sword bit deep into the Gorgana's shoulder.

She screamed until I cast Bolt and electrocuted her before using Hoarfrost to chill her out. Her scales near me turned to ice and she clawed my shoulder angrily, welts of green raising where she touched, but I grit my teeth and pressed on.

"Merlin, any time!" I grunted as the strength from the tail began to wane, but the poison bubbling up in my shoulder and chest grew to be unbearable.

"On it!" he snarled back, and rushed over my back to grab his sword and slam a slab of stone down on the creature's head. She cried out as he latched onto his sword and fell with it before jumping back up and slicing toward her exposed throat.

The blade bit in and slowly the body slumped forward, a slow drip of blood sloshing from the growing crevice that was becoming her wound. Her head flipped from her neck and shoulders, landing with an audible *thump* and a sort of sticky, gross sound of sludge hitting a solid before the humanoids she had summoned screeched as one and died.

Galaxy launched herself from my left and began to slowly unhinge her jaw as the shadows deepened, her and the mantle likely racing to see who could consume it first. *Manny, you take the corpses from the pawns, she gets the main chick except for the head.*

Manny grumbled inaudibly inside my head and I just rolled my eyes. Galaxy consumed the body as swiftly as she could and soon all the dead were gone. Cassia came over to see to my wounds, but luckily the swelling and pain had died down since boy wonder had lopped off the wicked witch's head.

"Now can we go home?" Arden groaned, her clothes

covered in gore, her hair sticking to the nape of her neck and out like it had bloody gel in it.

"Soon." I sighed and glanced toward where Cassia had come from. The dead were still there but there were hundreds of them, maybe more given how thick the trees and foliage were around here, hiding plenty from view. "Galaxy, you get anything decent experience-wise from the shambling ones?"

No, and they taste like crap, but it all adds up. For every three or four, we get a few points.

That was a problem, but likely because they were something else's entourage and not the boss themselves. Kind of like how in some games a summoner gave the experience, but killing their pets did little more than irritate them.

Though speaking of the summoner, I turned toward the ziggurat where the two giant fuck all monsters were still locked in a knock-down-drag-out brawl and they both looked only minimally worse for wear. There was no way we could get in there and kill one without either getting in the way, or killed in the process.

"Knowing when to flee is… humbling." Cassia huffed as she stared longingly at the Rot King and the Elder Dryad while they fought it out. "That would be a fight to enjoy, but not as low a level as we are right now."

My vision bobbed as my head did—she was right.

"Amabala, do you think we can get the hell out of here?" The woman stood with her hands on her knees as she fought to catch her breath. Aside from some minor cuts and bruises, and one nasty-looking snake bite on her shoulder, she looked alright. "You gonna make it?"

"Did you see me fighting?" She looked so proud of herself as she stood up, a big, cat-like grin engulfing her face. "I killed one of them and distracted her just like you asked."

Cassia appeared in front of her, blocking her from view, but I could hear her say, "You did good, kid." Then she punched Amabala in the chest and knocked her straight onto her ass. "But you got a lot to learn."

Amabala glared up at the Oni woman until Cassia offered her a hand and cheerily added, "And I can't wait to teach you all of it."

She helped her new friend to her feet before Amabala looked at me and replied, "I can, but I don't know where a portal that won't be heavily guarded will be."

If you can't get back to the Human realm, I can help you get to where you need to be, I think. Manny sounded uncertain, likely wishing he could have consumed more. *If we keep our flights brief and everyone can get along, we can make it that much faster and in a little more safety than if we were to try to do anything as hasty as building a portal to Earth ourselves.*

I blinked and frowned at that. We had a portal we could likely use, but it was overtaken by the Wardens. I almost facepalmed as I fought to keep myself from cursing up and down the air itself, then bent and scooped up the Gorgana's head. "We don't need to find one at all, we can go back in style with this."

"The Wardens are hunting us though." Amabala frowned, then turned to the others with an edge of panic in her voice. "How can we trust that they will let us through even if we come back with evidence that he passed his trial?"

"We can't." Arden crossed her arms and stared at me strangely, like she was trying to gauge where my head was.

"Nope, we sure can't." I grinned at them. "But they probably aren't expecting him to show up with proof he passed. And they sure as hell aren't expecting that he shows up with the Wild Hunt."

Cassia grinned as she put one of her massive arms around Amabala and Arden, the jinn woman shaking her head with a feigned sigh before she chuckled. "You're diabolical, you know that?"

Merlin just shook his head and eyed me before realization dawned on his face. "Does that mean…? Wait, you can't do that to them!"

I just grinned as the shadows beneath my feet darkened and

grew, Mako having come up to stand guard behind me. I just shook my head. "I'm not doing anything other than offering them a chance, but the consequences will be a little worse than they might think."

Mako's deep bass growl nearly drowned out his protests as the plot formulated in my head.

CHAPTER TWENTY-FIVE

The sun beat down on us where we stood in the plains no more than fifty yards from the portal back to Old Man's Cave where we had originally come from, but you would think we had stepped into a Renaissance Faire. Tents marred the horizon line from where we stood, the canvas died darker on the bottom than the top, but the tangle of hastily built domiciles stood between us and the portal itself.

That wouldn't have been a problem with Amabala, she could sense it as if it was the easiest thing in the world. No, the problem was the two dozen Wardens who stood outside and within the little village of tents watching us.

We stayed there for about half an hour, hoping that someone would have the stones to come and speak with us, but there was nothing from them except stony silence and drawn weapons.

Finally, I motioned to Merlin and he pulled the Gorgana's head from his inventory, lifting it above his head and away from himself for all to see. "I've passed your rite and have earned my place among both the Orders of the Staff and Sword. Let us through so that we can report to Ventricle Theodorous and we can all be on our way."

The Wardens watching us just sneered and stood firmly where they were, watching us, waiting for something.

Amabala hissed violently, "Portal!" She crouched and pulled her weapons. "It's a trap."

Sure enough, a portal opened twenty feet behind us and another dozen or so Wardens flooded from it with Mohawk at their rear. I chuckled at the sight of him and his green hair as it flopped to the side a little limply.

"Looking a little flaccid, buddy." I jeered at him, calling his sword from my inventory. His eyes burned as they fell on his weapon, then rose back to mine. "Yeah, I think I'll start a collection."

"Give it back, you worthless rogue." He shoved his buddies out of the way until he stood at the fore.

I shrugged. "Sure, I couldn't appreciate it the way you could anyway." I stabbed the blade into the ground easily. "Let us go back home, and you can have it."

"Not going to happen." He actually grinned at that, crossing his arms almost triumphantly. "You all die here."

"You sure about that?" I raised a brow at him and he nodded slowly. Amabala hissed again and this time two more portals opened and other Wardens slowly made their way out of it. Some carrying swords and other physical melee weapons, others sporting staves or wands. All of them trained on us.

Cassia says she's ready whenever we are, Galaxy whispered through my mind and I sighed theatrically.

"Give up, and all we will do is take you in and dissect you." Mohawk guffawed and stared at us, some of the other juveniles joined in and even some of the older ones smirked along with him.

"Tell you what—come take your sword back, Mohawk." I nodded to it and kicked it hard enough that it fell onto the flat of the blade with the hilt facing toward him. "After that? You can all surrender and let us through."

"You talk a lot, old man." Someone behind the front line of Wardens shouted and I had to fight not to break my bearing. "Just shut up and get on your knees."

"That's what your mother said last night!" Merlin snarled in return and flipped the random voice off.

Arden nearly doubled over she laughed so hard, and I had to admit, the vehemence and timing had been perfect. A familiar voice rang out from within the village, "Take them!"

Without skipping a beat, Cassia surged forward and punted the hilt of Mohawk's sword hard enough to send the weapon careening toward him and his friends. Some of the less brave Wardens ducked and flinched, giving us time enough to allow Merlin to throw up a shield for us.

Spells sheered the air like Scud missiles, whistling arcs of fire blasted at us with lines of electricity and other elements thrown in. They began to blend and clash for even greater effect, shattering the barrier as the earth around us burst straight up into a physical barrier around us.

"Mako!" I roared over the din, the black drake flinging himself from the tattoo on my arm into the casters and sword swingers on our left. Their screams confused the Wardens for a heartbeat before someone shouted orders for some of them to break off and kill him. "Cassia, Arden, protect Amabala."

Merlin appeared next to me as the wall of earth in front of us melted away. "Time to hunt?"

"Time to kill!" I snarled, my voice deeper than it should have been, but the mantle understood my purpose and will better than I thought.

You have a little time with the power I can muster for this, so go nuts. Manny laughed maniacally as shadows coalesced all around us, Mako roared and time slowed as I cast Mana Blade.

My sword became a scythe once more and we stepped into the light. Every step I took could have been a leaping bound and it was hard to get used to, even though I had done it once before. Cloth ripped and someone grunted as they split in two, their upper body landing by their feet.

"What the fuck is he?" I turned in time to catch a sword on the ebon haft of my weapon and kicked out with my right foot. My heel caught my attacker in the face and blood flecked the Wardens who were too slow to realize what was going on.

"I'm the Huntsman!" I growled, and the statement felt *right*. "I am judgement."

Mohawk sprang at me, but Merlin intercepted him and rammed his fist into the opposing Warden's stomach, knocking him to his knees. Chaos reigned behind us, Cassia laughing with Arden and Amabala calling out targets like they were skeet shooting or something. I left Merlin to his own devices and went back to my own work.

The portals had all closed by now and the Wardens who fought us were losing, badly. The dead piled up and the only thing stopping Manny and Galaxy from feasting was my concern that Mako would accidentally trample them.

The beast of a drake rampaged like a herd of bulls with teeth like daggers and the cold intelligence of an enraged toddler. His claws raked across his victims and his teeth crunched bone as the Wardens screamed and died, tail slapping those smart enough to try to flank him.

More spells seared the air and he just ate them like the tank of scales and hatred he was designed to be before turning and breathing a torrent of acidic bile at them. They didn't have the time to do anything other than erect magic barriers or die, and the majority of them who survived looked drained and ready to fall over.

So I helped them.

My scythe slashed and the blade caught one of the mages in the shoulder, lopped off the arm, then sailed back through his collar bone with ease, two of the others fading from view with personal portals saving them just in the nick of time.

Cassia crushed one of them under her foot and turned to savage another with the spikes on her forearms before she bounded back toward Amabala and Arden.

Water splashing drew my attention to the makeshift tent

village barring our path to the portal. Blades of liquid slashed through them like they were leaves falling before a blade, breaking objects and tattered remnants were all that remained from Arden's attack.

Galaxy and Manny, you both get half of the dead. The shadows that coalesced around me died down and I held the sword in my hand as the mantle went to work eating. *Galaxy, anyone who survived our little rebellion—drain them of everything but what they need to live.*

Alright, but don't kill them?

I shook my head at her question and she went to work draining the survivors first.

"All of you who didn't fall, listen closely." My command was such that they couldn't do anything but look at me anyway, but the deep growl from Mako cemented their attention on me. "The Wild Hunt has returned, and those who prey on human and supernatural creatures alike will answer to me and my riders."

I closed my eyes and did my best to ignore the chills running through me as I spoke on. "I don't hold a grudge against the Orders for acting as childishly as they have, but it does piss me off that you treat people so poorly. I would suggest changing that." My gaze swept across them all slowly. "Some of you use your power to help people, I'm sure."

My eyes fell on Mohawk, where he stood with an air of disgust and contempt surrounding him. I stared at him and found that I could see how he felt about me over his shoulder. **Murderous hatred.**

My mouth twitched as I regarded him and pointed to him with a knife hand. "And some use their power to try to bully others."

"You have no idea, and that mantle won't be yours for long." Mohawk sneered, his sword appearing in his right hand.

"We'll see about that." I shrugged and turned my back to him, announcing, "We're going home, to speak to the Ventricle Theodorous, and if I see you again, you die."

You would do well not to leave an enemy at your back, Manny whispered to me as if I didn't already know that.

"You have no right to try to threaten me, rogue." Mohawk sneered and raised his voice. "You don't know who you're messing with! The Order of the Sword will hunt you down for being a threat to humanity."

I glanced over my shoulder in that general direction, careful not to actually look at him and raised an eyebrow. "You're right, I don't even know your name. Nor do you even rate one to me. I took your sword once, you wanna let me take it again?"

He spat and from Galaxy's point of view, I could see what he was going to do. I just let it come. As he closed the distance, I gathered my mana and willed it all to explode behind me with Hoarfrost, the action of it nearly as easy as breathing for some reason.

The shadows around me deepened with my authority as the Huntsman and I raised my scythe, my voice taking on the demonic edge that I was beginning to associate with the Huntsman's force. "Ah, I see you."

His eyes widened, the majority of his body frozen completely solid from the spell that I had cast. There was a thin barrier around his body that kept the ice off him physically, but the barrier was trapped and him with it.

His sword was straight up in the air, the ice having climbed up itself to capture him where he hovered over the ground. His attack likely would have cleaved me in half if the straining muscles in his body and the aura around it were to be trusted.

"I'm a man of my word, kid."

My sword raised until the blade lay parallel to the ground, then I slid it forward as fast and hard as I could, the ice fracturing and falling away as the magic weapon slid through the barrier and up into his heart. He managed a grimace and the hatred in him boiled over until I twisted the blade and pushed a little deeper before allowing it to fade with a flex of my will.

I cast Wisp as he bled and died, to melt the ice around his

fist and his sword. "I think I'll keep this as a reminder of this little occasion."

The other Wardens watched in horror as the shadows rose around the dying Mohawk and consumed him, ice and all. I felt stronger. My whole body thrummed with energy that only seemed to be affecting me until Manny rejoined me and the others in my party started to glow with dark energy.

This is the bond you share with them. Your power grows, and flows to them, and the same for them to you. Together, you are stronger.

Thanks for that, Manny. I blinked and shook myself out a little to clear the tension in my body as I recovered from the brief buzz of power. I pointed to one of the Sword Wardens and then another of the Staff. "After we leave here, you'll wait an hour and leave as well. You're to keep as much of this circulating as you can—the Wild Hunt has returned and we will tolerate little. We will be in touch with your superiors."

Their shadows lengthened and rejoined mine, Mako making his way to me where he thumped his head against my shoulder and faded from view. Everyone but Arden joined me in my swagger toward the portal to Earth and we found the jinn interrogating someone just this side of the center of the tent town.

She let the girl fall and turned to us. "Order of the Staff has the portal under lock and key on the other side from what she says." She shook her hands as if they hurt. "We go in there, it's going to be a trap."

"What can we suggest?" I glanced around at the others and waited.

Cassia poked a finger at Amabala. "Can you teleport to places you can see?"

The cheetah woman thought about it, her eyes flicking side to side as if she were reading something before she nodded. "But only to places I can physically see with my eyes, anything like a painting is too abstract."

"That should work." Cass grinned and added, "All we

would need to do is weaken the trap or buy her the time to cast a teleport to get us out of the line of the fight."

"You want to avoid a fight?" Arden raised a teasing eyebrow at her friend and was met with a punch to the shoulder. "Hey!"

"I want to get home to people who matter—*with* people who matter." Cassia crossed her arms and stared at all of us. "You guys are family and I want to make it home to drink and play games with you all."

I nodded in her direction and she turned toward the portal. "I'll go first, Amabala with me, then Merlin and Arden and finally we can have Marcus come through. As soon as we're through, Amabala gets her bearings and preps the spell to get us out and we fight our way through if we have to."

"Sounds good to me." Merlin huffed, then pulled out the Gorgana head. "Just in case they want to listen to reason."

All of us turned and marched through the portal in order, and when we exited on the other side, there had been a massacre.

Blood and viscera covered the stone-strewn ground in what could have been a massive puddle. There weren't even any bodies left to identify anything, just a pool of blood on the ground and gouges in the stone walls surrounding us.

At our feet were steel bars and bindings that lay shredded and shorn like something had come through here and murdered anything with any sort of form or solidity to it.

This is hardly a good place to be right now, Marcus, use the power of the Hunt and get us all away from here now. A low, mournful cry rose in the distance that set every fiber of my being on high alert, the hairs on my body rising as goosebumps flooded my flesh. *Now. Right now—run!*

Stone cracked and electricity zapped through my veins as I shouted, "Commence the Hunt!"

Shadows surged in unnaturally slow motion as rocks toppled behind us, something skittering over the side of the mountain behind us and heading right in our direction. Mako sprouted from beneath me and we lifted away from the bloody grounds near the portal on our shadow mounts as fast as we could but the creature closed the distance.

"Arden and Merlin, nail it down!" I commanded and the two bringing up the rear turned in their shadows and shot back magic strong enough to almost blind me. It would have looked like a streaking comet to anyone looking at the sky day or night.

In the flash of light, I could see the hulking figure had hands all over its body that reached and grasped, some of them clawed and others holding small weapons. But they all belonged to the one, ghastly and twisted form.

Flames splashed against the creature. It screamed so loud that the ringing in my ears just wouldn't clear and it was all I could do to stay in the saddle.

Pure arcane energy lanced through the flames and pierced it to the ground as it tried to reach for us, then Merlin slumped forward in his saddle and we fought on through the skies. Arden galloped through the air beside him for a few minutes to ensure he didn't fall out of it and we finally made it far enough that I didn't feel like we were in immediate danger anymore.

"Is he okay?" I called and got nothing right away.

Mana fatigue. The fox showed him a way to use more than he has for spells and that one cost a lot, but it bought us time. Galaxy swirled inside my head for a few more moments and finally she said, *This power is not so foreign to me somehow. I can feel a resonance within it that calls to me.*

I feel it too, and it's frightening, Manny whispered quietly.

Why is this just now coming up?

Manny went to speak but instead growled and remained quiet, so Galaxy offered, *We could be growing accustomed to each other. Growing familiar to the point where we see similarities? Or it could be the change in magic density and type here on Earth. Whatever it is, I feel drawn to him.*

Since we don't know what would happen if you consumed him, let's hold off on that, okay? Sensing her agreement, I watched as the city moved into view. "We should set down outside the city in case someone sees us."

No one will see you. The shadows will convert ambient mana in the air to make it so that nothing below will see you, especially humans. Manny's response was quick, and I could almost feel a tension in him as he spoke to me. *I don't want to be consumed.*

Ah. There was that. *We will do everything we can to grow stronger.* It wasn't likely that he wanted to hear that at all, noncommittal as it was, but it was better than pregnant silence.

We rode on, coming to our destination before the sun had even begun to set, which was odd. How long had we been in Grestal?

We landed in the parking lot behind the High Table, Arden providing a suitable haze for cover as we did so and the woman who sat in the entry to the lot panicked, bolting from her seat as her eyes nearly popped out of her sockets at us. Her wailing screams were unintelligible, but it was easy enough to under-stand why she had reacted that way. We still had the shadows of the Hunt wreathed around us, so I willed those away and called Mako back into me as a tattoo.

It was so nice to be back here once more.

A horde of men and women sprinted down the sidewalk toward us and Cassia stepped forward. "One hell of a return party, huh?"

Those in front ground to a halt, the largest one an Asian man with long black hair pulled back into a tight bun against the back of his head, his features were tight as if he had been prepared for a fight to break out, but when he saw us, he relaxed. "Sissy Cass, bubba Marcus!"

It could only have been Kenshi who greeted us and pulled both me and Cassia into a hug that made me wish I had lungs made of iron. The man just squeezed and squeezed until all I could do was grunt and heave to try to get a lungful of air.

"Bubba Kenshi, let go!" Cassia hissed, shoving her brother away. The Oni-in-human form dropped me and soothing air helped to lessen the amount of black dots floating in my vision.

"I forget sometimes." He shrugged simply. "Here in time for karaoke! Come!"

He grabbed his sister and someone took pity on me and helped me to my feet, where I then limped theatrically toward the door of the High Table.

The world felt so new and I knew that I needed a shower. The shadows stopped a lot but I was more than certain that they didn't stop me from sweating, based on the faces some of the lycanthropes around us made. All of them huddled around Amabala who was having a truly hard time blending in, apparently unable to hide who and what she was just yet.

Merlin reached out and took her hand in his and she shimmered before a glassy image of nothingness replaced her and it was as if there was a Predator wading through the crowded Columbus sidewalk in between four buff powerlifters.

"Thanks, Merlin," I muttered and he just nodded and plodded along happily behind us.

"How long were we gone, Kenshi?" I asked softly, slightly worried that the time dilation would be something crazy.

"A week?" He looked to one of his cohorts who nodded and then back to me. "A week, sissy. Jolly need time."

"For what?" She wondered, but the look he gave her shut her up and she glowered at the sidewalk for a moment before muttering, "Fine."

Keith sat at the door, his grin widening like he'd won the lottery. "Hot dog!" He whooped and hollered until Cassia cut him with a glare and he managed to tone it down just a little. I waited for a moment as the others marched into the place without me and he winked at me. "You won me a lotta green, Marcus."

"That why you were celebrating?" He nodded shamelessly and I just shook my head at him—incorrigible, this one. "What all's happened while we were gone?"

"Well, your phone was going off like crazy when Yen checked it, but other than that?" He shrugged and eyed me knowingly. "If I said anything, Yenasi would kill me. Go on inside. The man's been... not himself since you've been gone."

I grimaced and made my way into the bar where the crowd

that had been there greeted the others boisterously. An unshaven and disheveled Uncle Yen sat at the end of the bar, a t-shirt slack over his frame as he nursed a tall, frothy mug of beer. He didn't even look up at us when we approached him.

"Damn, Uncle Yen, what the hell happened to you?" I muttered softly before I watched him blink and mutter something to himself. I grunted and spoke a little louder toward him, "Someone die?"

Yen blinked again and just huffed, slammed down his beer and closed his eyes. "All I hear is the boy, he's trying to reach out to me even now!" My eyebrows shot up as he turned to blearily glare at me, his head wobbling as he did. "Don't you *dare* mimic him, you bastard."

Galaxy, sober him up please. She hopped up onto the bar and hissed at him, batting him with a paw and his glassy eyes cleared visibly. "You okay now?"

His lip quivered and his eyes began to water as he whispered, "You're back?"

I snorted and put my hands out to show him I was real. "Sure am."

He launched himself at me, wrapping his arms around my shoulders, gripping me as much as he could before I gagged at the stench of him. He retched and turned his nose up at me. "Oh, you need a shower."

He looked down at himself and bashfully added, "Apparently, I do too." He cleared his throat and patted my shoulder after staring into my eyes for a few seconds. "Glad that you're back, son. Don't worry, we'll figure something out about the council. They may try to out you, but it won't be advertised by any of my people here, you can take that to the dragons."

He pointed to the Oni around us. "Pack up his things and be ready to move at a moment's notice."

"What are you talking about, old man?" Arden growled with a questioning eyebrow raised at him as she crossed her arms and shifted her weight onto her back foot.

"Well, you all returned." He chuckled. "No one ever

returns, so I just assume you all wised up and returned from your fool's errand."

It was my turn to snort and just grinned. "We found it, Uncle Yen." He stared at me as if I was daft, so I coaxed a little of the Huntsman's power into myself.

The shadows around us deepened and began to crawl up my body to cover me in the shadowed armor of the Hunt. My voice, the same demonic growl it had been before. "You're looking at the new Huntsman."

The entire bar was so quiet that you could have heard a fly fart upstairs, even with all the noise from the outside. The shadows dropped from my body in a cascade that reminded me of smoke, but I kept my voice cheerful as I addressed all the onlookers in the High Table. "I'm still getting used to it myself, but I mean to use this power for the good of us all."

Whispering broke out among the various creatures in human guise, even among the staff. That was, until Kenshi blinked and got his bearing under control—then he was all rage. "All staff know Marcus is bubba!"

He turned on his people and snarled, "You trust bubba Marcus before—trust him now!"

Some of the staff and security looked remorseful, but who could blame them? The boogeyman had essentially shown himself to them where they likely felt the most safe in the world.

I patted Kenshi on this shoulder. "It's okay, buddy. I understand how they have to feel."

He grunted and Uncle Yen took my arm. "You go take a shower while we get things sorted out down here. You can start working again in a couple days." He turned to the crowd of patrons and employees and bellowed, "Two rounds on me!"

The whole bar exploded in cheers and the smell of alcohol intensified. On my way toward the stairs, Cassia stopped me by grabbing my wrist and asked, "Can I join you in a few minutes?"

I scoffed. "You don't need to ask that." I winked at her as

her face lit up a bit. "Just make some noise or shout before you hop in so I don't freak out and attack you?"

She looked genuinely excited by the idea and I tried to grab her as she let go of me. "Wait! Don't do that, come on!" She just shoved her way through the crowd and was gone as I tried to keep an eye on her.

She's going to try to scare you now. Galaxy teased while I trudged up the stairs and summoned my room key to let myself in.

My room was clean and tidy, my phone on my desk with a note attached to it that I would look at after I took a shower. My bed was made, even had the corners they taught us in the Marine Corps in the sheets.

I grinned and patted the bed. "Great work, Seamus. I owe you some buckeyes, buddy."

A round of soft, snorting laughter greeted me from beneath the bed and I just chuckled as I made my way into the head to hop in the shower. Stripping my stank clothes off was a relief, and it would be nice to get under some hot water for a little bit, but I needed to shave first. The stubble was getting to be too much, even for me, and though I could rock one hell of a freedom beard, I liked being clean shaven more.

After scraping the stubble from my chin and tinkering with the idea of a goatee, then a mustache, I wiped off the residual shaving cream and came up to find Cassia standing behind me with a massive shit-eating grin. "Fuck!"

She cackled at my dismay and grabbed me around the waist. "That was funnier than I thought, but I thought you said you were going to attack me?"

I growled and turned in her grasp until she stood chest to chest with me before I pushed her back up against the wall and leered down at her. "Let's go then!"

She giggled and I shut the door to the bathroom before we got into the shower to clean off.

CHAPTER TWENTY-SIX

The mirror in the bathroom was foggy and my skin a little darker red due to the heat of the shower and other things, but otherwise I felt refreshed.

Galaxy sat on the bed in a pair of loose shorts and one of my tank tops with my PlayStation controller in her hands and a grin on her face as I grumbled, "Just couldn't wait, could you?"

"Nope!" She chuckled and stared at me, towel around my waist and quirked her head. "I needed a distraction, so I just popped in here to relieve some stress. By the way, you have a couple of messages."

I grunted and tossed my chin toward the paper under my smart phone and she nodded. "As well as a letter from what I assume is one of the Councilmembers."

I blinked at that and decided that getting dressed could wait just a little longer than my curiosity could and stepped in front of the TV to retrieve my effects.

Galaxy hissed at me as I crossed her line of sight to her game and I just chuckled as she tried and failed to kick me out of the way.

The letter was what I wanted to open first, so I did.

Hello, Mr. Bola,

I hope this letter finds you well. If you are reading this, either you have returned a coward with your tail tucked firmly betwixt your legs, or you have succeeded. It is my truest hope that the latter has come to be.

I would like to extend congratulations if that is the case, and allow you the first opportunity to truly test your new powers. Attached is the current phone number at which I might be reached, please call me at your earliest possible convenience.

Councilwoman Serpath.

Post Script: I do hope that I do not have to inform you that if you have failed and do not intend to try to retrieve the mantle again, that you should not contact me.

"Wow." I grunted and sighed. "That was rather... terse." I pulled the folded sheet of paper out next and read over it. There were texts from family, Mom and Dad reaching out for important family events that had happened, but nothing pressing. Though the last one was a little mysterious and was from a voicemail.

Bola, call me

-E

I listened to the voicemail, then recognized that it was Sergeant Major Espinoza and he sounded... worried? I couldn't tell, but I was going to have to try to call him back.

I pressed the call that had been missed and the phone began to ring through. Then stopped and someone answered whose voice I didn't recognize, "Hello?"

"Hi, I must have the wrong number." I hung up hurriedly and took a deep breath. Espinoza said that he would try to get a hold of me through the nurse that he trusted, hadn't he?

Why would he call me directly? My phone started to ring again and it was the same number I had just called. I ignored it and let it go to voicemail, then brought the paper with Serpath's number on it.

I dialed it and lifted the phone to my ear, letting it ring through until someone on the other end answered in a language I didn't understand, but sounded close to Pashto or another

Middle Eastern dialect. "Hello? I'm calling for Councilwoman Serpath?"

"Ah, Mr. Bola, my friend!" The man on the other end sounded genuinely excited to hear from me. "My queen will be with you as soon as she can. I will hang up with you and she will come to you. Goodbye!"

I stammered, "Wait, wha—" The receiver clicked and the line went dead just as the phone began to ring from the first number again. I rolled my eyes and answered it. "Look, I'm sorry that I hung up so abruptly, but I had a voicemail from someone at this number."

"Ease it back, Bola," Sergeant Major Espinoza warned and my eyes widened.

"I thought you were going to call through our mutual friend." My tone was even but had to be dripping with concern.

Espinoza was quiet for a moment too long, then sighed and informed me, "Kali is dead, Marcus. She was found on the running trail on Ft. Meade, torn apart as if by some kind of great cat or something. Her tongue and fingers were taken."

Specialist Kali had been instrumental in my recovery and sanity, and to find out that she had been taken down by something like that was just a lot. Galaxy's button mashing stopped and she stilled so that she could hear more through me as I spoke, "I take it that you wouldn't call me for something like that unless you thought something foul was afoot."

He was quiet for another moment then said simply, "She was murdered. I'd swear it on my chevrons." There was a thicker emotion in his voice this time as he added, "They were just covering up their tracks by taking her fingers. There were defensive wounds all over her, Bola. Shit that wasn't right. There are no great cats, here, sergeant. And if I had to think on it, she was the only one that connected you and me."

"What can we do then?"

"I need you to keep your damn eyes open." Espinoza growled, his voice lowered after that. "I'm onto something where I am. I had to call in a lot of favors from all over the world, and I'm pretty sure that I may owe someone a kidney after all this, but I've got some information lined up on what went down. All you need to do is stay safe and help me when the time is right, okay?"

"I'll keep a low profile until then if you don't need my help." Cassia came out of the bathroom with a towel wrapped around her waist and one over her shoulders, draped so that it covered her. She looked at me curiously and I turned my focus back to the phone. "I'll be okay where I am now."

"These guys got to Kali on a military installation, Bola—I don't think they care about wherever it is that you are." He sounded worried but I just shrugged to myself. He had no clue. "Stay cautious and keep your head down, Marine."

With that, the line went dead and I was left to wonder how he had gotten my phone number. Chances were good that he had found it at Kali's if she had been at all close to him like he had made it seem. He really trusted her, and she had said nothing but good things about him, so I had believed it all. What could he have been closing in on though? And who could have done that to Kali?

"You alright?" Cassia moved closer and I shook my head. "What happened, was that Serpath?"

"It was my former Sergeant Major, and he just told me the nurse that had helped me recover after coming back from overseas was murdered." I pressed the heel of my hand against my head just to break the tension that I felt.

I had power now—*real power*—and people were still dying needlessly. And for what? This shit had to stop. Soon.

"Whatever it is that Serpath needs us to do for her is going to be the first step to us making ourselves known." I rolled my shoulders as the anger and frustration washed over me, glaring at the girls in the room. "We're going back to the temple to try to figure out what the hell went on there so that the target is off me and the other survivors."

"Do you really think that someone is after you like that?"

Cassia frowned at me and then turned to Galaxy. "You were there, is that the case?"

"Likely so." She cast her gaze down, then back up toward me with determination in her eyes. "My captors just might have a hand in this as well, and I would like to find out more about them."

I smiled at her, though she wasn't prepared for the savagery of it I guess, because she flinched and blushed. I blinked at her and said, "What?"

"You looked like you were ready to eat her or something." Cassia snorted and put a hand on Galaxy's shoulder to steady her. "I think you're getting a little pent up—should we fight?"

Galaxy and I snorted in unison and she looked even more concerned as she stated, "I'll beat you up!"

That made us both laugh harder. I choked out, "Oh, I know you will."

She frowned and eyed us both. "Why are you laughing if you know you'll lose?"

"Because your greatest concern is still violence." I marched closer to her and took her chin between my thumb and index finger so I could stare into her eyes. "You care about me enough to beat me up, I think that says something."

She smiled at me, her nose crinkling as she said, decidedly, "Well, Oni don't really love the way humans do. So, I'm still figuring that out. But I do know that I love you—I think?"

I raised an eyebrow at that last bit and she grinned more. "Gotcha." She leaned into a kiss and then leaned back. "Oh, Luci is gonna be pissed that he wasn't there for that."

Galaxy cackled, making us both look down at her as she wiped tears from her eyes and heaved a loud sigh. "He's down-stairs waiting for you all now. He's pissed that no one has called him to warn him that you'd arrived."

Cassia and I glanced back toward each other and exchanged worried looks before a thunderous "Where are my friends?" broke the silence and Galaxy cackled some more.

A clattering downstairs made both Cass and I bolt for the

door, only to remember we were wearing only our towels. We dressed, then made our way into the hall and all but leaped down the stairs to land in front of a very upset Lucifer.

His arms were crossed in front of his chest, then his nose twitched and he leaned forward to speak softly over the din of the music. "I do hope I didn't interrupt anything?"

"Nothing that a good drink wouldn't cure?" I offered him with a smile, his gaze leveled against mine and he smirked. "You okay, buddy?"

"I am better than okay." He turned and raised his arms. "My friends returned from Grestal—we drink tonight!"

Once more, a deafening roar lit up the bar and the music came back to full blast before Luci turned back to us. "You'll have to tell me everything, okay?" His eyes bounced back and forth between us. "Every last detail."

Cassia swallowed uncomfortably and I just chuckled wryly; he would get it out of one of us. "Certainly!" I patted his cheek and nodded to the bar. "Let's start with a drink, shall we?"

A few drinks in, Galaxy sauntered down the stairs to join us, her clothes as they always were—stylishly clinging to her curves and artfully painted on. Her black jeans and yellow crop top were lovely against her dark skin and her smile as radiant as she could be. Her knowing grin only grew as Lucifer followed my gaze and fixed her with a smile of his own.

We've only just started the telling of what happened, don't blurt anything out, okay? She rolled her eyes at me mentally and let the devil hug her and offer her the cocktail menu.

She pointed to a margarita with various fruits she wished to try in it and Luci ordered it before asking, "And how did you enjoy *your* time in Grestal, dearest?"

"Oh, I had a wonderful time." Galaxy purred, her smile on me as she spoke. "I learned a lot about myself, and others. Had quite the adventurous menu and a few unbelievable experiences, but I wouldn't want to take away from Cassia and Marcus telling their side of the story."

Lucifer narrowed his gaze at her, then turned toward us. "Then by all means, do tell what else happened."

I started to speak again when Arden, freshly showered and her hair up in a messy bun draped herself over Cassia and me, crooning, "Hey love birds, filling Luci in?"

Cass and I stiffened as Lucifer's face went through various episodes of slowly dawning rationalizing until he finally settled on indignant shock. "*What!*"

Arden's confusion and Galaxy's rampant laughter only incensed Lucifer more as he struggled to articulate what he was trying to say.

Finally, Cassia had enough and stated, "I love Marcus. There, I said it. You all know it, and now it's out there." She stared at all of us as if any of the people gathered near us would challenge her, then she pointed to Galaxy and said, "So does she."

Lucifer's eyes widened and it was all he could do to keep from pulling his hair out, it seemed. His mouth moved but no words came through until he finally broke down, shoulders fallen and simply said, "How?"

"Things get complicated when you live inside someone else, don't they?" Galaxy offered with a shrug. "It's just what I— Cassia and I, I suppose—both feel. It doesn't help that the Huntsman's mantle can gauge and display relationships and their status to him in real time."

Lucifer blinked and stared at me. "Can you see how I feel about you?"

Too powerful for me to get an accurate read of him, sorry. Manny glared out of me and just stared until he couldn't focus anymore. *I will need to eat a lot more, and the bonds you have will need to be more deeply explored if you want to be able to read him, or even gods for that matter.*

I was about to say something to him in regard to that, but he stopped me and said, *Gods at full strength, she does not count and she is a part of you.*

Fair. "Sorry, the mantle can't get a read on you—you're just too strong." I winked at him and he almost seemed relieved. "We are friends though, right?"

"Oh, honey. Of course we are!" Lucifer patted my shoulder comfortingly. "Absolutely, we are. I was just curious is all. No worries."

I smiled at him. "Cool." I glared at Arden. "I know someone who owes everyone a round of drinks."

She rolled her eyes and shook her head at me before sighing. "I can afford it easily, but you can't blame me for you two having beaten around the bush."

She walked down the bar after that and began to order some things to drink and I even saw her eye the menu before returning. "I took the liberty of providing something to eat too —happy?"

I grinned, suddenly famished, but growled, "It's a start."

We all laughed, continuing to just hang out and fill Lucifer in on our adventures. Two hours or so later, my pocket began to vibrate violently. I pulled out my phone to find a blocked caller ID notification.

"Hello?" I waited until the voice started to speak but could barely make out what was said. "Sorry, I can't hear you!"

I blinked and suddenly stood in the middle of a small, beige, and bland meeting room with the phone to my ear and a glass to my lips, Councilwoman Serpath seated opposite where I stood. Her gaze was less than enthusiastic as she stared at me. She wore simple, but well-made clothes, colorful cloth ribbons draped from her long and pointed ears that complimented her green skin and hawk-like eyes as she continued to stare at me expectantly.

My drink lowered and I grunted, "Well, I guess I can hear you now."

"I need your *undivided* attention for a few moments, Mr. Bola," she hissed angrily.

"You got it." She eyed me steadily and I continued to stare back until an uncomfortable amount of time passed, then asked, "Should I go?"

"One typically speaks a little more respectfully to their elders and those who outrank them, am I wrong?" She lifted a rather large file from her lap and slapped it onto the table. "I do not expect the deference, bowing and scraping that used to be the norm of our positions as councilmembers, but I had come to expect a modicum of decorum from someone who reportedly served in the military. Especially one as well known as the Marine Corps."

"I've relaxed on a few things, and I don't know what you want either." I continued to watch her as I explained, "I won't bow to anyone, and I scrape for nothing. I've fought for my country and as I stand to serve your organization, I expect the same courtesy you are accustomed to giving people who are of use to you."

A slow grin spread across her face. "Excellently said."

"And it's far from all I want to say, but I'll hold off on that." I set my drink down and pressed the button on my phone to blank the screen. "How can I be of service to you?"

"My patrons are dying." She skipped all pretense and preamble and got straight to the facts—I could work with that. "I don't know exactly what is killing them, but it showed up recently and it's killing them gruesomely."

I frowned and she eyed me expectantly but I stayed quiet. Finally she closed her eyes and steepled her fingers, saying, "I can imagine you wonder why it is that I cannot hunt this creature down myself."

"Hadn't crossed my mind, actually." She looked caught off guard, but I explained before she got uppity. "You're powerful in your own right, I have no doubt of that—especially with the abilities I've seen from a certain Dhampyr. But while I was in Grestal, I learned that every creature, person, and being has their place in the grand scheme of things. Your place is to lead and your skills may not be what's necessary to hunt down the culprits, and I respect when someone knows their limitations and how to stay in their lane."

She nodded and finally I added, "And what better way to

test the Huntsman than to send them after something going bump in the night?"

Her surprise turned to savage glee as she growled, "*Exactly.*"

"Then I'll need you to send me back, and I'll need you to send me all the information that you have so that my friends and I can come take care of this issue for you." She lifted her hands and her mouth opened, but my own hand raised to stop her. "I held up my end of the bargain—I did the thing no one thought I'd be able to and became what was needed. What's in this for me and mine?"

"Other than the opportunity to test yourself and continued allowance to be a part of the High Table?" Her eyebrows raised almost impossibly high as she spoke, once again expecting something of me that I couldn't quite place. I nodded once and she sighed. "I will compensate you as best I can, but if more of my patrons die, then I can do nothing for you and face separation from my branch."

I eyed her for a moment longer then nodded once more. "Fine."

"How long will you need to prepare?" The exasperation in her tone was enough to make me stop messing with her so much.

"One of mine is having issues with the Warden Orders presently that I plan to try to take care of tomorrow. How often are the attacks?"

She frowned and pulled out a sheet of paper, then a pair of glasses so she could blink at the scrawling script on it before answering, "One or two a week, with seven of them having been torn limb from limb, their blood completely gone and their eyes and tongues missing." She folded the paper, thinking for a moment before she tapped it twice and a copy of it appeared next to the original in a puff of white smoke. "Here, take this."

I grabbed the sheet and folded it to put it into my pocket. "I can have my party ready in a few days. How do I reach you for transport?"

"Logistically speaking, you will be permitted to use my private jet and you may stay in my summer home near the scene of the latest murder in Cairo." She must have noted my confusion because she growled, "What?"

"You brought me here to you, why not just teleport us?"

She snorted and rolled her eyes. "Touched are always so interesting and easily disquieted by simpler magic." She touched her head and winked. "This is merely a meeting via the theater of the mind. It's easier for me to do these small things over a distance as opposed to coming to you or bringing you to me. Call me when you are ready; my jet is already waiting. See you in a few days."

She lifted her hands and shoved toward me, a sudden force jolting me hard enough that I came to standing as I had been when she took me. The drink that had almost been to my lips spilled as I flinched and spilled on myself.

"Uh oh!" Cassia whistled and laughed at me. "Marcus is drunk."

I sighed and wiped myself off, dabbing the bar where my drink had spilled as well while grousing, "No, but I wish I was. I just spoke to Serpath and she's going to bring us to Cairo for our first Hunt on behalf of the High Table."

"Oh!" Arden leaned closer and blinked at me with excitement building in her eyes. "I miss Cairo so much! I wonder how everyone is. Did she tell you what we'll be after? Is it a mischievous Sphinx or something?"

"It's someone brutally murdering her patrons there. She gave me a sheet of paper there with some details, but it was all in my head so I don't have any more information just now." Cassia's fingers slipped into both of my pockets, my eyes widening as she did so and I grunted, "Woah now."

"Hold still," she growled and pulled out the same sheet of paper that I had folded and put into my pocket. Cassia held it up between her fingers and raised a brow. "This?"

"Yeah," I whispered, mesmerized and irritated that I couldn't do something like that. "Man, magic is so cool."

The others chuckled to themselves at my humanity and began to read the script on the page, Arden finally speaking as she read along, "… Gutted and their eyes and tongues removed. Exsanguination as well? That could be a vampire, but the other bits are stranger, and less them." She frowned. "And they're leaving the bodies hanging for other supernatural creatures to find."

"That's weird," I muttered and finally just shook my head to refocus. "We can worry about that when we get there, though I'll need Galaxy on lore duty to see if there's anything in the myths and legends that could do that kind of thing. Right now, we need to ensure that Merlin is taken care of as far as the Orders are concerned."

"He should be fine that no one else is standing in his way, right?" Arden frowned over her drink as if she truly wasn't certain. "I mean, there was so much blood when we came back, but there can't have been anything that would be pinned on him, right?"

"I don't know, but I don't trust them either." Cassia's voice was low, but she mirrored my thoughts and feelings exactly.

"I wouldn't put it past the others in the Sword to try to make an example of him, including Jetlo himself." I growled at the memory of the asshole pulling his sword not ten feet from me; the rage it brought to mind caused Mako to get restless.

I checked my phone and the clock said it was plenty past time to go the hell to sleep. I winked at Galaxy as she yawned and nodded to Luce. "I hate to say it, but we have a potentially big day tomorrow and I need to be in top form for it." I patted Lucifer on the cheek. "Stay classy, Satan."

"Who do you think you're talking to, Marcus?" His grin widened and he put a hand to his chest, suddenly wearing a snazzy outfit with a well-fitting jacket over it. "I'm one handsome devil."

I snorted and nearly fell off my stool at the suddenness of it, then caught myself and laughed. "And the costume change to boot? Damn, there's no one here fresher than you."

We all said our goodbyes a little more tamely than that and I made my way to bed with Galaxy following closely behind. I stripped into my boxers and hopped into the freshly made bed and sighed, nothing like coming home from the field to your rack—nothing could beat it.

That was until Galaxy stuck her cold foot on my leg and I released an indignant yowl that made her laugh and say, "Sorry."

"How does someone who can shapeshift into a cat have cold ass feet?" I stared at her in mock rage and she just ignored me in favor of getting comfortable. "You think Merlin will be okay?"

"He's currently in the gym with Kenshi, who is chasing him with a blade as large as his forearm and almost as thick—I'm more worried about him now." I smiled at the thought and she knew my next question. "She's currently being taught how to browse the internet by Keith and it's... not pretty. Amabala will be okay. Though it will take her time to be able to shift her shape as Cassia and Arden can."

"Thank you."

She cuddled closer to me and sighed contentedly. "Of course."

I watched the blooming heart over her shoulder throb and deepen, then smiled and just put an arm around her waist to hold her as we both fell asleep.

CHAPTER TWENTY-SEVEN

Someone screamed downstairs, outside.

It was still dark, the moon shining through my window as clouds lazily drifted over it and I stumbled out of bed and toward it. I peered down at the sidewalk and saw a few drunken college kids stumbling down the way. My pulse slowed, adrenaline subsiding as I realized it was okay. Then something flickering across the street caught my eye.

The street lamp flickered again as I focused on it and the shadows darkened in the area; a figure stood there, watching the kids moving on and out of sight. Then it started to follow along, wherever it walked close to the lights, they flickered and failed as if the person's presence alone drained the electricity from the lights.

That wasn't good.

Galaxy, come on, I growled mentally, rousing her from her sleep. She faded and her presence flowed into me. I tried to call to Manny too, but there was nothing from him. As if he felt drained.

I dressed quickly, just pulling on the t-shirt and jeans that I had worn, then pulled my sneakers on. I didn't bother with the door, knowing I'd lose even more time, so I opened the window and hopped out.

The landing was a little jarring, but otherwise I was fine and started jogging behind the drunk kids until I was close enough that I could keep them in sight without arousing suspicion. The shadowy figure walked along, view uninterrupted by anything as most cars were off the streets by now.

The further from the High Table they walked, the longer the lights stayed off until we closed on the larger grounds of the campus near Eleventh. The students started across the street and the shadow just stood there, waiting. They didn't even see it, but it was there just waiting.

Damn it. I spat loudly and coughed before calling, "'Scuse me! Can y'all spare some money, please?" They turned and saw me walking toward them and the ruse worked as they walked opposite the direction I was walking so that we wouldn't make it to the same place on the other side of the street. "Oh, come on! I'm not some stalker or somethin', honest!"

They moved a little faster and the shadow just watched them leave before turning back to get a face full of me.

It had missed me casting Embodiment of Lightning and now I stood nearly on top of it, grinning. "Hi, can I help you?"

It hissed at me and threw a punch but I ducked and struck out at the creature's inner knee with my open palm. My hand went straight through it as if it were just shadow.

Marcus, it's the mantle! Galaxy warned and sure enough the shadowy drake stepped out from beneath it and swung his tail at me.

"Shit!" I hopped over the tail only to have what I assumed was Manny shove me so that I landed ten feet away and skidded on my ass as Mako charged forward. *Galaxy, go eat Manny!*

But what if that destroys the power of the Hunt? The genuine stress of it all was concerning, but if I had to worry about him going hunting while I was asleep, there would be nothing I could control anyway.

She understood that and surged out of me, her body larger

than normal and more powerful. She and the shadow creature that was Manny collided and began to fight each other, then Mako was on top of me.

I socked the drake in the chin angrily and growled, "You don't remember the beating I gave your friend last time?"

That was the Huntsman! Galaxy corrected me just as vehemently.

I howled, "Not helping!" Mako reached down and managed to grasp my leg in his teeth painfully and yanked up, my jeans ripping and my body following along. "Woah!"

The drake tossed me and I slammed into the light pole above him with an *oof* and began to fall as Mako turned toward where the two struggled.

Galaxy's claws were ripping the shadows to shreds faster than they could return and she was beginning to win, but Mako would fuck that up. I managed to grab the pole and cast Bolt at Mako before I planted my feet into the wooden frame and shot myself forward at him.

I snatched his head on the way by, rolling and trying to take him with me, but just twisted my arm and ended up letting go.

The distraction worked though, since the drake's head was aligned on me and not Manny and Galaxy.

I hopped up onto my feet and summoned my Mana Blade, muttering, "I really don't want to have to kill you, Mako. Finding a new mount will fucking suck—stand down."

The drake snarled and reared his head back, a rumbling breath filling his chest just before he stilled and the shadows that wrapped around his body slid away like water from a duck's back.

He blinked his reptilian eyes at me and suddenly I could feel how confused and irritated he was. We both turned as a grunt drew our attention and found Galaxy, bloody and sitting on the ground, smiling at us. "Did it."

"Are you okay?" I stepped closer to her and Mako joined me, but as soon as I stilled, so did he. "Are you going to try to eat me if I go to her? We cool?"

Mako did that weird double blink thing that reptiles did and shook his head, then tilted his head at the last comment, confusion more prevalent.

I reached out my hand and willed him to come to me, his immediate obedience another good sign. His body faded as soon as his scaled, beak-like muzzle touched my palm and the draconic tattoo returned to my forearm.

"That's still so cool." Galaxy grunted and tried to stand only to fall back onto her ass. "Ouch."

"You got into one hell of a fight, kid." I reached down to her and hefted her up into my arms as if she weighed absolutely nothing. "How are you feeling?"

"Hello?" She motioned to herself weakly and grinned. "I feel better than ever."

I fought not to yell at her for the sarcasm, but the fact was that I could tell she wasn't trying to be unkind. She was telling the truth.

"I'm stronger than I was before, like he clicked with something inside of me and just *fits*." She shook her head and stared up at me. "I feel one step closer to being whole, Marcus."

I couldn't help the smile that came to my face as I stared down at her. "I'm happy for you." I looked around at the damage to the street, the blood from my wounds having flecked the ground and more than a couple new potholes in an otherwise shit road. "We should get the hell out of here so we don't get caught."

She nodded and we hurried off, Galaxy still in my arms for some reason since she didn't seem to want to go back to being a cat, or just ride along inside me.

We made it to the High Table before Cassia found us, her breath coming in heaves. "Merlin with you?"

Galaxy and I shook our heads and she pulled out her cell and barked, "Arden!"

The device rang and the jinn picked up almost instantly. "Raiding—what?"

"Merlin at your place?" Cassia's voice was deeper now, and her skin began to turn red in splotches.

"No, I thought he was in the guard quarters getting some rest." She sounded unconcerned when she'd said it, then bellowed, "That little shit!"

The phone went silent and three heartbeats later, Arden stood in front of us in a pair of loose shorts and a tank top. "What the fuck is he doing?"

"I don't know, but we need to find him." Cassia was shaking, she was so pissed off. "I woke up and had a bad feeling and when I couldn't find any of you, I tried to find him and he was gone. Bed didn't look like it had been slept in at all."

"Do you think he could have gone to meet with the Orders?" Galaxy whispered and blinked up at us. "He had to know how dangerous that could be."

Cassia stepped closer and bore down on Galaxy. "Don't you know what all of us are thinking when we think it? What is he thinking right now? Where is he?"

"Cass, cool it." My tone was gentle, but I left no wiggle room for an argument. "We'll find him."

"Why are you two outside, and why is she bloody?" Arden frowned at us and then stiffened. "Someone just summoned a jinn."

"What?" Cassia growled as Arden's hair blazed behind her. "Where?"

Arden didn't say anything, she just took off down the street toward campus and we followed as fast as we could, her blazing trail lighting the street and setting car alarms off.

It took fifteen minutes for us to get to where she had stopped, and by the time we got there the grass had caught fire and she was weaving spell after spell at someone who stood behind an impenetrable wall of blue energy.

Xehano laughed and watched us, with Merlin unconscious on the ground behind him and the stone fox standing guard over his body.

Galaxy called to all of us mentally, *He's alive but something's wrong. I sense another presence here.*

"Getting real tired of you Wardens and your fuck-fuck games." My voice was a growl that probably could barely be heard over Arden's flaming rage. "What'd you do to the boy?"

"Less than I mean to do to you!" Xehano slapped his hands together, then separated them and lifted them above his head before shoving toward us. The flames in front of him met a wave of wind that ate their force and darkened the area considerably. "You had to get in the way. Had to make a nuisance of yourselves. No more."

He reached down and pulled something off his belt and held it up. It looked like an old-fashioned oil lamp, kind of like the ones that I had seen in a certain movie before.

Arden lost her absolute shit and roared, her magic lashing out at the air around her as she lifted from the ground. "Don't you *dare!*"

He rubbed the lamp as her flames whipped forward and slashed at the barrier in front of Xehano to no avail.

A smoky figure flowed from the lamp, manacles on their feet and hands that connected to each other, and then to the lamp itself, flowing inside it with heavy metallic clanks.

The voice was cool. "Master."

I couldn't make out what they looked like, but Arden screeched with renewed fury and her attacks crashed into the magic in front of him and the barrier began to crack.

"Kill them," Xehano ordered and I half expected to feel my heart explode.

The voice simply stated, "No. I cannot kill with the power of a wish."

"Very well, I wish for *that one* to be bottled like you!"

Arden's magic went absolutely wild as the voice quivered and said, "As you wish."

I roared, "No!" Mako crashing from my arm and toward the barrier as the shadows around us flowed forward. "Commence the Hunt!"

Shadows burst from the ground all around us, even Arden, as the jinn wrestled with her. The jinn yelled, "No!" The shadows wresting his target from him.

Cassia lunged forward, grasping the spectral figure around the waist so that she could arch her back and slam his head into the ground; the suplex worked and he was stuck there.

"Mako!" The drake turned toward the sound of my voice as his tail thudded into the barrier and cracked it further. Other Wardens had arrived and they all carried staves and wands in their hands. "Protect Merlin!"

The drake opened his mouth and roared so hard that the ground beneath him shuddered and his eyes glowed fiercely as he barreled into the interlopers.

Xehano huffed and snarled, "What the hell is this?"

I chuckled as I stepped closer to him. "You didn't know?" I motioned to myself as I summoned my Fae Frame into my right hand, the cool metallic kiss of the grip pleasing after wanting my guns for so long.

Shadow Weapon upgrade: yes / no?

Galaxy? My question made her stir and she just selected yes for me.

Shadows slid from my hand and wrist until they covered the pistol, reinforcing it with magic until the pistol had become a sort of shadowed hand crossbow. She must have sensed my distaste, because Galaxy growled, *We can work on aesthetics later. End this before he can make another wish.*

"I'm the Huntsman now, and this is about to get really shitty for you." His eyes narrowed and he touched his barrier to flood it with mana, but I squeezed the trigger anyway and a small bolt of shadowy hate burst from the muzzle and speared straight toward his barrier and the center-mass targets beyond it.

The barrier chipped and started to fall away, my joy at the sheer awesome display of power overcoming me. "Fuck aesthetics, this shit is amazing!"

I fired two more rounds and noted that each shot cost me about five mana, not terrible. The barrier fell completely, but like any good magic man, the Warden used pure mana to shove the worst of the damage away from himself and scrambled to respond with a spell of his own.

Mako roared again, the screams of the other Wardens echoing in the darkness of the light and my power swelled. For everything that Mako consumed, Galaxy fed as well, and he ate like he was a starving man at an all you can eat buffet.

You'll want to get in closer with him if you want to have a chance to keep him from casting heavier spells. Galaxy's warning was appreciated, but I knew how that could go.

Arden and Cassia fought the jinn almost to a standstill, Arden pleading with the poor creature to stop fighting them, but he just returned, "I have to fulfill the wish."

Merlin still lay unconscious on the ground with Rocky standing guard, jaws blooded and his sharp stone teeth bared at the Wardens who came too close. His tails swayed behind him as he made his fury known.

The scythe would be too much, and the chances of a sword made up of pure mana working on a wizard of Xehano's level weren't high. But Hoarfrost?

That could do the trick.

I used Embodiment of Lightning and stepped forward so that I was a blur and slammed my fist into Xehano's chest, the amulet that had fallen from his plain robes flaring to life and flooding our surroundings with power that lashed out at me. My fist ached, feeling like some of the knuckles had been pulverized and the bones shattered.

Galaxy thickened the shadows at my wrist for me like a brace and my lycanthropic healing took care of the rest. I flexed my left hand and grunted. "Magic is pretty damn cool, isn't it, old man?"

He just sneered at me. "You have no idea." Then flicked his wrist at me, a bolt of unseen power slamming into my right leg.

The pain was intense, bordering on debilitating, but I grit my teeth and covered the wound in ice with my will. I caked my left hand from the forearm down with Hoarfrost, the ice flowing and making blades on my forearm like a certain comic-book hero of Gotham and the ice on my fingers forming spikes at my knuckles before they finished with claws at my fingertips.

I shot at him with another couple rounds, no purchase made other than the minute distractions I needed to close the gap. His magic swept toward me and I rolled aside and shot again, catching him in the thigh, his snarl of pain making me grin.

Another Warden shouted something, blue and red lights flashing in the distance as sirens wailed.

Draw on the bonds of the Hunt to fuel you, Marcus, Galaxy insisted as some of the Wardens were closing on Merlin and the others, more having flooded the area as we fought.

I wasn't sure how at first but the moment I thought about them, the bonds themselves appeared before me, some of them thicker than others, color coded as well. The thickest ones, crimson and about as thick as a bass guitar string went to Cassia and the other into the pit of my stomach. The second thickest, a cool blue one that led to Merlin on the ground starting to rouse. The last one was to Arden and it was thin and looked to be unraveling as we went.

Each of her strikes was flurried and her begging had long since stopped. All she wanted was to put the jinn out of his misery it seemed, and the flaming hammers in her grasp rose and fell like she was going to crush a nail.

I snarled, wondering what the right thing to do was, when it dawned on me. I shot my crossbow at Xehano's head and cast Embodiment once more, appearing behind him at hip height and tackled him.

His magic slammed into my waist and lower back with a sickening crunch, forcing me to let go. He started to mutter something but a gushing blue light ate at him and he had to counter it, ruining his building spell.

I grinned to myself as I tried to get up but couldn't, when Merlin stepped into view.

Xehano spat and cursed before he patted his hip, but my

laughter drew his attention as I lifted the lamp in my grasp, "Looking for this?"

"No!" He tried to rush forward but Rocky rammed himself into the man's knee, a soft pop making him crumple and fall screaming.

I rubbed the lamp and Arden bellowed her rage at the enemy being gone into the air as the jinn appeared next to me. "Master." Whispers of power and fortune rushed through my head. I could see mountains of gold and jewels in a massive house to contain them all. Servants all over bringing the finest food.

"I wish for my friends and I to be healed." I blinked and the numbing pain in my back was gone. "Thank you."

"Stop!" Xehano snarled and Mako made his way over to the fallen Warden of the Staff. "Don't make any more wishes, and I will leave you alone."

I laughed as I climbed to my feet and rolled my eyes. "This ain't about you, old man."

Merlin clapped his hands together and muttered a few arcane words that escaped my ability to understand, when a cage of blue energy appeared around Xehano.

The old man waved a hand and the cage dissolved, but Mako slammed his head into the man and he screamed before Merlin put the cage back and pulled Xehano toward him. The cage crushed inward until a golden coin floated into Merlin's grasp.

I turned toward where the sounds of flesh hitting flesh and grunting came from, finding Cassia barely holding Arden back from me, the heat in her gaze such that it should have fried me where I was.

"Stop, Marcus, stop now!" Arden tried to press forward but Cass rocked her in the chin with a wicked right that snapped her head back.

"Trust him!" Cassia snarled, but didn't dare chance a glance back my way, as the attack wouldn't have hurt her friend too much in her state.

"I can't have you summon other lamps with jinn in them, can I?" The jinn figure stood there quietly, not saying anything or making so much as a motion of affirmation or decline. I shrugged, glad I hadn't wasted a wish. More images of power and riches flooded me, but I grimaced and spoke clearly. "I wish I knew where to find my friend Ardent Flame's bottled family. A map or list of the places would do wonderfully, mister jinn."

"As you wish." A detailed list popped into my hands and the jinn stepped closer. "Your final wish, master?"

"Marcus, stop!" Arden screeched and surged around Cassia, only to have the jinn physically stop her. "Stop, please. No more wishes."

She's forbidden to say what will happen upon the final wish, but from what I can piece together of her memories, she was able to use a loophole in her master's final wish to escape.

Thinking on it, I finally looked at the jinn and said, "I wish you free and ask that you hold no enmity or ill-wishes toward anyone here, or that we care about."

The manacles attached to his wrists and ankles burst in a rainbow of colors and bright lights. The chains slithered back into the lamp and the jinn surged forward, a grin on his face as he crossed the few feet and grasped my wrist.

The chains almost met the lip of the lamp when the jinn grabbed the lamp and heaved it into the air, a bolt of earthen power slashing through the air and powdering it instantly. He turned to me, the golden energy around him coalescing into the soft brown of sand in the desert, eyes of amber and honey staring into mine. "Thank you for freeing me, but if you hadn't been so careful with that last wish, you would have been the next prisoner of the lamp. Do not summon my kind without caution, friend Marcus."

He disappeared, flowing into the ground as easily as a swimmer might drop into the water.

Arden sobbed and collapsed to the ground, her hands covering her face as Cassia and Merlin went to comfort her. I felt like an asshole, but I'd had a plan. Or at least she could have thought that I would have thought of something, she could have trusted me more.

She cared enough to stay through her trauma to be here for you and her friends. She fought someone who had been enslaved—just like she was—to try to keep you safe, and was almost put back into chains for it. Galaxy appeared in front of me wearing a flowing dress of midnight that touched the ground at her feet. "You would do well to remember that trust goes both ways, Marcus."

I frowned. We had won, but why did it feel like a loss once more? I turned my gaze to the list in my hand and frowned as I quickly scanned it. "These places are all over the world, but there's one in the Middle East near Cairo, I think."

Arden's head whipped up and she stared at me, so I stared back and said, "I told you I would help you find your family, Arden. That didn't stop with your brother."

Her lip quivered and she smiled up at me, the gauge over her right shoulder filling steadily until it went from **friend** to **trusted friend** and finally stood on the precipice of two options. **Love** and **family**.

I smiled at her and held my arms out to the side. "We're family now, Arden. I'm trying to meet Mom and Dad, and my new siblings too."

She laughed and stood up, walking forward to stand close enough that I could see the gauge become a small group of figures huddled together and confirmed it was **family**.

Just as I was about to try to hug her, her fist crashed into my chin and snapped my head to the right, knocking me onto my ass.

My ringing bell cleared as she growled, "Then don't you ever ignore your big sister Arden and do some dumb shit like that ever again, or so help me I will fucking end you, Marcus." She leaned down so she could capture my eyes with hers, filled with mirth but still somehow serious. "I mean it, boy."

I just chuckled and tried to move my jaw as I said, "Yup, got it."

CHAPTER TWENTY-EIGHT

Getting back to the High Table without being seen wasn't too hard thanks to being able to use our newly strengthened bonds to travel through the air. It only took seconds anyway.

Bloodied and tired, all of us walked into the bar to find four Wardens in hoods standing there with Uncle Yen in his pajamas staring at us.

"Do we really have to kick more of your asses tonight?" I growled and rolled my shoulder, trying to get the rest of the fatigue from my system quickly.

Theodorous spoke from behind us. "Quite the contrary, I was just here to celebrate your triumphant return and happened upon these four skulking about in the shadows."

He leaned against the doorframe to the entrance as if he leaned on everything all the damn time and that smug look on his face made me want to yell at him to get his shit together. Maybe I was a little more tired than I thought.

"Young Merlin, I take it you have proof of your having completed the rite of the Sword?" Merlin nodded and went to produce the Gorgana's head but grunted and his eyes widened slowly. "What's wrong?"

"It was stolen from me." His words sounded like they must have tasted like ash on his tongue and I was pretty damn pissed myself.

"How truly unfortunate that is." Theodorous sighed and shook his head. "Well, I guess if you can't join the Sword, but the trip to Grestal didn't kill you, I find myself at a loss as to what to do."

"If it hadn't been for Xehano and all the other Wardens having interfered with us, we wouldn't have had any issues." I tried to keep the rage out of my voice but it was just so damned hard. "We just finished kicking Xehano's ass and setting free the jinn he was trying to use."

Theodorous didn't look surprised, instead staring at Merlin. "A good Warden does not use excuses but produces results. I trust you have evidence to substantiate these claims?"

Merlin pulled the coin with Xehano trapped within and flipped it into the air. Theodorous caught it with ease and stared at it before shaking his head. "I told you not to interfere, old man." He pocketed the coin and stared at Merlin. "I can't allow you into the Sword without proof you passed the trial. And I cannot let you just do nothing, and I take it you have no interest in joining the Heart?"

Merlin shook his head, confusion and anger prevalent on his face.

"Then I suppose I have no choice but to ask that you no longer refer to yourself as a Warden Trainee, Merlin." The boy flinched as if he had been struck, but Theodorous wasn't done. "I'd say you killing more than thirty Wardens and capturing your old mentor in his prime when he had been disobeying a direct order from me is more than enough to call yourself a fully-fledged Warden."

Merlin's face was overcome with joy as Cassia and Arden grabbed him and lifted him up to celebrate.

"I've been wondering if we shouldn't restructure for some time, but I'm not sure what category you would fall into as of yet." Theodorous winked and motioned for the other Wardens in the High Table to leave. He stepped aside so they could move past him. "No one else will come for you from any of the Orders, and if they do, I trust that you will leave them bloodied enough to at least be sent back to me?"

Merlin nodded once and Theodorous clapped his hands and smiled. "Good man! Well, everyone, I look forward to hopefully working with you again in the future. Please do take care of our young prodigy?" He winked and left whistling a merry tune, and that was it.

I snorted and turned to Merlin. "How'd it feel?"

He grinned at me and said, "Pretty damned good."

"Good." I stretched and yawned, then looked to Uncle Yen. "I hate to say it, but Serpath asked that the Hunt goes to Cairo so that we can try to stop whatever is killing her patrons. That okay?"

Uncle Yen stared at me, then nodded. "Yeah, we got coverage. Just keep me in the know and I'll have shifts for you when you get back. Good job, Marcus."

I offered him a smile and turned to the others. "We have today and maybe tomorrow to get ready, then we're on a jet and on our way to the land of Sphinxes and sand. Get your shit in order and get some rest."

They all nodded and Merlin piped up, "You think we'll really see a sphinx?"

Arden snorted and rolled her eyes. "I hope not, they ask all kinds of shitty riddles and try to eat you if you don't want to play."

We all turned to our various preparations, and for once, I was a little more prepared to go overseas than I ever had been.

Grinning, I found Galaxy and Cassia waiting for me in my room, Cassia handing me a controller. "Let's game a little before we have to go, okay?"

Galaxy laughed at me as she kissed my cheek and I settled in for a long ass night of wishing I could be asleep, but this was where I belonged now, and I wouldn't trade it for anything. I just wished Connell could have joined us.

Thinking of my son, I wondered what he was doing and resolved to call Aeslyn tomorrow. Hopefully I could see him before I had to leave again on another hunt.

But, if I had the forethought to think about it, I should have guessed that the Hunt was really just beginning, wasn't it?

ABOUT CHRISTOPHER JOHNS

Christopher Johns is a former photojournalist for the United States Marine Corps with published works telling hundreds of other peoples' stories through word, photo, and even video. But throughout that time, his editors and superiors had always said that his love of reading fantasy and about worlds of fantastic beauty and horrible power bled into his work. That meant he should write a book.

Well, ta-da!

Chris has been an avid devourer of fantasy and science fiction for more than twenty years and looks forward to sharing that love with his son, his loving fiancée and almost anyone he could ever hope to meet.

Connect with Chris:
Facebook.com/AxeDruidAuthor
Twitter.com/JonsyJohns

ABOUT MOUNTAINDALE PRESS

Dakota and Danielle Krout, a husband and wife team, strive to create as well as publish excellent fantasy and science fiction novels. Self-publishing *The Divine Dungeon: Dungeon Born* in 2016 transformed their careers from Dakota's military and programming background and Danielle's Ph.D. in pharmacology to President and CEO, respectively, of a small press. Their goal is to share their success with other authors and provide captivating fiction to readers with the purpose of solidifying Mountaindale Press as the place 'Where Fantasy Transforms Reality.'

Connect with Mountaindale Press:
MountaindalePress.com
Facebook.com/MountaindalePress
Twitter.com/_Mountaindale
Instagram.com/MountaindalePress

MOUNTAINDALE PRESS TITLES
GameLit and LitRPG

The Completionist Chronicles,
The Divine Dungeon, and
Full Murderhobo by Dakota Krout

King's League by Jason Anspach and J.N. Chaney

Arcana Unlocked by Gregory Blackburn

A Touch of Power by Jay Boyce

Red Mage and
Farming Livia by Xander Boyce

Space Seasons by Dawn Chapman

Ether Collapse and
Ether Flows by Ryan DeBruyn

Bloodgames by Christian J. Gilliland

Threads of Fate by Michael Head

Lion's Lineage by Rohan Hublikar and Dakota Krout

Wolfman Warlock by James Hunter and Dakota Krout

Axe Druid,

Mephisto's Magic Online, and
High Table Hijinks by Christopher Johns

Skeleton in Space by Andries Louws

Chronicles of Ethan by John L. Monk

Pixel Dust and
Necrotic Apocalypse by David Petrie

Henchman by Carl Stubblefield

Artorian's Archives by Dennis Vanderkerken and Dakota Krout